NOV   2005

Brian in Three Seasons

Brian in Three Seasons

Patricia Grossman

Copyright © 2005 by Patricia Grossman

Library of Congress Cataloging-in-Publication Data

Grossman, Patricia.
  Brian in Three Seasons / Patricia Grossman
      p.   cm.
  ISBN 1-57962-122-8 (alk. paper)
     1. Chelsea (Manhattan, New York, N.Y.)—Fiction. 2. Cerebrovascular
disease—Patients—Fiction. 3. Parent and adult child—Fiction. 4. Graduate
students—Fiction. 5. Fathers and sons—Fiction. 6. Art historians—Fiction
7. Middle West—Fiction. 8. Gay men—Fiction. I. Title.

PS3557.R6726B75 2005
813'.54—dc22   2005048940

Printed in The United States of America.

for Michael Cooper, and for Helene

autumn

❧ 1 ❧

No time seems quite so hushed and suspended with promise as the pre-dawn hour when I walk home alone. Dark though it is, I can sense the approach of daybreak, and it lightens my step. In the fifteen years that I've lived in my studio apartment in New York City—a decent-sized studio on Twenty-Second Street in Chelsea—I've become fully accustomed to the effect of shadows, from both sun and street lamp, on every stoop along the way to my building. Before dawn I love my block with a singular devotion. Arriving here after a night out always seems to me a happy accident, as if I've been delivered on the crest of a wave.

Tonight I'm especially happy to turn up my block and let myself into the building. The night was not an absolute success. The second man I followed into the Shackle's back room, a powerfully built man with bushy blonde hair, refused to wear a condom. It made me think of what Toulouse-Lautrec said when his mother made him see a priest about his frequent visits to the brothel at 24 Rue des Moulins. "I am digging my grave with my cock," Henri is supposed to have told the priest. In some awful way, it's a comfort that a man who lived in the nineteenth century and wore a waistcoat and a bowler hat made this remark, and that he pronounced it in the same insolent tone as came from the good-looking man tonight, the one who snapped at me, "Live fast, die young."

Lately, my thoughts have returned to Toulouse-Lautrec. By quitting the doctoral program before I completed my dissertation—yes, on Toulouse-Lautrec—I made a conclusive statement. I had been neither in a first-tier school nor ranked at the top of my class; there had been no hope of pursuing a real academic career. Yet even though I know the world has all the information and myth on Toulouse-Lautrec it needs—an artist too popular to earn the serious attention of my professors—Henri's short and dissolute life, with its improbably delightful paintings, continues to fascinate me. I sometimes imagine that the bar *I* tend, the Barracks, is actually the bar at the Moulin Rouge. In the course I teach, a nineteenth and twentieth-century art survey at Jersey Tri-Community, right across the Hudson, I find myself lingering over slides of *A la mie* (Down to the Crumbs) and *Le Baiser* (In Bed: The Kiss). I find myself drawn back to that neglected dissertation, to my unfulfilled curiosity.

Lately I've been thinking once again about the parallels between my New York back in the 1980s and Paris in Lautrec's era, parallels I drew in my dissertation. Daddy Decency, for instance. I remember from my research that Senator Béranger, the senator they called Daddy Decency, was popular in Paris in the 1890s. He led a group of conservatives who were out to preserve the rectitude of all Parisians. Toulouse-Lautrec and the others were a threat to the common morality. The parallel to our eighties was obvious: a government unable to mind its own business.

Inside my apartment, I switch on a lamp by the front door and check my reflection in the mirror. I don't look so bad, considering the number of hours I've been awake. Now I have to sleep. Who cares about the social parallels between one century and another? My Murphy bed is still open at the center of the room, a thoroughly welcome sight.

I wake at nearly four in the afternoon, dressed in last night's jeans. My lips are parched from the early heat that pushes up the riser, heralded by a clanging noise like a hammer smacking metal. The whole Shackle incident comes back to me. Rather than brood over it, I get up, drink half a liter bottle of lemon-lime seltzer, then take a shower and shave.

Shaving is something I do only a few times a week. My father, Avery Moss, shaves every morning of his life. He shaves on Sundays, too, even now that he's retired, because he loathes and fears bums (what he calls the homeless), looks upon them as a concept, the clear fate that awaits the undisciplined man. I shave when I feel like it. I find the scraping sensation, softened by lather or shaving cream, pleasantly bracing. I enjoy the necessary command over my own safety. I enjoy too the manifest evidence that I am starting anew. For me, shaving is enjoyable because it is not an imperative in my life. Now I shave to go out. It's Monday, and I don't work. Wednesday is my teaching day, and I'm off from the Barracks on Mondays.

The sound of my sister Beryl's voice on the answering machine interrupts my shaving. As always, the sound of her voice startles me.

Even now, in 1995, both of us thirty-nine years old, Beryl's voice manages to mock me as I know myself to be. Yet I always pick up when it's Beryl. I picture her standing in the kitchen of her big house in Scottsdale, Arizona, where every other day her maid stocks the huge ceramic bowl on the kitchen table with ripe mangos and bananas.

"Hi, Brian," she says. "It's me. I . . ."

"Hold it, I'm here . . ."

"Dad's with me for a while. He wasn't faring so well in Cleveland, so I thought I should bring him back."

"Really? I thought he was okay. Or just about."

My father, who still lives in the house where I grew up, on Periwinkle Drive in Cleveland, had a small stroke three weeks ago. A little lacunar, the doctor told Beryl. He'd had numbness during it, giving the doctor reason to believe he'd had other such strokes without knowing it.

"You know Dad. He refused to have a nurse or anyone to look after him. He probably doesn't really need a nurse, but I think he needs someone. He seems to have lost a little self-reliance at this point."

I don't answer right away. I know that this hesitation, this considered pace that has been mine since childhood, annoys Beryl. "In what ways?" I ask.

Even Beryl waits a second. Perhaps she doesn't want to be the one to enter the first event on a timeline of our father's decline. "He's just not himself. There've been certain changes. It would be different if he would get someone in."

"What kind of changes? Was the stroke worse than you said?"

"No, but I think he still has some recovering to do. It's easy to have him here. You know Seth. And after a while, Dad'll decide he has to go, and he'll be off."

Seth, my brother-in-law, evinces patience in all situations. He may not be a man with whom I have an affinity, but his mellow temperament has been a boon to Beryl, and to me as well.

"Do you think I should talk to Dad?" I ask. Beryl will know I don't want to, but of course Avery won't want to talk to me, either. The attempt would be excruciating for us both.

"I don't think you have to. I just wanted to keep you abreast," she says. She has assumed her business voice.

"Thank you," I say.

"There's one thing that's really puzzling. Eerie, actually. He's become obsessed with us when we were children. Especially our being twins. He keeps reminiscing over our matching pogo sticks and scooters and tricycles. And those saucer sleds, remember them? He never even picked those things out for us; Charlene did."

"I was thinking of her the other day," I say. "I'm going to look her up."

Charlene Wright had been our part-time housekeeper until my mother died, and then she started to work for us six days a week. Beryl and I were only five. If someone woke me up in the middle of the night and asked me who'd raised me to adulthood, I wouldn't have to be out of my REM cycle for five seconds before I'd answer, "Charlene Wright."

Beryl ignores my reference to Charlene. "Anyway, now Dad wishes all that stuff was still around so he could have it bronzed. Especially the pogo sticks. He's really obsessed with them."

"So you think he's had a personality change?" I ask stupidly. She has just described a total revolution.

"It would seem so," says Beryl.

I can tell she has something to add, but her daughter Melissa has come in from somewhere, and she says good-bye to me.

What remains of the day is mine. I put on my scuffed-leather bomber jacket and walk out.

Smoking a cigarette, I head toward the Hudson River. I think about Lautrec—digging his grave with his cock—and about Charlene Wright. For her, Toulouse-Lautrec must have been just another in a legion of people, past and present, who needn't be concerned with the details of survival.

It's a compulsion of mine—this rounding up of the people who swarm through my thoughts, positioning them together, forcing them to regard each other. A tic, maybe, a driving little compulsion that occasionally threatens my sanity, yet a thing I have always done.

I stop at my coffee shop, The Aegean, for dinner—eggs over-easy and Canadian bacon—then walk south to the pier. Late September, the light is already dim. There's a damp chill in the air, a threat of rain. Still, several men on rollerblades are doing fancy maneuvers, clearly pleased at how the velocity they produce combines with the smooth rotation of their hips and the tightening of their buttocks as they strike one foot and then the other to the side. Their style is expert. I wonder where they practice to attain the perfect form they show off along West Street and the pier. Watching the bladers in their sleek tights, I think that in a way Avery would be the ideal father for these men. He had always been uneasy about me showing any undeveloped skill in public. Fumbling, or the threat of it, terrified him. These men, who've kept their bungling private, who've emerged into public only as masters of their form, would have been the right sons for Avery.

The bladers and I establish our reference to each other instantly. The swift looks we exchange have only one objective—to be the first to register disinterest. Our mutual rejection is sullen, even hateful. I suspect the bladers know I would fumble.

Clomping a bit in my thick-soled boots, I walk past the bladers. I light another cigarette and let it dangle from the side of my mouth. I close one eye against the smoke. Gray water slams against the piling; its sight depresses me, but I look anyway. Why, after ten years, am I thinking again of my old dissertation? Should I return to it? If I do, will I just abandon it again—finding my talent wanting, my drive inadequate?

"Cigarette," says a voice in my ear. A demand, not an offer. The man knows from the shape of my back and the way I brood over the water that a demand can be made. I feel warm breath on the tip of my earlobe; the man is tall. From the inner pocket of my jacket, I remove a package of Marlboros. Together, we watch the water. I give up my thoughts to join this man in observing the shadowy waves that charge the piling. How much passes between us on what little basis! Neither of us speaks. I don't look at the man, but with each fleeting moment his physicality deepens. His stillness begins to describe him—his darkness, his capacity for reverie, his indifference to words. There is little more I need to know. We leave, smoking, neither of us leading nor following. Three bladers do figure eights nearby. We find a place we both know. I'm excited when the man withdraws from under his own leather jacket a set of handcuffs—standard register NYPD, as I recognize them—for I know it's part of what is to be, what follows the demand of the cigarette. The cuffs are attached to the man's belt by a hook on a scarred leather strap, and as he pushes back the hook's release with his broad thumb, I get hard; I know to expect resoluteness sooner from my penis than from my character. I look around to make sure our outpost is ours alone. A flash of dull steel whirs by as the man forces both my arms about a sodden post and locks the cuffs in place. My taste has grown rougher

11

since the necessity of latex has intruded its unwelcome tameness into my nights. Now, occasionally, it's the combination of threat and latex that entices me. Partners who are tough, yet self-preserving. In the end, the man takes my money clip and the bills contained there. Rather than leave, he grips my elbow hard, guides me away from the place, towers over me as we pass the bladers once more. Then, without so much as a glance, he departs.

I wander around a bit longer. Thinking about the man at the Shackle last night and the one who ripped me off tonight is too depressing to bear. These men I see drifting around me at the piers, the obviously cruising ones, hold no allure. For so long I've been coming here, and yet I haven't figured out how to keep safe, how to psyche out the really nasty ones, the ones bound to make me feel as I do now. I want to do nothing, to take no action, to occupy as little space as possible. At most, I want to go home and open my window so that I can hear the music that comes every night from my downstairs neighbor's apartment.

Molly Winfield, a Brit in her seventies, has lived in my building for thirty-five years, twenty years longer than I. I've never been all that fond of her, and I sense there's something about me she dislikes. Yet my great fortune is that I have the freedom to appreciate the best of Mrs. Winfield without speaking to her. Her wonderful garden, which my apartment overlooks, is a bit of rare luck in a city whose very earth seems to judge flowers more impertinent with each passing year. She's planted bluebells and foxgloves where litter and crack vials could have been. And there's more good fortune. Mrs. Winfield has a superb sound system, a better one than I could afford, on which she plays her opera CDs nearly every night.

I cross West Street and head home, vaguely hoping that tonight it will be Callas singing Puccini. It's still early, and I have no particular plans. Maybe I'll just sit at my kitchen table with a seltzer or a beer and listen to Puccini and look at the ivy, illuminated by footlights, climbing up Mrs. Winfield's garden wall.

❧ 2 ❧

Before it opens, the Barracks is as cool and silent as a sanctuary. Luis and Jordan and I keep largely to our stations, moving no more quickly than our duties or the approaching hour demand. Sunshine, if there is any, comes through the oblong upper windows of beveled glass. It illuminates the air's dancing lint and lands over my bar and the leather seats of several high-backed stools.

The Barracks is a neighborhood bar, bourgeois and friendly enough to open as work lets out. It serves thick grilled hamburgers with sweet pickles and shoestring fries. Over half the alcohol I pour is beer on tap. Jordan cooks the hamburgers and Luis busses tables. Norman Brinsky owns the Barracks, but he lives in North Babylon, Long Island, and comes by only once or twice a month, usually with an appointment book and ledger pad in his briefcase. He sits down with me to check the inventory and do the ordering. We're not exactly each other's style—Norman wears gold chains and a sapphire ring and is always flying down to Tampa for the dog races—but we've managed to cooperate over the years. Luis is just a kid, and Jordan, who was married for twenty-five years, used to work as a short-order cook in a family restaurant in New Jersey. We all get along fine, and we seem to regard the Barracks as the fulcrum upon which to balance the real weight of our lives. Each late afternoon when we meet inside the bar we enjoy a lovely, somnolent silence; this is the time and place to do small tasks and think our own thoughts.

I think now about Toulouse-Lautrec and the bartender who set up each night at the Moulin Rouge. Did Henri come in early, have the bartender pour him a drink before he laid out his pastels at his favorite table? Did he and the bartender observe the same lazy silence we share here? Proceeding in a synchronous dance with the others, I would like to fully indulge my musings of another place and time, but my thoughts return to yesterday afternoon's call from Beryl, to her report of Avery's strange behavior. I don't want to ruin everyone's reverie—our quiet little ritual—yet I feel a powerful urge to draw them in.

"My father had a stroke," I announce while I'm cutting limes.

"Jesus, that's rough," calls Jordan from the galley kitchen. "Trudy's old man died of a stroke. Massive. Got him inside fifteen seconds."

"Wanna cigarette?" asks Luis.

I'm frequently out of cigarettes, and Luis always has an oversupply. Cigarettes are what he gives; in his own sweet way the grandmother with the bottomless stash of hard candies.

"No thanks."

"So what're you going to do?" asks Jordan. He has come out to the bar.

"It wasn't major." I know this is no answer.

13

"I went to my father-in-law's funeral. It was pretty awkward, considerin' I had just left six months before. Trudy was still majorly pissed off. I was already living with Frank."

Jordan, who must be in his late fifties, left his wife for Frank Cantore, a carpet salesman from Passaic, New Jersey. Frank used to come into Jordan's restaurant for coffee between his appointments. On weekend nights when Jordan was off, the two of them started going into the Village. They came, in fact, to the Barracks. Now Jordan and his wife are friendly. It's touching how Jordan frets over all that worries her, how instinctively protective he is, but his attachment to Frank is never for a moment less than blissful. I am amazed by Jordan's adjustment to being gay, by his innate grasp of the contradictory rules of intimacy between men.

"So what're you going to do?" Jordan repeats.

"He's with my sister in Scottsdale."

"You going out there?"

"It was minor," I repeat. I bend down to check my stock of Red Label. "I think he's okay." I stop talking. Mentioning Avery has brought no relief. Other people go flying around the country when their parents have strokes. I know this. It's simple; I've spent so much time flying away from Avery I can't picture myself flying to him. I wish that I could fully support myself on this one, that I could be defiant. I love defiance. I adore the notion of Toulouse-Lautrec telling the priest he was digging his grave with his cock—a splendid show of defiance. Yet I don't delude myself. As much as I admire defiance, admire the ones who in Lautrec's time would have thrust rapiers into their oppressors' hearts, my own defiance finds expression mostly in conversation with like-minded friends. My defiance is of a conforming nature, a paradox that can be achieved in my era. To be defiant alone, to charge upon Avery with a string of accusations, is just not my style.

Jordan leans against the bar. "My old man's been dead for fifteen years," he says. His voice goes flat. "I probably never would've gotten together with Frank if he hadn't'a died."

I look at the burly Jordan in his black sweatshirt, curly gray hairs peeping out to form a fringe at his throat. It's hard to imagine that this man had a father, let alone one who cowed him.

"My old man is just some passing dick," says Luis. "Some brainless dick, and if he came in here today and didn't like what I do with mine . . . t-t-t-eh!" He snaps the air with a dishtowel.

14

Yes, I think, Luis's is an example of the kind of defiance that does a person good. Free of public opinion, a person can be sovereign. Toulouse-Lautrec once again. Defying insult and denigration to end up in his studio, the one place where he could acknowledge that which is fragile. The next night, charcoal and pastels in hand, out again onto the streets of Paris, into the bars and brothels. Often the bars were for lesbians; La Souris, near Place Pigalle, was very butch/femme, a bar where women smoked cigars and quarreled theatrically. I don't know if Lautrec ever went into bars for men. Certainly he flaunted his prurience in all other arenas. Like his father the count, he reveled in exhibitionism and appeared in drag with impunity. But Henri Toulouse-Lautrec would probably never have entered the likes of the Barracks, for people would have drawn immediate conclusions. I suspect that for all of Henri's defiance, he would not have found it amusing to be the object of that particular insinuation.

In truth, the Barracks might not have even drawn Henri; it does not host the swirl of colors and extremes of self-expression that he relished. It is in fact called by some "Uncle Tom's Cabin" because the men who come here tend to be seemly, occasionally toadying homosexuals, attracted to relatively sedate companionship and to their own kind.

"Fathers are a whole other discussion," I say as Luis flips the Closed sign on the Barracks' door to Open.

It is not five minutes before Gerald comes in the door. Gerald is an accountant for Sony Music and Entertainment. He often leaves work early. "If Ms. Ratchet doesn't stop busting my ass, boys, I'm outta there," he announces. He's already exchanged his suit for jeans and a black polo shirt.

"Listen to *her*," says Luis, just to annoy. "From my perch, she's got the whole world in her hands." Luis wants nothing more than an M.B.A. He's getting a correspondence degree from a business school, working, he's told us, toward one day getting his M.B.A. "Blow Gerald," Jordan has advised. "Show him you know how to play ball with the big boys." Luis has blown Gerald, but doing so did not get him an intern spot in Sony's planning division. Ever since Gerald refused to put in a word for Luis, he has become "she."

"I mean it," Gerald says. "The woman is nasty to the core. I hope that tonight her tits take a nose dive. I hope that tomorrow our CEO calls her into his office and she shows up with her jugolas hanging over her hip bones. This would be fair and just."

"Gerald," I say. "We trust that you confine your misogynist spoutings to within these walls."

"Oh, heavens yes. Just here and the Sony men's room, where misogynist spoutings always come two to a stall."

There are several coteries of men who come into the Barracks together, or gather once they're here. Gerald belongs to one of them, several guys who carry on a sort of staged misogyny, complaining about female bosses and relatives as protozoa who change speed and direction depending upon what time of month it is. It's all a riff, a parody of an ancient stereotype, a diversion that I hope will soon pass.

The cliques that thrive at the Barracks remind me of my long-ago days at Sandover High School, where groups of boys went through ritualistic bondings: whipping each other with flaming towels, branding their girlfriends' initials on their asses, bumper hitching down the main drag after midnight, reading Kafka aloud in dingy, smoke-filled basements. All fads, passing amusements that I observed with disdain, even as I stood in reverent and stark admiration of the way these boys moved and thought as one, color gaining in their faces at the same moment, the veins in their necks rising in unison. Reckless, swaggering boys orchestrating their impact on the world. I'd been stunned by their insistent and exclusive claim on virility. I'd had to wait to find mine. Yet today I have no inclination, like some of my customers here, to go back in time, to insinuate myself into a group and participate in a gay version of straight male bonding. No half-facetious misogyny for me, no midnight rollerblading, not even any iron pumping. Just as in high school, I watch and listen. The gossip and the petty intrigues might be beneath my participation, but not my attention. I play host to both the loners and the cliques gathered around the Barracks bar watching the news, arguing, wrecking each other with their steely, lonesome gazes. I serve them drinks and lean across the bar to allow them to step into the aura of my familiarity. I'm the home base they run to touch when the hunt becomes too heated, the game too costly. I sometimes think of myself as a benevolent house master in a boys' school; I've seen each boy cry alone at night, yet later I stand back, edgy but rooted, when that same boy approaches another with the bravado fashioned on a bright playing field. At the Barracks, I'm valued for exercising discretion, for whisking away the evidence of defeat, for conjuring the air of forgiveness around all who require it.

Tonight, though, I'm not quite present for my customers. Thinking of Beryl's call and of Avery, I'm out of sorts. I bide my time until I can bring the security gate down over the Barracks' front door. Avery, I know, deems the biding of time a dangerous pursuit. Yet I can only continue to stand here, pouring drinks and wiping glasses, because I'm in fact being paid to bide time. If I suddenly heat up with self-loathing and bolt out the door, I'll be all but jobless and, unlike my comfortably retired father, entirely unable to pay my way.

At 2:00 AM I pull down the gate and head for the Shackle. I stand near the juke box, under the blinking Miller's sign. In a moment, I see the man from the other night, the one who said, "Live fast, die young." He's leaning on the bar, talking to a guy with a dyed-platinum buzz cut and two rivet studs in his right earlobe. He's gripping the guy's knee. In a few minutes they're up and heading toward the back room. I suppose I could amuse myself with betting on what will transpire. Will the guy with the buzz cut emerge right away, incensed that the other refused to use a condom, or will he stay back there? Still another possibility: Will a condom be produced, as it was not for me? And if so, why? When they pass, I look at them, but the man from the other night shows no sign of recognizing me. Why should he bother to recall an unconsummated encounter? Still, when he passes I feel the ticking of multiple pulses.

I go to join the smokers flanking the door outside. Three of them know one another. The other one, who might not be a smoker at all, is getting ready to leave. He zips up his jacket, a jacket like a cosmonaut's, cinched at the waist, billowing in the wind. I can make out beneath the jacket the long arch of his back; the width of his shoulders is obvious. He doesn't mind hair, has not shaven his head to declare the proud form of his skull. Apparently he doesn't feel the need.

I search for an opening line, but come up empty. The man is oblivious to me watching him from the other side of the door. He turns up his collar, walks away. His night, his early morning, is over. I linger a moment, think to go back inside, then change my mind and start home.

Along the way, I see a couple of cab drivers drinking coffee in the Aegean. Elena's at the register. I rap on the window and wave to her before turning up my block. Elena Pitsaros is over sixty, has two grandchildren. She shouldn't be doing the late shift. I hope there's a gun beneath the register.

It's Wednesday afternoon, and I stand at the head of my airless classroom. I have just turned on the overheads after showing some slides.
The ugliness is back: scratched fiberglass desks, dirty white walls,
cheap turf carpet that maintenance is due to remove because last month
(last *month!*) a swastika was carved in the area where I must stand. In
the stark light, I seem to be the only one who requires a moment of
recovery. I never expected Jersey Tri-Community to offer me a seminar
room with mahogany wainscoting and amber lampshades, but this win-
dowless box could be the common room in a state penitentiary.

Today's lecture is on the prints of Toulouse-Lautrec and his contemporaries. I have just shown Vuillard's *The Bakery,* one of Maurice Denis's
prints from his famous *Love* series, Toulouse-Lautrec's *Jockey*, Mary
Cassatt's *By the Pond,* Bonnard's *Little Laundry Girl.* This is the fourth
meeting of our class. It is the first of two classes I'll use to tell my students
about a pivotal time in the history of French printmaking, the 1890s. I love
this time; experimentation in lithography pulled the most interesting
painters of the era out of their cloistered studios and into the social milieu
of the Imprimerie Ancourt. There, the master printers Père Cotelle and
Henri Stern worked directly with most of the artists whose works I have
just shown. It was the first time prints were produced as original works of
art, and it was during this time that the concept of limited editions was
born. French artists built on the techniques of the Japanese artists that they
had so admired, and a substantial market sprang into being. Prints were
suddenly the thing to own; they were possible to own in the form of
posters, song sheet covers, menus, and for their own sake. The artists so
skilled at creating these prints, most famously Toulouse-Lautrec, worked
together many times. The Imprimerie Ancourt was an exciting place to be.
Occasionally, an artist's model would visit the studio to watch inked
rollers pass over a stone bearing her image. I imagine the model watched
through all the proofs until Père Cotelle or Henri Stern pulled the first
completed print, and then she saw something she'd never seen before: a
convincing image of herself rendered in only three flat colors.

I have done my best to create the sense of excitement that I imagine
accompanied these times. As always, I try to draw out my students'
impressions. But my eyes are slow to adapt to the harsh light. When they
do, I notice features of my students I don't care to dwell on—Carrie

Phillips' perennially wounded expression, Darius Johnson's dagger tattoo, Matt Parnell's untreated acne.

"I have to apologize," I tell the class, "that the only woman whose prints I can show you is Mary Cassatt. But the fact is, she was the only woman making prints during this time."

Automatically, I scan the faces of my female students. They are, without exception, impassive. One girl, Felina Diamond, has her marketing textbook out. Lucille Marcovi is checking the messages on her cell phone.

"Lucille. What did you think of *By the Pond*?"

She smirks and replaces the cell phone to her backpack. "Which one was that again?"

"The Mary Cassatt. I was just saying that Mary Cassatt was the only woman making prints at the time. Certain feminist art historians have their feelings about Mary Cassatt. About her imagery. What did you think of the imagery in *By the Pond*?"

"What was it, again? Sorry."

"Does someone else want to answer that?" I ask. Maybe I'll go back to the Shackle tonight. I usually don't go on Wednesdays, but maybe Wednesday is the night the man in the flight jacket goes.

"The woman and the child," answers Damon Craig. "With all the green around them. Really nice shades of green. I don't see what's wrong with the imagery. Why shouldn't she paint women and children? Half the world are women, and a whole lot of them have children."

Two or three students laugh. I look again at Lucille Marcovi. Imagining herself off the hook, she has begun to examine her split ends. Girls in my college days had the same habit. It is the single sign of continuity between our two generations. "Damon's right," she says. "It's perfectly fine." She glares at me. She knows I'm in the extreme minority, and it wouldn't occur to her that the opinion of an underdog is worth listening to.

"Whatever one thinks of Cassatt's imagery," I say, "it's important to see how absolutely society restricted her choices."

"Isn't that what society *always* does?" calls Felina Diamond. "That's what wrong with society."

A good teacher, I think, would find this remark opened onto a plethora of opportunities. A good teacher would say, "That's a broad charge, Felina. How do you think society is restricting women artists

19

today?" I am merely hoping the Path train will not be too crowded when I get out of here.

"How did the male artists treat her?" asks Damon. "I mean, did Toulouse-Lautrec and Bonnard and all those guys treat her like an equal at the printmaking place? It sounds like they probably did."

"That aspect of the French printmaking revolution is not covered in the texts," I say. Then I can't resist, "But I don't imagine they beat her."

Regrettably, the whole class laughs. It has taken this cheap shot to wake them up, and I don't expect their attention to last. After all, these are marketing and accounting majors who are taking my course for easy credit.

"Last week I showed you many paintings by some of the same artists. Would someone like to compare the paintings with the lithographs I showed you today?"

"They're flatter," offers Damon.

"And? Anyone?"

"Not as good?" tries Carrie Phillips.

"What do you think, Carrie? Do they seem less skillful to you?"

Carrie looks baffled. She's trying to gauge the right answer. "I'm not sure. Maybe. They're flatter, like Damon said. That's not so good, is it?"

"Think about the technique involved," I say. "Drawing with lithographic crayon on limestone. The limited methods of creating texture that I told you about. *Flat* is a characteristic of the medium. It's important when comparing works of art in different media to account for the identifying traits of each medium. Darius," I try, now a bit desperate, "what can you tell me about Toulouse-Lautrec's 'Jockey' print and the T-shirt you're wearing?"

Darius Johnson looks down at his T-shirt, which advertises an M.C. Hammer concert, plucks at the cloth in an effort to see it better. "Oh, yeah," he says, "silkscreen and lithography, man. Not that far apart." He looks excessively pleased with himself.

By now no one but Damon and, to a lesser extent, Carrie, are listening. Perversely, I go on. "Printmaking today is both commercially useful, as in your T-shirt, Darius, and still an art form. Since the printmaking revolution in France, artists' prints of all kinds have thrived and the techniques have grown more and more sophisticated. But prints are still multiple editions, so they don't sell for as much as paintings. Some people think that prints don't have the same artistic worth, either. I think this a moot point. People should appreciate a medium on its own terms."

"I don't think it's a mute point!" declares Matt Parcel, temporarily awake. "Mass-produced versus original? No contest. Of course mass-produced is worth less."

I'm obliged to let the word *mute* go. We're advised to be selective about correcting them. The ethos of this community college revolves around not doing further damage to the students' self-esteem.

"Yes, Matt, there's no question prints are worth less money than original works. They're not mass produced, but they are always multiples, so it stands to reason they're worth less. I'm talking about their artistic value."

"The prints are simpler than the paintings," says Damon, getting back to the original question. "I like that about them."

I nod. If I don't encourage this one student, what am I doing here?

"I'm not sure they're as rich," he continues. "Because of their different surface. But on the other hand, they're more clear. They must be simpler because if you tried to do on stone what you did on canvas, it would never work. The process would take, like, forever, and everything would get all muddied up. But I like how you can really tell where one shape starts and another begins. It makes everything crisp, and I like that. Crispness."

I nod again. "This is all good, Damon," I say.

He runs a hand through his black, almost curly hair—from the crown to the nape of his neck, which he cradles with his palm. His expression is serious.

To bring back the rest of the class, I say, "How are you all doing with choosing the topics for your term papers?"

Some students groan, some don't bother to react.

"Talk to me," I say.

"It's hard," complains one girl at the back of the class. I think I know everyone's name but hers.

"What specific trouble are you having?"

"Choosing," she says.

I have given them a list of ten possible topics, all of which necessitate the citing of certain texts and articles they'll read this year. They also have the option of choosing their own topic, and I've promised to meet with those students privately to approve the topic and discuss what I'll require of them.

"Well," I say, "if you budget your research and writing time well, you still have a couple of weeks before you need to choose."

"I think I'm going for my own topic," says Damon Craig.

"Those of you who want to do your own topic should fill in an appointment time. The sign-up sheet is on my office door. So I guess we're done for today. I look forward to seeing what topics you all settle on. See you next Wednesday."

They file out, and I follow them, just as happy to depart the room that always seems to bring out my priggish side. I am aware that I'm passing over the swastika. The student who did it was never caught; for all I know it's one of mine.

* * *

Returning from Tri-Community, stepping into the lobby of my building, I see Hector Diaz leaving Molly Winfield's apartment. Hector works as a registered nurse at Episcopal Downtown Hospital, but his need to give of himself appears to be boundless. I don't know what drives it: religious faith, uncompromised love of humanity, guilt. (Hector's down at the bars plenty, and before that it was the baths.) For whatever reason, he has befriended Molly Winfield, and he brings her home remedies for her rheumatoid arthritis, listens to her complaints about the neighborhood, runs errands for her, does all that I should probably do, living as I do on the floor directly above hers.

"How is she?" I ask.

"Oh, fine, considering. You know, lots of joint pain. What's there to say? We'll get there, too."

Strange remark. Hector and I have been neighbors all throughout the epidemic, but neither of us has asked the other's HIV status.

"Well, you're definitely getting points in heaven. And while I'm flinging around clichés, what goes around comes around."

"And you reap what you sow!" declares Hector. A non-native speaker, he's fascinated with American idioms and loves to practice on me.

I slap him on the back. "Good going! I almost mistook you for Uncle Sam."

"Oh, yes, that's me. Uncle Sam of Color. What's up with you, Brian?"

"The same. Oh, except my father had a stroke." Why do I say this? I'm not sure I've ever talked to Hector about my family.

"Oh, no!" he exclaims. His face is radiant with concern. I want to abduct this facial expression of Hector's. I want to feel what he's feeling, this apprehension over all our fates, this willingness to alight at once on the source of a person's trouble. Hector's innate sense of compassion seems extraordinary, and I suspect he's had it his whole life. His mother, Rosa, had it, and she loved Hector, so there was no question he would simply absorb her compassion, as if the air around her was just more of the nourishment inside her womb.

"It wasn't that bad," I say. "It could have been a lot worse. Just a little lacunar. One arm is weak, not quite normal, but otherwise he's going to be all right."

Hector nods. He probably sees the effects of lacunars every day. "It's a blessing it wasn't massive," he says.

"Yes. He's convalescing at my sister's."

"I'm glad," he says. "When they don't have a place to convalesce, it's not so good. I see it at Episcopal. If they don't have people to help them convalesce, they're more likely to be back. Complications of some kind."

Hector has not relaxed his solicitous expression. His intensity is unnerving. "My dad's well cared for."

We linger for an awkward second. "You want to come up and order in Chinese?" asks Hector.

"Sure," I say. "I'm pretty tired, though, so just as long as we make it an early night."

Hector's apartment is in the same line as mine. With all his furniture and knick-knacks, though, it looks smaller. He favors heavy overstuffed chairs. He has a pull-out couch covered by a crushed velvet spread and many brocaded pillows. Candles are everywhere. There are some ex-voto paintings on his kitchen wall, small paintings giving thanks to the saints in whom Hector believes, and he knows I love these little pictures. We've joked that if he doesn't bequeath them to me, I'll contest the will.

Hector and I slept together fifteen years ago, when I first moved in. I remember that we laughed a lot. The sleeping together was my initiation to the building. I liked Hector, he liked me. We got it out of the way.

Hector calls Szechuan Palace on Ninth Avenue and goes to take a shower. We're like that in each other's apartments; no standing on ceremony. When he's gone, I notice he's added a new picture to the collection of family portraits on his credenza. It's of his mother and him at Hector's graduation from nursing school.

When Hector returns, a towel around his waist, I hold out the picture for him to see. "Is this new?"

"My cousin sent it after the funeral."

Hector's mother died last year in their hometown of Taxcla in Chiapas, Mexico.

"She couldn't look a whole hell of a lot prouder," I say.

Hector beams. "All day, she kept breaking down. I'm the first to go through college, let alone beyond."

This is as close as I've heard Hector come to expressing pride.

I shake my head. Hector's feat amazes me. Ninety-five percent of the students at Sandover High went on to college. Of those, I'd venture that ninety-three percent of their parents paid the full tuition.

"My family wants me back in Taxcla."

"You're kidding."

"There's a hospital that needs a head of nursing. I'm not going. My God, can you see it?"

We laugh. We've talked before about how Hector's family wants him to marry one of his second cousins, a pretty girl of borderline intelligence.

"I would've returned for Mama. But now? No." Hector starts to tear up. He's virtually tortured himself over the circumstances of his mother's death last year. Rosa had visited him here, had stayed in our building, sleeping on the pull-out while he slept in a chair. She was here for a month. He threw a party for her, showed her the sights, took her dancing once a week in Spanish Harlem, brought her to Bloomingdale's so she could pick out a ring with a real gemstone. He'd had every minute planned. A week following her return, Rosa Diaz died in her sleep. Hector is convinced the trip was too much. Too much stimulation, he kept lamenting. She died from over-stimulation.

"Hector, it was bound to happen. Who knew she'd had a heart problem all along? Are you supposed to read minds? What you need to remember is that she had a wonderful time here. She really did."

"I know," he says meekly.

The buzzer rings and I take in the Chinese food. Hector sets the table. He's silent now. I shouldn't have asked about the picture.

After we're seated, he says, "I was the favorite. Out of ten children, I was always her favorite. It's not right to say so, but you have to understand, Brian."

"I do," I remark, although I don't.

"You know, she loved you," says Hector.

What does this mean? It's true, I spent time with Rosa during the month she was here. Lots of Hector's friends did. She liked having people around, and one night she cooked for eight of his friends, making a whole meal in Hector's tiny kitchen. Now when I run into one of Hector's friends, we invariably bring up Rosa's *ceviche*. And one Saturday afternoon I rode the Staten Island ferry with Hector and Rosa. But love? No, I won't accept the overflow of Rosa's maternal love, a love so facile that it can, by happenstance, sweep up a stranger.

"Are you keeping up your group?" I ask.

He serves me some moo-shu pork, then heaves a sigh.

"What does that mean?"

"I'm keeping it up! Yes, correct, that's what you do in this country. You shoo away your parents and then when they die, you go to groups. Death and dying. Ber*eeeeeave*ment."

What is there to say to this? I roll a pancake, use the back of my spoon to spread on a little plum sauce.

"She was in my heart always. Every day for two years after I left Taxcla, I thought about returning to her. And still later, she was always with me. I'm not ashamed to admit it; she was my best friend. What is a group going to do about that?"

It was Hector's supervisor at Episcopal Downtown who suggested the group, not me. I don't know the answer to Hector's question.

"I'm sorry, Brian. You got me on a bad day." He reaches out to squeeze my arm. "And you of all people. Most of your life a motherless child."

"Come on, Hector," I say, "one thing has nothing to do with the other." His constant consideration is oppressive. I need to get out.

"You're right. All this sorrow at the dinner table," Hector says. Then he gives me an impish little grin. "I should turn in my hostess card, don't you think?"

"I'd say so. The sooner the better."

* * *

Downstairs, I flop down on my bed, close my eyes, and, feeling entirely useless, consider once more whether to return to "The Theme of Dissolution in the Works of Henri Toulouse-Lautrec." Besides the artistic censorship of the two eras, I'd drawn on the parallel of syphilis and AIDS. One caused by a microorganism—a pathogen—the other a virus, but both diseases incited the people in power to lay down the law, to curse the evils of free thinking and bodily pleasures. Because of the new drugs, AIDS is quieter today, more decorous. But the Senator Bérangers, the Daddy Decencies, they are still hissing and sneering behind their hands, still sermonizing to their constituencies.

In my dissertation, I'd stressed that both diseases were thought to be scourges spread by society's undesirables. After I'd read about how in Lautrec's time the Ligue Morale raided bars and houses of prostitution, I pointed out that over a hundred years later New York City closed down the baths frequented by scores of gay men. And the parallels didn't stop there. Spirited characters in Lautrec's time (Henri himself) upheld the right to rule the nature of their intimacy, to protect themselves or to dig their graves with their cocks, as they chose. In the '80s in New York, many men joined together to take command, to make themselves obnoxious rather than slink away in their assigned role of pariah. In both cultures, as society clamped down, defiant voices rose, concerned citizens acted up.

Yet for months, the conclusion of my dissertation had eluded me, until—I remember the weather was turning balmy—its whole premise struck me as embarrassingly obvious. Thinking back on it, I'm not sure I've much revised my opinion. Yet somehow ideas keep swirling around in my head.

❧ 4 ❧

Between serving drinks at the Barracks, I pick up a library book called *The History of Striptease*, which has a section on La Goulue, the quadrille dancer whom Toulouse-Lautrec made famous.

A country beauty who escaped to Paris, La Goulue eventually brought throngs to the Moulin Rouge. Years later, a broken old woman, she sold peanuts outside its door. Melodramatic stuff, by any account. So many of them—the entertainers and the pleasure seekers—died penniless in slums or mad in asylums. They might have been characters in a morality tale.

"You look pretty serious," I suddenly hear. Luis is standing in front of me with his tub of empty glasses.

"Oops, sorry." I replace the book and take the tub from him.

"Pec check," I tell Luis. I'm not really interested in his gym routine nor the development of his pectorals, but we have hours to go.

26

Luis pulls down the neck of his tank top in an automatic way. Usually he delivers the details of his gym regimen in a fey monotone I find irritating. Tonight, though, he lowers and replaces his shirt swiftly and without a word, as though he has been spurned or has decided to extend himself only as far as civility demands. I try to prod him about the machines: weights, sets, reps, levels of resistance. I'm embarrassed because I'd grown used to thinking of Luis as incapable of detecting my insincerity. Finally, moving beside me to place the glasses in the sink of soapy water, he says, "Have you talked to Jordan?"

"Not yet. He hasn't been out here."

"I know. But he's not back there cleaning the grill."

"What's he doing?"

"Making long distance calls. To everyone. About Frank. How old is Frank, anyway, sixty? Old enough to test negative fourteen times. Not fifteen, though."

"Oh *shit.*" I can't manage more. I don't want to say more, not to Luis. Jordan is the sort of man I've sometimes wished myself to be. Steadily kind and caring, yet not conspicuously so, as Hector can be. Jordan doesn't pile up good deeds or make fusses over people, but I've always sensed his good will. He's the slowest of us all to crack jokes at the expense of the customers. I've even grown an affection for his body, and I've come to take comfort in his total disregard of it. There is the big stomach that begins high and strains against his striped muslin apron. It jiggles when he laughs, and he pats it in a protective way. Jordan is the sort of man who I would not want to imagine walking into an empty apartment alone. He must have people around him; people to accept his kindness, to harvest his charm; people whose expectant smiles inspire him to tell stories about movie stars and super models. These are unverifiable stories that he's heard from the minor actors and other theater people who come into the Barracks, but he passes them along with a sense of authority. Everyone likes Jordan; no one would want to see him alone. He waited twenty-five years and gave up his beloved wife Trudy to come into his true passion; his solitude would be black and unjust. It would not be like mine; I would much sooner bear my own solitude than witness Jordan's. This is something I know.

Luis brings over new glasses, and I begin to load them into the sink. "Why'd he come to work?" I ask. "For Christ's sake, why didn't he just call Norman, make him get off his ass and come to his own bar for a change?"

27

Luis shrugs. "Where else is Jordie going to go?" he asks. "Frank's not even home. He's at his sister's house in Passaic. He's telling his sister and his niece."

When some people find out, they transform themselves into the town crier. They gather together their world—the nearby friends, the scattered relatives, the dry cleaner clerk, the high school drama teacher. They gather these people together, and they bellow the news. They stay up for seventy-two hours, and so do various of their friends. The news, although never entirely unexpected, is still a blast, and its force keeps them awake longer than they have ever been. Later, they fall into a fractious and haunted sleep.

Then there are others who, when they find out, tell no one, and they *will* themselves to sleep. For seventy-two hours, they perceive nothing. Upon waking, they imagine themselves still asleep. They reveal what they have found out slowly, with great selectivity.

I have no idea into which camp I would fall—the town criers or the sleepers. Jordan's partner Frank, though, is entering his seventy-two hours as the town crier. He is telling a sister and a niece that I didn't even know existed. And Jordan will stay up, too. Now he's on the phone in the kitchen. People's hamburgers will be late tonight. I tell Luis to relieve me for a minute.

Jordan has his back to the door. He's talking on the wall phone, and supporting himself with one hand on the door jamb. I'm struck by the sight of the spatula in that hand, its stem quivering against his thumb. He's held a spatula most days for over twenty years. How many times has it shaken in his grasp? Quite possibly none. I open the refrigerator and take out the jumbo jar of sweet pickles. I help myself, taking my time about it, and Jordan hangs up. He puts down the spatula and kneads the back of his neck. "It's all too much, Brian," he says. Lacking animation, his face has become indistinctive—the face of a working class white man in his fifties, a face on a billboard in an old Communist country. "I can't even begin to cope."

I'm ashamed of an impulse to engage Jordan, to get him going as I always have. With Luis, it's "pec check." With Jordan, it could be a tidbit on Liza, or Sotheby's Faberge egg auction, or whomever is appearing at Rainbow and Stars—items I pick up from the Chronicle section of *The New York Times*, that mannered little column that hovers over gossip but never quite lands on it. The slightest tidbit can prompt Jordan's merriment.

28

"I'm so sorry," I say. "Maybe he'll be a slow progressor. I know two of them. One's been asymptomatic since he found out nine years ago. You know it's not like it used to be."

"His T-cells are already in the toilet," Jordan says. "And it's not like he's been the healthiest. He could lose thirty pounds, plus the diabetes and the kidney stones."

"Well, yes," I say, "but don't wish away the thirty pounds." I can barely hear my voice.

Jordan absently pats his own stomach. He turns and looks at me full in the face. There are chalky streaks along his jaw. I wonder if he wears makeup, then hate myself for noticing. "What would you do?" he asks. "If you were me? How would you try to make his life good?"

Forthright questions of this kind always leave me speechless. I'm embarrassed and fascinated. I want nothing more than to answer, since I admire the perfection of spirit that delivers them. I'm above such questions, yet unequal to them. "I can't imagine you doing better than you are already, Jordan."

"What am I gonna do, Brian? I got some money saved. Maybe we can go to the Nile. Or the Himalayas."

I say nothing. Jordan and Frank have season's tickets to a musical theater in Long Island. The performances are in a tent. When Frank picks up Jordan at the Barracks, they wave and say they're off to the outer reaches. They love nothing more than to eat at Spanky's, the restaurant around the corner from their apartment. They know all the waiters. Frank would hate Egypt. He would be miserable with the Himalayas towering above him.

"There's gotta be something," he says. "Jesus, something." Jordan has been a short-order cook for as many years as Frank has sold carpets. They have imagined, whether in words or through rushes of energy that purl through their thoughts, the extravagant show they would attend if time were running out. Now I can see that Jordan has lost his love of the flamboyant; he can imagine nothing.

"You'll come up with something," I say. We hug each other. I return to the bar, and Luis moves around the floor with his Rubbermaid tub. When there's a break in the conversation at the bar, we can hear Jordan slapping burgers on the grill.

* * *

29

It's way beyond midnight when I head for the Shackle on the off chance the man with the flight jacket will be coming or going, or—if I'm really lucky—standing by the juke box waiting for something to happen.

Amazingly, I'm quite nearly that lucky. When I walk in, I spot on the rickety coat rack by the door an olive-green nylon jacket with fleece lining. It's time, I alert myself, to take a risk. Two possibilities from the first time I saw him; he was tired and perhaps satiated and didn't see me, or he saw and dismissed me upon a single scan.

Unlike my father and Beryl, I lack the temperament for taking risks. My throat tightens, I detect a faint heaviness in my chest, I'm aware of a pulsating in the most delicate of my veins. My face heats up well in advance of any risky action.

The man is dancing by himself. Solo dancing, as I've seen it, suggests a level of narcissism I refuse to engage, even for the prospect of a night of great sex. This solo dance is an exception. Not because the man is the world's most sexy dancer—he doesn't stand out—but because he's so clearly not preening. He's removed from his surroundings, as I've often wished to be while standing on this same rutted floor. He's merely cheering himself with his own company. There's a wall mirror not five feet away, yet as I watch he doesn't once check his reflection.

I enter the dance. This is a pick-up bar, not a dance bar, and so it's only the two of us dancing to some Lou Reed song. For me, the first half minute is a torment. I'm a suitor who has encroached on the territory of a potential mate, and—like a suitor in the wild, a big cat or an exotic bird—I've no choice but to wait to see if I will be accepted as worthy.

"A little late to ask," I say, "but do you mind if I join you?"

He neither smiles nor turns away. His eyes open a touch wider than they'd been, and even in the dim lighting this tiny gesture accentuates his air of ease.

After five minutes, we leave together. He's coming home with me, and I can't believe my luck. I love the way he looks in his flight jacket, and I love the soft waves at the back of his neck. Outside the Shackle, I touch these waves. We don't say much on the way, but twice we stop to kiss in a warehouse doorway. His lips are softer than I expect, yet the force of his embrace is literally breathtaking. Impossible though it is, his embrace seems heartfelt.

In my building, I need to lead him up the steps and down the fluorescent-lit hall. He has the advantage. I'm a couple of inches shorter than he, and my walk, a bit high-stepping, is not my greatest draw. I've been in this position before, when some frailty of mine becomes evident, and my strong attraction turns on me, berates me with a livid glimpse of my own unworthiness.

In my apartment, he looks at some of the prints and paintings I've acquired through the years. He looks carefully, but says nothing.

"Would you like something?" I say. "Seltzer? A drink?"

He nods no, and scans my apartment, clearly looking for a bed. I go to open the Murphy cabinet and lower the bed. He smiles, a smile that affects me the same way as when he widened his eyes back at the Shackle. "Great," he says, and then pulls me onto it. He's determined and he's forceful. My response makes him more so.

It's not until a couple of hours later that I realize he might have hurt me. There might be a bruise or two by midday tomorrow.

He sleeps beside me, but I know he'll be gone before daybreak. I touch the waves that cling to the back of his neck, three loose brown curls too sweet-looking, perhaps, for this man's head.

He wakes within the hour, right as I'm falling asleep. He dresses and looks for his flight jacket.

"In there," I say, pointing to my tiny vestibule, where the coat tree is. Most times I don't want their names; his name I want. "What's your name," though, is the ultimate kindergarten question. How can I ask it, aching as I still am from the onslaught of his passion?

After he's gone, I can't go back to sleep. I pick up *Helen Croft: The Baybridge Manor Years* at my bedside, right at my elbow. I hope he didn't see it. It's one of a little-recognized genre, the spinster novel, that I find myself reading regularly. There is a surprising quantity of these novels on dimly-lit shelves of used book stalls. Most have cloth-covered bindings, and some have crumbling spines that leave behind a brittle powder on my fingers. This one is the second of a trilogy I bought last month at the annual St. Luke's Church book sale, and I already know it will end with Helen living in a rectory in a scantly-populated Sussex village.

The first volume, which I finished last week, took up Helen's youth and adolescence as the daughter of the cook at a convent school. Quickly scanning the pages, I grow concerned for what will happen to Helen in this second volume. Raised among girls better heeled than herself, Helen has assumed some pretensions that might undermine her role as governess to the children of Baybridge Manor. I'm not surprised that by page thirty Helen has fallen in love with the Master of Baybridge, a London banker. She suffers every time the Baybridges entertain at home, especially when she catches a glimpse of the master petting his wife's cheek or extending his arm to usher her into dinner.

After reading almost ten pages, I know that the second in the trilogy will be as good as the first. I think I can probably fall asleep.

❧ 5 ❦

Although my sister Beryl's house in Scottsdale is a one-story faux adobe, its interior has much the same hale and optimistic tone of our Tudor style on Periwinkle Drive. This is my second visit to Scottsdale. My first was six years ago, when Melissa was in pre-school and Beryl and Seth had separated because Beryl could not stay away from Greg Visconte, another condominium developer, a married man whose over-groomed good looks appeared on interstate billboards and post-midnight TV all over Phoenix and Tucson. Every night for a week Beryl had called me, her shamelessly amoral brother, and in a moment of open-heartedness I had flown out here to indulge her, to try to parlay her episode of lost control into something of an emotional renaissance. Predictably, it now seems, Beryl renounced both her lover and the dark, wavering part of her character he had unloosed. Our communication had swiftly regained its crisp, half-strangled cadences.

I'm here now because Beryl said she wanted my first-hand opinion on my father. The very fact that she is turning to me for counsel is a sign that Avery, always her chief advisor, has lost some reliability.

When I arrived at the Phoenix airport last night, I shook hands with my father. He had said little in the car. At Beryl's, I looked around the rooms, decorated so like the ones of my childhood. The living room carpet has the same fresh vacuum cleaner tracks over its acrylic nap as did our wall-to-wall pure virgin wool on Periwinkle Drive. Some fibers of Beryl's viridian pile sparkle, suggesting the cooling surface of a mountain lake. The drapes are whorls of aquamarine and turquoise. The color scheme has been calculated to offset the dusty and pallid tones along the desert highway. The only hot colors are in the huge Western paintings on the family-room wall. One is of an Acoma chief in full regalia, gold-leaf highlighting the feathers of his headdress. I simply don't look at these paintings that I know have been insured by Lloyd's of London.

I arrived last night, and now I sit in the family room, cooled by central air conditioning, a cup of tea before me. I cross my legs carefully, trying to avoid the edge of the mosaic-topped coffee table. My father is in the bathroom. Seth, who is an assistant principal at the district middle school, has already left for work. Melissa is in sixth grade now, and she rides in with him in the morning. Across from me, Beryl sits in the path of the sun coming through the skylight. She wears a white linen suit with short sleeves and gold-rimmed buttons, and a Cartier watch. Her permed hair is wet, and she keeps scrunching it in her fingers so it will dry springy in the sun coming through the skylight. She's going to drive over to her new development, Far Horizon Vista, to interview a prospective groundskeeper. I will be here alone with my father before she returns to take us out to lunch at the Desert Pavilion Mall, a quarter mile away.

Here I sit in my black jeans, Doc Martens, and my gray T-shirt from the Army/Navy store on Christopher Street. I could be a tradesman discussing an estimate for ceramic tile work around the adobe fireplace. I am some kind of worker, commissioning myself to houses where the men wear a coat of clear polish over their square nails, as does Norman Brinsky, owner of the Barracks, to distinguish themselves from laborers.

"So what did you think?" asks Beryl. She means last night, shaking hands with Avery in the airport, his silence on the way home.

"When did he start dressing like that?" I ask.

Beryl shrugs. His style of dress is of no consequence to her. That he has traded in a lifetime of the finest materials for the convenience of synthetic fibers—last night's stiff collar, the yellow of a Fiestaware plate, a shiny barrier girding in the loose flesh of his neck—does not bother her. Beryl and I have always been set off by different things. She's called me to Scottsdale because Avery has taken to mumbling to himself and harping on our childhood. I'm not all that worried. But that Avery should start dressing like any senior citizen wandering the Desert Pavilion Mall, that he should quietly turn in his beautiful wardrobe for the most conventional resort wear, little more than rompers for the elderly, leaves me humiliated for him.

"Wait till he starts on the twin thing," Beryl says.

I look down at the mosaic, my eyes jumping from one cobalt glass stone to another. The pattern is of parrots lined up along a perch. It's hard to look Beryl in the eye. Perhaps it just seems to her that my father is obsessed with our being twins because we allude to it so infrequently ourselves. "Maybe he won't do it with me," I tell her.

Beryl's hair is almost dry. As she rises, she arranges it so the coils frame her head evenly. She looks at her watch and frowns. "I'll be back around 12:30," she says. "It's good you two will have some time together. It'll be interesting."

The ever-clinical Beryl. The phlegmatic twin who even in childhood found the volatile one an interesting specimen. At age six or seven she would stand off to the side, her head cocked, watching me wail over some perceived slight. Now I wave my fingers to wish her good-bye, a deliberately faggy gesture, and then I just sit and listen as she pulls her BMW out of the driveway. When she's gone, I wander about the family room, taking everything in, reviewing first one object and then the next as if they were all curiosities in a Diane Arbus photograph. The objects in my sister's house are so standard in a house of its type that they inspire in me an inverse reaction; I am spellbound by everything. Every decorative item makes me feel for Beryl and Seth, who have chosen soulless objects to make intimate statements about themselves. It is much the same as looking at a Diane Arbus photograph of rich people; I feel for them.

Just as I pick up a blown glass paperweight, my father walks in. He's wearing tan slacks and a white polo shirt, better than last night. I must look relieved. "So, Mister," he says. "You wrenched yourself away from the Big Apple."

"How're you, Dad?"

"Not bad. I had a minor stroke, you know," he says, as if to a stranger. "So now this arm's not itself." He holds out his left arm. "Golf swing's shot to hell. Sometimes I can't remember words. But lucky, considering. So you wrenched yourself away from the Big Apple. Is that how they dress there? Like construction workers? You look like one of my guys at the old sites, Moss Development's old sites, do you remember some of them? Sandover Square?"

Of course I remember Sandover Square. My father had developed one of the first full-scale shopping malls on Cleveland's south side. Thirty-three years ago; I was only six. That part of town has been declining in recent years. I'm surprised Avery mentions it. I just nod. I'm thinking about one or two of the construction workers on later projects. Avery should only know.

"I'm going to get some coffee. Mind if I get some coffee?"

"No, of course not." I still have the glass paperweight in my hand, but by the time I put it down my father has left for the kitchen. He hasn't asked me to join him.

I remain in the family room, picking up and replacing various objects. There are several framed pictures of my sister's family. Seth and Melissa are often together; my sister must have taken these shots. Seth Edwards is a good-looking guy who seems indifferent to the wealth accumulating around him. In his spare time, he and some friends play Scottish folk music at bars in Phoenix and Tucson. Although I've never felt close to Seth, I've always liked him. During the time of Beryl's affair with Greg Visconte, I listened to Beryl's complaints about Seth's passivity, but I've always read him as a guy with a generous spirit. I'm sure he's a better father than most. I loved the role Visconte played in Beryl's life, what might have grown out of the only episodes of self-doubt my sister has ever shown, but I always knew she'd be better off with Seth, a man who had openly hoped for a daughter, who had never shaved off the beard of his hippie days, who was a Young Socialist for a time, a Vista volunteer after that. Now I look at a picture of Seth and Melissa; his beard is graying and Melissa seems to be wearing lipstick. They look a little in love. Time is passing. I put down the picture and go into the kitchen.

"Good coffee," my father says. "You know all these designer coffees they have now. All these damn coffee bars. Do you think the natives in Colombia know they're picking coffee beans for these asinine places?"

"Natives?" I say.

"The people who live in the place, for Christ's sake. Natives. The original inhabitants of a region. Get out your *Webster's*, Brian."

My father has always regarded dictionaries and encyclopedias as the cornerstone of a developed culture. When Beryl and I fought at the dinner table, he'd send us away to continue our linear journey through the *World Book*. Since I was generally considered to be the one at fault, I completed Z before Beryl began on D.

"There's more," Avery says, nodding toward the Braun coffee maker.

"That's okay. I'm a tea drinker," I say. "So what about this stroke, Dad? Honestly. Do you think it's changed things for you?"

My father doesn't answer. He stares at me in a way he has never done before. It's rude; I don't know where to look. "Beryl can't remember those roller skates of yours," he says. "The ones with the little keys for adjusting the size. Big thick metal wheels, remember? Now they have these roller blade things, like Melissa has, that's all you see. Those old skates, though, Beryl could really move on them. You, I don't think they were so much your thing."

I remember the skates. They were matching, like most of our toys. Charlene had taken us to the May Company to buy them. My father had given her the money. "Charlene got us those," I say.

"You know, I think about her," says Avery. "It must be the retirement."

"I think about her, too."

What I think about the most is those two weeks I lived in her house, but I don't say this. I stayed there with all of them, her husband Lloyd, her foster sons Mosley and Rudy and LeRoy. Once Avery drove over and sat in the car while Beryl came to the door with a big fruit basket. It had been wrapped in turquoise-tinted cellophane and stapled at the top with a ribbon and card that said, in the handwriting of Avery's secretary, "To the Wrights, with warmest wishes from the Mosses." When Beryl had handed the basket to Charlene, the cellophane had crackled. Beryl had tried to get me to come home, and I knew her words had been scripted by Avery. While she talked, I read a paperback book, I remember it, *The Mystery of Treasure Cove*. She had finally said, "You think they want you? You're a rich white boy to them. You must be out of your mind; I can't believe you're doing this. I can't believe you think this is an okay thing to do."

"So why don't we just pick up the phone and call her?" Avery asks now.

He couldn't mean it. "I doubt we'll find her," I say. "It's been twenty years. Over. I'm sure she's long since moved."

"She's still there," my father says with authority. I know he has not bothered to verify this. He picks up the phone. I see him punch in the familiar 216. In a minute he's asking for Charlene's number at the old address. He pronounces it with a flourish; he's being cocky. When he gets the number he writes it down with the most casual of smiles, a blasé expression that underscores his superior understanding of the world.

Without consulting me first, he punches in Charlene's number. I want to flee, but I also want to stay. My father will find the voice to carry him through this telephone call. I would lose mine, yet even after his small stroke, Avery's voice is readily available to him. He has no reason to doubt it.

"Yes, hello. Is this Charlene Wright? . . . Well get ready for a surprise, this is Avery Moss . . . no, no kidding. I'm just fine, just *fine*. How are you doing?"

There is a long pause, during which my father looks at me with a forbearing expression.

"We don't know what life's going throw our way, do we? We're all really shortstops, trying to catch those ground balls before they get past us."

I wince. Avery listens some more. "I'm sorry to hear it, Charlene," he says. "Lloyd was a good man. One of the unsung heroes. . . . Uh-huh, that's right. . . . You know who I have standing here beside me? Brian! He's here in Scottsdale, we're both visiting Beryl. Everybody's all grown up now, and we were wondering about you, just sitting around and wondering about you. . . . That's right, sure. Listen, I was thinking. Do you have any of those old pictures of the twins on their roller skates? You know the ones I mean? We were just talking about those."

This is terrible. I have to put a stop to this. To my own horror, I start to fidget in my place; I am the irrepressible child with the right answer but no permission to voice it.

My father lets out a belly laugh; it is rich and deep, but I can't believe it's not perceived as insincere by all who hear it. I have heard it countless times, especially coming from his study in the Periwinkle house, a room where Avery sometimes made business calls in the evening. It is the laugh that shows things are going his way. "I knew you'd hang onto them," he says. "That's just great. Tell you what. When I get back, I'll just swing around and pick them up. I'll call first, of course. I don't want to put you out with stamps and post offices and all. I'll just swing by. Now Brian, here, he looks about to bust a gut, so I'm going to put him on."

My father hands over the phone, a Panasonic cordless that I cradle in my palm as I walk back into the living room. I must put it to my ear and speak. Will Charlene remember how Avery's smugness offends me? Will she remember the hours I spent sitting at the kitchen table as she ironed, asking her questions about her life at home, about Lloyd and her boys, frantically trying to counteract my father's message that our own family must stand at the center of her universe? Or rather, in the years that have passed, years in which I've so rarely called or sent a card, had Charlene come to resent me?

"Charlene. My God. It's Brian."

"Now would you listen to that voice?" says Charlene. "A man's voice, all right."

"You sound wonderful!" I burst out, relieved to hear the welcome in her tone. She sounds the same, and therefore wonderful. "But please do me a favor. Just forget about this picture business." I hear Avery behind me, but I keep walking, to elude him, around to Melissa's room. "My dad's had a stroke, a small one, and he's not thinking clearly. I really don't want you to put yourself out."

"Now what trouble is it to look for a couple of pictures?" asks Charlene. "I mostly sit here all day. They tell me I need a new hip, but I say if the good Lord wanted hips to be made of plastic . . ."

"Who's there with you now?" I ask. "I mean, who's living there?"

"Oh, I've got my Mosley here. He drives a bus for the schools, you know, for the little ones, and he stays in the room at the back here. The rest of them is gone. My Lloyd. Did you hear me tell your daddy? Before he died, he sent in the last payment on this house, God bless him."

"I'm so sorry." I want to ask about LeRoy and Rudy, her two other foster sons, but I don't know what to say. Finally, I come up with, "I still remember your stuffed veal breast. I remember LeRoy and Rudy loved it, too." This is as far as I can go in alluding to our two weeks together.

"Oh-h-h, I haven't made that in years," Charlene practically sings. "That took some *time*. Now, how's Beryl? It's Beryl you're out there visiting?"

What she means, I think, is how far have we moved toward accepting each other. Charlene is made sad and jumpy by dissension between siblings.

"Beryl and her family are fine. She's in real estate," I say. "With both feet."

Charlene laughs. "Oh, my!"

I laugh, too. "Our worlds have been pretty different. But that's no surprise."

"And you've been taking care of yourself?" asks Charlene. "You've been keeping safe?"

It's more than my father or Beryl has ever asked. "I'm fine, honey," I hear myself saying. "And don't think because I'm such a lousy correspondent that I don't think of you. Not true. Not true at all." My voice is about to crack, and Avery is upon me.

"Tell your sister Beryl I'm taking good care of her Duchess Regina," says Charlene. "She's sitting here on the radiator without a chip on her. You remember the duchess, don't you?"

"I do, although I'm not sure I want to."

Duchess Regina is a pink china poodle that Beryl had the nerve to sell to Charlene for fifty cents one summer evening when the two of us had a sidewalk sale of our old toys.

"Now let's not insult the duchess, she's truly a regal thing," says Charlene merrily. "She graces my living room."

"Here's my dad, again, sweetie. You take good care of yourself, and say hello to Mosley. And to the others, too." I hand the phone back to Avery and flee as quickly as I can to the bathroom, where I turn on the water full blast, not knowing what else to do, and wash my hands until I'm sure my father has hung up the phone.

At the Desert Thai Palace, I report on Duchess Regina. I tell Beryl that Charlene has not lost an iota of her saintly temper. As I speak, Beryl firmly nudges my foot under the table. She's upset that we called Charlene; she doesn't understand why I have participated in the very folly she invited me here to help her squash. She switches the topic to the groundskeeper she just hired, Jesus Mendez. He has seven children, and so she offered him more than she usually pays groundskeepers. I say nothing, but Avery puts his hand over hers on the checked tablecloth. He leaves it there for a few moments, and I see Beryl's eyes mist over as she looks down at it. I am astonished by the beauty of his hand and the precise consideration of its placement over Beryl's. The resolute masculinity of Avery's hand has evolved into something tentative and modest; his hand seems breakable over Beryl's, with its chestnut tan.

"Good girl," says my father.

The old Avery would have chastised her for letting her heart get in the way of her common sense. But Beryl has witnessed his transformation at closer range than I, and she knows, as she always has, what to say to please him.

We order, and then Beryl asks my father a business question. I suspect she knows the answer; the question has to do with capital-gain taxes, but she is clearly out to preserve their early roles. There is no patronizing here; Beryl still needs to receive my father's advice more than Avery needs to give it. He answers her readily enough, but then he leans back and beams at us. "This is really something," he says. "My twins together. What'd you think of Charlene, Brian? What'd I tell you about her staying put? You know that house is paid for. Damn fortunate situation. Think of where she could've ended up."

I do. I think of exactly that, and wonder how much Avery would have had to put himself out to provide for Charlene's old age. I think of his own pension, and of Beryl's. I think of Charlene and, more frighteningly, of myself, me without someone like Charlene's Lloyd.

"Soon as I get back," says Avery, "I'm going to swing around there and pick up those snapshots. She's got you and Brian on your skates, Beryl. Black-and-white evidence to back me up."

"Dad. Let's forget all that. Let's talk about the future. Why do you want to stay in Cleveland with those terrible winters? You could easily move right into Far Horizon, one of the deluxe units. We're happy to keep one open for you. Seth and I have already discussed it."

I didn't know this was coming. I wait.

"Debbie Shuster could come, too," Beryl adds. "We have some efficiencies left."

Debbie Shuster has been my father's girlfriend for over twelve years. He puts her up in a luxury building by Lake Erie. We generally don't allude to her. Whenever Beryl and I do mention her, it is with the understanding that my father does not particularly like her, but that it is too much trouble to put an end to their arrangement. I can't believe, though, that my sister is now openly treating her as chattel and that Beryl has further devalued her by offering the efficiency.

"Debbie's fine where she is," says Avery.

"But you're not, Dad. We're worried about you. Aren't we, Brian?"

Beryl has never asked me if I'm worried about my father.

"The decision is ultimately his," I say uselessly.

Beryl scrunches up her hair. Although it's perfectly dry, her gel makes it look wet.

As if to secure his claim on independence, my father begins to elaborate on his answer to Beryl's earlier question. He speaks with greater facility than he has, apparently calling on a dormant instinct, and his features seem to shed their cloudiness. The very pace of his speech quickens, and his pronunciation becomes crisp. I'm not attuned to what he's saying, so I watch this as the estimable defense strategy it is. I decide he should stay in Cleveland. Before I leave Scottsdale, I'll tell Beryl what I think.

The food comes, Pad Thai for me, squid for Beryl, beef with basil for my father. Their business discussion continues. I ask a question or two, which Beryl in particular attends to meticulously. Neither of them asks me what I'm doing, what's new with me.

As I finish my Pad Thai, they talk about tax shelters. Then I lean back in my seat. I'm tempted to do something I haven't done in years—push back so far that the front legs of my seat lift into the air. As a child, I was virtually unable to sit in any other way. With some regularity, the rear legs of our dinette chairs succumbed to the pressure of my weight, depositing me on the slate floor, my head spinning and the booming notes of Avery's anger ricocheting off the kitchen walls. It didn't matter how many times I was warned. I fell the most at Saturday morning breakfasts, when Avery read the business section of the paper and absently twirled Beryl's hair as she sat beside him reading one of her *True Romance* comic books. Finally, wanting to eat in peace, my father agreed to sign me up for a Saturday drawing class at the Cleveland Institute of Art. I'd been lobbying for months.

From the moment I entered the studios that were occupied during the week by real, matriculating art students, adults possessed of the most advanced ideas, as soon as I wandered about the vast cement-floored studios with their chemical smells and divine disorder, I felt at home. I was eight years old and had detected the redolence of bohemia. I remained in those classes for five years. During the first two years, I began to see what it would be like to recreate on paper the objects before me, to show perspective and use shadows to suggest form, to animate with a skill that made people nod their heads in recognition. I glimpsed what having this capacity would feel like, how it could grant me the most beguiling future, but then I stopped improving. When my father picked me up in front of the Institute, he found me glum, sometimes tearful. He wanted to withdraw me from classes. Wise competitors, he told me, know when to concede. Yet I insisted on returning to the Institute every Saturday, until the fall I was thirteen and Avery said that he was going to give Beryl piano lessons and I would take the coronet, and there'd be no arguing about it.

For three months I played Revelry upstairs and Beryl played Greensleeves downstairs, neither of us progressing much, until Avery allowed us to stop. After a few weeks, Beryl joined the French Club and I started smoking joints on Saturdays with Ned Tanning, a sixteen-year-old pot-head down the block who fancied himself a troubadour. Ned strummed a mandolin and recited poetry, and I just let my mind wander, or read library books I was too stoned or too young to appreciate, Vasari's *Lives of the Artists* and Gauguin's *Noa, Noa*. Ned was the first homosexual I'd ever encountered, although he didn't know he was one. I developed an aversion to his mandolin and his receding chin, and soon enough I spent every Saturday in my own company.

Five years ago Avery sent me Ned's obituary from the *Cleveland Plain Dealer*. It said that Ned had twice toured Europe with an early music ensemble called Victoria. It said he was thirty-eight years old and had died of pneumonia.

"I don't see the down side," Beryl is saying now. "You'll have your independence, and you'll have Seth and me nearby. You won't have to always worry about hiring people to shovel the driveway. Promise me you'll think about it."

"Thinking costs nothing," says Avery. "Does it, Brian? You're a big thinker."

"Doesn't cost a thing, Dad. Unfortunately, doesn't pay for anything, either."

He smiles. "You thinking a lot these days?"

"Oh, yeah sure. Always thinking," I say.

Beryl signs her name to the lunch bill, and my father nods, his expression again soft, his eyes glazed.

Back at Beryl's, Seth and Melissa have returned. Everyone is in good spirits. The novelty of my presence cheers them. Seth shakes my hand heartily, and although Melissa is shy, she sneaks me open-hearted glances. I have never said or done anything to alienate them, and our family is small. It is incumbent upon all of us to be charming.

Now Beryl announces she's not going back to work, and we should all go swimming. They have a built-in pool behind the house. Transplanted cacti are lined up behind the deep end, along a cerulean wall. In the spring, I'm told, these cacti bloom and the play of fuchsia and apricot yellow against the wall is something to behold. (A touch of Mexico, says Beryl; the gardener is from Puebla.) Someone has stretched a net for water volleyball across the shallow end. Everyone scatters to various rooms in the house to change. I'm the first outside, and then my father, who wears boxer bathing shorts and an open terry cloth jacket. His chest hairs are white and sparse, and his stomach muscles sag, but he's not as heavy as he once was.

Beryl comes out in a Speedo tank suit, just a blur of tan limbs and royal blue before she dives into the deep end. When Seth joins us, his graying beard bobs comically against his bare chest as he walks, carrying a folder stuffed with school papers. Melissa startles him by jumping on his back for a piggy-back ride. She's small, but too old for this. She's wearing a two-piece suit. After Seth tells her to get down, she sticks out her chest and proudly sashays off. In a moment of silence, we hear the swishing of Beryl's even front crawl, an inviting sound. She stops at the shallow end and asks us all to join her. At first my gray T-shirt fills with water and swells, then collapses, soaked, and clings to my chest. Melissa points and says, "Hey, I think Uncle Brian forgot something!" She giggles.

"I'm delicate," I tell her, and make sure to smile. "Sunburn, sunstroke, the whole works. My sensitive New York skin."

The smile was a mistake. Melissa swims over and tries to remove my T-shirt. I stop her by grasping her upper arms, too hard. I feel my strength and am startled by it, but I can't let her lift the shirt. It was only last week that the man in the olive-green flight jacket was over, and he left a bruise or two after all.

"Ow!" she yells.

"Sorry," I say, hushed, and then everyone is upon me, Avery and Seth and Beryl; for a moment they all look at my face, to weigh my intention, and then at my T-shirt, to wonder what it conceals. If Beryl and Seth have ever paid enough attention to the AIDS epidemic to know about KS lesions, they probably *haven't* paid enough attention to know that KS has been treatable for some time. Maybe they think there are KS lesions under my shirt.

"Missy, what's with you today? Just leave everyone alone," says Seth.

Offended, Missy ducks under the water and emerges a minute later with an explosion of breath.

For the rest of the visit, just another two days, we eat and swim and go to movies and play backgammon at the game table. Once I find myself alone with Beryl in the kitchen. She's pouring us all sodas, and I'm laying out crackers and cheese on a plate.

"You know, Dad seems basically self-sufficient to me," I tell her. "This twin thing is a little out of character, but I think he has a ways to go before we worry about having to take care of him."

"Maybe," Beryl says, "but I'd just rest easier if he'd move into Far Horizon Vista."

"The choice is ultimately his," I say. I know I am being obnoxious by repeating this truism.

"I just worry. I might look like a flurry of activity," she says with an awkward glimmer of pride, "but you should know I worry about everyone in the family." She looks at me pointedly.

"Let me be one less worry," I tell her. "In case you've wondered, I'm HIV negative."

Since I've arrived in Scottsdale, Beryl has done nothing but parry around any allusions I've made to my life; still, she deserves to have this information. Right away, I realize that she has assumed me to be ill. Perhaps in her imagination she has attended many versions of my demise. I watch as she takes in a new reality. This is a manifest process, I believe, only to me. It is the single way in which I've experienced the purported telepathy of twins. Beryl hardly moves a muscle in her face, yet I can virtually see her concealing the evidence that she was harboring a mistaken impression. I can see her thoughts, like solitary footsteps, hasten to catch up to this new reality, this updated version of what is real. She is our father's daughter, and she developed early the habit of concealing any signs of foundering. As a young child, she learned not to speak before hearing all the facts. Only I could tell, I don't quite know how, when she was harboring the wrong idea. I never exposed her, less out of nobility than fear of reprisal. Yet now Avery has grown unexpectedly sentimental and vague, and it is not so essential for either Beryl or me to get our facts straight.

"Getting yourself tested could not have been an easy thing to do," says Beryl. She returns the soda to the refrigerator and stays behind its door, fussing with something inside.

Clearly she's avoiding having to look at me, but in truth I am the one who doesn't want to pursue this conversation. I still remember what Beryl said when we were thirteen, one Saturday after Ned Tanning left our house.

You know there's something wrong with him, don't you, Brian? Can't you tell? It's so obvious. All that waving around he does, he's such a girl.

I'd already begun to develop an antipathy for Ned Tanning. Despite my admiration for his mandolin playing, despite his intelligence and his piquant take on the social structure at Sandover Middle School, the most amorphous instincts had started to drive me from him. When my sister articulated what was behind these instincts, what had left me feeling so unsettled, so out of control, I told Ned Tanning that I didn't want to be friends anymore. I hadn't offered an explanation, and had resisted his appeals for one. I simply fell silent and watched as Ned replaced his mandolin to its velvet-lined case. The strain of trying to hold back tears altered his face; his lips became soft and blubbery, his long lashes fluttered rapidly—all proof that Beryl had been right, Ned Tanning was such a girl.

Now it's up to me to transcend this ancient history, to encourage Beryl to let me know who she is today. I know this. And I know that today she wouldn't dream of saying what she had about Ned. Yet this trip has been difficult, and I don't want to burden myself being the gracious host while she shows me the credentials of her newly acquired tolerance. The truth is, I just want to go home.

Back in the den, I take my place at the ivory-inlaid game table. In years past, my father would have long since jumped up and gone to attend to some paperwork. Now, though, he seems content to think about the game and listen to the shrill song of the cicada beyond the plate glass door, near the pool. He looks up and smiles when Beryl places a soda by his elbow. The obliging smile is an expression surrendered as barter to get along at his age. It is sorrowing and resigned, nothing like the smile I long ago courted, so broad it revealed most of his gleaming teeth and so affirming it charmed his staunchest detractors.

⮞ 6 ⮜

Among all of us at the Barracks, I am known for starting the shift in silence. Sometimes I begin speaking only when a customer demands my response. Gerald from Sony once said that he fully expected Hindi to emerge from my mouth once I got around to talking. Then he had walked away in disgust. This Tuesday evening, though, I cannot contain my pleasure at walking through the door and seeing the sconces with their warm yellow glow. Luis has also lit the votive candles in their little glass cups and placed them at the few tables along the windows. The dark wood of the bar is covered with nicks, and the mirror above it is tarnished and foggy. "Everything," I say, holding out my arms, "is so blessedly old!"

"He's back!" calls Luis, rushing from the kitchen. "And he speaks!"

"Have you ever been to Scottsdale?" I ask. "Here's the breakdown: 85% Caucasian, the rest Other. Other serves Caucasian. Buildings older than ten years are landmarks. You drive forever. The sun always shines. Pure hell."

"I would probably like it," says Luis. This is his stock response to the mention of anywhere but here; he has never been out of New York.

"You can have it," I say, thinking that Luis would be Other, would work in Scottsdale but live in some deteriorating neighborhood in Phoenix. "Maybe you can get your MBA out there."

"Brian, come in here, will ya?" The voice comes from the kitchen. It's Norman Brinsky's voice. I look at Luis. His lovely brown eyes are sad. "Jordan's in Passaic, at the hospital. Frank got sick when he was with his sister."

This is so startling that I think, irrationally, if Frank had not gotten himself tested, he would not have gotten sick. Who tests positive and gets sick the next day? As I walk in to see Norman, I am absurdly angry at Frank. It is Frank who has forced me into the unpleasant company of my boss. Norman Brinsky is no Charles Zidler, destined to build just another night spot, the Moulin Rouge, into a legend. Norman will continue to water down the vodka and count up the receipts I send him express mail every two days. He will do this and nothing more until a recession forces him to sell or he gets sick himself. Passing over the hardwood floor to the kitchen, I remember that this philistine has to some extent held sway over my destiny. My life is tolerable because he is largely absent from it. By the time I push through the swing door to the kitchen, I'm so livid that I know I've assumed the pout of a recalcitrant child.

"You're supposed to have a backup system here," says Norman. "Luis and me couldn't find anything. A Filofax, a list, nothin'. How'm I supposed to cope with this?"

"Don't get so excited," is all I can think of to say. My thoughts have turned perversely global; Norman says he can't cope with Jordan's absence for one night, and I immediately think of disasters that require real coping: earthquakes, famines, massacres. This jump I make from the trivial to the momentous is something I did as a teenager. It was a

rambling and evil twitch of mine; I used to bring up Bërg﹀
the Crusades when Avery complained of contractors not shov﹀
time. It was quintessential adolescent behavior, and Avery onc﹀
my allowance for it.

"We'll get through," I say. "How hard could it be to flip a couple
of burgers?"

As it turns out, it is as difficult as Norman makes it. After no small
amount of vacillating, he takes the logical course of placing me behind
the bar while he takes Jordan's place behind the grill. Everyone outside
hears a good deal of banging. Every time Luis comes through the swing
door from the kitchen, the sizzling on the grill is inordinately loud. Luis
says this is because Norman puts vegetable shortening on the grill
before he slaps on the patties. Luis has been dabbing at his eyes and
waving the air each time he emerges from the smoky kitchen. He says
Norman has done nothing but criticize Jordan, from the brand of
ketchup he orders to the way he braids the twist-tie on the ten-pound bag
of frozen fries. Nor does Norman approve of the martini I mix for him
as he cooks. My first night back from Scottsdale has not presented the
much-needed evidence that I am in command. When I leave the
Barracks, I see on the street only escapees from a world of claustro-
phobic families.

I want to go to the Shackle. The juke box there glows a lurid red and
blue against dusty blackness. Outside, steam rises from gutter grates.
After three days of steadfast radiance, I crave the gloom. But I'm not
ready to go, to possibly run into the man in the flight jacket. I head
toward Twenty-Second Street.

At home, I call Jordan, whom I've never called at his apartment. If
he is not in Passaic at the hospital, though, I'm certain he'll be up.

"Everything's fine," I say, since probably the ring has given him a
jolt. "It's just me, Brian. I'm calling to see how Frank is."

"Brian, you doll! He's not doing too bad. It's PCP, but they have it
under control. You know he wasn't taking anything. How could he, poor
shubble, he didn't know he had it."

Jordan has been calling Frank "poor shubble" for years. It's true that
something about Frank invites the epithet. He's small, and it's easy to
tell his formality with people is an attempt to mask his shyness. I've
always thought it strange that between the two of them, Frank is the
salesman. Jordan's effortless social ease virtually envelops Frank whenever they are together.

"When is he coming home?" I ask.

"Soon. They don't keep 'em in these days unless they're sultans. It's okay. They'll treat him and then get him started on a cocktail. But he'll be fine here. And he's got sick leave coming from Hudson Rug and Carpet. We'll get along."

There is a business-as-usual quality in Jordan's tone that angers me. I don't know precisely why I called, but it was not to hear the flat tones of Jordan's acquiescence. Frank will rally and flag, rally and flag. He might respond for a time—even for many years—to protease inhibitors, but he will still rally and flag, and then he will die. Jordan seems now to accept this as an inevitability that can be borne.

"How are his spirits?" I ask.

"Better," says Jordan. "His sister was good about it."

Good about it, I think. The best Frank can hope for from his sister is a moment of forgiveness for his being ill.

"Well, I just wanted to check in. We missed you tonight. You would've gotten a kick out of Mr. Ineptitude manning your grill."

Jordan laughs. "You're home early," he says. "It's only 3:00. No Shackle, tonight?"

"Forget it, I'm too worn out from watching Norman."

Jordan knows that I prowl around, and he has an idea of my haunts, but I am a mystery to him. He is a man who owns and uses porcelain egg cups, who polishes his kitchen sink with a chamois cloth and irons his jeans. He loves his life; I don't think I even intrigue him.

"Brian," he says. "When are you ever going to fall in love?"

"I'll have to check my calendar."

"I bet it's not on there. If you ask me, there are reasons why you don't fall in love."

Jordan's awful sincerity, his perfection of spirit, is taking aim at me again. I feel my pride rising, as well as my loftiness, my insistence on the essential complexity of all human dealings. He cannot possibly get away with so direct a statement. (How would Toulouse-Lautrec have responded? So clearly not meant for domestic love, what did he do when vapid strangers wondered at its absence in his life? Probably, I think, he unscrewed the handle of his hollow cane, took a deep, osten-tatious swig, and stared them down with his long-lashed brown eyes— his only comely feature.)

"It seems to me," I say, "that we were talking about Frank."

"You know," says Jordan in a confiding tone, "all those years with Trudy, working at the old diner, I'd see guys come in together, real swishes sometimes, but I never thought anything of it. And I knew where I was headed, too. I just said to myself, 'Hey . . . the world's a roomy place.'"

This is why I have never called Jordan at home, I think.

"Frank and I have this line with each other," he continues. "'Me, Tarzan, you, Jane.' It's not a role-playing thing. It means just because he's a certain way, doesn't mean I have to be that way too. And vice-versa, of course. Some of the guys that come into the Barracks, Brian, you're not them. They shouldn't bother you so much."

"Who bothers me?" Again, a child's defensiveness. It seems I can't stop. "I mean, besides Gerald, who bothers me?"

"It's not that you make it so obvious. Everyone loves you. You're a great listener, people trust you. You're definitely king of the bar. But you got a major love block, Brian, and if you ask me it has something to do with one or two flying pinkies in the world. If you want to be happy, you gotta get over it. I say this as a friend."

Why do people in couples so often appoint themselves heirs to the moral high ground? I want to say this, but Jordan's beloved Frank is in the hospital, and I must listen politely. I must not give in to my rising anger.

"You're saying, then, that although I'm a bartender at a well-known queer bar, I need to be outed."

"Okay, so you think this is none of my business. But lemme tell you why I like working at the Barracks. It's because every time that kitchen door swings open someone's heat drifts in. Most guys might be in there killing time, like straight bars the world over, but there's always one guy, doesn't matter his age, his looks, nuthin', who's so in love he doesn't have a face or his own brain cells. He's being pulverized. He could be in pain or in, you know, ecstasy, but I feel his heat every time Luis swings open that door. Lemme just say, it's a heat with a pulse. All these years, Brian, you're the only one who has stayed cool at the Barracks; you're the only one with a pulse no one's allowed to hear."

"It's my job," I say. "Me, the consummate professional."

Jordan sighs. He is frustrated that I won't be drawn in. Yet he is urging love upon me as he looks ahead to losing his own—a privation I cannot begin to fathom.

"I know you get hot in those bars by the water. That counts for zip in my book."

'Go polish your sink,' I want to say. My call, though, was supposed to be solicitous. I say instead, "Well, you Tarzan, me Jane, honey."

Jordan laughs. It's his wonderful, shaking laugh, and I say a cheery good-bye as its chords are still rumbling in his throat.

On nights like these, my English ladies' novels are the only soporific I can rely upon. I've built up a tolerance to most sleeping pills, but my discovery of tales that unfold in rural English villages has made a difference. I can always sense the threads tying together, and whether they will offer up an ultimately consoling message or a somber one is of no consequence; it is the very tying up I'm after. Feeling it around the bend puts me into the uniquely trusting state I require to fall asleep. Lots has happened in *Helen Croft: The Baybridge Manor Years*. The master of the manor is doing more than kindly tolerating Helen's youthful crush. It is Christmas, and he is shopping for her on Bond Street. He is weighing the merits of several weaves and materials. It is quite a stretch to believe that this dashing upper class banker could even momentarily respond to Helen's awkward flirtations. She has a wonderful enthusiasm and goodness, but she is, frankly, plain. Yet I read that the master's exquisite young wife is inordinately conscious of germs, and I am meant to extrapolate. Right as the possibility of romance gains credibility and I wonder how Helen might react to the master's expensive Christmas present, she is called back to the convent school to attend her ailing mother. At this point, Helen must struggle mightily with her conscience; her sweet mother has entered a decline right as Helen is on the brink of soaring into a new world. I finally get drowsy, and this is the perfect place to put the book down. There are chapters and another volume to go before Helen winds up in her scantily-populated Sussex village, and I can't imagine how the author, R.W. Dodson, will get her there.

On the way to the bathroom, I see the red light on my answering machine flashing. After talking to Jordan, I'd turned off the ring so that I wouldn't be awakened in the morning. The caller could be Beryl with news of another stroke; it could be Jordan to announce a sudden bad turn.

I have to replay the tape to recognize the voice, and when I do a warm satisfaction spreads through me; it's him, the man in the flight jacket. We hadn't exchanged numbers, so he must have gone to some trouble; he must have remembered I'd said I tend bar at the Barracks.

The message begins casually. He uses my name. He says he's the one from about a week ago, chuckles at the foolishness of this, then gives a few identifying characteristics, including the flight jacket. I hear in his voice a slight waver that surprises me. He says his name is Neil. (At last, no longer the man in the flight jacket.) Next he says what he wants to do to me. No longer does he sound nervous. He says he will do it until I beg him to stop. His intonation makes it clear that the bliss, not the pain, will be unendurable. Just listening stirs an erection. I think of Neil as an alpha animal, myself as his cowering prey, dependent upon his mercy but longing for the flares of coercion that make his mercy pools of grace. Then I press Replay, and transpose our roles. As I listen, I recall his sedate good looks—almost proper—a quite ordinary handsomeness that, unlike the rough trade I've picked up lately, belies his urgent need. He leaves his number. The challenge, of course, is to wait just long enough before using it.

* * *

Today I have arranged my lecture around a theme, the collection of the picture dealer Ambroise Vollard. Although I've given this lecture before, I've never done so this early into the semester. But why should I carry out the second session of the history of French printmaking class? It was headed for failure. Of course, I'll have to improvise later in the year, but I won't think about that now. Today we'll dip into the economics of it all—the mind-set of the people who represent artists and those who patronize them. It is the only angle that might hold a little interest for these kids.

I show slides of paintings and lithographs by Manet, Denis, Caillebotte, and Redon; sculptures by Aristide Maillol. I repeat what I've told them about the rejection of many of these artists' work within their time. Caillebotte, who I tell them is one of my personal favorites, could not give his paintings away; the Musée du Luxembourg rejected his bequest of seventeen canvases. I do not, as during other classes, linger on points of form and composition, theme and color. I slept only two hours this morning, two fitful hours that have depleted me more than would have no sleep at all, so I make it easy on myself. I tell my class that Vollard acquired paintings for practically nothing in his era of

51

unperceived masterpieces, that he purchased Manet's *Woman on a Sofa* for fifteen hundred francs and put the price of four hundred francs on a Renoir, *Femme Nue*, in his own shop. I tell my students that this last canvas is priceless and now hangs in the Rodin Museum; I tell them what *Woman on a Sofa* is worth today in American dollars. As I predicted, my students are fully with me. After I explain about dealers' percentages, they figure the margin of profit. Spittle flies from Matt Parnell's mouth as he announces his sudden interest in international art dealing. He will check out some web sites.

Nathan Weinstein, Chairman of the Humanities Department, had told me when he hired me that all of us in the tiny department must commit ourselves to exposing these students to a world beyond bleak practicalities. He thinks we are their only hope. I have succeeded on occasion, but I am failing now. They have shanghaied my class. I am surprised to hear them discussing Sotheby's and Christie's, auction houses I would not have expected them to know. They are arguing about reserves and commissions. Amazingly, one student knows the names of the chief financial officers at both houses. I have underestimated them. This was easy enough to do. Jersey Tri-Community is hardly Harvard Business School. It trains, at best, students who will one day reach the status of middle manager in the offices of unglamorous industries— plumbing supply distributors, novelty manufacturers, office supply companies. Do my students have any idea what it takes to trade in old masters? From where have they acquired their inflated view of themselves? Who has given them their great readiness for the world, their apparent certainty that one need not have a cultivated mind in order to deal in fine art?

When I began to teach at Tri-Community, I was committed to building my students' self-esteem. I have long since seen my obligation as rather to carve their self-regard to meet their capabilities. Now I have developed the perfidious desire to instill in my students a genuine self-doubt.

Rather than risk opening my mouth while in this foul mood, I sit down and let them talk. Cezanne's portrait of Zola is projected on the wall, but they are not looking at it. The portrait is dark, slippery, brooding. They are telling each other the likely financial workings of the auction houses and estimating the staggering profits of these houses. I give them a self-deprecating smile, showing I am out of my element.

When class is over, I go to my office overlooking the parking lot. It's not even mine, but more of a time-share allotted to the members of the Humanities faculty. In a moment, Damon Craig knocks on the door frame and walks in.

"You were quiet today, Damon."

"Sorry."

"No need to apologize. We all have our days. To be honest, the class got a little away from me today."

"Those guys . . ." says Damon, and shakes his head.

I want to agree, but can't. I look out at two boys from my class arguing over the open hood of a Subaru.

"Can we talk about my term paper?" asks Damon. He taps his finger on the sign-up sheet on my door. His is the only name on it.

"Good. Sit down."

He does, crossing his legs two different ways, finally spreading them apart and clasping his hands between them. I remember how the male models at the Cleveland Institute of Art always had trouble arranging themselves in a pose. Most times, the female models assumed a successful stance the first time; they knew how a garment would flow, how to flatter themselves. The men had no idea.

"It's not on your list."

"That's fine." I lean against the metal desk and wait for him to go on.

"You're not sitting," he observes.

"Oh, no, no. I'm not rushing you out," I say, and go sit behind the massive desk that makes me look shrunken.

"That's okay, Mr. Moss. Here's what I thought. I thought I'd do a thing about why it's okay for those women painters to paint family scenes."

I look at him, trying to figure out if Damon just wants a chance to air some feminist backlash. Or does he even think in a language that includes the words "feminist" and "backlash."

"You want to defend the validity of women artists choosing domestic subjects," I say.

"Right. I do. My girlfriend's a painter. She goes to art school in the city. She paints her sisters and her mother and things they do together. You should see her paintings. They're incredible. She already has a gallery interested."

I realize that Damon has probably taken my class to get closer to his girlfriend.

"How do you plan to approach the subject?" I ask.

"That's what I wanted to talk to you about."

"Well, first of all, which artists will you focus on?"

Damon blushes. "Definitely Mary Cassatt," he says.

I suspect he wants to focus on his girlfriend, but cannot say so.

"Okay. But you'll need to get yourself a context. You can't defend in a vacuum. Clearly, you feel you have to defend. You just said you wanted to write a paper on why it's *okay* for women to paint domestic scenes. Who says it isn't? And what female painters made it a point *not* to paint domestic scenes? Who have you read, and how is your viewpoint different from theirs? And what broader things do you intend to say about gender and domesticity? If it's okay for women to paint certain subjects, is it *not* okay for men? Many men during that era painted domestic interiors. Most of them, in fact. Vuillard specialized in them."

"But I don't want to talk about them. The men."

"I understand, Damon, but if I'm reading you correctly, I think you might be suggesting that you feel women are more entitled to interpret domestic scenes than men are, that it's their natural province. How can you prove this without comparing their work to those of their male peers?"

Damon stretches out his legs and puts his hands in his pockets. Deflated, he waits for help. He is a boy who knows how to ask for help and doubtless has a history of getting it. He seems sincere, yet he knows the power of his beautiful face. He has the bones of an aristocrat, if not the origins of one.

"Okay, look, you don't have to get into the paintings of Vuillard or the others if you're not interested. But I don't want this paper to be an homage. I'm going to give you some things to read. You're going to need a point of view to argue against."

I write down the titles *From the Center: Feminist Essays on Women's Art* by Lucy Lippard and *Framing Feminism, Art and the Women's Movement* by Parker and Pollock. "These should be available at the library. If they're not, let me know. And I have a copy at home of Linda Nochlin's article, 'Why Have There Been No Great Women Artists?' You need to try to get ahold of it, or I'll bring it in for you."

These texts were all assigned to me my first year in graduate school. I've never used them at Tri-Community.

Damon looks at me. Clearly this is all more than he bargained for.

"Where does your girlfriend go to school?"

"The School of Visual Arts," he says. "She's really good. I mean *really* good. She was just born with this power. She could paint you here now, and it would look exactly like you. But I'm not sure she's staying at SVA."

"Why not?"

"Most of the time she's against the grain there. They don't appreciate her. I think they're just jealous."

I think of my father's axiom, "wise competitors know when to concede." But they also know when *not* to.

"Sounds to me like she has too much talent to quit," I say.

"She wants to marry me," says Damon. When he looks at me, he struggles to keep the pride off his face. "This just happened."

Does Damon expect me, his teacher, to discourage him? I stuck it out well beyond college, to the all-but-dissertation stage of my Ph.D., only to find myself now still cobbling together a living. And that is with*out* marrying. "What do your families think?" I ask.

Instantly, his expression is troubled. "It's not up to them," he says.

We are moving into intimate terrain. Suddenly it is necessary for us to examine each other more closely, to evaluate our mutual trustworthiness. We do this surreptitiously, each in his own way. I need to decide how much I want to—or ethically should—draw this boy out. I look at his hands. They are recently evolved from a boy's hands, full-sized but still smooth, the fingers so long as to look a surprise to themselves. He moves his hands a great deal as he speaks, not for emphasis, but from nervousness, even cracking his knuckles once or twice. His entire countenance is that of one who thinks he's being judged. Yet there is nothing defensive about him. He wants to present himself to me as he truly is. And he looks at me with frankness. Has he heard I'm gay? It hasn't mattered before, but now he needs to know. He looks into my face, then away.

"I guess that's kind of sarcastic, the title 'Why Have There Been No Great Women Artists?'"

"You can decide when you read the article."

"Look at Mary Cassatt, though," says Damon. "You say that society restricted her choices, but I bet if it hadn't, she would have made the exact same pictures."

"We'll never know."

"Mr. Moss, I don't want to get you against me, or anything. I just maybe have really strong feelings because of the way the other girls at

SVA are about my girlfriend. Like, her subject matter and everything. I keep telling her they're jealous of her talent."

"Damon, I hope you're going to finish out school," I say. "Even if you do get married now."

Damon turns red again. "We're talking," he says. Regaining his poise, he runs his fingers down the back of his head and neck, stopping at his collar bone. His gesture. "So anyway, thanks for approving my term paper idea. You did approve it, didn't you?"

"Of course," I say. "How could I turn down a term paper born out of such chivalry?"

As I'm about to leave the building, Nat Weinstein, my department chair, stops me in the hall. He nods toward his office, a halogen-lit room with green metal shelves overflowing with books and binders. Theater posters hang on the glossy-painted cinder block walls, as well as a framed and autographed picture of Uta Hagen, with whom Nat once studied at the Herbert Berghoff School. Years ago, Nat got some interesting character roles in summer stock and a small part in a Broadway revival, but he stopped going to auditions when Jersey Tri-Community hired him. The Arts and Humanities department consists of Nat and me teaching drama and art history, and three adjuncts covering classic through modern literature. Four out of five of us are fags; Daphne Abbott is a straight woman with a lavish sense of camp. (At our last department picnic she insisted Nat dress like Edith Wharton. She came as Henry James, and behaved like a fuss-budget when the fried chicken was brought out without utensils.)

"Sit down," says Nat, removing a pile of *The Zoo Story* from the chair across from him.

"Uh-oh," I say. "This can't be good."

"I'll get right to it. The Board and Casey have been meeting all month. They're slicing down our curriculum to just what they can afford to get away with."

"I knew Casey'd send us to straight to hell," I say. Mike Casey is the president of Jersey Tri-Community. Our department was unanimously against his hire, especially when we discovered he'd once been associated with one of those business skill mills that advertise on the New York City subways. Our opinion was never sought, though, and Casey was hired last March.

"He can't get rid of us," says Nat. "We're tied to certification; we have him by the proverbials. But I'm afraid he and the others will have just a tad more influence over our curriculum."

"Mike Casey should die," I say.

"That would be quite handy," agrees Nat. "But it's not likely, considering his youth and hearty Celtic ancestry."

I wait. Nat has called me in here to discuss my role in this restructuring. The very fact that I'm waiting does not, of course, bode well.

"I wanted to give you as much lead time as possible. They want you to teach something next semester that they're calling 'Art and the Digital Revolution'. Basically, how computers have revolutionized all aspects of art, from fine art to commercial art. Especially commercial art."

"Jesus, whose brainchild was that? It would be one thing if it was a studio course, but to be taught out of the Humanities department?! It's ridiculous."

"I'd like to give you a pep talk," says Nat. "But I'm not feeling all that peppy."

"I'm not qualified to teach that class, Nat. What are they doing with my survey course?"

"Undecided."

"Oh, Christ, I don't believe this!" There goes my voice, I think, rising in that way I've always regretted. Panic made manifest. Never—in any situation—a good idea.

"What they want to come out of the technology course is to give kids a sense of the whole economic chain. You know. You examine the makers of the graphics software, what goes into the creation of these programs, the distribution outlets, the various applications, the user base, the product's consumer, blah, blah, blah. An overview of how it all works. It'll be one of those courses where all you have to do is stay one step ahead of the curve."

Nat is no less entrapped than I; like me, he is a white man just short of a Ph.D. who is making his way in academia. Simply staying afloat is a struggle. We have been reduced to making our sexual orientation clear to the rest of the faculty in the hopes of securing ourselves as a protected minority. Nat and I, as well as Brent and Rupert, the literature adjuncts, have all felt deflated by resorting to this self-flaunting, and we have all recognized its folly. It is assumed that the Arts and Humanities department has a greater than average number of gay faculty members; it has been so everywhere for generations. In their beneficence, our colleagues regard us offhandedly. They have no inclination to set us apart from themselves. They think they live in an ideal world, but Nat and I know they think with little depth and perception; they are incurious about the myriad differences that set us apart, differences that we alternately celebrate and are guilty of concealing. Nat is shaking his head, and we can't think of much else to say to each other. For the moment, we are captives in their unshaded world.

Finally, he says, "I'll help you get together a syllabus. And you know I'm here to support you."

"Thanks, Nat," I say, and slap him collegially on the back. "I do know that."

Before I leave, I ask about Sam, if he's on a trip. Sam is Nat's partner. They own a house not far from the hospital in Passaic, where Frank Cantore is now a patient. A culinary cruise company recently hired Sam as a maître d'. Before I'd met Nat, I never would have imagined such a company existed.

"Oh, I think he'll manage," says Nat. "Last night he had baby lamb and hearts of palm and a vintage Muscadet. For me it was meal-in-a-pouch time. I wasn't ambitious enough to do a stir fry."

I smile. "It could be worse," I tell Nat. "For me, it's the Aegean coffee shop or starve."

"Starve," muses Nat. "It's not pretty what we have to do to avoid starving, is it?"

"Nasty," I agree. "And I can't even say I wasn't warned. My father used to warn me all the time. 'What do you think it's going to be,' he always said, 'a picnic in the park?'"

⮞ 7 ⮜

Saturday morning, and I am thinking about La Goulue's breasts. I'm looking at a photograph taken in 1929, the year of her death at age 59. During her later life, her breasts were huge; they fell like saddle pouches over her ample sides. In the photograph, she wears a shapeless dress of the kind Charlene used to pull from her canvas bins. La Goulue, Jane Avril, May Milton—they and so many of the other artists' models led their own lives of dissolution.

58

A cigarette burns in the crevasse of a blue ceramic ashtray to my right. There's a notebook before me, but I've written nothing. For over a year, La Goulue and Toulouse-Lautrec's other models played a central role in my dissertation. I was interested in their enslavement. They were all enslaved. Henri's brush and his lithographic crayons indentured them to his service.

After the poster "Moulin Rouge—La Goulue" was plastered all over Paris, the free-spirited performer La Goulue was no longer her own woman. The director of the Moulin Rouge, Charles Zidler, wrote into her contract that she must pose for Henri; doing so became a condition of her employment. No posing, no dancing. From Zidler's point of view, La Goulue could be exchanged for any trollop off the street. Toulouse-Lautrec, though, was irreplaceable.

Before she died in penury, the fat and prematurely aged La Goulue tried to make a comeback. She set up as a belly dancer at a street fair, and Toulouse-Lautrec painted her canvas tent. Today its panels are in the collection of the Louvre.

And then there was the cabaret singer Yvette Guilbert. She despised how ugly Henri made her in his drawings; he did it again and again, without her permission, but what could she do? Her singing career thrived because he'd chosen her as his subject. Through Henri's paintings and lithographs, Yvette Guilbert's long black gloves became as famous as La Goulue's hairstyle, the golden helmet. After awhile, Toulouse-Lautrec took to painting the gloves alone.

One year after "Moulin Rouge—La Goulue," came "Divan Japonais," the poster that brought crowds to see Jane Avril dance. She died years later in a public asylum. What did the people who had clamored for her encores care? Too bad she squandered her charms, they thought, and bought tickets to see the performer next in line. It was the same for La Goulue and Yvette Guilbert; the men in their audiences regretted their departure for the time it took them to button their spats. The women were glad to see them go.

The exploitation of his female models was a motif I'd woven through "The Theme of Dissolution in the Works of Henri Toulouse-Lautrec." I still have a passing interest, but today the point I was making seems as stale as the parallels I drew between syphilis and AIDS.

As I get up to refill my tea cup, the phone rings. I plan to call the man in the flight jacket, Neil, later this afternoon, yet I hope this is him calling me.

"Hello." I aim for a mellow-yet-resonant tone.

"Hi. Is it okay that I call you?"

To my surprise, it's a young girl's voice, and it takes me a moment to realize it's my niece, Melissa.

"Missy? Sure, of course you can call me." She has never called before.

"Pops left. He went back home. Mom said I should call and tell you."

"Uh-huh. I'm glad you did. Is he okay? Was he okay when he left?"

"Yes." She says no more. Maybe she is suddenly shy.

"Are you upset or glad that he's gone?"

"Umm . . . both, I guess. I'm not supposed to mind that he's old, but I do."

"It's too bad you didn't know him when he was younger. He was quite a . . . vivid presence."

She says nothing. This last might be too abstract for her, but I get a kick out of the image it conjures of my father—a swashbuckler, a grand orator, a visionary. Avery in his prime *had* been a vivid presence, but one honed on the tension of not knowing who he was. He insisted on seeing himself as he ensured the community saw him: a civic leader and a dutiful father, always highly eligible but never quite ready to remarry.

"He was here for five weeks," she says.

"Really, it was that long? Well, it was good of your folks to have him."

"Why didn't *you* take him?" Melissa wants to know.

I take a breath. It must be written somewhere that one should turn the other cheek when being judged by a twelve-year-old.

"Long story," I say.

"But can *I* come visit you?" she asks. "My best friend Amy's been to New York three times. So have lots of kids been up there."

"I guess it's up to your parents," I say, but I don't encourage her to ask them. I can imagine this bright-eyed twelve-year-old in her designer jeans climbing the crumbling steps of my tenement. Hector Diaz could be sitting on the stoop, wearing his dog collar. Seraphina, the transvestite down the block, might be returning from a shoplifting spree. She will want to show me her new tank top, and she'll be particularly charming with Melissa, maybe giving her a pair of dangling earrings or a Lucite bangle. Then we'll walk through my fluorescent-lit hall that will smell of two-day-old curry and into my apartment that is smaller than her bedroom in Scottsdale. Its dark woodwork will introduce her to a melancholy she never knew existed. As consolation, I will show her

Mrs. Winfield's garden, but I will realize too late that the season is over and there are nothing but haggard junipers and dry stalks. Melissa will politely ask to call her parents. From the bathroom, I will hear her lose control, sobbing and hiccupping, and then there will be silence while Beryl counsels her to stick it out.

"They'll let me come," she says, confidently. "They're on this thing about maturing experiences."

"They might raise a question or two about my qualifications as a maturing experience. How's school?"

"Fine." Small, deflated voice.

"How's your jazz dancing?"

"Okay."

I don't know how to end this conversation, and I'm not in the mood to talk to Beryl or Seth. "Do you think Pops is home yet? Maybe I should call him. I really should get off and call him, honey, and make sure he got home all right."

"Okay."

Her voice is now that of a much younger girl. It twists through me. "It was good talking to you, honey. I'm glad you called. You can always call. Anytime, okay?"

"Okay. Well, thanks." She hangs up while the phone receiver is still tight and warm against my ear. Finally I replace it, but instead of calling my father, I call Neil, in my mind still the man in the flight jacket.

It's after 2:00 AM on Sunday. Jordan and Luis and I are leaving the Barracks. Luis is going uptown to Washington Heights where he lives with his sister and her boyfriend. Jordan is going home to Frank, who has been back from the hospital in Passaic for two days. As Luis and I turn our collars up, we listen to Jordan talk about setting the alarm to go out and get Frank fresh croissants from the bakery and a rose from the all-night green grocer.

We say goodnight, and I walk in the direction of the Shackle, then remember about Neil and turn away, not wanting to run into him there.

Neil has asked me out on a date. Given his message on my answering machine, the list of what he wanted to do to me until I begged him stop, the last thing I'd expected was for him to ask me out on a date. Embarrassed for him, I'd said yes. It would be more than a little awkward to go to the Shackle now and see him emerge, a little dazed looking, from the back room.

Instead, I go to the Aegean Coffee Shop. Athos, Elena Pitsaros' son, is waiting tables. "You're the best, Brian," he says wearily. (He's been saying this for fifteen years.) "What you have tonight?"

"Hi, Athos, how've you been?"

He just nods and waits. His resentment is so tightly compressed it could unfurl with my very next word.

"The feta and tomato omelet," I say.

"Nothing but the best," answers Athos, and leaves.

In the booth ahead of mine sit two men and a red-headed woman. The young woman is all over her boyfriend. Her hands are constantly upon him, plucking at invisible pieces of lint, wrapping both her arms around his one when he so much as shifts in his seat, tucking his long hair behind his ears. My stomach tightens at her constant nearness, her focused anxiety. I look at the boyfriend. He's checking me out.

They're talking loudly about a party in New Jersey.

"I'm not tired," says the man whose back is to me. "Let's go."

"Joey," says the girlfriend, "I don't want to go."

The boyfriend Joey ignores her. "Hey," he calls to me. "What do you think? Are you tired? Want to go to a party in New Jersey?"

We all laugh at the absurdity of me, a stranger, accompanying them to a party in New Jersey. They're a little drunk.

"I guess we're all nocturnal," I say.

"Not me," the girlfriend answers. "My circadian clock is normal. " She looks at Joey pointedly. "*Nor-mal*."

"Well, you're odd man out," Joey snaps, and I cringe for her. She releases her hold on him, crosses her arms.

"I'm two-thirds serious," calls Joey. "It's right across the GW Bridge. A good friend of mine is in a jazz band. Do you like jazz?"

"I do," I say. What am I doing? They are about the age of my students. This could just as well be their first time staying out all night.

"It's too late to go to bed anyhow," says Joey. He rises. There's a tip on their table—all coins. "Come on. You can take the express bus back," he tells me. "The night's shot anyway."

"Sure, why not?" Increasingly, I've felt faded at this time of early morning, bewildered. I should go home, I should act my age, but Joey is fairly gorgeous, and his ambivalence excites me.

I leave twelve dollars on the table, almost twice the cost of the omelet, and stand up.

The other man has been quiet, but now he shakes my hand. "I'm Kyle," he says. "This is Joey and Sarah. I'll drive."

I end up on the back seat with Sarah. I watch her in profile as she leans forward to nibble on Joey's ear. She acts low rent, but she has a decidedly patrician look. It's the cheekbones, the brow, the way she rakes her fingers through her hair. There is nothing genteel about Joey; he is her insurrection.

Suddenly we're there, at an apartment complex in Fort Lee.

"Hey!" says Sarah when Kyle pulls the car into a parking spot marked with a number. "What's going on with you guys?"

"Let's go in and get wasted," Kyle says. "Then we'll hit the party."

Joey gets out with Kyle and they go ahead. I'm not sure what to do.

"It's *Kyle's* place," says Sarah, disgusted. She yanks the door handle and leans her weight against the door to open it.

I've ridden here in the hopes of arriving at a large party and disappearing with Joey into a remote bedroom. Getting wasted does not interest me. By now I'm so tired I don't care what happens, as long as I get to flop down somewhere and sleep.

But Joey and Kyle's pleasure, it turns out, is to see me with Sarah. Sarah's pleasure is to please Joey. They know, the two young men tell me, that my cock can rise with whole Navy fleets looking on; their goal is humble, just the two of them want to watch it rise for Sarah. It doesn't. How could it? There is no arousal where there is no freedom of choice. I don't start to get hard until Joey pulls off his shirt, unzips his fly, and tells Sarah to bend over.

Toulouse-Lautrec flashes through my mind as he does, mystifyingly, on these unlikely occasions, a spectator from another century. Unable to see my dilemma, he marvels at my luck—the red-haired Sarah. He becomes like a manic cartoon artist, his paint brush swiping the air as he cheers me on.

It turns out that Sarah's capacity for humiliation has its limits; she will go only so far to capsize the expectations of her well-off parents. She manages to break free of Joey, gives him the finger, goes over to her pocketbook and removes a package of cigarettes. She offers me one, consolation, I suppose, and I take it. As Joey passes by, he tells us we're pathetic. He pours himself another bourbon. Sarah, smoking and weeping, sits on a futon. Her arms are wrapped about her knees and her lips are tightly shut, but her shoulders shake and her tears stream.

I sit next to her. "I'm sorry," I say, though we both know tonight is not my fault.

She tells me Joey would be better off if he were like me, if he would just admit it already. She's stopped crying and has the hiccups.

"He never will," I tell her, for I have seen others like Joey, and I predict he will go through a period of tormenting gay men, then relent to a spiritless life of convention. He will be particularly proud of his kids, as if startled by their existence, and maybe in later life a gentleness will settle over him. I don't want to judge Joey, but I do tell Sarah that she'll get over him and find someone who will appreciate her.

"That would be a first," she says, picking a fleck of tobacco off the tip of her tongue.

I smile. "I guess we didn't think we'd wind up being allies tonight, huh?"

She raises her hand to drag from the cigarette, but it's trembling, and she breaks out sobbing again. I take the cigarette and snuff it out. "I can't stand it!" she blurts out.

"I know," I say, but I'm struggling to keep my eyes open. I stroke her hair.

"He's so awful!" she says, "So . . . *mean*."

The simplicity of this goes right through me. It's been years since I've singled someone out as mean, even longer since I've been hurt by a mean person.

"Give me a hand here," I say, and pull her up. Together, we unroll the futon. We lie down side by side, and she wriggles tight against my chest. "It's going to be all right," I repeat, until she stops weeping. Soon I hear a light wheezing. We sleep for less than three hours. I wake up with an aching neck and a dry throat, and slip away from her.

It's almost noon, Sunday, when I get home. After my shower, I pick up *Helen Croft: The Baybridge Manor Years.* The new chapter opens in drafty quarters above the kitchen at the convent school, where Helen's mother, Bernadine, is laid up with an unnamed intestinal disorder. It's too depressing to continue. I want to jump ahead to the scene in which the Master of Baybridge will present Helen with her woolen cape trimmed in lush velvet. (I want to hear bells ringing!) But rather than skip ahead, I replace the book to the nightstand. I bury my head deep into the pillow and exhale hugely, as if in its release my breath could dash the effect of the night's experience, leaving me longing only for the sweetest connection to another human being. I think of the fresh rose Jordan put at Frank's place this morning. I wonder if it took Frank by surprise—if it was, for him, like going to the Nile, or looking up at the Himalayas.

❧ 8 ❧

Debbie Shuster has left my father. I get this news on a sheet of paper Beryl has folded around some family photographs taken during my trip to Scottsdale. It's the Wednesday after the ill-fated trip to Fort Lee, and I've just returned from Tri-Community. The note says, "Dad came home to a rough time. Debbie Shuster broke up with him. She must have found someone else to put her up by the lake. Dad's upset. Give him a call?"

At age thirty-nine, Beryl now tempers her orders to me with insincere question marks, such as the one at the end of the command, "Give him a call."

Fleetingly, I consider calling Avery. My face blazes at the thought. Even the Avery Moss of Scottsdale, the new Avery who slips on wash-and-wear and pauses to listen to the song of the cicada, would not know how to respond to my expression of sympathy.

For as long as I can remember, my father has been a man of unlimited choices. Women pursued him shamelessly. After my mother died, remote female acquaintances invited him over for dinner, took Beryl and me to play miniature golf, suggested picnics with their own children. My father dated an endless stream of divorcees and widows—trim women with beehives, bubbles, and French Twists. He spent money on these women, opened doors for them, guided them with a light touch to the small of their backs. He made reservations to a supper club featuring a jazz quartet, then encouraged them to wear whichever cocktail dress most flattered their legs. He did not date women with thick ankles, and he moved among slim-ankled women with little upheaval. If a woman demanded more of his attention than he was prepared to give, he cut her off, beckoning the next one in line. He kept Beryl and me out of what he called his "dating scene," simply arranging to pay Charlene time-and-a-half to stay with us after work.

The truth is, I am too humiliated for Avery to call him. Always circumspect about his women, it would be easy enough for him to avoid

65

the subject of Debbie now that she has broken up with him, and I'm sure he would find it spiteful of me to bring her up.

The phone rings. Half hoping it's Neil calling to cancel our date, I pick up.

"Hey, Roy Rogers," Avery says, hale and hearty as a cruise director.

"Dad?"

"You remember, don't you, those Roy Rogers and Dale Evans outfits you and Beryl used to go tearing around in?"

I have to strain to remember the scrub-faced, distinctly untough cowboy of my youth, to remember that I was Roy Rogers and Beryl Dale Evans, and we had the costumes of their franchise to prove it.

"I was just thinking of you, Dad. I was just going to call you."

"I'm back safe and sound on Periwinkle. Quite a visit we had, don't you think? A good visit; a good, solid visit."

The last time Avery called me was six years ago, when Melissa fell off a palomino horse, the first horse she'd ever ridden, and Beryl had called Avery from the hospital and told Avery to call me, to let me know that Melissa had broken her collarbone and if the break had been a quarter inch over, she would have been a quadriplegic.

"Sure," I answer Avery. "Good visit. What's going on, Dad? Is Missy all right? I just spoke with her; she called me to tell me you'd gone home."

"Missy's a doll, isn't she?"

I wonder if Avery has called to tell me about Debbie Shuster. I haven't taken off my jacket yet. Sweat rolls down the pit of my chest.

"She's a good kid," I say. "Seth sure loves her."

"Beryl loves her, too," my father booms. "We went over some things. Beryl's doing some good planning. Couple of annuities ought to pay for Missy's college. I told Beryl I'd finance undergraduate or graduate school, her pick."

"Melissa's only twelve," I say. What if she wants to be a waitress, I think. What if she wants to be a goddamn bartender in a neighborhood dive? Then I remember: Melissa's probably never seen a dive, let alone been to one.

"College is just six years away," he says. "That's nothing. When you get to be my age, you'll see that's a nano-second." He pauses. The old Avery would have taken this opportunity to point out my disregard for the future, and for Seriousness in general. I see that Avery has given up on me, has fully transferred his aspirations to the females of his descent.

I say nothing, but unzip my jacket and pat my fingers reassuringly on my chest.

"Guess who I swung by and saw earlier today?" asks Avery.

"How is she?" I ask, deliberately stealing his thunder. "How did she look after all this time?"

"You know, pretty well. The same, really."

I doubt Avery had ever looked much at Charlene.

"But that son of hers—Mosel, Moses, whatever—he's shot to hell. I remember when he was a good-looking guy. Powerful build. Now he's got a gut and he gave me this none-too-welcoming stare. What the hell, I didn't come to see him. She was a lady, though. Served me those little Stella D'oro cookies, not so bad, really, with chocolate sprinkles, and some black tea. The tea I couldn't stomach, so I just let it sit there. Then she got the pictures. I'm looking at one right now, Roy Rogers, you and Beryl on those skates you don't see anymore."

"You sound good, Dad," I say. I try for a little intonation; I emphasize *good*, put a punch of incredulity in it so that Avery will realize I know about Debbie Shuster. It's not necessary, I think, for me to actually mention her. Avery may be seventy-one with a minor stroke behind him, but he's got time and money. His marketability has not declined.

"I'm pulling together a little project. All the pictures of you two, with captions. I'm going to have them printed on rag paper and bound in a slip case. Good cowhide, a little tooling. I can get ten copies printed up. Remember Dan Sharp? My main printer for years. Moss Development put his kids through college."

At what age will the pictures of me stop, I wonder, at age eight when I started showing a bit too much interest in art? This interest would have been acceptable had it not shown in my face, giving me a solemn and faintly insalubrious look, a questionable way of pursing my lips when lost in my new reflections, my new habit of looking at objects as elements of a composition.

"Well, go ahead, Dad," is all I can think of to say. I feel a rage building. My father has forsaken his intelligence. He is no longer in the hunt, and his sense of alacrity has vanished. He makes no demands. It would no longer be a source of pride that, upon his order, I years ago completed the final entry in the *World Book's* WXYZ. I am tempted to remind him of this accomplishment. Ask me what zymoscope means. You, arch proponent of expanding one's mind, do *you* know what a zymoscope is?

"I'll send you a couple of albums," he says.

Whom does he think the second copy will be for?

"I don't have a lot of room, Dad," I say.

"What, for a couple of 9 x 12 photo books you have no room?" There is that exasperated tone that signals an outburst, but he gets himself under control. "Well, you ought to come visit, then. Plenty of room here."

"I will, Dad."

"Not much new since I got back. Remember Debbie Shuster? You met her, I remember we went to the club once. We decided to call it quits. One of those things."

There is a terrible hollowness in Avery's voice. This man who has always scorned compassion, who becomes fidgety around any show of solicitude, has left a light under his closed door. I see his shadowy feet moving back and forth, worrying a trail in the carpet, and I want him to turn the light off, to block his fretful pacing from my view.

"You'll find a sharp-looking woman in no time," I tell him. It's an expression from my childhood, 'sharp-looking woman,' his expression.

"I'm not worried," he says.

"You have no cause for worry," I say. "I'm really sorry, Dad, but I have to get off and go to work now."

"Work? Now? Oh, you're still at that place."

"Thanks for calling, Dad. I'm glad you're back safe."

* * *

Cool evening, with a decent wind. I love that. I'm on my way to meet Neil for the date. Nothing too imaginative, just dinner, then maybe a walk, if it's not too cold. On my way to the restaurant, I can't help recalling my most recent dates. There haven't been many of late. My second-last one was with a guy named Mitch, a junior-level architect who spent the whole evening dissecting the politics in his office. My last date, even worse, was with a terrifically handsome man I'd met at The Barracks. I'd been so smitten that I'd made an exception to my no-intense-flirting-on-the-job policy. His name was Lance, but Jordan and Luis called him Sir Lancelot. He'd invited me out to the Metronome, a club and restaurant, to hear a new jazz band. There was great promise in the air. When the bill came, first one, then the next of his credit cards was rejected. Right out of a Grade B movie. I had to walk to the closest cash machine while he stayed on, enjoying the most expensive port on the dessert menu.

Although Neil is not wearing his flight jacket, I spot him outside the door of the restaurant where we'd agreed to meet. I have a quarter block to go before I reach him. I always hate the approach—the endless walk toward. Too much can be revealed during this approach. When we meet up, we kiss briefly. Both of us blush, and this is a bit thrilling.

After the waiter takes our order, Neil says, "I wanted to apologize for the other night. After I left, I realized I might have really hurt you."

"Well . . ."

"I'm sorry if I did. I hope you don't get the wrong idea. It's been . . . quite a while."

This is fairly implausible. After all, I've seen him twice at The Shackle.

"I'm not sorry. I mean, maybe you did hurt me a little, but it was just a . . . byproduct."

"A *byproduct*?"

We laugh, clearing the air. Then he tells me that—unbelievable as it is, even to him—he has very recently broken away from conversion therapy.

"You don't mean what I think you mean."

"'Fraid so."

"Really? I didn't think *any*one in New York would . . . feel the need. Are you religious?"

"No. I was raised Methodist, a none-too-gay-friendly religion, but my parents were barely observant, and I'm not at all. That's not why I did it. There were a lot of factors. To tell you the truth, AIDS was one of them, but only one. Anyway, we don't need to get into it now. I only wanted to try to justify my overzealousness the other night."

"Really? You think you were overzealous? I think you were wonderful."

Neil looks down, then directly at me.

"And what about the last message you left on my machine? That didn't sound *so* awfully repentant. Shall I repeat it for you?"

"No, no, that's okay." Now he's genuinely embarrassed; his phone self has outdone his live self. He takes a sip of water. "Maybe I'm giving out some mixed messages. I'm sorry, I hate it when people do that to me. But I asked you out hoping we could get to know each other a little better."

I feel the blood rush to my face, and the skin behind my earlobes grows hot. Harmless though his proposition sounds, he's opening us up to all kinds of conjecture. My first impulse is to ask, "Why?" I don't. I say nothing.

"Now *you're* embarrassed. We're not doing so well here."

"We're doing fine."

I say this because it's what's expected. I didn't come here seeking to know Neil. I came here because he asked me, and because I thought it might be a condition of taking him home again. Even now, as we eat in this noisy restaurant, I am adoring the way he looks, his broad face and almond-shaped eyes, his unusually long lashes, his mouth that would be the shape of good will and bemusement if those qualities had a shape.

Despite my mounting desire, we stay at the restaurant for a long time. My curiosity about his conversion therapy grows, but he doesn't bring it up again. He tells me that for ten years he worked in real estate, but now he is in his last semester of training to be an acupuncturist. He spent all last year studying traditional Chinese medicine in Nanjing. I like this, find it intriguing. And he tells me his age: thirty-six.

When it's my turn I talk about teaching at Tri-Community and my unfinished dissertation, my recent thoughts about returning to it. He already knows about The Barracks, no need to mention it. Neil asks about my family. He wants to know how my mother died. "Car wreck," I say, but then turn away as I do when I can see in people's eyes that they are thinking about the burden of such a loss coming to a five-year-old. This turning away is reflexive—I wouldn't know how to do otherwise.

Finally, we are back at my apartment. I've left the 1929 photograph of La Goulue on my kitchen table. The box containing my old dissertation is there, too. Neil glances down.

"Some of what I'm working on," I say in a tone I hope doesn't invite further inquiry.

"You're planning to redirect it?"

I nod yes. "Theoretically, that's what I'm planning."

I open the kitchen window. We hear Callas singing Casta Diva from the first act of *Norma*.

"My neighbor's an opera nut," I say. "But actually, I'm lucky. She has a first-rate sound system. Sometimes I just sit in my chair and do nothing but listen."

Still standing, Neil briefly closes his eyes. I'm reminded of his solo dance at the Shackle, his capacity to quickly transcend himself.

Taking a chance, I go to pull the Murphy bed from its cabinet. I lie down and wait.

Eventually he comes to sit on my bed. "Do you paint, also? Did you paint some of the pictures you've hung?"

All these questions. I've been with guys where we've kept up the anonymity for months at a time. With one, we've never exchanged even first names.

"Let me see you," I plead. "Take off your shirt."

Neil starts to unbutton his shirt. He's slow about it.

I touch his leg. "What is it? What's the matter?"

"I'm not sure."

"You brought up this conversion therapy thing pretty fast. Why did you tell me about it?"

He looks at me. "I just got so unhappy. I knew from the beginning it wouldn't work."

"But why did you want it to work?"

"There's this odious side to me that just wants to conform, that's sick to hell of all the inside jokes and the never-ending wit and drollery, the having to come out every time you turn around. The holding *back* from coming out every time you turn around. All of it. And then all my bad feelings just got worse when I moved to China."

"I bet."

"I loved Nanjing, and before I came home I also spent time in some hospitals in Beijing, observing traditional Chinese medicine practices. I loved it all, but I was lonely every minute, and I resented having to be lonely."

"So when you came home . . ."

". . . I started looking around, and I found this guy, this therapist, and I figured I'd try it, it would at the very least be interesting."

"So what *was* it like? I imagine some deprogramming thing, like they do for people in cults."

"A little more subtle. The shrinks who do this are trained. That's what's so insidious. They aren't all religious zealots or quacks in polyester suits, believe me. There's a whole association and the president teaches psychiatry at Albert Einstein Medical College. There are members all over the country, and they think of themselves as mavericks bucking the psychiatric establishment. They want to get homosexuality reclassified as a developmental disorder. They're undaunted by the lack of empirical evidence."

"And you went to one of these guys."

"I went to one."

I open the drawer of my bedside table. "Want to smoke a joint?"

"Okay. Ordinarily I'd pass, but now you've got me off my stride." He smiles.

"Someone gave me this. I'm not all that much of a pot-smoker, either." (This is true. Luis gave me this joint before I went to Scottsdale, but I forgot to take it with me.) I light it and pass it to Neil.

"Do you want to say more or is this making you too uncomfortable?" I'm rubbing inside his unbuttoned shirt as I ask this, circling his nipple with two fingers.

Neil leans over and holds the joint to my lips. The feel of the smoke passing down my throat, harsher than that of cigarette smoke, reminds me of my first joint with Ned Tanning, the mandolin player who died of AIDS long after we'd ceased to have contact. I close my eyes; it's easy to give myself over to the illicit rush that accompanies that first toke, the adrenaline kick that spills a formless dread within me. When I open my eyes again, Neil is lifting his shirt over his head. He takes both my arms and manages to get me under him on the bed. He straddles me, the inside of his solid thighs tense against the outside of mine so I can't move. Now nothing is rooted to its place in my apartment, for I have no need of the fundamentals around me. Molly Winfield's garden has grown silent, and the quiet remains until hours later, when the notes of Casta Diva rise once again with the early light.

Neil opens his eyes and groans. "Oh God, not again! What time is it?"

"She's a little obsessive," I whisper. "It's probably a new CD." I get up to shut the window. "Go back to sleep," I say.

Neil looks at me until I grow nervous, probably visibly so, then closes his eyes.

❧ 9 ❧

No bruises, and the few from our first night together are fading. I finger the one along my ribs, notice a sallow shade has appeared at its center; the bruise will soon be gone. When Neil left, neither of us said anything about a next meeting. My breathing is rapid, I notice, and it is thin.

Afraid of embarking on the day, I throw off the blankets and jump from bed.

After I shower, I clean and arrange things in the apartment. Then I decide to call Charlene. The Wrights' phone rings for a long time. I have an image of Charlene struggling out of her armchair to get to the phone, the one phone, in the kitchen. She will be slow, avoiding the resolute step whose vibrations would land as stinging pain in her hip; maybe there is a cane or even a walker, so I let it ring.

Finally it is Mosley who answers, and I want to slide the receiver soundlessly into its cradle. Instead, I become my father's son. "Mosley Wright," I say heartily, and pause. "Brian Moss." Good, adamant tone and the manner of a first-string varsity player. I want to applaud myself. I haven't spoken to this man since he was the boy who wanted me out of his mother's house, the boy who made up the couch with sheets from the deep freeze and scooped Spanish Rice from my plate onto his the moment Charlene turned her back.

Silence at the other end. Then a chuckle, impressively neutral. "You don't say."

"I'm calling from home. New York."

"It's raining Mosses these days."

"Yes, I heard my dad was there. How're you, Mosley?"

"Hangin'."

"Good," I say, though I suspect he is toying with me. I want to ask about his job driving a school bus, but the question is too lame. I hope that he'll ask what I'm doing so I can say I'm tending bar, but he doesn't. No doubt Avery told him I was teaching college.

"Your mom around, or did I catch her out?"

"She's around."

I wait. He's still there, breathing.

"I was sorry to hear about your dad, Mosley."

"Uh-huh. Thanks."

"Lloyd was such a gentle guy." I say. "He was always good to me."

"He was not one to say 'no,'" is all Mosley says.

I hear the resentment there, of course, but why respond? Instead, I flash on Lloyd's hands, how as a boy I could not reconcile their size—huge, thick-fingered, rough-knuckled hands—with his sweet temper. Yet Lloyd's hands seemed to be a burden to him; they dangled apologetically at his sides in a way Avery's hands never would, for when Avery's hands had been idle they had retreated becomingly into his silk-lined trouser pockets. "So your mom's around?" I repeat.

"Hold on."

Waiting, I think of Neil, how he looked back from my doorway and could not decide what to do next.

"Yes?" There might be a tinge of dread in Charlene's voice.

"I hope I'm not disturbing you. It's Brian. Did Mosley tell you?"

"Well, of course you're not disturbing me, Brian! This is my hot-chocolate time is all. Nestle's hot chocolate and three baby marshmallows. Seven mornings a week since Lloyd passed. Did you ever have a silliness you clung to?"

"A whole host of them," I tell her. "I'm just checking in. To see how you're making out. How's your hip?"

"Just perfect unless it's rainy or sunny," she says. She probably says this on the church steps every Sunday morning. I am sure she manages to attend services. When she worked for us she went to the First Pentecostal on Superior every Sunday. Lloyd never went. To get out of it, he teased her that he didn't want to stand in the way of her romance with the preacher.

"I may come to Cleveland before long," I say, announcing news to myself.

"My, wouldn't that be something? A treat for your dad."

I listen for the hint of sarcasm in her voice, but there is none. I am humbled that I know someone who uses the word *treat* without a certain tone.

"I understand my dad was by," I say. "I was hoping he would drop that picture business."

"We struck a deal, the two of us. I gave him the picture and he promised to give me one of those special books he's printing up."

This is too much; I can't even pursue it. "What did you think about all his changes, Charlene?"

"Now, I'm not sure. One thing is, never in the years I worked for you would I *ever* have imagined eating Stella D'oros across from your dad. And that's even with me knowing about his powerful sweet tooth."

"Look," I say, "me either." I wonder if Charlene registered the change in his style of dress, but I think she would be uncomfortable if obligated to remark on it.

"I never said your father was unfair," she reminds me. "That was one thing I never said."

"No, maybe not unfair, . . ." I answer.

In the most basic matters of survival my father was even-handed; he raised Charlene's pay regularly and he gave her a generous bonus every Christmas. In his mind, this forgave what he was unable to control—how he would snap at her for no greater reason than walking slowly, as fast as she could manage considering her forty or fifty extra pounds. He never said anything overtly offensive, but he snapped without provocation and, worse yet, his face assumed a long-suffering expression if ever he had to repeat an explanation to Charlene. To witness these brief episodes as a small child was to know, if for a moment, the obliterating solitude of the powerless.

"Did he behave himself when he was over there?" I ask now.

"Oh, yes, he really did," says Charlene. "So how've you been out there in New York?"

"Fine, thanks. Managing. I have a couple things going."

"Are you still making those drawings of yours?"

"My ball point wonders, you mean?" The desk in my room had always been strewn with the complicated abstract designs I'd drawn with an endless supply of Bic pens. On cleaning days, Charlene had gathered these drawings and placed them in a neat stack on a shelf where I kept my motorcycle models and board games and trading cards. Every week, without fail, those drawings traveled from the place where I was meant to do homework to the place where I was meant to entertain myself.

"I have almost no time for drawing anymore," I tell her. "But you know I teach art. Teaching art's not what it used to be, but I guess I can say I teach art."

"Is that right? To little children?"

"Their *bodies* aren't little."

Charlene laughs. "They don't grow up these days. I got a giant-sized one in the other room." She sounds weary.

"I'm going to let you go now, honey. But I'll call if I come to Cleveland soon, if that's all right."

"My, I would hope you wouldn't have to ask," she says, the perfect answer.

* * *

75

Rather than replace the carpet in my classroom, Tri-Community maintenance has used some sort of tool to try to etch out the swastika. It looks horrible—like a swastika that has been scratched over.

"How lovely," I say when I enter the class. "And what a *creative* solution."

Some students laugh. While they probably had nothing to do with the swastika, they regard it as merely the high jinks of a spirited fellow student.

I'll have to say something to Nat. This little economy is shameful. The remains of a swastika is just as bad as a clearly delineated one. Worse, in a way. I can't believe I teach in this dump.

Today will be devoted to the paintings of Gustave Caillebotte. If I have to teach something as discouraging as Art and the Digital Revolution next semester, I'm going to teach what I please for the remainder of this one. If that means pressing my personal tastes on my students, so be it. I'm thoroughly sick of this alleged college that will not direct a single beam of light onto that which is not useful.

There is perhaps a two-thirds attendance today. The class is talking loudly. Some students are eating snacks from cellophane bags. I walk to the back of the room, project *Floor Scrapers* onto the front wall, and say nothing. I simply look. Let them continue their talking, their eating; I'm not their baby-sitter. It's particularly galling that they regard my class as an opportunity to discuss their upcoming Accounting Practices midterm.

I look ahead at the projected slide and ignore their chatter. This is not difficult for me; I've been blocking out conversations my whole life. What was my choice—listen to Avery explain the fine points of commercial real estate development to my sister? Listen to Beryl and her friends' exhaustive study of clothes and makeup? Zoning-out is a survival skill that no longer requires my cultivation.

Gustave Caillebotte's *Floor Scrapers* features three shirtless men on their knees. They are removing by hand layers of old varnish off a wooden floor. In the foreground is an open bottle of wine set on a hearth. A few tools are scattered about. The wood shavings are the most sensual part of the painting. Their texture is described by the arch of their curls, and it's easy to conjure their sylvan smell. All three scrapers lean forward, and I can feel the pleasant ache in the muscles of their arms. All three have what could be described as a fairly typical French male body, slim and small-boned, pleasing tautness rather than classic musculature.

Sinewy, lean—one kind of male body to which I've been repeatedly drawn. The floor scrapers' resemblance to one another increases the power of Caillebotte's composition, an elegant one in which the viewer is a choreographer crouching across from his dancers.

"It's impossible not to feel you're right down there with them," I say.

A few students stop talking and look up.

"Do any of you know this painting? It gets its share of attention."

No one says anything. There's a murmur from the front of the classroom.

"Lucille," I boom.

She pushes a couple of buttons on her cell phone and replaces it to her pocketbook.

"Why would you think I wouldn't mind you talking to your friends in my class?"

She shrugs. Nat has told me that he and a few others have tried to get cell phones banned from class. Amazingly, administration and faculty did not agree on it. We are permitted to tell students to turn off their phones, but we are not to insist they leave them behind. I can't imagine which civil liberty such a ban would violate. Nat thinks administration is afraid that the commitment of Tri-Community students is so provisional a cell-phone ban would drive them right out the door. I'm not sure he's joking.

"This is probably Caillebotte's family home in the Batignolles section of Paris," I continue. "The unusual perspective is typical of him. Matt, what do you think of the perspective?"

"I like it. I mean, it's cool how you feel you're down on the floor with them. But those guys could've saved themselves a lot of trouble if they'd rented a floor-sander from Home Depot."

Everyone laughs. I do too. At least someone can bring my class together.

I have grouped several paintings that show a similar perspective: Caillebotte's most famous *Paris Street, Rainy Day*, his *Dahlias: The Garden at Petit Gennevilliers*, *Perissoires*, and *Oarsmen*. All of them make the viewer approach the subject head-on. Caillebotte's technique was to create space by using converging diagonals, I tell my class. Some of his contemporaries imitated this use of perspective. Take for instance Toulouse-Lautrec, in some of his posters.

Unusually polite, my class takes up the discussion. Some students even offer up comparisons with the perspective used in other paintings

I've shown them. I can't understand why they're paying attention. Am I so obviously weary of them that they feel sorry for me? Or have they finally reached a saturation point with their own lazy-mindedness? Whatever the reason, we are briefly aligned in appreciating the beauty of Caillebotte's paintings, and even in longing for gardens and boat outings and apartments that open onto stately avenues.

Toward the end of class, we talk about their term papers. Most of them have chosen their topics, but none have started the necessary reading. I give them a little lecture on time management. (I, who never finished my dissertation.)

The class files out, stopping to comment over the scratched-out swastika. As they leave, someone who has been standing in the hall knocks on the open door. Looking up, I see a large man with thinning dark hair and an overly ruddy face. It's obvious he has something on his mind, and he wastes no time.

"Are you Brian Moss?"

"Yes."

"I'm Bill Craig, Damon's father."

"Is he all right?"

Bill Craig waits for the last of my students to leave the classroom. "He's married!"

I wait.

"He says he's quitting school. He knows there's no way they're living in my house if he quits school. And she's talking of quitting, too, not that some art school is going to get her anywhere. No offense about the art."

"None taken."

"One day my kid's setting himself on the straight and narrow, the next day he's fucked himself over."

"I'm sure that's a little extreme." I'm waiting to see why Bill Craig has come to see me.

"You don't know my kid," he says, then leans on one of the desks.

"No, not very well."

"Well, believe me, it's not extreme. He's headed straight for the toilet. This was his last chance."

I have to restrain myself from laughing. "How old is he, nineteen?"

"He's been a mess since he was twelve. I had to pull some real strings to get him in here."

It never occurred to me that anyone would have to pull a single thread to get a kid into the likes of Tri-Community. Damon Craig must have done something terrible. "He's a bright boy," I say.

"He's trouble," says his father. "He's supposed to be *in recovery.* I'm supposed to treat him like he's fragile as hell. They tell me he's 'troubled,' but I tell them he *is* trouble."

It's easy to piece together Damon's story. He got into drugs or alcohol or both when he was in high school. Maybe even middle school. Some crime was committed, hopefully not a felony. A judge ordered rehab. Time passed, he fell back once or twice, then got himself fairly together and ended up at Tri-Community. There are others here with the same history.

"I haven't seen any withdrawal papers on him. This is all news to me. What are his plans?"

"Plans? My kid? He'll get some shitty job, and she'll do those paintings of hers, and they'll think they can live on cheese doodles and sex. It's a big fucking delusion. He has no idea, and there's no way of getting through to him."

"I understand the girl is quite talented."

"That's loverly if your parents have a Swiss bank account," Bill Craig says. "Hers don't. Her father's not even in the picture."

"I'll admit I'm disappointed," I say. "Damon has showed some real interest in my class."

"He could do plenty more than show an interest if he wanted to. He's an ace at working below potential. Very experienced. Been doing it for years."

I look at Bill Craig, trying to get him to see that I still don't know why he's here.

"Half the damage has already been done," he says. "But here's my thinking. There's one thing out there in the world of pyschobabble bullshit that might have something to it. The tough love show-down. It worked to get Damon into rehab. So it's worth a try to get him to stay in school."

"Maybe . . ." I say.

"I'm thinking you and a couple other teachers here, and me and my wife, and an uncle he cares about. He's mentioned you. Seemed to like your class."

"Mr. Craig, this is not a usual situation. I'm not one for determining the life course of people I hardly know. I'm for giving people their own lead."

"What—that empowerment crap? You have to earn your self-confidence. You don't sprinkle it over yourself like talcum powder."

"I teach art history here. I'm not the college counselor."

"So? Do you care about your students, or not?"

"Please don't put me on the spot this way."

"Okay. At least I know where you stand."

"I stand at not liking to be bullied," I say.

"I already talked to Nathan Weinstein."

"And?"

"He's thinking about it."

"Then so am I." ("We pansies stick together," I want to add.)

Damon's father nods, as if he's made his point. He extends his hand. "We'll leave it that you'll talk to your boss, then," he says. He straightens up. "Weinstein said something to me about boundaries, but I told him that if we don't violate Damon's fucking boundaries, he and that girl will end up sleeping inside the boundaries of a homeless shelter. I think he got it."

Not five minutes after Bill Craig leaves, I walk into Nat's office. "Want to go out for a beer?" I ask. "We're supposed to talk."

"Oh Christ, he found you. Never a dull moment around here. Sure. Give me a minute." He throws me the keys to his car. "I'll meet you. I bought a new Barbara Cook CD. It's on the dash."

Rather than wait in Nat's Toyota, I lean against it and smoke a cigarette. By the time I finish, he's coming toward me. We decide to go to a local straight bar, since the nearest gay one is a dive twenty miles away.

Once in Pete's Spot, we settle into an uncomfortable booth. Nat gets right to the point. He thinks we need to go along with Bill Craig's idea. He says that Mike Casey, Tri-Community's president, fixates on every student who drops out. He calls in all of the kid's teachers, one by one, to find out what went wrong.

"Like it's our fault," I say.

"Casey's not going to last, Brian," Nat assures me.

"Maybe, but we're here now," I tell him. "And I don't think we should get involved in the Craigs' private affairs. It was ballsy of Bill Craig to even ask. I don't believe it takes a village to raise a child, not in New Jersey. There's nothing we can do to make up for the Craigs' bad parenting."

Nat has listened patiently. "It really *is* a shame Damon's dropping out. He's doing well in all his classes."

"His father's a thug, as you saw. This could go anywhere."

"No, because the moment it gets out of control, we leave. This meeting won't take place at Tri-Community."

"That's worse, Nat! It seems even less professional if it's off campus."

"No, it gives us a safe egress. Like the personals. You don't invite the guy to your house."

You don't, I think.

"I'm not going to do this. It just feels wrong to me. I like Damon, but I don't want to get involved in his family dynamic."

"Okay," says Nat. "That's fine. Whatever you decide."

"So you're going to do it? Who else?"

"I'm still considering. Two others are doing it—Business Communication I and Network Management." (Nat and I never remember the names of the instructors who teach these courses.)

"Well, I don't want them to think I don't care about Damon. It's not about that."

"Oh, Christ, Brian, they're not going to think twice if you're there or not. Let's drop it. What's going on with you these days?"

I briefly consider telling Nat about Neil, then dismiss the idea. "Nothing much new. You know, I already told you I'm looking over my old dissertation."

"Oh yes, 'The Theme of Dissolution in the Work of Henri Toulouse-Lautrec.'"

"Your memory's amazing, Nat. Definitely the only person alive who knows the name of my dissertation."

"It's the ginkgo biloba."

"It's you."

"Dissolution is a beautiful word," he says. "Fine, evocative word. Wiser and more colorful than dysfunction. And *darker* in all the right places."

"Absolutely," I say. His brand of awareness is just what I need at this moment. "These kids today, they drink plenty, but they're not dissolute. They wake up in the morning and repent by pouring soy milk over their puffed millet balls. They take anti-oxidants. Something scarier than dissolution is going on with these kids. Something that doesn't even have a name yet."

"Hypocrisy comes close."

"It's certainly inconsistent, but it's not quite hypocritical, because they're not preaching anything. I think they have more of a choice disorder. They see all these options, and instead of choosing one, they embrace them all. It never occurs to them they're meant to choose."

"Right," says Nat. "The culture stimulates them at a hundred miles a minute, welches on its responsibility to hone their critical skills, then diagnoses them all with ADD."

"You got it. Of course, I don't purport to being much better off. I just have the worthless attribute of insight."

Nat raises his beer bottle. "Here's to dissolution," he says, and we clink our bottles together. "Do you think I can take ginkgo and still be dissolute?"

"I don't know," I say. "Can I be a mannerly little social drinker and still be dissolute?"

"We're such losers," Nat moans, and we clink bottles again.

"We're no better than these kids we teach," I say. "*Really* losers."

"Watch it," he says. "You're speaking to a distinguished department chair at a top-flight university."

❧ 10 ❧

For the first time since I've lived here, Beryl is coming to New York. She's bringing Melissa. They're coming now because Beryl is attending a seminar related to taxes and condominium development. The seminar is probably not all that important to her. I suspect she has compromised with Melissa; they will visit me together. They are staying at The Plaza. It would have been easier for me to meet them there, but I have come to LaGuardia Airport to pick them up because they expect it. They have no idea what meeting a plane at a New York airport entails; I've switched subway trains twice and taken a bus to get here. The bus inched along for a mile and a half of the Brooklyn-Queens Expressway until, near the entrance to the Kosciusko Bridge, it passed four Chassidim gathered around the open hood of a stalled station wagon. Smoke rose from the car's engine. Everyone on my side of the bus glared out the windows at the Chassidim. Before the bus was finally able to pick up speed, I could feel the tension of twenty people suppressing a religious slur.

My muscles still stiff from the bus ride, I run toward the crowd of people waiting to meet passengers from arriving flights. Just in time, I see Beryl coming toward me. She must have had her hair fixed an hour before she got on the plane. I'm glad to see that Melissa's hair is just Melissa's hair; it's pulled back with one of those scrunchie things girls her age wear. I kiss them both, briefly, and tell them we can take a cab back. I know Beryl will pay for it.

The drive to the city goes quickly and the taxi lets us out in front of the Plaza. "I wish I'd known you were coming sooner," I say as we walk past the Palm Room to the Plaza's front desk. "I would've scheduled the painter for another time. My place is full of drop cloths. I'm staying a couple of nights at a friend's."

This is a lie, of course. I don't want them to see my building or my apartment. From the Plaza to my studio apartment is quite a socio-economic distance. We would all three of us suffer the bends.

Melissa stops at one of the glass cases displaying gold jewelry set with precious stones. "What would keep someone from just breaking the glass and reaching in?" she asks.

I don't think either she or Beryl has heard my explanation about my apartment. "Alarms, hotel security, the cops just outside," I say. "It would never happen."

"I don't really like any of these," says Melissa. "They're just too— *too*." She shakes her head delicately and wrinkles her nose, her impression of a snob.

I smile. Beryl tells her that the appreciation of rubies is acquired. You have to know something in order to appreciate.

"I don't see why I have to know about rubies. Uncle Brian, how far is the Empire State Building?"

"Close. Walkable, if you brought warm enough sweaters." I look at my watch. "It's still pretty early."

"Can we go, Mom?"

"I haven't been there since I was a child," she says. "Let's go. It would be nostalgic."

Beryl does not acknowledge that I was on that trip to New York, too. Avery had taken us, along with one of his girlfriends, to see some Broadway plays.

They check in and go upstairs to change their clothes. The lobby is mine now; I have relatives staying here. I walk about with my hands clasped behind me. As I approach an immense flower arrangement, a man in an Armani suit leans over to examine one of the orchids. "Miltonias are my favorites," he says, then permits himself a quick scan of my body. I walk away, simply because I can. He's not a bad-looking guy, and I used to be impressed with wealth. No more. For me, impeccably-groomed men are the easiest to resist.

Beryl and Melissa appear in the lobby. Even Beryl is dressed suitably, in a denim jacket and a pale, gauzy scarf she's wound about her neck. Melissa cannot contain her excitement. She wraps both her arms around my one arm and thumps her head against my shoulder. "The Empire State Building, the Empire State Building," she chants. Another hotel guest looks at us and smiles.

Walking down Fifth Avenue, we are happy. We are in the part of Manhattan featured in travelogues, a stage set of pleasures to meet every civilized taste. We drift in and out of stores, purchasing and browsing being all of a piece. On the first floor of Bendel's, Beryl buys a perfume called Aspire. We take Melissa into F.A.O. Schwartz, with the intention of getting her something, but she is content to wander in awe, stopping to stare up at a nine-foot stuffed giraffe, watching a group of boys use remote controls to maneuver race cars with high-tech names. She is twelve years old and can't let herself give in to the regressive pleasure of playing with toys. I see her fighting the impulse to lose herself among displays that look like enchanted storybook sets. Suddenly she says she wants to leave, and her tone has a finality to it, as if we have led her into a den of iniquity to test her character and she will now emerge triumphant. Once again, we enter the stream of pedestrians along Fifth. It's snowing lightly. We stop to watch the skaters at Rockefeller Center, and then, remembering I have to be at work at 5:00, I hurry us along.

Inside the Empire State Building, the allure of New York on display drains instantly away. We must go down to the basement to get tickets to the observation deck. The basement of this historic building is a vast dinginess. The line is long, and people are stepping out of it and cursing the slowness of the clerks in the ticket booths. Tickets are being sold to the observation deck and to something called SkyRide, and it is not clear where to buy what. After asking two people, we find out we can get a combination ticket, which Melissa is eager to do. She probably thinks that this wait and this ugliness will be redeemed by whatever a combination ticket has to offer.

"Is it always like this?" asks Beryl, and I see Melissa tense up.

"These must be school groups," I say.

When we finally have our tickets in hand, we agree to go to SkyRide first. I lead us to the escalator that will take us to this tourist attraction on the second floor. I'm feeling pressed by the bodies around me, and hot in my leather jacket and sweater and thermal undershirt.

"It *can't* always be like this," says Beryl again. We have reached the top of the escalator and she is trying to take off her jacket, but the press of people makes it difficult. "Missy!" she shouts, though Melissa is practically next to her. "You stay right with us the whole time."

I expect us to go right into the SkyRide, whatever it is, but we follow the crowd into another waiting area. Again, a maze of worn velvet ropes. Beryl manages to get her jacket off and drape it over her arm. This is not the line at the gourmet deli in Scottsdale's Desert Pavilion Mall. This line is composed primarily of Hispanics and blacks, races Beryl is most familiar with through her role as employer. She smiles valiantly and puts her arm around Melissa. A child in front of us shrieks, and we see bits of barbecued potato chip fly out of his mouth. The line moves forward at an impossible pace. Many of the adults wear a placid expression that makes me sad, but also amazes me. A teenager behind us has his Walkman turned up so high that we hear music and fragments of lyrics coming through his earphones.

"Gangsta music," says Melissa, and Beryl looks at her. Although her posture remains erect, she has stopped smiling. The facial muscles that usually work together to give my sister her ever-alert look have slackened. I see the faintest prevision of old age, a suggestion of jowliness. Surely she will have cosmetic surgery, I think. When I visit, people will be surprised that we are twins.

"You know that music?" asks Beryl.

"Oh, Mom," Melissa answers.

Now Beryl steps out of line to see what is taking so long. As she steps back in, a person in a gorilla suit seems to appear from nowhere to entertain the children. A two-year-old wails, and when the adults around him laugh, humiliation is added to the child's fear and his voice rises several octaves. The gorilla makes the mistake of kneeling down to the child's level and extending its leather-palmed paw. The screaming little boy stomps his feet violently and enters into a frenetic spin. The gorilla rises.

"That's just King Kong," the child's mother says. "King Kong is harmless. Look there!"

Ahead of them a little girl, about five, steps forward and offers her hand for the gorilla to shake.

"This is a living hell," says Beryl.

"Mom, come on. It's the Empire State Building. It can't be much longer."

It's touching, I think, that Melissa trusts that the Empire State Building could not let her down. Finally, a guard unlatches the velvet rope at the head of the line, and we move forward. I think we are going into the SkyRide, but instead we are herded into a large square room with video monitors. Some kind of holding tank. The lights dim. Frank Sinatra's version of "New York, New York" is piped into the room. Then Liza Minnelli's. We have apparently reached the last stage of our wait and the songs are meant to pump us for the excitement to come. The video screens flash, and Jackie Mason appears. Then Joan Rivers, Alan King, Jerry Seinfeld, Eddie Murphy, and a string of comics I don't recognize. The theme is the trials of living in New York. The last joke is about a woman who will try to advance the science of cryogenics by being unfrozen twice a week to move her car to the alternate side of the street. Melissa looks up at the screen with an open mouth. She laughs along with the crowd, wanting to be in the know. Beryl looks around her. She is pale and obviously living only for the purpose of getting through this experience.

The lights rise and a woman's hearty voice comes over the speakers. "Ladies and gentlemen, welcome to SkyRide. May I remind you that people with coronary artery disease, pregnant women, and anyone who experiences vertigo are not encouraged to go beyond this point. Anyone falling into one of these categories, please stay behind when the door opens, and an usher will escort you out."

"This is unbelievable," hisses Beryl. "No warnings posted, no announcements made downstairs. Can you imagine waiting all this time in this hellacious line for nothing?"

Finally, electric double doors open, and we file inside. I'm disappointed as we enter a small screening room whose seats are mounted on a metal platform. This is what we've been waiting for? This is what you can't be pregnant for? We sit down and follow instructions to buckle our seat belts. Lights dim. A supremely masculine voice fills the screening room. He tells us he is the captain of our spaceship. His voice is that of the consummate father. If we put our trust in this man—his prowess, his judgment, his vast experience—we will be safely guided along our dangerous mission. His tone carries both command and great joviality—all a son needs to bloom. He is our captain. He will carry us forth on our journey. We are right behind the captain in the cockpit, and our spaceship charges forth. From the stratosphere we sweep just yards from the streets of New York and zoom back up again. Our spacecraft ranges out of control in New York's most popular locales—the Brooklyn Heights' Promenade, the Metropolitan Museum of Art, the Statue of Liberty, Rockefeller Center, Central Park Zoo. Everywhere, unsuspecting pedestrians must jump to the side. Sitting inside our spacecraft as the sound of the rocket engine roars around us, we feel the speed and the gyrations of each twist and turn. The verisimilitude is dazzling. Rocking wildly in my seat, I can virtually feel my adrenal glands secreting. I am thrilled; I don't want this experience to end. Returning to the Barracks to cut limes and wipe rings of moisture off the bar is a ridiculously barren prospect. Yet the rocking begins to slow, the captain's tone moves brightly toward his concluding words, and before I know it my seat has stalled and the lights have come on. A bodiless voice instructs us on how to exit. I look over at Beryl. She has lightened up and is smiling. Melissa has no identifiable expression on her face. I know I look goonish to them. I have overreacted, have let myself get carried away. As in many years before, I am my poised sister's overemotional brother.

"What did you think?" I venture as we leave.

"Okay," says Melissa. "There's something like it in Phoenix, but this was better because it's New York."

"I wonder how many times a day they can fill that theater," says Beryl.

"Where to now?" I ask them.

"The observation deck!?" says Melissa, balancing demand against entreaty.

"In your dreams," my sister answers. "I'm starving. Let's take Uncle Brian back to the hotel and get a late lunch. We can order room service."

In Beryl's rooms at the Plaza, I can practically smell the cloying scent of the gardenias that pattern the valences and drapes, drapes that fold their way to the floor like an emperor's robes. The suite is small— a bedroom and sitting room.

"Kind of oppressive room, don't you think?" I ask, dropping down onto a love seat. Melissa flops down on the carpet by my feet.

Beryl ignores me and walks over with a menu. The food, of course, is outrageously expensive.

"Parfaits!" says Melissa. "They have parfaits, Mom. Can I have one?"

"Want to hear a little story about Tennessee Williams at the Plaza?" I ask. "Melissa just made me remember it. It's from his introduction to a reprint of *The Glass Menagerie*. It's called 'The Catastrophe of Success.'"

"Sure," says Melissa courteously.

"This happened on the night after the Broadway debut of *The Glass Menagerie*, which made Tennessee Williams an overnight celebrity. The critics had raved and raved, everyone was talking about him. So to honor himself in his room at the Plaza, Tennessee ordered a filet mignon and a chocolate sundae. He was so ecstatic, so giddy over his longed-for success, that when his perfect cut of meat came, he poured thick chocolate sauce all over it."

Melissa giggles. Beryl smiles distractedly.

"Of course he wrote about this little incident as a metaphor for how he felt that night he became a celebrity," I say for Melissa's benefit. "The over-richness, the excess, the desolation of it all."

"Hmmm," says Melissa, trying to be adult, trying to piece my story together.

Beryl has gone back to scanning the menu. I feel like a pedantic asshole. "Sorry," I say. "It's the thirty-percent teacher in me."

After the food is rolled in and we've gathered around the room-service table, Beryl says, "We have to get Dad to come to Scottsdale."

I groan. "Not this again."

"I don't want to make any unilateral decisions, Brian. He's your father, too. But now's the time to do it."

I wait for her to begin a lecture on my lack of planning, a theme that goes back to our childhood. Beryl planned when most children who lived along Periwinkle Drive did not have the slightest concept of a future. She alone of us seemed to divine that the future would not be an extension of the present, that the patronage that kept us happily skating up and down Periwinkle each evening would evaporate, leaving us—unimaginably—to fend for ourselves. I'll never know how she understood this. She was the child who collected our friends' skate keys and kept them in a knit pouch clipped to her belt loop. And Beryl always brought a sweatshirt to neighborhood barbecues. Among all the neighborhood children, she was the only who foresaw the chill of the night ahead.

"I really think Dad just wants to be left alone," I say.

"Did you know he went to see Charlene? Did you know he's going to print up little books about our childhood? This is *Dad* we're talking about, Brian. He needs to be stimulated. That's all he needs. I'll make him a consultant for my company. It's not bogus; we could really use him."

"I'm sorry he's embarrassing you. I think it's sort of funny, actually. Who would have thought it? Dad in a mild, sentimental old age."

"I talked to Debbie Shuster. She's completely out of the picture. She kept him waiting on her for twelve years. He could have found someone substantial and gotten married."

"Beryl, have you ever seen Dad with someone substantial?"

"Damn it, Brian, we can't just let him stay there alone."

Melissa puts down the remainder of her hamburger. "When *I'm* old, I'm going to sit out on an iceberg and let the polar bears get me. That's the dignified thing to do."

Beryl looks at Melissa, then at me. "It's those World Culture videos they show at her school," she says. "It's Seth's fault, actually. He orders them."

"You can put me out on an iceberg too, honey, when the time comes."

In the brief pause that follows, my implication settles in. It will fall to Melissa to arrange my very old age. The prospect binds me to Beryl. I look away.

"Is Pops going to go into Desert Haven, Mom?" Melissa is worried.

"Never." To me, Beryl says, "Desert Haven is a nursing home on the edge of Scottsdale. There's an adobe wall around it. Melissa's afraid of it, but it's really fine. The director lives in one of my villas. But, no," she says, turning back to Melissa, "Pops will never go to Desert Haven."

I put down my turkey club. "Beryl," I say. "Dad has a house, plenty of money, and he's still capable of making his own decisions. We went over all of this in Scottsdale."

"He's *lonely*, Brian."

In my mind, loneliness is solitude denouncing itself. Avery has never been a man to seek solitude. There has never been a sense of quietude in a room he has occupied. For Avery, stopping work has naturally unfolded straight into loneliness. Still, I am at a loss. "Did he tell you he was lonely?"

"He doesn't have to!" she practically shouts.

"You two sound like little kids," Melissa interrupts. "Like, about five."

We look at her. For some reason, she chose the age we were when our mother was killed.

"Okay," I say, chagrined. "We don't need to have a major blow up. My position is simple. If Dad wants our help, he'll ask for it. If he wants to move to Scottsdale, he'll move."

"What about his regression? It's real, Brian. You've seen it."

"If you ask me, he was never regressed *enough*. I actually find his regression a bit piquant. I'm sort of excited to see what will come of it."

"What will come of it will be suffering."

"How do we know that?" I look at my watch, and get up. "I'm sorry, but I have to go to work."

Melissa rises, too. She hugs me tightly around the waist. "Thanks, Uncle Brian. So far, I love New York."

"Hey, thank *you*," I say. "If it weren't for you, I never would have seen New York from the inside of a cockpit."

* * *

As Jordan does a last-minute inventory check and Luis fits new votive candles into their glass cups, I talk about SkyRide. I praise the deftness of the illusion. I describe the captain's assured voice, and we speculate about his looks. I tell them that it was all thrilling, but that my sister was interested only from a business standpoint and by the end I couldn't tell what my niece thought.

"What did you tell us happened to your mother?" Luis blurts out.

I am annoyed. "She died in a car crash when I was five."

"So maybe your sister was upset. You know, traumatized. Because you could have all crashed into the street at any second."

Jordan looks up expectantly. The two of them are always trying to get me to open up.

"What would you have me say?"

Luis leans against my bar and folds his arms. "Just tell me what you think."

"I think it's boring, if you really want to know. It's been almost thirty-five years since my mother died. I don't buy into the repressed-traumatic-memories school. And we never saw the crash. To us, she just went to see her college roommate near Pittsburgh and didn't return. We got sent to my father's cousin in Sandusky for two weeks. When we came back, my father had hired our housekeeper Charlene to take care of us. That's what happened."

Luis and Jordan say nothing. I have made it clear that now we are to return to our small tasks and to our thoughts.

Ever since I moved to New York twenty years ago, the death of my mother, Lenore Rubin Moss, has become an item in the accounting of my identity. Yet each time I have reported on my mother in an imperturbable tone, I have felt a stranger to myself. As an adult, I am meant to state the fact of her death with hands in my pockets, nodding slightly so that my listeners know it's not necessary to respond emotionally—a tidy reciprocal nod will do. All adults, myself included, are in a pact to express with utmost parsimony the events that have shaped their characters. If I described the real relationship I had with my mother, even Jordan would feel embarrassed. My longing would pervade the air.

My mother was a beautiful woman. If I didn't remember her so, I could conclude she was beautiful because Avery demands that a woman be beautiful. Certainly she was slim-ankled. I remember her lovely figure, the hour-glass figure admired as classic at the time. She was the kind of woman about whom other women said, "She can really wear clothes." Had she lived at the end of the nineteenth century, my mother could have been one of the stylish patrons in Toulouse-Lautrec's Moulin Rouge pastels.

Certain of my mother's clothes she had identified as being from her trousseau. There was a rust-and-olive striped fitted suit, probably gabardine, with shoulder pads. There were Ship-and-Shore blouses whose patterns were woven through, raw-silk toreador pants, a wide patent leather belt, and a tight heather skirt with side slits. The crown jewel of my mother's trousseau was a Persian lamb jacket with a mink collar. If someone complimented my mother on any one of these articles, I remember her saying, "It's from my trousseau." When she'd defined trousseau for Beryl and me—the special wardrobe that a bride gets for her marriage—I had been struck by the awful inscrutability of the word. My parents, I knew, had a business relationship like the one Avery had with the men he introduced me to at his construction sites. My parents' nightly kisses were like the handshakes he gave these men, hasty pledges that served to seal their partnership. These kisses took place in the kitchen almost every evening, and I had thought they in some way fueled my mother, like gas fueled our Chevy Impala, because they set her on a speedy course, wiping down all the counter tops and slamming the lids of pots on the stove.

The thought of my parents' wedding, the event most connected to the word trousseau, had troubled me even more. From what I knew of weddings, the groom stood at attention next to the bride, his expression reverent and adoring. Such an expression on Avery's face was unimaginable. Yet more impossible to picture, so frightening that I hurled myself against my mother's legs, breathed in the slight chemical smell of her dry-cleaned skirt, was my nonexistence on the day of her wedding. I was forever trying to give form to this nonexistence: myself as a tiny seed floating in my mother's veins, circulating along with her blood; myself as the ghost of the dachshund next door who my mother said died on the day I was born; myself as the dander that rambled within shafts of sunlight all over our house. Only my mother could erase the terror that overcame me when I thought of her wedding, or when she wore something from her trousseau. My mother was the one who made my heart race with mortal fear, yet only her touch and the smell of her clothes could allay that fear. When she died, I was not surprised. I had seen that Avery and Beryl could live without her. My mother's death confirmed what I'd already been taught—that longing, like so much of what I expressed as a child, was indulgent. Longing was the worst; it was a punishable offense.

The three of us have been silent for a while, and now Luis walks behind the bar to turn on the stereo. Salsa music fills the room. When a commercial comes on, I hear a noise at the door. Frank Cantore is standing outside the Barracks. He is holding a big box.

"Jordan!" Luis calls. "Drop the pickles, your man is here."

As Frank walks smiling into the bar, I realize that I haven't seen or talked to him since his diagnosis. For friends, the routine has long been clear. For friends, I expertly handle the equipment of the sick room: oxygen masks, bedpans, catheters. But for acquaintances like Frank, there is no routine; they put me in a delicate situation. I have not wanted to make an acquaintance into a friend for the sake of his illness. I have not wanted to become, like some people I know, a foul-weather friend, a person who seeks intimacy around impending death. I usually do nothing with the acquaintances. When they die, I attend their funerals. I go to the service, but I don't return for the reception, the one where there is a buffet and, at the door, a pile of snapshots of the acquaintance tanning himself on the deck of a sailboat or dancing with his shirt off.

"Hi, Frank," I say. "You look great."

"Thanks. How's your dad, Brian?"

My God, I think. Who is Avery to Frank Cantore? People's goodness never fails to surprise me. "He came through pretty well. Not much in the way of residuals. What's in the box?"

Frank holds up a hand to stop further inquiry. He is smiling. Jordan appears from the kitchen. He has removed his apron. They kiss briefly, like my parents had, but their eyes linger on each other. "It's here," says Frank, and nods toward the box.

Jordan looks at his watch. "We can't try it here," he says.

"Sure we can. You don't open for fifteen minutes."

"Honey. What am I going to do with you?" Jordan looks up at me and Luis. "What the hell am I going to do with him?"

Frank asks me for scissors and sets the box on a table. I see a label from a company called Pamper Yourself. When Frank opens the box there is something mint-colored in plastic wrapping. "Do you like the color?" he asks Jordan.

"Is it what we picked?"

"Yes," says Frank. "Don't you remember? We thought the magenta was too jarring." He tears open the plastic and takes out a large folded square of something covered in an awful green flocked cotton. Next Frank pulls out of the box another plastic bag, this one containing a bulky set of controls and a wound-up cord.

"That's supposed to do everything?" Jordan asks dubiously.

"There must be instructions," says Frank, thrashing his arm inside the box. He brings out something else wrapped in plastic. "Oh, good," he says, "the pump. It looks pretty good. See, there's a pedal."

Together they remove the pump and fasten it to a spout at the end of the green flocked thing. Frank wants to be in charge. He starts working the pedal. Luis and I step back. The flocked thing unfurls a little, but then not much happens. "This might take a while," says Frank. He sounds disappointed.

"Let me try," Jordan says. He pumps a few times, and then the flocked thing starts to swell. It expands steadily until it is raft-sized. "Here we go," says Jordan happily. "Is it firm?

Frank crouches down to touch the air mattress. Luis and I move closer. Some kind of latticework is visible beneath the flocked covering. "Give it a few more pumps," says Frank.

Jordan does this, then closes the nozzle tightly. Frank plugs in the set of controls. "Lie down, sweetie," he tells Jordan.

When Jordan is settled, Frank pushes forward two levers on the control box. The raft begins to gyrate. Jordan clasps his hands behind his head. I see the loose flesh of his cheeks quiver. We all wait.

"This is *great*," he says. "I have to tell you, I thought this thing was going to be a turkey. But it's not!" He smiles broadly.

"Can you feel the warmth, baby?" asks Frank.

"No. Well, maybe. . . . Yeah, I think it might be starting."

"You guys are out of your minds," says Luis. "What *is* this thing?"

"It's a Pamper Yourself Massage Mattress," answers Frank. "Like magic fingers, only better. It vibrates all your kinks out, plus it's a giant heating pad. It's Jordan's present for taking such good care of me when I was sick."

"Gyration is the theme of the day," I say.

"Gyration is *my* theme every day," Luis says.

We are interrupted by an insistent knock at the door. Gerald from Sony leans into the glass. He glowers at us—we who have strayed from our nightly posts. Luis looks at his watch. "Uh-oh," he says. "A minute and a half past opening time. She's going to bust a circuit in her calculator."

"When's her cirrhosis going to finish her off already?" asks Jordan. Jordan, who never uses feminine pronouns for men.

Two mornings later, I call Beryl at around eleven o'clock. We have brunch plans. Beryl is going to splurge on the Palm Room.

"I left a message at your apartment," she says. "Haven't you been checking in?"

"Sure, but not yet today." This is half true. The lie is that I'm sitting on my Morris chair across from the Murphy bed. The truth is that I haven't yet checked my messages.

"I'm really sorry, Brian, but brunch is off. We're going back today. We have a 3:15 flight."

"You're kidding! What happened?"

"Melissa is in real trouble with me. And with Seth, too, when we get home." She keeps her tone stern; I assume Melissa is within earshot.

"You practically just got here."

"We're only cutting the trip short by a day and a half. And believe me, that's only the prelude to her punishment."

"Jesus, what happened?"

"Three hours I was away, tops. At my seminar. That *was* why we came here, if you'll remember. Missy was supposed to do her home-work in the suite. You'd think you could trust a twelve-year- old alone for three hours. But apparently I have a far less mature twelve-year-old than I'd thought."

All this is definitely for Melissa's benefit.

"So—what happened?"

"She went out. On her own. She's not even allowed to go into Phoenix by herself. But she walked right out of the hotel and went to the Empire State Building. That damn observation deck! Anything could have happened to her. AN-Y-THING."

"I can't believe Melissa just offered this up. How did you find out?"

"*That's* your question, Brian?" Here she lowers her voice. "'How'd you find out?' Are *you* twelve?"

It takes all I've got not to respond, *Shut up!*, that constantly reiter-ated command from my childhood, my single pathetic defense against all that revealed Beryl's disdain: her lectures; her cool and sometimes magnificent displays of reasoning; her put downs; her threats to expose my transgressions to Avery. *Shut up, shut up, shut up.* The mantra of the insecure child. As an adolescent, my mantra was embellished: *shut up, asshole; shut up, shithead; shut up, pizza face; shut up, corpse breath.*

"I'm sorry," Beryl continues when I don't answer her. "I'm a little out of control here. As I think you'd be if you found out your only child had wandered the streets of a dangerous city alone."

"But she's all right?"

"Physically, she's fine. Mentally, I wonder. I was up here in the room for forty-five minutes when she finally strolled in. Of course I'd already called hotel security."

"So what did she say?"

"She said there were lines to get up to the observation deck. Lines, Brian! If she was going to be so outrageously deceptive, you'd think she could have anticipated the lines. Especially after that first day, the line for the SkyRide. Or, you'd think when she realized what time it was, near when I was due back, she would've gotten out of line and come back. But no, she just had to get up to that observation deck along with a thousand other mindless tourists."

Thrilled with Melissa's little insurrection, I have to struggle to keep my voice even. "I'm just glad she's okay. Can I say good-bye to her?"

95

"No. I'm sorry, but I'm not inclined to grant her the slightest pleasure right now. When her punishment is over, in about three weeks, you two can talk."

I wish them a safe trip and hang up. I imagine Melissa passing down Fifth Avenue on her way to the Empire State Building. There are countless claims on her attention: old women made-over as young ones, lavish store window displays following themes she doesn't understand, the dissonance of car horns and shouts and belching buses from the avenue, blotchy-faced men in ragged clothes muttering to themselves, the frightening press of curbside crowds. She is horrified and enthralled. In line for the elevator to the Empire State Building's observation deck, she's in a state of suspended desire. The passing of each moment, the very fact of her aloneness within each big-city moment solemnly impresses her. And then she reaches the top. It's all before her: the rivers, the harbor, Ellis and Liberty Islands, New Jersey, and—best of all—the ocean, the Atlantic Ocean that she has never before laid eyes on. Her accomplishment is unparalleled in her experience. Her observations, she is certain, penetrate deeper than do those of any one else on the observation deck, for she knows that hers are inexorably connected to her future.

Sitting on my Morris chair, I long to be Melissa this morning—a child who has just roamed the greatest American city in no one's company but her own.

❧ 11 ❧

It's been two weeks, and Neil hasn't called me. I never got his last name, so after my shift at the Barracks on Tuesday night I head over to the Shackle, shake hands with Tim, the bartender, and order a Perrier. Tim and I have known each other for a few years. Tonight we talk about our bars, a recent spate of queer bashing in the Village, whatever topic is handy. I keep my eye on the front door. Men are coming in and out of the back room, but I don't look in that direction. It's very late, and I'm tired. I do what I mightily don't want to do.

"Do you by chance remember that guy I was dancing with a few weeks ago?"

"I remember. I never saw you dance, Brian. I figured you must have had something special going with him."

96

"Has he come in lately?"

Tim takes a moment. "He was in a week and a half ago or so. Left with some young guy I never saw, twenty at the most."

I nod, and change the subject. Tim has told me what I want to know, but I scratch him off my list. He's bulked up enough to work at the Shackle, but underneath he's one of those bitchy queens who live to stir up trouble.

At home, I'm comforted to see *Helen Croft: The Baybridge Manor Years* is where I left it on my night table. As I undress, I remember that Helen's mother has died from her unnamed intestinal disorder. Helen could not, or would not, stay away from Baybridge Manor long enough to nurse Bernadine during her dying days. She left that job to the dutiful nuns.

Once in bed, I take up the book and discover that Helen has at least managed to attend Bernadine's funeral. As the nuns hand Bernadine over to God, Helen closes her eyes and pictures the Master in his silk dressing gown knocking upon her door in the servant's quarters. She flushes with pleasure and is not brought back to the moment until her mother's pine coffin is lowered into the ground.

I think, as R. W. Dodson has intended for me to think, that Helen is villainous. Illicit sex, I'm to believe, will drive people to base behavior in the most unsuitable settings. The devil has inveigled his way into Helen Croft's young life, laid claim to her soul. Months or years later Helen will disown this brief era during which the devil possessed her.

I stop reading. Has Neil returned to his conversion therapy? Will he disown his two times with me, his dalliance with the twenty-year-old—wind up, as I know Helen will do with the Master, regarding these as his final lapses? The thought makes me queasy. No matter how tidy I try to keep my encounters, I am destined to eventually be at the mercy of another man. What alarms me most is that as I grow older a mere rendezvous can leave me feeling altogether malleable. Isn't this powerlessness in the presence of Eros the province of adolescents? Only a few times have I felt so . . . *amorphous* in the company of a man. The first time was with Daniel.

Almost twenty-five years ago, the very sound of Daniel's name had sent a charge of excitement like an internal shudder throughout my body. I met him in the second-floor arboretum of the Cleveland

Museum of Art, not far from the ceramic wishing well I'd loved to peer down as a young boy. The previous day I had turned fifteen. Taking stock, I'd found myself wanting. My most salient characteristic was that I possessed a keen appreciation of the talents and powers of others. I was virtually stalked by other people's potential, while suffering for the early defeat of my own. What were my options? I loved art, but didn't have a special talent for making it. The love of painting alone did not strike me as a gift to be respected, but merely as the sediment of a renounced ambition. When I wandered the galleries of the museum that afternoon, crossing several epochs in less than three hours, I felt nothing but remorse.

In the hour before the museum closed, I'd settled into a Breur chair in the arboretum, a jungle of green-black leaves, and opened a paperback copy of *Dear Theo*. In these letters, Van Gogh, an artist in his twenties, looked forward—ecstatic—while at fifteen I looked back. It is this miserable version of myself I see first when I think of Daniel, in all his weightlessness and beauty, drifting into the seat beside mine.

Daniel had sat silently, not looking anywhere, not reading. Several empty chairs and benches were nearby, making his seat selection a statement. I had seen him through parts of my body that were not my eyes. The longer he remained motionless beside me, the more animate those parts became. The bond between Theo and his brother Vincent increased not as I read, but as I thought about their closeness—and as Daniel stretched his legs, crossing them at the ankles. Finally, he reached into a backpack and removed a notebook. It had a Case Western Reserve insignia on the cover. When he opened it, I glanced sidewise and saw mathematical formulas, indecipherable to me.

"I'd rather be reading *Dear Theo*, if you don't mind my saying so," Daniel had said. "Are you an artist?"

"Not really," I told him. But I'd been struck by the question. It was not the usual question of one boy to another. It sought information on my appeal, not my level of prowess.

Daniel had told me how much he admired those with artistic talent. He said it took a lot of humility to try to replicate nature. This struck me as peculiar; I had thought the act of drawing to be purely ego-driven. I had even asked Daniel about the role of the ego, and he'd answered, although I no longer remember what he'd said. After the museum closed, we went for a walk around the lagoon in front of the building.

We circled it several times. Eventually I said I had to leave. Daniel invited me to come to his dormitory room the next afternoon.

When I arrived the next day, a Sunday, Daniel told me his roommate had gone home for the weekend. The two of us passed a hash pipe back and forth. For a few minutes we kept up the pretense that we'd made this date to continue our conversation, and then I was permitted for the first time to stare at a man's penis, to feel it as I had felt my own, to marvel at its sameness and its difference, to take it into my mouth while Daniel's fingertips bored into my scalp.

The mingling of our sharp smells had frightened me. Sensation had been suppressed, there was awkwardness and, most insupportable, shame. I had not been seeking the sex, but the atmosphere that led to it, an incorporeal place that brought out the most graceful parts of me, a place full of excitement for his being infinitely older, almost twenty-one, a place where I could possess the same measure of autonomy Daniel did.

At home during the several weeks I had been with Daniel, I was not able to stop myself from smuggling his name into every conversation. Beryl had been the first to figure it out, to connect my friendship with Daniel to the time I'd spent with Ned Tanning two years earlier.

Before she ultimately told my father the truth about Daniel, Beryl tried out a few approaches on me. The first was not so far from her customary stance, that of the worldly woman from whose example I would profit. She warned me away from homosexuality by telling me what she knew of it: that the men were called homos and the women dykes or lezzies. The homos made fools of themselves by wearing ascots and using ebony cigarette holders. The dykes slicked back their hair with Brylcream or Wild Root. Both were normal during the day, but then emerged as themselves at night. Beryl told me that society hated them, and that's why there were laws against being a homosexual. She told me that she had read some experimentation was normal, but that meant doing it once, and no more. "Get out of my room," I'd said.

Next Beryl tried pity. When I was in bed with the flu, she asked if she could sit down next to me. She told me she'd been thinking about it and had concluded I'd been more affected by our mother's death than she. "Mommy was always petting you," she said, although I remembered no such thing. "You were always clinging to her. I think maybe some crucial part of your development was interrupted." While talking, my sister stroked my hand, something she'd never done. My palms grew moist and clammy. I thanked her for spending time thinking about me, then told her I felt my fever rising, I needed to go back to sleep.

Finally, Beryl had taunted me. She wanted to know if had I seen Daniel lately, and she pronounced his name with a French accent. She told me people at school knew. "Thanks, Brian," she'd said. "You just blew my chances for being head majorette." I'd said if she got meaning out of life by tossing an aluminum rod into the air, I had done her a huge favor. That's when she told my father about Daniel. That's when she unveiled her theory connecting Ned Tanning to Daniel.

Meanwhile, Daniel and I had stopped meeting. There'd been no drama about the end. Daniel had left the seat beside mine as incidentally as he had taken it up. I knew immediately that this was the casualness I would be up against for the rest of my life. I accepted it without question.

Avery never directly addressed me about Daniel. He just looked up from his coffee one morning as I was leaving for school and told me he'd given up on me, he was through investing his energy trying to give me some character.

That afternoon I'd gathered together some clothes and hitchhiked to Charlene's. I stayed there for as long as I could. I stayed past the day Beryl had showed up with the fruit basket while my father waited in the Lincoln Continental—his dream car. I stayed until Avery turned up two days later and interrupted the Wrights' dinner (my dinner), to tell me he'd had enough of my tantrum, that I should be ashamed of myself for imposing on the Wrights. Trying to hold back the tears did no good; my outburst was louder and more pathetic for the effort. I can still hear the sound of it, and I can still see loathing in the eyes of Charlene's foster sons Rudy and LeRoy, the indifference in Mosley's eyes.

All this stirring up of old memories has kept me up, and now it's almost morning. I remove a package of cigarettes from the night stand and light one. I go sit at my wooden kitchen table and open the dissertation box pushed off to the side. Was Lautrec a smoker? Did he adore the focused distraction of cigarettes in the way he adored alcohol? How is it that I don't know this most vital of details—don't know or have forgotten? It seems unlikely that Henri would have abstained, given the life he led. I see him with a big, foul-smelling cigar, tobacco flecks sticking to his grotesque lips.

Flipping through the pages I wrote so long ago, I stop to read the part about Toulouse-Lautrec's death. There is nothing there but the telling, I realize. Anyone could have written it. Recycled information. Henri died of end-stage syphilis in 1901, at the age of thirty-six. He returned to his mother to die. He came back to Maman despite her having committed him to an insane asylum two years before. In the end, a stroke left him paralyzed and she was the one who cared for him. His father, the count, was useless. A man of full height, he was nevertheless a child. He sat in Henri's room and used an elastic shoelace to shoot down the flies that circled his son's deathbed. Not as exhilarating as a falcon hunt, but a distracting enough pastime.

The relationship Henri is said to have had with his mother, Adèle Comtesse de Toulouse-Lautrec, is a subject I avoided in my thesis. I'm not sure why. I'd learned from several sources how mother and son were each in his/her own way oppressed by their bond. Toulouse-Lautrec's periodic attempts to banish Maman from his life invariably failed. Outside her careful watch, he could not control his drinking nor his carousing. Repeatedly, Maman had to leave her château near Bordeaux to come watch over him. If she could not come herself, she hired a spy to follow him and report back to her. Yet however disapproving Maman was, she could be counted upon as Henri's measure of last resort. Forgiveness was always there in the end. For the span of Henri's life of thirty-six years, they were engaged in their agitated dance of charming and insulting each other. From all appearances, it was a miserable love affair.

My unfinished dissertation is like Henri's relationship to his mother, I think. Essentially it holds me back, but I can't let go.

A garbage truck screeches and sighs outside my building. It's the six AM collection. I snuff out my cigarette and return to my bed. Its springs tremble, then hum deep into my bones.

* * *

A temperate day for late November. I decide to walk home from the midtown branch of the New York Public Library. This is the branch that houses the art collection, and I've been reviewing my sources for a lecture I'll give to my class next week. While there, I also checked to see if there were any new acquisitions on art of the Belle Époque, but there were none. Most of the new books were on the contemporary art shelves.

After ten minutes or so, walking west on Twenty-Third Street, I spot Damon Craig. He's in front of the School of Visual Arts. A girl has just left him to go through its doors.

"Congratulations, Damon," I say. "Was that your wife?"

Damon lurches back, as if avoiding an insect about to land on his face. He blushes. "Mr. Moss!"

I look up at the entranceway. "Good school," I say. "Excellent training."

"I was just dropping her off."

I nod.

Damon asks me where I'm going. He doesn't really care, but he's still flustered. And he's not a rude boy.

"Home, actually. I live near here."

"So how'd you know? About me and Sue?"

"Things get about," I say vaguely.

Damon half-smiles, plays with his hair, then drops his hand.

"Have you started those books I told you about, *From the Center* and *Framing Feminism*?" Let him squirm, I think. Let him tell me himself.

"Not exactly."

"What're you doing right now? You could go to the library. I'm just coming from there, the midtown branch, the art and picture gallery on the third floor. You'll probably find both books there."

"Well, yeah, but I have some other stuff to do."

"Why don't you walk with me first?" I say. "I'm practically around the corner."

Damon looks at his watch. I wait, doubting that he has anywhere to go.

"I guess, if it's that close."

"Good!" I slap him on the back and we get going. "You know, I was really impressed that you thought up your own thesis subject. You were the only one who didn't choose off the list."

"Thanks."

"I'm sorry you weren't in class this week. But we can talk now. If you haven't actually started the reading, what have you been thinking about? Sometimes it's better to let a few ideas swirl about in your head first."

"I've been pretty busy. We had to get the blood tests and get a witness, and even though we were just getting married at City Hall, Sue wanted a few days to put together an outfit. She made this amazing-looking dress."

102

We turn onto Twenty-Second Street. It begins to drizzle and the breeze has turned colder.

"How're your folks reacting?" I ask.

"My dad won't let us live in his house. No surprise. He's, like, anti-romance."

I stop in front of my building. "Really? He's kicking you out?"

"Pretty much. Unless I meet his conditions."

I wait.

"Listen, you're not anything like my dad, but you might not get it either."

The rain starts in earnest, and the wind kicks up. It'll probably be brief, but we're both underdressed. "Why don't you come up? Have a beer before you do what you need to do. Let the rain stop."

Damon looks a bit panicked. He's only truly comfortable around Sue, I realize. "I suspect you really want to tell me what's going on with you and your father, anyway."

"Yeah, okay. For a couple minutes."

Inside my apartment, I toss Damon a beer from the refrigerator. While he's opening it, I remember my book-marked *Helen Croft: The Baybridge Manor Years* on my night table. I have to count on Damon's not looking in that direction. (It could've been worse; I could have left out *Prairie Boys in Chaps*, my other bedside reading.) Damon goes to sit on my Morris chair. He takes an old paperback copy of Ben Shahn's *The Shape of Content* off the nearby bookshelf and starts to flip through it. I pull up one of the kitchen chairs, turn it around, and straddle it, facing him.

"You've got a lot of books here."

I nod.

He looks about. "Is this your only room? Or is there another one back there?"

"This is it. Some people have pull-out couches, I have a Murphy bed."

"Cool," he says, but his tone is flat. I'm sure it's hitting him that if a man my age can afford only a studio apartment, he and Sue might be in for some trouble.

"Why don't you tell me what you'd like to tell me?"

"It's pretty much what we talked about in your office that day. I'm not going back to Tri-Community."

From the host of responses available to me, the great majority would sound parental. "And Sue?"

"We decided she's staying at SVA. For the time being, anyhow. Things have gotten better there. There's this instructor who does realistic work and he's, like, championing her. Most of the students are still pretty much a bunch of assholes."

"So what are you thinking?" I ask.

"What do you mean?" He avoids my eyes.

"First of all, exactly what did your parents say?"

"They said if I stay at Tri-Community, me and Sue can live in the house until I get my associate degree or transfer to a real college. That's my father's condition."

"Not worth entertaining?" I ask.

Damon looks directly at me. Those bones, I think. He's a beautiful boy. For the second time this week, I think of Daniel, about the same age as Damon is right now when I met him.

"You live here by yourself, right Mr. Moss?"

I look around. "Nah, I've got a big family. It gets kind of chaotic around here sometimes."

Damon laughs. "Sorry. That was pretty stupid."

"Really, I'd like to know your plans. I'm interested."

Damon starts crossing and recrossing his legs, as he had in my office. "I've got a couple of things in mind. I'm a really good carpenter. My dad taught me. He's got this construction company, not a big one, but he makes out pretty good. Of course, forget it, he'd never let *me* work for him."

Briefly, Damon's eyes well up. He looks away from me again. Because of his bones, his beauty will last. Many people throughout his life will want him. I'm impressed with how little he seems to be aware of his appeal. At the same time, I'm beginning to lack objectivity. I wonder if I should rush this visit to its conclusion. Yet I haven't accomplished my purpose.

"I'm going to take the liberty of being direct," I tell him. "It's interesting to me that you seem to think your love for Sue and staying in school are mutually exclusive. It's almost quaint. Young guys in the forties and fifties thought as you do. They thought they had to go out into the world and slay dragons for their wives."

Damon hasn't quite regained his composure. I think I see him wince a bit.

"There's a connection between your decision about how you must be with Sue and the thesis topic you chose. This clear division of gender roles. Have you thought about that?"

"Listen," he says, louder than he'd perhaps intended. "I know what's up. But I just want to make things easier for Sue."

I nod and ask him to tell me about her.

He checks my expression to see if I'm sincere. Slowly, he starts. "It was just a dumb thing that made me first notice her. We were at this guy's party—we actually found out later that we both think the guy's pretty much of a dork, but she was there, and she was wearing this . . . *thing*."

His fingertips brush his hips. I smile.

"This sarong thing. It was maybe five different shades of blue. And it was this material, almost like crepe paper, except even more delicate. I don't usually much notice what girls wear, but I had to say something. It was just so amazing. So then she told me she *made* it. I couldn't believe it. Plus she said she'd been to Indonesia with her best friend, and the sarongs she'd seen there had inspired her. And I got sort of fixated on that. Like, you see something, it inspires you, and right away you make one yourself, only, like, with your own imprint."

"That *is* impressive," I agree. I want to hear more. More of this tale of love springing from the appreciation of a sarong. More about a sense of protectiveness and a vision of the future spiraling out from the first sight of a sarong.

"And the other thing was, I didn't get, like, caught with Sue. I usually get caught after the first couple of minutes with a new girl. I mean, of course I've had girlfriends, but it always seemed more part of group mentality, if you know what I mean. And it was always weird when I first met girls."

So says this boy who by any standard is extremely attractive. I watch him as he speaks and feel an agitation I can't suppress, my body responding to the desire that won't be fulfilled.

"But with Sue it was different. It was like she wanted to make me comfortable and she wanted to make me go crazy over her at the same time. Not just, you know, with sex. Because then she started showing me her paintings, and they were incredible. So on one level I was looking at the paintings, but on another level I couldn't believe a girl who could do all this was interested in me."

"Why not, Damon?" You, I think, with that gorgeous head of wavy black hair, that unstudied and sexy five-o'clock shadow, those shoulders, that lovely, fetching smile, that slow and graceful way of comporting yourself.

"I don't know. It doesn't matter. You asked me to tell you about her. I'm telling you. She's beautiful and talented, and she loves me." He recrosses his legs.

That simple, I think. And then I remember what Neil has done, left the Shackle with some young guy, more than likely some moronic young guy. No different from what I've been doing for years, yet right in this moment, listening to Damon, the image of Neil prowling around is nothing more than evidence that chance will not be generous with me.

"I understand everything you've told me," I say to Damon. "I want you to know that."

Damon's face relaxes. He smiles an intelligent smile and invites me to nod with him in complicity, in brotherhood. He's not afraid to prolong the sense of our alliance by continuing to faintly nod as we link gazes. To my dismay, I feel my cock swelling inside my jeans. I'm grateful for my position on the chair, how its back partially blocks me from Damon's view. I consider what to do. My erection is growing intractable. Like a microchip in my ear, it's giving me directions, and I cannot keep myself from looking down at Damon's crotch. There is no straining bulge there; he shifts his position merely from nervousness. He has seen my gaze travel, confirmation of the rumors. He smiles—sadly, I think—but he shows no sign of being offended.

I get up from my seat, turn around, and take a can of 7-Up from the refrigerator. I busy myself getting ice and a glass. I'm not a kid anymore, I can control this. I resume my seat, drink from the glass.

"Here's a possible scenario for you to think about," I say. "You find some work as a carpenter, but it's sporadic. You want to work all the time, and you try, but you just can't make it happen. Sue gains more and more favor at SVA, graduates with top honors. You, being the lovely guy you are, are nothing but proud of her. The thing to do now is to move out of that small apartment you share with two roommates neither of you like, but—again—you just can't make it happen. Sue gets a not-so-bad receptionist job at a gallery, but the pay is terrible. She needs to paint at night and on the weekends, and there's no place to do it. She uses the apartment's common living room, even after the roommates lay down the law. You both get thrown out. The guy who owns the gallery starts hitting on Sue . . ."

"She'd blow him off," interrupts Damon.

"Maybe," I say. And then I decide to stop there. I'll say no more. "*Maybe*," I repeat.

Damon's expression is weary now, haggard even, as if the events I've described have already transpired. His jaw has tightened around the bitterness he directs either at me or at Sue for losing her resolve in my scenario. Thankfully, he does not look the least bit desirable at this moment.

"You're a bright boy, Damon, and a thoughtful one. Ultimately, I don't think Tri-Community is the place for you. But it's a stepping-stone toward bringing you into focus. Just as SVA is doing for Sue."

"Things with me got a little sidetracked before I started at Tri-Community," admits Damon. "That's why I'm there instead of someplace better."

No doubt he's referring to his addiction and recovery, but I don't pursue it.

"I mean, no offense. I know Tri-Community's good for some people."

"Want another beer?"

"No, I'd better go. But thanks. It was good talking and everything."

"You're quite welcome," I say breezily—as if our visit had cost me nothing.

winter

12

The Barracks is lively tonight, and we have lit the season's first fire in the small brick fireplace on the west wall. In one corner, Luis is entertaining a table full of men in the corner by singing, with melodramatic intensity, the lyrics to Cole Porter's "Love for Sale." He exaggerates his Cuban accent. Ten minutes later the men leave a big tip, which Luis tucks into his jeans pocket before going through the swinging kitchen doors to share his rendition with Jordan. I hear the trill of the first phrase, and I wait for Jordan to erupt in laughter. He doesn't. When Luis emerges ten minutes later, his smile has vanished.

"Is everything okay?" I ask, leaning over the end of my bar.

"Frank is one of the ones who can't take the cocktail. Not any of them. His bloods go haywire or he has diarrhea all day."

"Damn it. What are they going to do?"

"He's on AZT. Talk about yesterday's drug. Jordan must want to kill all those HIV born-agains. He must just want to murder them."

I say nothing.

"I would. I would want to kill them all. I don't care." Luis looks towards the kitchen door, and I wonder if he's on a cocktail, if he's guiltily keeping to himself that *he's* one of those HIV born-agains.

"Let's all go out," I say. "Let's you and me take Jordan out after we close up."

Luis usually heads back up to Washington Heights after closing. I don't know where he goes before letting himself into his sister's apartment. Jordan always goes straight home. We have never all three gone out together.

"Okay," says Luis, also solemn. "Where should we go?"

I suggest the tamest after-hours club I know, Quentin's. Yet even there, we will be surrounded by guys taking K and Ecstasy and Poppers;

the disc jockey will turn up the bass so high our teeth will rattle. But Quentin's has a balcony with several little groupings of high-backed upholstered chairs—a genteel parlor in a sink of vice.

When we pull down the security gate on the Barracks, Luis and I tell Jordan our plan. He needs a night for himself, we tell him.

"Frank might be having a bad time of it," he worries. "He gets up choking. We don't know why."

"Call him. Tell him you've gone out with us," says Luis.

"He'll think it's odd. We've never done it before. It'll worry him."

"No it won't," I say. "You underestimate Frank."

Jordan nods thoughtfully. I love this about him. He is more responsive to other people's viewpoints than anyone I know. He thinks they hold worthwhile lessons from which he can gain.

"Okay," he agrees. "Let me back in."

He goes back to phone Frank, and Luis and I solemnly shake hands, confirming a job well done.

Quentin's is on an upper floor of a warehouse building on Eleventh Avenue in the Twenties, not all that far from my apartment building. Just before 2:00, it's packed. We're lucky, for as we come in a group of men is vacating one of the prime seating arrangements; they are going down to the dance floor. Four of them are into body modification, and they look at the uncultivated, lumpish Jordan, clearly a duck who has strayed from his pond. We take over their seats.

Here on the balcony, we sit in chairs that look meant for sultans. We are positioned over the dance floor, where shirtless men of all ages, many with closed eyes, dance in a mass, making it impossible to see who is with whom. One man has opened his fly and let out his erect penis. He is pivoting from one partner to another, teasing them both. Unsurprisingly, the huge ones are the exhibitionists, and this guy is big. Jordan looks at him with an impassive expression. I wonder if our bringing him here was a good idea. He is so sad.

"Would you like to go somewhere else?" I ask. "The Empire Diner? We could just get coffee."

"Oh, no, this is fine."

He has come to please us. A waiter stops at our table and Jordan orders a ginger ale. Luis and I order beers.

"So what is the game plan with Frank?" I ask. An indelicate approach, but somehow right, I think.

110

"Just AZT for now. He was in this group for people who can't take the cocktail, but he says it turned into, what'd he call it . . . a whine-fest. So we got him out of there. I gotta say, though, I feel royally gypped. As if everybody but me and Frank are living in the new decade. Frank and me, we're still in the mid-eighties."

I nod. "It must feel that way. Has he tried all the combinations?" I ask, even though I know he has.

Jordan perks up for a moment. "But what's good is he's got a great doctor. Dr. Janus. And he's on the list for some protocols. So it's not like there's no hope."

"Good," I say. "Janus is supposed to be one of the best. I'm glad you're with him."

I want to kick Luis under the table, to bring his attention back to our conversation. He keeps looking at Jordan earnestly, but then his gaze drifts to the exhibitionist on the dance floor. Now he takes off his own shirt. "Hot in here," he says.

"How is all this going over with Frank's family? Do they know what's going on?"

"He just has the one sister, Trish in Passaic and her kids. She's divorced and she works for Hudson Carpet too, in the front office. Frank got her the job after her divorce. He's worried about what might happen to her. Afterwards." Jordan drinks from his glass of ginger ale. Unexpectedly, he smiles. "You know what I hate about these places? They never have any party mix or nuts or anything."

"Quentin's idea of appetizers don't come in Mr. Peanut's cans," says Luis. He has slunk down in his seat and hooked his thumbs through his belt loops. He is looking down at his clearly defined abdominal muscles. Absently, he strokes his stomach.

Jordan squeezes Luis's shoulder. Like a father humoring his adolescent son through one of his phases, Jordan has always poked some fun at Luis's obsession with musculature. "Best abs in the place," he tells Luis. "Hands down."

Luis blushes and looks away. It is unbelievable to me that he could have actually thought his vanity had gone undetected.

I light a cigarette. "Can Trish help you out? Or her kids, how old are they? Can they help?"

"Tad is fifteen, but he's a pretty messed up kid. Trish has her hands full with him. And Mindy is only nine. All along, Frank has been helping *them*."

I take a slow drag.

"He's not that sick," says Jordan. "Except in the mornings. Mornings he's sick." He rubs his face. Then he looks down at the dance floor, the pounding feet and the sweating torsos that project the appearance of robust health.

I have made a terrible mistake and it cannot be taken back. Jordan is looking down at the life he will be cast into when Frank is gone and, rightly, he sees its impossibility for himself. He arches his head back, away from my smoke. I snuff out the cigarette. A strained and accommodating smile on his face, Jordan still looks, glassy-eyed, at the great swarm of foreigners beneath him. I put my hand on his knee. "Let's get some fresh air," I say.

Jordan rises at once.

"I'll see you guys tomorrow," says Luis. He kisses Jordan, but his gaze is fixed on a spot on the dance floor, not on the exhibitionist, but on one of the men he is teasing, a Latino darker than Luis and very handsome.

Jordan and I leave together, unnoticed, and start walking. We pass two men stirring against the side of a building. I remember how Neil and I kissed on the way to my apartment from the Shackle, how surprised I'd been.

We walk another block before Jordan stops. He tries to move forward, but in this perfectly still night he is held back, as if by a blast of wind. I have to fight an urge to flee. He tries again to move on, but his shoulders begin to tremble; they are mountainous shoulders, and they are quaking. The sound that comes from him then is one that we are all called upon to restrain; it is a wretched mix of an animal in heat and a terror so convincing it draws other senses into its service, mine as well as Jordan's. The distant whoosh of traffic on the West Side Highway becomes the monotonous rhythm that precedes a deadly crash. The feel of the brisk air, the smell of chimney smoke, and the sight of steam escaping from the street below carries to us—I know to both of us—a foreboding of deep winter desolation. Jordan is bellowing, and I put my arms out to him. He is too big, much too big to take shelter there. Rather, he must reposition his arms to take *me* in, to smother me inside his warm, incautious embrace.

13

"Here we are, Brian," says Constance McCabe. Beryl has arranged her hire over the phone from Scottsdale. She is a handsome, large-boned Irish woman employed by Quality Nursing Service. "I hope you'll be comfortable," she says. "I put on fresh sheets."

"Thank you." I set down my canvas duffel bag and leather backpack. "I'm sure I will be."

In truth, I could never be comfortable in this room. It is my old room on Periwinkle Drive, the one I left over twenty years ago. Amazingly, Avery has preserved my childhood refuge: the very room where Charlene discovered pictures of naked men, the room whose door Avery had pounded, demanding that I stop sequestering myself. It is a door he once threatened to remove.

"I'll give you some time, now," says Mrs. McCabe, and leaves me. Rather than look around, I go directly to the night stand phone, my old black princess model, and call Nathan in his office at Tri-Community. When he answers, his voice is clipped, deeper than usual, as if prepared to rise in defense. "Nat. It's me. I'm calling from Cleveland. Actually, from my old room, if you can believe it."

"Uh-oh," he says.

"Daphne or someone will have to cover for me this week. I'm really sorry. My father's had another stroke. I won't be here long, but I have to see, you know, what's possible from here on out. My sister'll be up later this week, and hopefully I can get away then. Do you want me to fax Daphne my notes?"

"Only if it's convenient. Take as long as you need, honey. I'll make whatever arrangements we need to."

"Thanks." I mean for the "honey," as well.

After hanging up, I ache to pick up the phone again. Yet I have already spoken to Norman Brinsky, whose nephew is going to tend bar in my absence. My index finger veritably itches to circle the old rotary dial, to call who I used to call, my few old friends (about whose whereabouts I know nothing) and Ned Tanning, the mandolin player who died of AIDS. Most of all, I want to call Charlene, sure reminder of my existence in this Tudor-style house, this hushed, still toney suburb. Yet I can't. Avery is asleep downstairs; I can't very well talk to Charlene or start tracking down remote school acquaintants, people with whom

I forged a bogus connection in the first place, before I say hello to my father who has just had a serious stroke.

Still, I can't go down yet, either. I empty my clothes out onto my old bed, over the bedspread with its nautical motif of dancing anchors and life preservers. I have brought black jeans, a T-shirt, jerseys, a gray thermal pullover. A boy's wardrobe, I think, compared with the adult wardrobe I had as a boy. For most of our time at Sandover High, Beryl had laid out my clothes on this very bed. Each morning after breakfast I had allowed her to rummage through my closet. All my clothes ran along a style called collegiate when I was in high school: button-down oxford shirts, some pin-striped, some in pastel colors, V-neck lamb's wool sweaters, cordovan penny loafers, sports jackets with suede elbow patches. I owned a couple of ties, both with authoritative patterns—tiny polo players and the crest of the Danish royal family. I permitted Beryl to pick out my clothes because she seemed more capable than I of projecting my image into the world. She had a gift for assembling my presentation in such a way as to ensure my social standing. Consequently, all through high school, I looked the budding young capitalist. Today, I have a variation on the wardrobe I should have had then, the bad boy's wardrobe, unironed shirts, leather vest, scuffed Doc Martens. My appearance in this room twenty years later is a threat at last fulfilled.

As a concession to Avery, I go into the bathroom to shave. The slightest suggestion of beard is for him a menace—the entire underclass manifesting in the form of his son. I look straight at the mirror, trying not to take in the familiar oval sink basin, the glazed yellow tiles flecked with burnt ochre, the leaded window with its pebbly frosted panes, the window that always screeched when I tried to open it. I wish I had stayed at a Day's Inn and rented a car, charged both to my American Express card. I long for the lovely anonymity of a motel room, any room filled with generic amenities.

Downstairs, Constance McCabe is reading *Family Circle*. She fills my father's old Eames chair. The room that has always been noisy is quiet now. Where is my father's loud voice? His laughter, although infrequent, has always been full-bellied, his voice commanding. Televisions and hi-fis and my cornet used to blare here. Beryl's school friends practiced their baton twirling and dance moves all over the house. Charlene had vacuumed and yelled over the sound of the motor that it was time for us to get to our homework. Beryl's cat Rufus had yowled to get in and out.

Now I can almost smell the silence, and it seems that Mrs. McCabe is at its core. Yet I realize that this is an illusion—that the noise left when Beryl and I did, when Rufus died from diabetes and Charlene took another job. Before today, I had never considered that most of the sound in the Periwinkle house had subsided all at once. Perhaps it was not Avery's first stroke at all, but this sudden vanishing of sound that has turned him mild.

"Is he still asleep?"

"He's there in the den," says Mrs. McCabe. "He's waiting for you."

"The den" is her term. My father has always called the room off the living room his study. A pretentious choice of terms for a man whose work was developing commercial real estate. A set of Harvard Classics as well as the entire Modern Library and several thick volumes of the history of world culture and civilization fill the shelves of the room from which Avery sometimes made angry evening calls to the owners of plumbing and electrical supply houses. There were times he got so loud that Beryl asked me to go downstairs and investigate. Walking past the open door to my father's study, I would hear Avery's sputtering expletives, see his color heighten and his cheeks quiver as his frenetic gaze scanned titles by Plato, Aristotle, Voltaire, and Montaigne. Back upstairs, I would tell Beryl, "He's reading the classics again."

I sit across from Mrs. McCabe on the Danish modern couch. "So," I say, and wait.

"What would you like to know?"

"My sister's already told me some. I know about the paralysis and the slurring, and that he's on blood thinner. I know about some weird new laugh. There was already a personality change with the first one. A sentimentality that was definitely *not* my father. I hadn't known strokes could do that. It was pretty unsettling. I guess that neither one of us knows what to expect."

"I've been working with stroke patients for fifteen years," says Mrs. McCabe, as if in answer.

I nod.

"Once you know what kind of stroke a person has had and which part of the brain it affected, you get an idea what to expect," she explains. "With your dad, a lot of the damage was to the motor strip in the right hemisphere, so that accounts for the paralysis on the left side. He does slur some, but he uses all the right words and understands language fine." Mrs. McCabe pauses to drink from a cup of tea on the end

115

table. "That's a lot to be grateful for," she continues. "The bad part is that there was also some damage to your father's parietal lobe. That resulted in anosognosia, a form of a stroke-related condition we call Neglect. Have you heard of it?"

"No."

"It will complicate his treatment. It's an odd condition, or seems odd to us. Neglect patients just don't seem to care about their disabilities. Besides slurring his speech, your dad can't vary the tone of his voice. But he doesn't seem to be aware that he sounds any different than before. The most peculiar symptom of anosognosia, though, is that people tend to disinherit the side of their bodies that was affected by the stroke. Just this morning, for instance, your dad caught sight of his left leg and for a second he thought some stranger was sitting next to him. You can imagine how frightening that must be. But, really, it is not as uncommon as you might think."

I'm impressed by how much Mrs. McCabe knows about what has happened to Avery. Impressed, but not surprised. After all, Beryl is behind her hire.

"Would you mind going in with me?" I ask.

"If that's what you'd prefer," she says. Now her manner is correct and remote. I have become in her estimation one of the family members who shrink from unpleasantness. Mrs. McCabe has no idea what I have seen over these last years—whom I have fed, whose vomit I have collected in plastic basins, whose tacky brows I have wiped with cool witch-hazel compresses, whose toenails I have clipped. To her, I am just another son with a return airline ticket in my backpack. She doesn't know that it is not the new, enfeebled Avery to whom I am averse, but the old, healthy one.

She rises, and we go into the study together.

Mrs. McCabe immediately walks to my father's right side. "Oh, look what you've done," she says, sounding pleased. To me, she points over by the window and says, "When I left, he was over there."

To receive me with a measure of formality, my father has wheeled himself behind his desk. He has done this with one hand. It took some effort and some reasoning power.

"Hi, Dad." I don't go over and kiss him. I have probably not kissed him in twenty-five years. I stand where I am and ask, "How are you doing?"

The left side of Avery's face is pulled down and his left eye, too, is sagging and looks wetter than the other eye. I can only see him from the torso up. He's wearing a three-color nylon jacket that says *Nike*, the same kind of awful stuff he wore in Scottsdale. Avery doesn't answer me. I don't understand. I thought his hearing was still fine.

Mrs. McCabe motions for me to come stand by her. I do. Now my father looks at me. "You came in for your old man," he says. The words are blurry. He is drunk, I think irrationally, before I remember. "Number two twin."

He means that I was the twin born second, but the double meaning is obvious. "At your service," I say. "Beryl's practically on her way."

"I told her not to come. The opening of the new condo. I never missed an opening in my life. What the hell's it all for if you miss the openings."

I don't say much at first. Avery's voice has lost its timbre. He is making sense, as Mrs. McCabe said he would, but his affectless tone is jarring; he could be on Thorazine in some back ward.

"She's coming at the end of the week. We have a lot to discuss."

"Tell her to bring Missy." He turns to Mrs. McCabe. "My only grandchild," he says. He does not smile. I wonder if he can. At another time, he would have stressed the *only* and looked at me. Now his voice is dull, uninflected. He has lost a vital component in his artillery against me—the ability to allude to my problem without having to name it.

"I don't know if she's bringing Missy. Dad, can you move anything on your left side? Can you feel anything?"

"She says I can move my little finger," Avery says, referring to Mrs. McCabe. "But I don't see a damn thing. Half of me has died. Half of me is in heaven or hell. Which do you think, Brian."

"I don't think anything is dead. We're going to set you up for a course of rehabilitation."

"What the hell," says Avery vaguely. Then he laughs. I have no idea why, and it is not a laugh I have ever heard from him. It is nearly maniacal, so in opposition to his affectless tone that it is hard to believe such a sound could come from the same man.

"Lunch time," says Constance McCabe. "What can you do about wheeling yourself out from there?"

"Wrong way," says Avery, meaning he could navigate the right-hand turns to get in, but not the left-hand ones to get out.

"Try using your good hand with the other wheel."

This ends up a time-consuming activity. When my father's wheelchair finally emerges from behind the desk, I see that the ankle of his nylon pants has risen up. He is wearing thick stockings. I look at Constance McCabe.

"Support hose. Helps prevent blood clots," she says. She has stopped talking to me in full sentences, feeling perhaps that I am not deserving of the effort. She could well be right. My mind has already started to wander. I have projected myself back at the Barracks. Jordan and Luis are commiserating with me for my lost week in Cleveland. "It was worth it," I'm telling them, "to see masculinity incarnate in panty hose."

After lunch, Mrs. McCabe helps prepare my father for his nap. Then she drives her old Volkswagon Rabbit to the supermarket, and I find myself in my old room again. I have come to Cleveland to spring into action, yet I don't know what action to take. I lie on the made bed and stare at the milky glass fixture overhead. Dead insects, God knows how old, litter its bottom. My room is overheated, so I take off my shirt. The bruise from that first night with Neil is long gone. Part of me would have the bruise return. If Neil's mark was on my body, I'd have legitimate reason to think about him. As it is, I think about him anyway, try to remember if Neil ever said the name of his therapist, the one who was helping him go straight. I'd like to call him for an appointment, just to see what Neil is up against, see exactly how these sons-of-bitches work.

It's only 2:15, and Constance McCabe said Avery might sleep for two or three hours. I go to my backpack and remove *Helen Croft: Dawn of a New Season*. This is the final volume of the trilogy. I finished *The Baybridge Manor Years* on the plane. When Helen returned to her governess job after her mother's funeral, the Master had greeted her with the news that the Mistress would give birth in May. He'd hoped that Helen was looking forward to having a new little charge. Helen had congratulated him, then gone to her room to pack. The book ended with her strewn across her narrow cot, in tears.

The third volume begins two years after the second ended. I learn that Helen has grown God-fearing, that she embraces only the needs of those less fortunate. To support herself, she has resumed her work as a governess, this time for a family who lives near the northern edge of Hyde Park in London. Her current mistress, a Mrs. Shipley, is devoted to good works. Each year Mrs. Shipley arranges a jumble sale in front of the parsonage of the church to which she belongs. In the opening chapter of Volume III, Helen arrives at the jumble sale with the Shipley children, the twins Vanessa and Victor.

This is too much to bear. I put the book away, and lie down again.

Red-breasted robins, the ubiquitous bird of my childhood, are chirping nearby. I go to the window to watch three of them range across the frozen lawn in search of worms. It's been so long since I've seen a robin that I can't remember how they gather food in freezing temperatures. That's what I'm doing, wondering how robins forage in the winter, when Beryl calls.

"Oh, good, you're there! Have you seen him?" There is the sound of rushing air and a distant beeping over the line. She's in her car.

"Just for a few minutes. He looks pretty bad. It's hard to tell what's going on with him. Mrs. McCabe says he sees and hears fine, but he didn't know I had come into the room until I moved over to right where she was standing."

"That's the Neglect," says Beryl. "You have to move to his right side."

Here I am, the first one to come see Avery after the stroke, yet it is Beryl who talks about the Neglect as though she's known about it forever.

"It's so weird," I repeat stupidly.

"What do you think of Mrs. McCabe?" asks Beryl.

"She seems excellent. A real straight-shooter."

"Good. Now listen. There's a rehabilitation center just ten minutes away from me. Very, very good reputation. I think I can get Dad in."

"Uh-huh. Well, maybe that's a good idea. I just don't know. I don't think he knows." What am I doing here, I wonder.

"I have to go, but I'm glad you're there," says Beryl. "Dad really insisted I stay for this thing tomorrow night. So I have a flight for Friday midday. You'll still be there?"

"I expect so."

"Okay, I have to go now. I have to pick up the printing of the floor plans for the new units. So I'll see you on Friday, Brian."

Beryl is off the phone before I hang up. When I return to the window, the robins are gone. I lie down again, this time closing my eyes. To calm my mind, I try to call up several of my favorite Toulouse-Lautrec portraits, *Red-Haired Woman in a White Blouse* and *Emile Bernard*—strong, assured portraits that remind me of the simple beauty of the unwatchful expression. Yet the memory of these particular paintings sets me on edge; they call forth the dissertation sitting on my kitchen table, still waiting to be put on course. Finally I think of a painting by Lautrec's friend Pierre Bonnard, one of the languorous and lushly sad paintings of his wife Marthe submerged in her bath. This image of Marthe bathing becomes a purveyor of all that comforts me, an endless supply of English spinster novels and Aegean suppers, even of faceless midnight fucks.

It is dusk by the time I enter the sun room where my father and Mrs. McCabe sit. It is a sportsman's room in a house with no sportsmen. Avery's sun room is a tribute to the social sports, some from another era. The walls are hung with engravings of fox hunts and cricket matches. There is a stuffed and mounted bass that my father didn't catch. Its varnished scales have a smooth factory gleam. In the far corner of the room is a walnut cabinet with recessed lighting that is full of lacrosse and field hockey trophies. The trophies had belonged to Geoffrey Weiss, Avery's second cousin and my third, something of a family legend, a Rhodes scholar and star athlete who died of leukemia at the age of twenty-nine. I have never been clear on how my father came to acquire Geoffrey's trophies, but they are lit up now; the trophy cabinet is in fact the only source of light in the room.

"Why's it so dark in here?" I ask.

"Your dad says the light bothers his one eye," answers Mrs. McCabe.

I move to Avery's right side. "Dad. Does the light bother your eye?"

"Brian. How's it feel to be back home." There is no interrogatory tone. I have to supply it myself.

"Fine, Dad. The house looks good. You've kept it up."

"Did you see that I had Mrs. McCabe take out some of your old toys. Your old Matt Dillon rifle. There, over there." My father points with his good arm.

On a table by the door is the rifle, the box containing my old Roy Rogers costume, a few more guns. My father had always liked to buy me guns. Toy metal pistols, their handles inlaid with plastic colored to resemble ivory. Rifles endorsed by TV cowboys.

"Little boys today play with submachine guns," I say. "Not always plastic, either."

"You take everything too seriously," slurs Avery. He has said this many times before.

Mrs. McCabe excuses herself to prepare dinner. We sit in silence for a moment. I allow myself to look Avery over. I'm glad to see he's wearing a sweater made of real wool. Mrs. McCabe's taste, I suppose.

She picks out his clothes as Beryl once picked out mine, but I realize she must also help dress him. As we sit, he begins to slump to one side. Instinctively, I go to straighten him. I remember that when I touch his left shoulder he's aware of nothing, so I say, "I'm straightening you up now, Dad."

He doesn't answer. Then suddenly he says, "Debbie's got me by the balls." Avery must intend this as a biting pronouncement, but in his new tone it comes out as befuddled—nearly sweet for its lack of rancor.

"What do you mean?" I ask. "I thought she was out of the picture. You told me so yourself."

"She thinks she can sue me," he says. "Palimony. You know palimony, very handy in your world."

Very handy. My world. This stroke has given back Avery some of his old edge but has deprived him of the tone to claim it. I'm obliged to fill in the sarcastic tone of the barbs he aims at me. Still, some tiny advance has been made. Inferior though it may be, Avery has granted me my own world.

"Does she have a lawyer yet?"

"She has a lawyer, I have a lawyer, we all have lawyers."

This he does intend as a joke, so I smile. Yet I can't gauge his true level of concern over this lawsuit.

"Does she know you've had this second stroke?"

My father just looks at me, his perennially naive son. "Let her have 'em. They won't be of much use to her."

"Excuse me?"

"The balls," he slurs. I supply the exclamation point and the impatience.

"Beryl will talk to your lawyer," I promise. "Debbie Shuster must be a real viper. What were you doing with a woman like that, Dad?" Before he answers, I say, "Forget it. It doesn't matter."

"She might still be a good-looking woman," he says. "but believe me, she's ugly on the inside."

Until now it hadn't mattered to Avery if his women were ugly on the inside. He had always appreciated them for their ornamental value, and now he is paying. Sitting in a wheelchair, wearing support hose, eerily empty of expression, atrophied, afraid of his own left leg—paying, it would seem. Yet in truth, not paying. In truth, all event is random. If not, how could we defend ourselves from those who say AIDS is our punishment?

"I never met her," I say neutrally. Over the course of my father's twelve-year relationship with Debbie Shuster, I have not been to Cleveland and he has only been to New York once, alone. Beryl, though, met Debbie several times when she and Seth came back to Cleveland for visits. For years she has complained that Debbie is a real operator and it was a mystery to her that Avery couldn't see it. In Scottsdale, I heard Seth tell her to be grateful Avery had someone, and she'd burst out, "Please! Daddy could get anybody. All the time I was growing up, he had to beat them back."

"She was an attractive woman, but she hectored me to death."

"You can hold your own," I say, then realize he can't. I wonder how much this stroke was a response to Debbie Shuster's leaving him.

Mrs. McCabe reappears, steps to my father's right. "Shall we?" she asks.

I am unclear about the boundaries of her role. She is a nurse whom Beryl has hired to stay with my father for eleven hours a day, from nine a.m. to eight p.m. I have come here to take over when Mrs. McCabe is off. After dinner, Mrs. McCabe is to show me a few things about my father's care. Yet shouldn't I be the one to shop and cook? Tomorrow I will go to Heinen's to buy food for dinner, I decide. I will prepare it, and Mrs. McCabe will be our guest.

The teakwood table in the dining room is set. Mrs. McCabe has found the good china that was a wedding gift to my parents. When I look up from noticing this, she catches my eye, her expression confirming the importance of her choice. I smile to acknowledge her superior experience in these matters. The meal, though, is simple. It consists of soft foods—a soufflé, creamed spinach, hot rolls, baked apples. Only the right side of Avery's mouth moves when he chews. I wonder if he knows the left side exists. Who does my father think shares his mouth, friend or foe? There is no deficit on his right side. He eats with his customary gusto, his usual mechanical vulgarity. Like his character, his right hand is programmed to get the job done. When he pushes aside his plate, though, half the soufflé and the creamed spinach remain on its left side.

Sitting on Avery's right side, Mrs. McCabe says to him, "Mr. Moss, there is still food on your plate."

"What're you talking about."

"Bring your plate back and turn it half around. You'll see."

Avery looks at her, glassy-eyed.

"Just try it," she says. "What've you got to lose?"

"Impossible," says Avery. He might mean the act of turning the plate around; he might mean going on with his life.

"Come on, Dad. Trust Mrs. McCabe."

"Jesus," he says, but does as he's told. If the appearance of the food now on the right side of his plate surprises him, he does not acknowledge it. He eats as greedily as before.

"Lucky you're right-handed," comments Mrs. McCabe, then turns to me. "It can be a full-time job in itself getting a patient to favor their subordinate hand."

"Very tough to overcome a lifelong habit," I say.

"We'll have other lifelong habits to contend with," says Mrs. McCabe. She is preparing me. Is she also signaling her pessimism for my father's full recovery?

When Avery finally puts down his fork the skin of his baked apple folds in upon itself, sad and unavailing. My father pushes the plate aside. "Brian," he says. "Remember the sirloin at the clubhouse."

I do. The exclusive Brandywine Country Club, where we belonged for years, had an immense and plush clubhouse. Its carpet, woven with the club's seal, gave off a smell of spruce like fragrant steam rising off a forest floor. It had a bluestone fireplace that took up an entire wall. My father brought Beryl and me to Brandywine for every holiday dinner. When our meal was ready, we were surrounded by three black waiters, each of whom my father addressed by name. I knew his heartiness to be fueled in part by their servitude. Avery always ordered the Brandywine Sirloin, a huge, center cut piece of meat charbroiled on the outside. One of the waiters would cut a small incision so that my father could see and approve the red meat inside, the pink juices running into the gutter of the plate. From the time I was seven, Avery had insisted I also order the Brandywine Sirloin. Beryl was allowed to order our favorite, creamed chicken over biscuits. Then one day when we were teenagers, my father quit Brandywine. According to Beryl, he had been asked to leave. She said it was because of his girlfriends—their clothing, their gestures, the conspicuous shimmer of their fingernail polish, their cloying perfume. She claimed that someone official had spoken to Avery. I had thought this all a projection of Beryl's wishes, yet it was true that my father had quit the club with no explanation to me.

"Steak is off the menu for now," says Mrs. McCabe.

"Steak helped to get you here, Dad," I add.

"Don't give me that," he slurs. "I'll be good as new soon as soon as I get out of here." With his good hand, he slaps the arm of his wheelchair. Then he laughs that strange and barbaric laugh.

I look at Mrs. McCabe, but she is eating the last bit of her baked apple. When she is done, I rise to take in our plates. She insists I relax. "I'll need you in a few minutes. Before I go, we'll get your father ready for bed together. I'll show you how it's done."

I nod. This is a good woman; I owe her my cooperation. She need not know how alarmed I am by her plan.

Within the last ten years, particularly during the first five of them, I have tarried in Mrs. McCabe's world—kneading Jake's perennially sore limbs, turning Philip on his back and later on his side while he lay unconscious, shaving Lamont when he could not sit up, washing Benjamin's scrotum with a cool Babywipe. These men's bodies, all of which had merged with mine (three tenderly, one in a demented heat) became in the end my charges, charges I shared with other friends who had known them in the same way. Even in their greatest suffering, these men were courteous as we cared for them. Nursing my dying friends has not been difficult, has often been a privilege, but the prospect of undressing my father, of shaving his face to his standards, of applying a moist cloth to his sparse gray pubic hairs, terrifies me. Then I remember, with a torrent of relief, the power of Avery's right hand, the glorious section of intact brain that will deliver signals to his right hand, permitting him to guide both razor and washcloth where they need to go.

Avery and I sit in silence while Mrs. McCabe rinses the dishes and puts them in the dishwasher. I long to excuse myself to go smoke a cigarette, but I must wait. Finally, Mrs. McCabe returns, wiping her hands on a dishtowel, then placing it on the back of her chair. "The best way to learn is by doing," she says to me. "Mr. Moss, are you ready for bed?"

"What the hell," he says. He tries to get up.

"No," says Mrs. McCabe, behind him in a second. "You can't do it by yourself. Remember? This is a two-person operation now. Your son will stand by. He's our apprentice tonight."

"That know-it-all," asks Avery. Again, one of his old provocations loses its sting the moment it hits the air.

"Your sister had someone come in to fix up the bathroom while your dad was still in the hospital," she says to me. "Otherwise he couldn't have come home. You'll see. We'll go to the bathroom first, and then I'm going to show you how to transfer. We'll transfer him from the chair to the bed, but later you'll need to transfer him to the toilet as well."

I stand there with my hands feeling heavy at my sides.

"Let's go." Mrs. McCabe unlocks the brakes on Avery's wheelchair and pushes it to the threshold of the bathroom.

Shortly after I met Daniel, when no one was home, I'd come into this room to masturbate. I'd stare at the wallpaper—white calligraphic strokes on a muted gray ground—and then the strokes would multiply and go berserk behind my closed eyelids. A Mark Toby, I'd realize years later. I would come into one of the monogrammed guest towels, another wedding present Avery had kept, then run the single towel through the Maytag so as not to risk Charlene unballing it from the hamper. The same wallpaper and guest towels are here, but now there is an elevated toilet seat, a horizontal grab bar beside the toilet as well as a gleaming U-shaped one along the bathtub wall. There is a plastic chair whose legs are stuck to the tub's bottom with suction cups.

My father rears his head back; it falls a little to the left. "Christ, what is this, a command performance," he says.

"I'll wait in the other room," I say.

"Good-bye," Avery answers.

My father has to negotiate the wheelchair into the bathroom. Although the doorway has been recut, the clearance still doesn't allow for much maneuvering. Mrs. McCabe follows Avery in, then closes the door.

In the guest room, a hospital bed has replaced the old trundle arrangement. Everything Avery needs has been set on the right side of the bed: a pitcher of water; medication bottles; Kleenex; eye glasses; a battery-run buzzer, in case of emergency, I suppose. A portable radio sits on a tray table to the left of the bed. Against the wall is a laminated board balanced on two cane-backed chairs. I stand in the middle of the room to await their return. Dying for a cigarette, I weigh my chances of slipping out the kitchen door for two or three drags. Then the water in the bathroom is turned off and the door opens.

"Are you ready, Brian?" calls Mrs. McCabe.

"Didn't ever picture this in that great imagination of yours, did you?" says Avery. He is wearing pajama bottoms. I don't know how Mrs. McCabe managed so quickly.

She looks at her watch. We are keeping her. "Let's cooperate here now, Dad."

Mrs. McCabe removes a sling from a hook on the inside of the closet door and places Avery's weak arm inside its loop. "This is to keep his arm steady while we move him." She points to the board. "That's a slide board. There's another one in the bathroom. He's starting to get to the bed on his own, but this should be left here just in case. We'll use it now to show you."

Even after his weight loss, my father is a big man—broad shoulders, hefty neck, a wide and fleshy face. I already saw in Scottsdale that his stomach muscles now sag and his chest is more sunken than during my childhood, but he's still a big man. Mrs. McCabe looks no more than 5'3". I can't imagine how she'll get him from the wheelchair to the bed. Involuntarily, I move forward.

"No, no," she says. "He can manage. Your father does most of this himself now. Don't you, Mr. Moss?"

Avery says nothing.

"Let's get started," Mrs. McCabe says.

"Fucking palimony. She hasn't got a chance, has she Brian."

"Not my specialty, Dad. You'll have to ask Beryl."

Beryl is not a lawyer, but she has been involved in so much litigation over the years that she's become fearless and hearty in the face of lawsuits. Several times she's been sued by buyers who found small asbestos levels in the insulation wrapping basement pipes. Once she had to prove to the Scottsdale town board that she was in compliance with local sewage disposal ordinances. Another time a child tripped over a torn piece of astroturf on a communal deck and cracked his head open on the corner of a baluster. And she has found reason to counter-sue laborers who were suing her for contract violations. "Beryl's the one," I repeat. "Let's concentrate now, Dad. Mrs. McCabe needs your full attention."

Constance McCabe has already folded up the wheelchair's foot-rests. She checks to see that the brakes are locked. "Okay, feet to the floor now."

My father puts his right foot on the floor. The left remains in place.

"Afflicted foot, too," reminds Mrs. McCabe.

With his right hand, Avery pushes down on his left leg.

"Good. Strong foot in front of weak foot."

My father repositions himself.

"Excellent. Stand now."

Avery does. His good leg does the supporting. It trembles.

"Watch now, Brian," says Mrs. McCabe. She moves quickly, first removing the chair's armrests, then balancing the sliding board between

126

the chair and the surface of the bed. "Okay, Mr. Moss, you can sit," she says.

Avery obeys. His breath explodes out of his open mouth. I didn't expect him to be so exhausted. There's a film of sweat above his upper lip. We wait. After a moment he says, "Here's my specialty." His slur is worse; I can hardly understand him. He leans forward on the board, lifts himself slightly with his good arm and scoots along until he reaches the end propped up on the bed. His right bicep bulges. No competition for Luis, I think, but respectable for his age. "Can you do it one more time?" asks Mrs. McCabe. "Or do you need a rest?"

Without a word, he lifts himself again, and she removes the board. "No stage fright for you," she says. "How much can you get yourself settled?"

He frowns, but his right side manages to lead his left to the middle of the bed. Once there, Avery closes his eyes.

"This is no small task," Mrs. McCabe tells me.

"Helluva effort," Avery confirms, his eyes still closed.

Mrs. McCabe turns on the radio to his left. "Your news is on now," she says. "Listen to it and see what you can do to turn it off before you go to sleep."

In response, Avery snorts.

"Stimulation on his left side," Mrs. McCabe says. "There is a world to his left and it must be heeded. It takes training."

I smile at her unwitting double-entendre. "I tend to stand to his left anyway."

Before we leave, Mrs. McCabe removes a plastic urinal from beneath the bed and hands it to Avery. Once more, I give thanks for the healthy part of my father's brain that allows him to take hold of his penis and direct it where it must go.

"Sleep well, Dad," I say, and rush away to see Mrs. McCabe out.

Back in my room, I smoke a couple of cigarettes and snuff them out in the basin of a plastic trophy I got, along with every member of the Brandywine Junior Tennis League, in 1962.

The black princess has a rotary dial, so I can't call in for my messages at home. I go back downstairs and check on Avery. He's turned off the radio himself, an encouraging sign. In his study, I use the push-button phone. Three beeps. The first call is from Bill Craig, Damon's father. He got my number from Nathan Weinstein, he says, even admits to bullying Nat for it. Damon's going to stick it out at Tri-Community, he says, and he knows I had something to do with it. He's calling to thank me. He says he's sorry he was such an asshole to me and that if I ever need some home renovation work to call him—he'll give me a beautiful deal. The second message is from my dentist's office, confirming tomorrow's appointment that I'll have to remember to cancel. The third is from Jordan, calling to say he wants me to know everyone at the Barracks is thinking of me.

❧ 14 ❧

"Well, isn't this something," says Charlene Wright as I mount her front steps. I've called ahead. She holds open the door with one hand, leans on a four-footed cane with the other.

The door opens directly onto the living room. It looks as I remember it: overstuffed chairs with lace doilies patching their arms, hooked rugs, a profusion of house plants, ceramic and painted plaster animals on the radiator cover. On one wall is a photograph of Lloyd in a suit. I never saw him in a suit, nor assuming the solemn expression he must have thought appropriate to professional portraiture. I smell a spice from last night's dinner—cumin, maybe. The room is overheated.

I give Charlene the flowers I've brought. Dandy's, the flower store in one of Avery's old shopping centers, is gone. This is a grocery store bouquet.

"I just love these," Charlene says, pushing her nose into the tea roses and baby's breath. "Now, you sit down here and make yourself at home."

I do. "I just couldn't come here without stopping by. I hope you don't mind."

"Mind! How could I possibly? You just sit here, and I'll be right back."

She leaves, stomping along with her aluminum cane, and returns with her signature plate of Stella D'oro's. I get up to help her, but she says, "Sit doesn't mean like a Jack-in-the-Box. I'm just going to get the tea. You are such a welcome sight. Brian Moss as a man is not a sight I thought I'd get to see."

I smile, and watch her slow progress back to the kitchen. She didn't have a gray hair on her head when I left. And though she was always overweight, I don't remember this thick band of flesh at the back of her neck.

128

"How's your dad?" is the first question she asks when we are settled. "He sat with me in my kitchen just, when was it? Last month? Now, how bad was this last stroke of his?"

"It was definitely worse than the first. He's in a wheelchair. Lots of motor troubles, and some speech. But his mind seems sharp. In some ways, sharper than after the first stroke."

During this little report, Charlene's expression registers every piece of news. The solicitude on her face when she hears the word wheelchair is so genuine that I realize immediately she has kept her compassion alive in the company of friends, probably many friends with many troubles.

"How about you? How's your hip?"

"It's just perfect. Unless it's raining or sunny out." She smiles, but I see a shadow of misgiving. She is wondering if she has said this to me before.

"So you live here with Mosley."

"Yes. He's out now. He comes and goes. Got himself a girlfriend on Buckeye Road. Still, it suits him here. It's all paid off, did I tell you?"

"And the others? LeRoy and Rudy?"

"Aren't you sweet to remember their names? I did my best with those boys. Rudy I paid for his auto mechanics course, LeRoy I bailed out of all kinds of fixes. But I have to tell you honestly, the street got both of them. Even Mosley won't have nothing to do with them. He was always the gentle one. Too sleepy-minded, I guess, but maybe that's what it takes to stay out of trouble these days."

I nod. "He sort of kept to himself when I lived here those two weeks."

"That was really something, wasn't it?" Charlene says, handing me the plate of Stella D'oro's. That is her entire comment. During the two weeks I stayed with her, she took aside LeRoy and Rudy many times, and once I saw her holding them hard, her thumb pressing into each boy's upper arm as she spoke. They had looked at the floor. Once LeRoy had looked up at me, and there had been murder in his eyes.

"So now what will happen with your dad? You can't be here, and I guess Beryl can't either."

"That's what we have to figure out. Beryl wants him in rehabilitation out by her."

Charlene just nods. Who would pay for private rehabilitation if she had a stroke? They are the same age, my father and Charlene, and their bodies are following the same trajectory. She just listens and does not offer an opinion on where Avery should live and who should help him get through the rest of his life.

"Tell me about you and New York," she says.

"I can't imagine being anywhere else," I tell her. "I'm teaching, like I told you, an art survey course. And I also tend bar at a place not far from where I live. I never finished my Ph.D., but I've decided to go back to my dissertation. It's on the painter Toulouse-Lautrec. Somehow I never got it out of my blood. It's pretty embarrassing, actually, tinkering around with some vague idea forever while the here-and-now needs my attention. I'm afraid I'm just not a here-and-now kind of guy. And . . . what else?" I am growing nervous, unbound. "Lots of people in New York, lots of people I know, do a combination of things."

Why am I defending myself? Charlene of all people had no ambitions for me. In her view, children are to be loved and cared for and then released to their own recognizance.

"Toulouse-Lautrec. Isn't he that one who painted ladies of the night?"

"Exactly. But that's not all he painted, by any means," I say. "He was a fine portraitist. He painted all kinds of people."

Charlene laughs her wonderful laugh I remember from my boyhood; it just rolls over you and carries with it the magic of its permission-granting. "It was *France* he was from," she says. "I know about those French."

"It is so interesting to me that people can be systematically killing themselves all the while they're creating the most exquisitely beautiful things. Painting themselves out of a hellhole. A cliché if ever there was one, but I just have this stubborn fascination."

"Well now, if I was a painter, I would paint pictures of places I could never go."

Charlene knows exactly what drove Lautrec. I am surprised I am having this conversation with her. Then I am not surprised. I remember Charlene as the person to whom I could say anything.

"His life was really so dreadful. And in many ways he was such a dreadful little man. There is a picture of him defecating on the beach. Can you imagine? He asked one of his friends to take the picture. This was his idea of amusing. Yet when he sat down in front of a model he could unveil the most submerged aspects of character. Maybe there's something wrong with me, but I just can't reconcile all that vulgarity and delicacy in the same person."

130

Charlene sinks further into the worn armchair. "Honey, you haven't been married."

I laugh.

"You used to talk to me about art when you were a boy. I don't remember which painters you took up. That Toulouse-Lautrec might have been one of them. I remember you spotted a book at a garage sale I took you to. It had lots of paintings by different artists, and you used your allowance money to buy it. You looked downright pious holding that book."

The book Charlene refers to was one of those Time-Life volumes that wrapped up a movement in eighty-five pages and had an insert of color plates. I remember the book was called *The Post-Impressionist Years*, and it rose imposingly on the shelf above the John Tunis and Matt Christopher sports novels Avery bought me. When he came in to say goodnight, Avery sometimes eyed *The Post-Impressionist Years* with suspicion.

"I remember that book! You and I used to look at it together. You called it my milk-and-cookies book, and I was offended. But it's true, you sat down with me when I had milk and cookies and we looked at it together."

"Lots of people wearing fancy clothes," remembers Charlene. "And having picnics."

It is not within Charlene to say, in a prickly tone, "*white* people wearing fancy clothes."

"And ladies of the night," I remind her.

"Oh my, I had you sitting down looking at ladies of the night and drinking milk and cookies?" she asks. "Why, you could've turned me in."

"I wouldn't have." I look at Charlene, the new furrows in her brow, the afghan on her lap, the Stella D'oro in her hand. Her flickering eye-lids betray a struggle to stay alert.

"Do you remember your art teas?" she asks. "This was when you were a little older, already taking those Saturday classes. You borrowed slides from the library there and sat me and Beryl down. Before long it was just you and me. We had tea and you told me things."

"What a pretentious little prig I was. The worst of it is, I'm still doing the same thing."

"No, Brian! I learned things from those little teas. You told me how certain colors are made, and you told me . . . what else? You told me lots about that one painter who went to Tahiti and painted the topless women. You wanted to go to Tahiti."

"Tahiti is no tropical paradise," I say. "It's full of all kinds of problems. But there's a part of me that still wants to go there."

"Me, I'm happy right here," says Charlene. "My house that's paid for, my one son who stayed, my church friends. If it weren't for Lloyd's passing. . . ."

"I can't imagine," I say. "How long were you married?"

"Fifty-five years." She sighs. "It's a terrible irreverence, but I did always pray to be the first one to go."

"Fifty-five years," I repeat. "That's incredible."

"It's a piece of time, all right."

"My parents had only been married for a year when Beryl and I were born and you came to work for us, right? So all together they were married only six years."

"But only because of the tragedy. Tragedy struck your household, Brian. I was there that day."

"I didn't remember that you were there."

"You were only five. But it was on one of my two days that your daddy got the call. I hope I never see a white man turn that much whiter again."

"We used to talk about my mother, didn't we? I mean, in the days before I held those mortifying 'art teas.'"

"At first, honey, we didn't talk about nothing. You were in no mood for talk. No one could get you to say a word. I would've given my eyetooth to bring you back your mama. You were the saddest little boy alive. It wasn't natural; it tore my heart out."

I reach out to touch Charlene's knee. "That must have been a burden for you. On top of all the worries you had with your boys."

"Burden. That wouldn't be my word. But after I came on with your daddy full time, right after, I sure did witness the worst case of the blues every time I caught sight of you."

"I'm sorry."

"That can't ever be nothing to apologize for. I was sure glad when you finally started to talk about your mama, though. You two had a terrible bond. Some women get that with their children, though your mama didn't have it with your sister Beryl. I gotta say I always thought it would cause trouble one day, the way you two adored each other, but then when she died the trouble landed *that* day. Terrible. Just terrible. Your daddy, bless his heart, didn't know what to do with you."

"But then I remember I started trailing *you* around all day. I do remember that."

"I didn't mind that one bit. I knew you'd stop when you were ready to stop. And you did."

We're silent for a moment, not long at all, but Charlene's head dips down till her chin hits her chest. Then she pops up again. "Oh, I'm so sorry," she says. "It's those pills for my hip."

"Are you in a lot of pain, sweetie?"

"The Lord doesn't hand out more than we can bear."

Of course He does, I think. On a constant basis.

"Think what you may," she adds, reading my mind. "He has a definite plan in mind." Following the doctrine by rote, Charlene sounds meek. Yet she is Pentecostal, the worst, and for her to accept me unconditionally as she always has, she had to have asked herself some questions along the way.

I rise to leave and am surprised that my legs feel weak. Charlene is too tired to answer any questions about my mother; my asking them now would be in some way indecent.

We look into each other's eyes as she struggles to get up with me. I have not had enough of looking at her—her hands, her knuckles now gnarled from arthritis, her fleshy, pocked arms and her black eyes and her lips that I know to be slightly livid beneath their coat of bright red lipstick. An unparalleled sense of familiarity is settling in; I am remembering how often I clung to her, plying myself to her side as Beryl raced off on her scooter or did somersaults on the front lawn. I am just now remembering Charlene's rose water and cigarette smell, the feel of those polished cotton shifts she pulled from the deep canvas bins of discount stores.

Charlene holds my gaze, but it's impossible to tell what she is thinking, or even if she is pleased that I came. Once she is safely up, she makes her way to the radiator and comes back with the ceramic poodle, Duchess Regina. "Here she is," Charlene announces. "Not a nick on her, just like I said. Do you think Beryl would like to have her for her daughter?"

"I think Beryl would say a deal is a deal, sweetie. And as I remember, she didn't give you any kind of a break."

Charlene laughs, and my heart lurches at the sight of the space between her two front teeth. I wish that *I* had given her Duchess Regina, this fussy pink poodle with its rhinestone collar who has sat in Charlene's company all the nights Rudy and LeRoy were out where she didn't want them to be, and later when Mosley was at his girlfriend's, and the night Lloyd died.

I reach out my arms, and our hug is as strong as it was so many years ago. But as I walk back to Avery's Volvo, I wonder if the hug came upon Charlene like a gust, a blast of air against which she had to brace herself in order to stay upright.

* * *

My arms are full of grocery bags when I return. Inside are some staples and the ingredients for tonight's soft dinner—creamed chipped beef over mashed potatoes, a marble cake mix, and Pillsbury chocolate frosting in a can. A thoroughly retro meal that would be the fare of a '50s theme party in New York. Still, this is pretty much how we used to eat, Avery and Beryl and I, and the meal promises a pleasurably nostalgic excursion, something I didn't think possible here on Periwinkle Drive. Avery will surely be pleased. Constance McCabe, though, glares at me as I unload the bags on the counter. "Oh come on," I say, before she can respond. "This won't kill him."

She opens her mouth to answer, but I say, "So what did you do this morning? How is he?"

"We did range-of-motion exercises. Stretch and flex. I'll show you later."

"My father exercised his whole life," I tell Constance McCabe.

She has picked up the can of frosting and is reading the ingredients. I appreciate the ironic look on her face.

"He ran laps at the high school three times a week his whole life."

"That's good," she says. "Who's to say he wouldn't have had this stroke twenty years ago if he'd been sedentary?"

"I guess that's true." It flashes through my mind that twenty years ago I would not have minded if Avery had had a stroke. "Why don't you take some time to yourself?" I say. "Until dinner. Go shopping, or go home for a while. Whatever you like. I'm here."

"I'll just go read inside," she tells me.

It occurs to me that Mrs. McCabe would be liable for leaving Avery in my inexpert care during her watch. But I have cast her away, and it's too awkward to ask her to come back and talk to me. It seems too intimate, and I don't think Mrs. McCabe much likes me. I suppose she is

134

used to negotiating her presence in houses where she is always the outsider. Like Helen Croft, I think, she is essentially a servant, expected to neutralize her personality to accommodate its stage.

Alone in the kitchen, I bake the marble cake. I mix the flour and savor the sweet chemical smell inside the packet of chocolate. Later, when the cake is cooling, I make the roux for the chipped beef and go into the sun room to tell my father and Mrs. McCabe to get ready. They are watching a game show together. I have never known Avery to watch a game show.

At the table, which I've set with the good china, Avery does not look well. His face is colorless except for a pink rash along his jaw, possibly from the Coumadin.

"Her goddamned lawyer called my goddamned lawyer today," he says.

"I can't believe she's going through with this," I reply. "The woman's a piranha."

"Let it go all the way to the Supreme Court. I'm not giving her a penny."

Mrs. McCabe has brought in a bowl of the thick lentil soup she'd made for lunch. She is eating this, leaving most of my chipped beef untouched. "Excuse me," she says. "Mr. Moss, would you like some soup? I reheated it."

"What are you talking about."

I wince at his rudeness. But tonight Mrs. McCabe is seated on Avery's left. He is not aware of her bowl of soup.

"I brought in some lentil soup, and I'd be glad to share it with you."

"Oh, no thanks," he says. He is eating my chipped beef happily. "Haven't had this for years. This was our Sunday night special, remember Brian."

"Yes. Look Dad, I think the best thing to do would be to settle right now with Debbie Shuster. You don't need a legal mess in your life right now. Just cut your losses."

"Who're you, F. Lee Bailey? I have a lawyer for legal advice." Among my father's most irritating enthusiasms has always been his admiration for F. Lee Bailey.

"I'm sure Beryl would say the same. You can afford a settlement. Otherwise this will drag on for years."

"Debbie thinks this stroke has made a patsy out of me," Avery says. Again, I must supply the declarative tone. "And this is a matter of principle. I don't run from matters of principle."

I try another tack. "How old is Debbie? What is her work experience? Maybe you could help her get a job. Call Dino. See what he can set up."

Five years ago, Dino Zinetti bought out Moss Development. He had been working just short of a full partnership with my father for years. Always the heir apparent, he had cheerfully stayed on. Dino and Avery are still in close touch. The huge arrangement of gladiolas in the foyer and the forced narcissus bulbs on the stair landing are from Dino.

"You don't know what you're talking about. Beryl knows Debbie. She would never take a job at Moss. It's not her style. No. She's going to go for broke on this one. She's a fighter."

If my father's voice was capable of intonation, I think his tone over this last remark would have expressed admiration, despite himself.

"What *is* her source of income?" I ask.

Avery's face seems even slacker than when he came to the table. He says nothing, but takes a mouthful of mashed potatoes. Traces remain on his lips.

"There's a bit on your mouth, there, Mr. Moss," says Constance McCabe.

I am still unused to my father's affectless expression. If his muscles were working right, would his face register his humiliation? Slowly he puts down his fork and picks up a napkin. I have laid out my mother's Madeira linen.

"I think perhaps you should postpone this subject," Constance McCabe tells me.

"I'm sorry. You're right. Dad, let's talk about this another time. You know, I saw Charlene today. Do you know how long it's been?"

Avery says nothing. Although I might have asked this question of anyone—it is essentially rhetorical—Avery probably perceives it as an insult.

"It's been over twenty years. It was wonderful to see her. Of course it was upsetting too."

"She's a good woman," says Avery. "An excellent woman. I should give *her* the goddamn palimony money."

This is one of the least likely paths for my father to take. It's a thrilling leap of good sense. "You should," I say. "She wouldn't use it to take herself to Aspen."

"I'm going to clear the dishes," says Mrs. McCabe, a warning. "Then we need to have another round of range-of-motion exercises."

She turns to me. "We have to keep his muscles from contracting. But most of all, we have to constantly stimulate parts of your father's brain he hasn't used before."

I look at her quizzically.

"Your brain has had a serious injury, Mr. Moss," she says to Avery, putting her hand over his, "but the brain has remarkable recuperative powers."

Turning to me, she explains, "It's called cross-modal plasticity. Basically, when the cells that are responsible for a certain action have been destroyed, the brain finds a detour around them."

As Mrs. McCabe finishes up in the kitchen, I get my father settled back in the sun room. In a minute, Mrs. McCabe joins us, and I watch as she works on Avery's left side, gently bending the joints of his limbs and his fingers and finally his toes, still bound in their support hose. She does this slowly and with patience, explaining to me that this routine must be followed three or four times daily. She reminds Avery that when he is alone he should use his right arm and hand to take his left side through these motions.

Mrs. McCabe hands me a cassette from her pocket. She asks me to put it in the sound system for her. Walking to the other room, I see that it is a tape of new age music. I fiddle around with Avery's tape player, finally getting it to work. The tape features tinkling bells and pan pipes. My father has surely never been exposed to such music. He is a man without musical tastes, and he listened to—or tolerated—whatever Beryl and I put on the tape player as young teenagers: The Band; Crosby, Stills, and Nash; Buffalo Springfield. When I get back to the sun room, Constance is guiding the first stretch-and-flex exercises. My father is staring vacantly ahead, and I marvel at his submission to Mrs. McCabe's authority. She tells Avery it's time for him to take over, and she motions for me to follow her out to the foyer.

"There are just a few things I want to tell you before I leave," she says. "You probably noticed the red ribbon around your dad's left wrist. I also put a strip of Day-Glo orange tape on his left shoe. When you go back in, you might also notice that your dad smells like a pine tree on his left side." She smiles slightly. "That's because I rubbed lotion on his left arm. I left the bottle out if you want to use more. It's all part of the process of getting him to be aware of his neglected side. It seems strange at first, but you'll see its value.

"Now, if you leave your dad alone, keep his right side at the place where there's the most stimulation. If you put his right side by a wall and then he is perceptually cut off on his left side, he will panic. Imagine. It's like being in an isolation cell. But if you are going to stay in the room and work with him, then address him from the left. We can't cater to his right side. He has to begin to train himself to register us on his neglected side."

I nod obediently. Mrs. McCabe lives in a world where people sometimes only recognize half of themselves.

"Do you think you'll be okay?"

"I think so," I say.

She puts on her coat, a good worsted wool, and reaches into her pocket. "Here," she says, handing me her card. "It's fine to call me at home if something comes up."

"You really go beyond, don't you?"

"It's my job," she says, and opens the door onto the cold December night. "Oo-o-o," she says with some pleasure, "flurries."

When she leaves, I look at the card. She lives two blocks from Charlene; I probably passed her house this morning.

When I return to the sun room, Avery says, "So, Brian. I've been thrown a real curveball."

"I guess you have, Dad. But it could be much worse. You'll just have to work really hard to recover. That's okay. You've already started."

His right hand fidgets on the wheelchair's armrest. He is starting to slump again to the left.

I go to his left and pull him back. "Hey, Dad," I say. "What's this?" I hold up his left arm with the ribbon on his wrist.

He doesn't look.

"What's this?" I repeat.

"A helluva curveball."

"Dad. Look to your left."

He does.

"What's this?" I ask again.

"A goddamned bracelet," he says.

I take this in the way that Avery intends it. I want to point out that he is wearing nylons, too. Instead, I say, "It's not a bracelet. It's a red ribbon. I suspect you know that. Mrs. McCabe is trying to get you to respond to your affected side. She's first-rate. I think you should work hard for her."

"She knows her stuff," says Avery. "Beryl hired her."

"Look down at your foot, Dad. What do you see?"

Avery looks at his right foot. "What I've seen my whole life when I look down at my foot," he says. "My foot."

"Your left foot, Dad." I snap my fingers by his left ear. "Look down at your left foot."

He does. "Uh-huh," is all he says.

"Do you see the Day-Glo tape on your sneaker?"

"I see it," he says.

I don't know whether to keep this up. I drag over a chair and sit close by on his left. "Dad," I say.

"Yeah?" he responds.

"Good!"

"The biggest curveball since Lenore left."

Avery hasn't spoken my mother's name, at least to me, in years.

"She didn't leave, Dad. She was killed in a car accident. Thirty-four years ago." Has the stroke caused more cognitive damage than we realized?

"First, she left. You were five years old. You didn't know everything. Still don't."

His slur is more pronounced, as I have noticed it tends to be past eight o'clock. I have to strain to understand.

"I'm coming over to your right now," I say. I do. It is like moving out of the shadows. I come into view for Avery; he crystallizes for me.

"She left me when you and Beryl were five."

Because his remark is stripped of intonation, it reflects none of Avery's usual tactics of subterfuge—his sarcasm, his false buoyancy, the sense that his next remark will be a preemptive change-of-subject.

"When she went to visit the college roommate that time. Near Pittsburgh. She was going there to think."

"About what?"

"Me. Leaving me for good." As usual, there is the monotone, but his voice has also receded. His left eye is watering.

I take a Kleenex from the box Mrs. McCabe has left nearby. "I'm wiping your left eye now, Dad. Your eye waters on the affected side."

"Uh-huh. It's because I was seeing a woman. I can't even remember her name. I hadn't seen her more than five, six times. But your mother found out about her because of something with the woman's mother. The woman's mother was crazy, she was trying to pawn what's-her-name off on me. How did I know I'd picked up with a woman whose mother was some kind of a case . . ."

He stops when he sees the look on my face, how desperate I am to leave the room.

"Sorry," he says. "I guess I should keep quiet."

Amazing. My father has apologized to me. "It's all right," I say.

"This woman was nobody, Brian. I don't even remember her name."

I nod. They have all been nobody.

"Precursor to Debbie Shuster," I say, hoping to return to the subject of Debbie Shuster.

He rests for a moment. Then he says, "You know, your mother wouldn't have minded about you."

I just look at him. In the scheme of things this might be the most generous thing Avery has said to me in twenty-five years, but he must not be allowed to think it sufficient. "Of course she wouldn't have minded," I say. My voice brims with authority. Intonation virtually floods my tone. I want Avery to marvel at the unique sense of command my words carry. I want him to covet the resonant timbre that surrounds my words, and so I repeat it: *"Of course she wouldn't have minded."*

He stares ahead, stuck there, no doubt surprised that I have exploited my advantage. Finally he says, "Your mother had a strict sense of fair play. She said that she had been a good wife and she had the right to expect fidelity. She said she was going to visit the roommate, and decide what to do. You wouldn't have known me, Brian. For two days before she left I kept begging her to tell me what she was going to decide. I became this person I'm not, this little boy about as old as you at the time. I kept following her around and begging her, and she kept saying how could she tell me if she hadn't decided, and finally, right before she left, about seven in the morning after I hadn't slept all night and you and Beryl were starting to make a ruckus down the hall, she said she would probably decide to leave."

"Jesus," I say.

Absently, Avery begins to do his stretch-and-flex exercises. He clenches his fist and brings it towards and away from his shoulder, as if he is holding a free weight.

"Those two weeks were a nightmare. I sent flowers. I called. I told her the woman was out of my life forever, and I had learned my lesson. I told her I'd get help. I pulled out all the stops. She always said the same thing—we'd talk when she got home. Once or twice her voice was tender and sweet, and then I got my hopes up, but most other times she was cold as hell."

This is the most sustained talking Avery has done since my arrival, and he looks utterly depleted. Pale, except for the rash that is more pronounced and has spread to his forehead. Watching him, I see for the first time a liver spot that looks parched on his bald pate. He begins to tremble. He has slipped again to the side.

I go to straighten him up. "It's okay, Dad. Let's not get excited now. You don't have to talk about this. We can talk about it another time. Here," I say, placing his left hand on the right side of his lap. "Remember what Mrs. McCabe said. About using your right arm to exercise your left one."

Automatically, he takes hold of his left hand and begins raising and lowering it.

"Look at it, Dad," I prompt.

"What the hell is this."

"It's a red ribbon. Mrs. McCabe tied it there."

"I don't need it."

"Just humor her," I say.

He doesn't answer. I hear his strained breathing. I kneel down in front of him and pick up his afflicted foot. It's heavy in its sneaker. I untie his laces and remove the shoe. I begin to rub his foot. The support hose are a scratchy nylon, already snagged. Beneath them, his foot is icy. I rub harder. "Can you feel this, Dad?"

"What. Where the hell are you."

"Here, I'm down here. I'm rubbing your foot. Can you feel anything?"

"Get up," is all he says, and I do.

"You know the rest," he says. "The car crash. Thank God you kids weren't with her. At first there was some talk about you going with her to visit the roommate. That really scared me. I thought then there'd be no chance of her coming back."

"So afterwards we went to your cousins' in Sandusky," I say. I have never talked much to Avery about my mother's death, and I don't believe I can do so now, no matter how extraordinary the circumstances, nor how depleted are his powers. I suck in my stomach and hold my breath, as if without these measures some part of me inside might escape through my pores—a superstition carried over from childhood.

"Yes, right. You two went to Sandusky," he repeats.

"So all these years you have never known what Mom decided." I have to say this. It is simply required of the moment.

"She was going to leave me," says Avery. "I found out from the roommate. And it wasn't just because of the woman. She'd been thinking about it for months."

I say nothing, but wonder what it would have cost the roommate to lie.

Avery's right hand drops his left arm. I pick up his left hand. I untie the red ribbon from his wrist, and then hold his hand. It, too, is icy. I reach behind me for the pine-scented lotion and put a little on each palm. Between my two hands, I rub his left hand vigorously. "Can you feel this, Dad? Can you feel any of this? Even a tiny bit of friction? Can you smell the lotion?"

"Brian."

"Yes. What?"

"I have to piss. You want to take me, or you want to get the thing."

"I'll take you."

Looking for an extra pillow in the guest room closet just after midnight, I come across my mother's mink-collared Persian lamb jacket, the plum of her trousseau. On the hospital bed behind me, Avery snores. There in the closet, inside a clear wardrobe bag, is the Persian lamb jacket. When I open the bag, its atmosphere is released—the stagnant climate of thirty-four years of disuse. The closet lighting is dim, but I recognize the shiny textured lamb fur. The mink is dyed black. Shiny black on dull black.

In his prime, Avery could easily have afforded a full-length mink, many full-length minks, but he purchased this jacket before his prime. In the early '60s, this little jacket was a starter fur. Advertised, I would not be surprised, in the bridal magazines. My mother went for it. She pictured, I imagine, Saturday nights at the symphony. Avery bought the jacket as a wedding present, but he never took her to the symphony. The only place he took her was to the parties of Moss Development's business associates.

I had watched my mother dress for these parties. Beryl and I had both watched. Each of us lay on one of the twin beds. I watched my

142

mother lift a black satin full-length slip overhead, and although I had never seen the slips of other mothers I knew hers was the only correct one to wear. It was simplicity itself. I watched her make up her face as she sat in her perfect slip. Her make-up, too, was minimal, although I understood her shade of lipstick and her eye shadow were for evening and not daily wear.

From Avery's bed, Beryl would chatter along on a variety of subjects. From my mother's bed, I merely watched. Next would come the swift fall of her good black cocktail dress. For this, she pressed together her lips. The dress cascaded down. Crepe de chine, silk netting over the bodice, a collar trimmed with a slender bit of organza. Beryl and I took turns zipping this dress up, and I had a perfect memory for whose turn it was. After the zipping, my mother put on her earrings. Real emeralds in a gold circle setting. Clipping them on always made her wince.

Finally, my mother would enter the foyer, Beryl and I following. There, Avery whistled at her, and he held out the Persian lamb jacket with the mink collar. As if waiting to have his picture taken, my father would strain to keep his smile constant. The foyer was redolent of Old Spice and Chanel No. 5. My father's fixed smile gave away his regret over not desiring this beautiful woman, his wife. At five years of age, I knew the reason for Avery's sad smile.

As my father placed the Persian lamb jacket over my mother's shoulders, the baby-sitter always materialized from somewhere inside. Whenever this happened, I began to wail—a sound that ignited my parents' steps so that I heard their dress shoes tapping urgently down the walk. Then I heard nothing until Avery started the engine of his newly-waxed Pontiac Bonneville. Beryl would follow the baby-sitter to play "Old Maid" in the family room while I sat pressing my forehead to the bubbled glass panel set into the front door, imagining disasters that would prevent Lenore's return, including the one that actually came to pass just before we turned six and she was driving home to tell my father their marriage was over.

The marriage had been a mistake from the beginning. How could it be otherwise if my mother talked about her trousseau more than her wedding? But Avery Moss was a man who thought that there were women to marry and women to seduce. Sleeping fitfully behind me now, incapable of rising on his own, he probably still believes this. Yet as a child, I saw his pride that my mother was his wife. He revealed it in a myriad of gestures—holding out the Persian lamb jacket, a guiding hand on Lenore's back, opening the car door for her, squeezing her shoulder as he watched Beryl and me splash merrily in the wading pool at the Brandywine Country Club. He fulfilled his desires away from home, and was oblivious to Lenore's longing when he returned to Periwinkle Drive. Periodically my mother would bang pot lids on the countertop or grind out a cigarette with vehement finality or slam the bathroom door or even swear at him—"You bastard!" Beryl and I heard all of this from our rooms, but we never heard his response. I imagine his amazement at Lenore's outbursts; I imagine him finding them completely irrational. How could this attractive woman who had a husband with a growing business, a handsome house, and a set of twins—the jackpot, one of each gender—how could she find the time to allow rage to mount inside her? Doubtless Avery gritted his teeth during these lapses, chalked them up to hormonal surges. He did not see how the towering heap of discarded *Cleveland Plain Dealers* on the bedroom floor or his jockstrap carelessly left on her vanity table or the gum wads he perennially stuck in ashtrays could be anything other than quirks that his wife's affection for him would lead her to dismiss. It would not have occurred to Avery that the absence of his passion for her would instead lead Lenore to regard the newspapers and the jockstrap and the stale wads of gum as his droppings—like the turds Toulouse-Lautrec left on the beach, I think now. Avery's gum wads were a "fuck you" to the required civilities of an agreeable life. Still, he didn't understand Lenore's outbursts. He expected each to pass in time, but from my room I knew her outbursts came from a place within her to which he was indifferent. Avery might be happy to hold out Lenore's mink-collared jacket, he might be proud of her beauty, but he was not interested—as I was—in watching her dress.

Whether my mother would have really left him upon her return from Pittsburgh is another matter. Despite what the roommate told Avery, I suspect their marriage would have gone on. A child of the early forties, Lenore Rubin had not been raised to become a twenty-nine-year-old divorcée dependent on alimony and child support. With an undergraduate focus in art history, she would have had few prospects. And there would have been shame. No matter what the roommate told Avery, I believe my mother would have stayed. If she had lived, she might even be in this room tonight, checking Avery's breathing, turning him on his side, picking up the fallen newspapers on the right side of his bed.

* * *

144

Upstairs again, I'm still not sleepy. From the bottom of my backpack, I take out *Helen Croft: Dawn of a New Season*. I'm ready to give the Shipley twins, Victor and Vanessa, another try.

The twins are six years old. Although they bear only a slight resemblance to each other, they are always dressed alike. In the new scene, Helen suffers pangs of conscience as she admits to herself that she dislikes her wards. Despite the piety of their mother and the seriousness of their businessman father, the twins are spoiled children. Diabolically enough, they seem to have spoiled themselves. Regarding their twin status as some special endowment, they are always ready to accept admiration. Indeed, Helen thinks, they do whatever they can to rouse it. They are not above inclining their heads together in a fetching way to elicit the affection of passersby. She tries to be charitable, but it turns Helen's stomach when they do this. How can they be such little show-offs? She has always been a kind and patient governess, but Helen finds herself falling under the recurrent temptation to strike the Shipley twins. She must pray.

It doesn't take long before I'm downstairs again, checking my messages on the phone in Avery's study. This time, there's only one beep signaling a waiting message. One more chance, I think, but the call turns out to be from Daphne Abbott, reporting on how my class went in my absence. She makes a couple of dry remarks on the level of intellectual curiosity among my students. She would readily make the same remarks about the students in her Victorian literature class, so I don't take it personally. I smile and make a mental note to bring her some little thank-you gift.

Returning to bed, I see on the hall table a large package addressed in bold marker to me. When did this package arrive, and why didn't Constance McCabe let me know it had? The writing on it is not Beryl's; I don't know whose writing it is. Maybe Nathan or Jordan's. It is wrapped twice in brown paper and tied with twine, giving it an old-fashioned look.

Sitting on the side of my bed, I tear off the wrapping to find a natural wooden box with the words *Real Artist's Oil Paint Set* across the top. When I open it, I see it's just the kind of set I longed for when I was a boy. It includes ten tubes of color, one large tube of Titanium White, linseed oil, paint thinner, three assorted brushes, a palette knife, a canvas board, a wooden palette, a color chart, and an instruction booklet. The inside cover of the box is inscribed with the signatures of famous artists, including Toulouse-Lautrec's stamped monogram. The set must have been quite expensive, yet it is so much the amateur's idea of all it takes to make a painting that it's practically kitsch.

The paint set, it turns out, is from Neil. He's taped a note to the bottom of the box. In it he says he got my father's address from Jordan at the Barracks. He says that he knows this present might seem odd, even presumptuous, but he would love to see me start painting again. He's signed his name, his whole name, Neil Beck, and under that he's written his phone number.

What am I to make of this gift? Can this man—whose last name I haven't known until now, whose touch has a wandering madness to it, who during sex has grabbed my hair and twice knocked my head against the wall to force me to acknowledge his passion for me—can this same man have sent me such an impossibly naive gift?

I'll never use this paint set that I wanted when I was thirteen. Yet its belated arrival in my old room has created an irony that makes me wonder if there really are no coincidences—a notion I've always dismissed as just a little too new age.

❧ 15 ❧

No more than an hour after Beryl and Melissa's arrival, we are all sitting at the dining room table discussing the Debbie Shuster problem. Or rather, my sister and father are discussing it. Melissa and I eat Lorna Doones from a box at the center of the table. Mrs. McCabe is off for the day, and when Beryl and Melissa came in an hour ago, Avery was in the living room by himself. His head was inclined to one side, accentuating the droop of his left eyelid and half his mouth. His fingers were curled into a half fist. Bright nylon running pants made a cruel parody of his thin, inert legs. He could not smile when Beryl and Melissa walked into the room, and when he spoke the excitement aggravated his slur. Beryl must have been shocked. Missy fell silent and stared.

Now Melissa and I watch the two of them. They are at their best when they are breaking down a problem. It is a process that allows their most competent selves to emerge. My father's stroke has made him no less ebullient in the face of tough propositions. And if anything, Beryl's fear over Avery's stroke has made her more eager to seek his counsel.

"I've done some looking into palimony," she announces. "And I think you're going to be okay."

"Deevers took her case," says Avery. "He's a top man. He wouldn't take a case he didn't think had merit."

The left side of Avery's lip gleams with spittle. I've grown used to this, but Melissa keeps looking at it and then away.

"Do you know about the Marvin case?" asks Beryl. "Michelle Marvin sued the actor Lee Marvin. She must have taken his last name, but they weren't married. The proceedings dragged on forever, from trial court to California State Supreme court and then to a couple of appeals courts. Eventually, the ruling was that non-married couples don't have the same rights as divorcing married couples. In other words, Debbie has no right to your property or support just because the two of you were together. She has to prove some underlying basis for her claim. Say, for instance, she had been an unpaid employee for Moss Development."

"She wasn't anything," says Avery.

"It's definitely good you two didn't have a contract, but she's probably going to argue there was an implicit contract."

"No written contract, no contract," says Avery, impatient—I'm sure—with the fine points.

"But you should know about this, Dad. Somewhere in all of this, one of the courts awarded Michelle Marvin about $100,000 to get, quote, *rehabilitated*. Apparently rehabilitated means to learn employable skills. But then another court sensibly reversed that decision. I don't think she ended up with a thing."

"It should have been thrown out of court in the first place," says Avery. "If you can't see a contract, it isn't there. The woman gets nothing."

"You supported Debbie, didn't you, Dad?" I ask. "She went to all your business functions and everything?"

"Brian. Don't get Dad upset. They were together!"

Melissa cannot hide her fascination. I can't imagine what this conversation sounds like to her. She's probably still stuck on trying to connect her nascent images of sex with her grandfather's jowly neck, his asymmetrical features, his bald head.

"She could have worked," Beryl argues. "Would I give up working just because Seth has a job? Would you give up working because someone . . ."

147

"That's beside the point," I say. I don't tell her that, yes, I would give up work, why not? Does the world need me to pour out draft beers four nights a week so that on Wednesdays I can beg young jocks and future actuaries to appreciate Bonnard's experiments in delayed perception?

"I think Dad should settle with her," I say. "If you ask me, this rehabilitation concept is just. Debbie Shuster's not in our generation. She's not prepared."

"You've never met her, Brian. She's a user from the word go. And besides which, she's not so far from our generation."

"What's palimony?" asks Melissa.

"Oh, God, sweetie. Weren't you listening?"

"I'm sorry. I don't get it."

"Melissa. Don't make me go through it again."

Missy reaches for another Lorna Doone. She tosses her long blonde hair over her shoulder in a flip gesture, but it's not effective. Her face reddens, her eyes well up. In the short time since I've seen her, she has changed. There is a scattering of tiny colorless bumps across her forehead. She tends to look fretful. I suspect there is nothing new in this incident; Melissa is not as quick as Beryl, and Beryl cannot hide her irritation.

"Palimony is like a divorce suit," I tell her, "for people who aren't married. They could be gay or straight."

Beryl just looks at me, but Melissa nods her head. "See?" she challenges. "Uncle Brian doesn't mind telling me."

"Missy," interrupts Avery. "Come give your Pops a kiss."

Melissa looks at Beryl and suddenly I see Missy's six-year-old face; she is awaiting a signal not only of what she should do, but how she should feel.

Beryl gives Melissa a neutral look, sufficient signal for her to rise to kiss Avery. I see her eye the bit of spittle, as if defying it to move.

My father pats his left knee with his right hand. "Here," he says. "Sit down on pops's lap."

This time Melissa looks at me.

"No, Dad. You had a stroke, remember? Your left leg can't sustain any weight. You have to remember these things."

Avery's head rotates towards me in a painfully exact line. As it does, he gains years. He ceases to be a reduced version of his handsome, blustering, well-built self. Fully facing me, he is an ugly old man with

148

unsettled scores. The color he had reclaimed during the period Constance McCabe and I cared for him has drained from his face. "You. I have to take advice from you now. Mr. Artiste. Mr. Gay People's Rights. Mr. Overgrown Boy." His slur has not totally mangled the words, but his straining to give them expression has caused a vein to rise and pulse at his temple.

"Dad," cautions Beryl.

Melissa just stands at her place, grateful, perhaps, for her reprieve, yet clearly frightened.

Beryl and I rise also, but it's too late. Somewhere through the scrambled circuitry of Avery's damaged motor strip, an instinct has emerged. He manages to stand on his right leg. It wobbles uncontrollably. We are both reaching for him when his leg gives way, dumping Avery onto the parquet floor in front of his wheelchair. He is sprawled half under the teakwood dining table. We all crouch down around him, and he struggles to move freely within the nylon jacket that has become twisted around his torso. A wet stain spreads over the top of his bright blue running pants.

The instructions that seem to ricochet around the dining room—*Call 911; don't lift him; give him space*—are coming, surprisingly, from me. It is Beryl who is dumbstruck and Beryl who is crowding Avery. I see her mouth go slack, as it did when she was a girl and someone teased her with a fanciful question that led to a deeper mystery, a question such as a *pourquoi* tale might pose: "How did the leopard get its spots?" Such questions had stolen from Beryl the certain set of her jaw and left her briefly stranded, just as she is now. She throws her arms about Avery's neck. Melissa and I watch her kiss his bald head, applying her lips so fiercely to his age spot that it is clear she would rout it out—if only she had the power to do so. My father screams, and since a scream cannot be without affect, its sound is a complicated growl, spasms riding the airwaves, a sound unlike any I've heard before.

Melissa runs from the room crying, and I empty Beryl's purse to get to her cell phone.

* * *

Avery is back in the hospital. I have called Quality Nursing Service to let them know. They will reassign Constance McCabe. She is the noble knight, charging in and out of people's lives, never pausing for so fruitless an activity as accepting a family's thanks. I ask the woman who takes my call for Constance's address, but she is not permitted to give it out. Then I remember I have her card, so after I hang up I order a dozen roses to be sent to her house. There are many reasons to do this—among them is that after Constance spends the day with her new patient, she will return home and think of Avery, and of me, too. She will check us off on her mental inventory as one of the decent ones.

Avery's right hip is badly fractured. Bone fragments have become displaced. The doctor he's had for years—Marvin Kastle, whom Beryl and I used to call King of the Kastle—is not optimistic. He has prescribed Demerol and a sedative. We are outside Avery's room. Dr. Kastle explains that this is one of the worst things that could have happened so soon after a stroke. He pauses long enough for me to think it pointed, that he is accusing us of negligence. This without knowing the worst of it—that we were right there, stunned for a split second yet also, each for his own reason, hopeful that Avery might stand on his own.

"I'll be honest. If we just bind the femur to mend on its own there is a likelihood of complications, and even with the Coumadin, a blood clot is a concern. Recovery will be a very long, drawn-out process, and it will be harder for him to get the kind of rehabilitation he needs for the stroke. The usual course would be to operate, to realign the fragments using plates or, at Avery's age, to replace the hip. Eventually his hip would be good as new. But he's not a great candidate for surgery; I can't tell you otherwise. I'm sorry," he says. "It's not an enviable choice to have to make."

"We'll operate," says Beryl. She has always taken the choice that offers the highest possible return, despite its risk.

"I agree," I say. Pivotal as this decision is, this time I need to accede to her; she's the one driven beyond reason to see him regain his powers.

Dr. Kastle nods. He tells us he'll rush a couple of pre-op tests. He tells us there will be papers to sign. Throughout the years he has been acquainted with us he has rarely smiled or casually touched us. Avery has defended Kastle's remoteness as a mark of his professionalism. But Kastle smiles now, sadly, and squeezes Beryl's shoulder.

* * *

In the sun room of the house on Periwinkle Drive, Melissa and I sit with the television turned to a soap opera. Beryl is in the living room, talking to Seth. I hear her weeping. To my surprise, her tone then slips into the cadences of baby talk. Melissa might hear too, but she seems unfazed. At the commercial, I ask her what we're watching.

"*Charting Our Way*," she tells me. "A bunch of us watch it. It's addictive."

"It's supposed to be," I say. (No need for her to know that if I were alone I'd be upstairs reading *Helen Croft: Dawn of a New Season*.)

She starts to roll her eyes, then seems to think better of it.

"I've been wanting to ask you. How did it all work out when you got home? Did they ground you?"

Melissa switches the TV to mute. "Yep. And things have gotten worse, too. They don't let me do anything." She looks at me, clearly determining if I'm trustworthy. "I really hate Scottsdale, Uncle Brian. It's totally, like, a money pit, and all the people are alike."

"You'll get out eventually. I can tell."

Melissa brightens. "You think? Well, maybe if they ever stop grounding me. I like *sneeze* and they ground me."

"Really? They don't seem that unreasonable." I have to be careful here.

"Actually, I'm grounded now. I wouldn't be here if it weren't for pops's stroke. It's because I went down to Nogales, and they didn't know. But it's only because I'm so *bored* in Scottsdale."

The trip to Nogales surprises me. She just turned thirteen a couple of weeks ago. There's no question this breakout to the Mexican border town was a bold act for a barely thirteen-year-old. Even I would have grounded Melissa for this. "That's hardly a sneeze, Missy. You didn't go there alone, did you?"

"No, a friend of mine drives."

"Your friends are four years older than you?"

"Some of them. We were fine. Mom and Dad wouldn't have even known if Chrissy's stupid mother hadn't called them when we got back."

I look at *Charting Our Way*. A woman in a tight red sweater is yelling at a contrite-looking blonde man.

"It was so incredible down there, Uncle Brian. I couldn't believe it. How could it be so close to us, but still be so different? Everything. Like, first of all, the smells. All this pollution and fried stuff and beer and maybe bad sewers. And there're all these incredible colors, like the houses and bars and everything are painted in blue or yellow or pink. The other Nogales, the U.S. one, is nothing, just depressing."

I've heard the Mexican Nogales is a tacky tourist town. "Further into Mexico," I tell her, "Oaxaca, Chiapas, Tuxtla—all those places are much more authentic. And even more colorful."

151

Without hesitation, Melissa says, "I wanna go."

"Maybe you and I *could* go sometime. To central Mexico."

"Yeah, like they would really let me." Melissa gives me the look of one who's been put upon longer than she's been alive. Then she looks down. "Uncle Brian," she says. "Did you know your hands are sort of shaking?"

She's right, I see. I put my hands in my jeans pockets.

"Are you scared?"

"Concerned," I say.

Missy comes to sit by me. "I guess at times like this it doesn't matter if you've always hated each other," she says.

I laugh. "You're right. But it's more complicated than that."

"Mom says pops was mean to you growing up."

"Did she?"

"She says he was disappointed you didn't want to do anything but draw all the time. It's too bad you didn't have my dad, Uncle Brian. He thinks all kids should play music and do art and stuff. He's on this committee at school. He says that the arts makes kids citizens of the world."

"Your dad's a good guy," I say.

We stop talking and absently watch *Charting Our Way*, until Melissa asks, "Is pops going to die?"

"I don't know what will happen. But whatever it is, it's not going to be good."

Melissa is thinking. "So if he doesn't die, his life will be, like, really, really sucky?"

"He doesn't have a lot of inner resources," I say.

"What does that mean?"

I'm too tired to attempt an answer. "It means he never took music or drew as a child," I tell her.

"It was awful when he fell. He peed in his pants."

"I know. I hope he wasn't aware of it."

Beryl enters the room. She drops down on the other side of me. "Everything hurts," she says. "You'd think *I* fell."

Melissa turns the sound back on, loud. We all laugh when the red-sweatered woman slaps the blonde man and a piano chord is struck and held.

* * *

152

The next time the three of us are in the sun room is five mornings later. We are eating breakfast and watching two squirrels chase each other through the rhododendron bed, their tails stirring up a shower of snow each time they course through the leaves. Three days after his surgery, Avery died of a cerebral hemorrhage. This is our last day in Cleveland. I've been gone just over three weeks—the Barracks and Tri-Community have both done without me. A few days ago, Nathan and Sam sent a fruit basket. I haven't seen a fruit basket since the time Beryl carried that huge one to Charlene's door—barter for my release.

Norman Brinsky's condolences were clumsy but well-meant. He told me his nephew went back to school, but he'd keep my bar running himself until I was able to return. Jordan and Luis sent flowers and a note. A magnanimous gesture, considering what must be their nightly hell with Norman tending my bar.

Beryl and I plan to come back at the end of the month to see about the house sale and to meet with Avery's lawyer and his accountant. All three of us, though, are booked on evening flights out of Cleveland Hopkins Airport. Now Beryl and I finish our coffee, and Melissa reads *The Giver* for her English class. For the first time since early last week, Beryl has dressed in a suit and silk scarf, and she's washed and gelled her hair. She is wearing make-up. I'm greatly relieved. We all have our unreasonable fears, and I have learned that one of mine is the sight of Beryl off her game.

Soon Charlene and Mosley will be here. When I called Charlene two days ago to tell her about Avery, she'd let out a gasp. I had to explain why he was back in the hospital in the first place. I could virtually hear her thanking the Lord that she hadn't had her own hip replaced.

Charlene is coming to pay her respects. Perhaps it is the house she is coming to see. She knows it better than we do. She knows the corners where dust balls gather, which mold stains can be scrubbed away and which are permanent. She knows the effects of sunlight on each fabric in the living room, the source of the noxious smell in a remote corner of the basement, the moment to protect the kitchen sink against clogging, which birds tend to roost in the eaves. In the summers, she knew which hornets' nests buzzed with life and which were abandoned shells. There is an animism in this house that arose when Charlene worked for us. In the ways that count, the Periwinkle house is hers. Yet she hasn't seen it in over twenty years.

"What should I expect, Brian?" asks Beryl, as though she is attending a business meeting for which she needs briefing.

"Well, you know. She's about Dad's age. I mean . . . you know what I mean. Her health isn't great. She uses a cane, I think sometimes a walker. She has diabetes. She hasn't gained any weight, but she hasn't lost any either."

"Do you think she honestly cared about Dad?"

"Jesus, Beryl, I wouldn't blame her if she didn't. He could be hard on her. But he was fair, too. She wouldn't be coming here if she hadn't at least respected him."

"Uncle Brian. Why did pops decide to get cremated?"

Beryl sighs. She has sighed constantly during the last two weeks. She sighed when the men from Home Care Network came to take back the rented hospital bed. She sighed all day as we sorted through Avery's closet and drove to Goodwill to donate his clothes.

"Avery always wanted to be cremated," I tell Melissa.

"He told you that when you were *a kid*?" she asks.

I look at Beryl. "I guess he did."

Beryl nods. "He was just that way. He told us things like that. It's not unusual to get cremated, Missy. Lots of people do it. It conserves on land."

All the more for you to develop, I think.

"I'm going to get mummified," says Melissa. "And they'll bury me with Fitzhugh, just like the ancient Egyptians did."

Fitzhugh is the miniature schnauzer Seth got Melissa for her last birthday.

"Missy," warns Beryl.

"*What?*" she demands.

"What have we said about thinking before you speak?"

"What did I do wrong?"

"You're old enough to control your impulses. There are times to be whimsical and times not to be. You should know which is which."

Missy looks down. Her straight blonde hair falls over her eyes.

I look at Beryl, but say nothing. The timing of Melissa's little fantasy is so clearly a cover for her anxiety that only my sister could miss it.

"I'm going to be buried," Melissa repeats, nearly a whisper, "just in case." She says no more, but I know she means just in case she is not really dead. I remember she also wanted to sacrifice herself to a polar bear, but I don't point this out.

The exuberant notes of the doorbell chiming out our welcome are jarring this morning. Going to the door, I remember that Charlene has heard these lilting notes countless times. She was the one to pay the newspaper boy and the milkman, and she took money from Avery's petty cash fund to give to the annual collectors for muscular dystrophy and the cause of world hunger. For all the years she worked for us she let herself in the side entrance. I wonder if she has ever stood outside the massive walnut door and listened to the cheery notes ringing inside.

"Hi, sweetie. It's good to see you. Be careful up that step."

Charlene is well-bundled in a full-length woolen coat and a mohair cap rolled down over her ears. Behind her, Mosley wears only a lumber jacket. His head is bare. I put out my hand. "Mosley," I say. "Come in."

The last time we saw each other we were adolescents. It's impossible not to remember that Mosley and his brothers were my sworn enemies, with me at the clear disadvantage, but we both smile—just a small resigned smile that leaves me surprisingly happy.

Inside, Beryl and I help Charlene get seated. She has brought her walker, which Mosley holds aside. Seated, Charlene winces, then quickly smiles. She looks around. "My, my," she says.

We introduce Melissa, who shifts her weight from one foot to the other.

"Now really," Charlene says, "could you be much prettier?"

"She thinks she could," Beryl points out. "I suppose it's part of the age. What can we get for you, Charlene? There's tea and coffee and plenty of fresh bagels and some donuts, too. I'll just bring it all out." She hurries off.

When she is gone and Mosley is seated too, Charlene talks about the surprise of Avery's death. It seems her mission to confirm its total unpredictability—his death as an accident. I have seen this preoccupation in elderly people before. It is important that she call such a death entirely unexpected.

Avery died, I assure her, because of a series of complications, small mishaps that added up to his accidental death.

Charlene nods eagerly. It is the first time I have sat with her in the Periwinkle house and seen her exhibit a concern for herself.

Mosley is seated on the bamboo couch next to Charlene. He holds on to her walker in front of him.

"So you're driving a school bus?" I say to him. Back in New York, talking to him on the phone, I had resisted asking this question. It is a mistake to ask it now. How could such a question sound free of conde-scension?

"Thirteen years now. They get rowdier every school year, and I'm not allowed to smack 'em."

We all laugh, but Charlene puts her hand on Mosley's knee to shush him.

Beryl returns with a tray full of coffee mugs and a steaming pot. She tells Melissa to bring out the bagels and donuts. When we are all settled together again, Charlene twists one hand with the other, clears her throat, and says, "The Lord has His reasons for taking people when He does. Your daddy couldn't stand on earth but he is standing in heaven. I'll light a candle for him. I worked for him for a good long time and saw you kids grow up. Men aren't meant to bring up babies. Every year I expected him to bring home a bride, but he never did."

There is nothing to say to this. Melissa takes a half bagel and asks Charlene, "Did my mom ever do stupid things when she was a kid?"

"Your mother was the smartest girl on this here block. She had all the other children in hand. Remember that bowling alley of yours, Beryl?"

"What bowling alley?" asks Missy, excited.

"Down there in the basement. Your mama and your Uncle Brian ran a bowling alley."

"Not me," I say. "I was a mere wage earner. Five cents an hour as I recall. And I had to ask for it every Sunday night."

"Your uncle and mama got a bowling set for their birthday. All the pins, and miniature balls, and an alley that was really a rubber mat you rolled out. So they opened a bowling alley with a snack bar. Your Uncle Brian was the chef, isn't that right?"

"Right," I answer. "Milk with Bosco. Crackerjacks. Grilled cheese sandwiches that *you* made and I brought downstairs."

"Anyway, this boy Petey next door, he got a little carried away one afternoon and he played himself fifteen games in a row. How much was that, Beryl?"

"I hate this story," says Beryl, but she is smiling. "Twenty-five cents a game. Three dollars and seventy-five cents altogether."

"That's right. Well, at the end of the game, Petey only wanted to pay for the games he got strikes in. I can't remember . . ."

"Four," says Beryl.

"He said the rest of the games was rigged, isn't that what he said Beryl? Wasn't that the problem between you two?"

"My God, Charlene, what a memory."

"That's right. So he gives your mama $1.00 and gets set to go home."

"I remember he took this little plastic Howdy Doody wallet out of his pants pocket," says Beryl. "It was *stuffed* with money. He was an only child and his parents gave him a huge allowance."

"I'm an only child," Melissa points out.

Beryl ignores her.

"So I hear some yelling and I come downstairs." Charlene says. "By the time I get there, your mom is sitting on Petey. 'Course a boy can't possibly cry if he has a girl in a flouncy skirt pinning him down. But he was purple all right."

"What about Uncle Brian? What was he doing?"

"Cleaning my counter," I say.

"It didn't end there, neither," says Charlene. "This Petey was a slippery little boy and he managed to wriggle away and run out of the house."

"Then what?"

"Your mama disappeared upstairs to her room. When she came down, she had this fancy-looking piece of paper."

"It was a subpoena," says Beryl.

"A what?" asks Melissa.

"A legal document that requires someone to appear in court."

"And it worked, too," says Charlene. "That little Petey must have been scared to death. Your mama went over to his house and she came back with her two dollars and seventy-five cents all right."

Everyone laughs, including Mosley, who is eating a honey-glazed donut.

In the next moment, though, Charlene looks ashamed. "Your daddy was so proud of you when he found out," she says. "He laughed and laughed."

Beryl sighs. Her eyes today make her look older than usual; there is a slackening of her upper lids.

We all sit drinking coffee and eating. For Beryl and Melissa and me, it is a second breakfast. The room is filled with mid-morning sunshine. Avery is dead, I tell myself. Avery is not sitting in his chair or in his wheelchair, a little agitated and gripping the arm rest, a little uneasy with his son in the room. Avery is just not here; I am hosting a condolence call for him, and everyone watches the two squirrels that are once again chasing each other through the rhododendron and up and down two dogwood trees. The sunshine grows brighter still. The variegated bark on the trees sparkles, and the definition of slender branches against the clear sky is beautiful.

Before Charlene leaves she says she supposes she won't see me again. I tell her I'll call her next month when Beryl and I return to talk to the realtors. She looks forward to it, she says. When I hear a catch in her voice, I hug her tightly. Her lashes, blinking tears away, tickle my neck, and I involuntarily pull away. Her face is full of dread, but suddenly its muscles relax, and she calls out to Mosley not to lay the walker on top of her special banana pudding. They're on their way to a church potluck, she tells me. Just what she needs—more food.

Later that afternoon, we are all in different rooms upstairs, packing our things. In my old room, on top of the bedspread with the nautical motif, I stuff everything into the duffel bag and leather backpack I brought three weeks ago. Then I go down to the guest room and take the wardrobe bag with my mother's mink-collared Persian lamb jacket, the one Avery had held out for her and she'd slipped into with the coolness of a practiced performer.

❧ 16 ❧

Just a few steps into my block I recognize Seraphina in what she calls her "hermie" garb—this time a thrift shop raccoon coat with shoulder pads, a brooch of semi-precious stones, jeans and combat boots. I have never been happier to be home.

"Vacationing on the islands?" she asks.

"Right. That's why I'm this lovely shade of bronze. How've you been?" I reach out to squeeze her arm. No need to tell her the truth. Seraphina and I will probably grow old together, but we don't talk.

"Don't ask. Especially if you've ever had root canal."

I wonder how Seraphina can afford a root canal. She alternates between working as a secretary in seedy law offices in the Bronx or Washington Heights and collecting unemployment. Until she gets the final procedure ("the botched circumcision," she's fond of calling it), Seraphina still goes to work as a man, and her employers always find out that the strange something they sensed during the interview is that Seraphina—Marshall to them—is transsexual. They know enough to lay her off rather than fire her, and she always collects unemployment.

"My first mistake was going to that shitty public dental clinic. I may be a maverick, darling, but I have learned that my dissident ways don't extend to operative dentistry. Give me a Park Avenue man with shiny noiseless tools and a wife and kids in Connecticut. In fact, give me one, anyway."

I laugh and squeeze her shoulder, then go on my way. I know nothing of Seraphina's romances—if her fantasies ever surface in her daily life, or if she just roams the west side piers being witty for tourists and lending herself to salesmen returning to their low-rise headquarters over the George Washington Bridge, aging men who ascribe no significance to their fleeting, mechanical encounters with Seraphina, men who in fact enforce the speed of these trysts, hoping to outpace the process of making memories.

Once I am inside my apartment, my joy at being home dissipates. The Murphy bed, modern novelty in a '40s movie, is a necessity here in this studio apartment. It's folded up and enclosed within the cabinet I had built for it. The old Morris chair, covered in stiff velveteen, is pushed back against the wall; the faded dip in its bottom cushion stabs at me with its sense of waiting to be of service, to bear my weight.

Have I been corrupted by, of all places, the house on Periwinkle Drive? Worse, now that Avery is dead, have I internalized his disapproval, his insistence that I've deliberately impoverished myself within some endless adolescent rebellion? *Mr. Artiste. Mr. Overgrown Boy.* Never before have I returned from days away to wonder why I live here. I have always known why I live here, have always felt privileged to hold the lease on this little haven at the center of my world. For fifteen years I have been aware that while others might declare this room insufficient, it has within it all I need—warmth, morning light, a satisfying shape, and enough wall space to hang my revolving gallery of prints.

But now I am afraid of my apartment, afraid of being alone here even for as long as it takes to hang up the wardrobe bag containing my mother's Persian lamb jacket. The utter stasis of this room sets my adrenaline surging just as if I had walked in upon a great and violent commotion. I'm grateful that it's dinner time, time for The Aegean.

159

Athos is still on his shift. He has just placed a cup of coffee before a young woman at the counter. When he sees me, he pantomimes applause. "You're the best, Brian. Where've you been, Brian?"

"Feels like around the world," I say. "What's good tonight, Athos?"

"Everything for you is good, because we make everything the way you like it. Special order." He has followed me to my favorite booth, a two-seater by a window looking out to Ninth Avenue.

"I'll have the spinach pie," I say.

Athos nods, then cocks his head at me. He's been waiting on me at The Aegean for years. We have our routine, our patter. But here is his dilemma. He has gotten used to me; I'm perhaps like the distant cousin from Salonika who lives on his block in Astoria, a familiar fixture in his world, one who he may not like but to whom he is bound by shared experience. Athos worries that I may one day—tonight, even—take advantage of our long familiarity to confide in him. Yet he is a man who respects the slow building-up of history. It is the passage of time between people, not who they are, that commands Athos's loyalty. So he stands over me and waits.

"I went to Cleveland to help my dad. He had a stroke."

Athos frowns; everyone knows the hardships that come with aging parents.

"But then there were complications, and he died," I add.

Now Athos moves a little closer and extends a thick hand, flesh swollen around his wedding band, to squeeze my shoulder. I can tell he wants to say something that will comfort me to my bones. "You're the best, Brian," is all he manages. His customary hale tone has slipped away, has been replaced by a raspy whisper.

"Thanks, Athos. Thank you."

"You're welcome." He proceeds to the front. "Gimme a spinach pie," he yells to the kitchen, an order like a tragic pronouncement.

I'm not one to read in restaurants to detract from the fact that I am alone. No paper, certainly no spinster books. Other than occasionally reviewing students' papers, my habit is to watch the avenue or just let myself do nothing.

Athos returns with a plate of three small meatballs covered in tomato sauce and stuck with toothpicks. He is holding out the plate so the steam doesn't fog his glasses. "On the house," he says. "Nothing's too good for the best." His robust, here-to-serve-you tone has returned. The shoulder squeeze, I decide, has marked the zenith of our long connection.

Watching the people on Ninth Avenue, I acknowledge to myself that tonight everything is different. I am no longer anyone's child. I pop a meatball into my mouth without my father on this earth.

What does it mean that Avery, his imposing physicality, is no more? I have stayed away from him all these years because of what I detested about him—his blind conventionality, his temper, the ludicrous way he patronized women, his rigid view of what makes a man. Yet I've always feared that some extreme circumstance would force me once again under his roof, under his domination. What if *I* had been the one to get sick? I remember how at the end of Toulouse-Lautrec's life he had attached himself to his mother, needing no one else. Had I been the one to get sick, Avery might have become for me as Maman was to Henri, a measure of last resort. *Mr. Artiste. Mr. Gay People's Rights, Mr. Overgrown Boy.* Avery had called me all these things. Yet what names would I have called him had his face been the last one I knew I'd see? From my early adolescence, we could not have disappointed each other more.

Athos brings the spinach pie. When I look up at him, I imagine he has read my swiftly falling thoughts, but he just takes the empty meatball plate. "Good," he says, "You liked."

It would be wise to wait until morning, yet I call Neil as soon as I get home. Before an hour has passed he is at my door. We know not to speak of his absence or mine, or the gift he sent me while I was away. Speaking would civilize us, and we are not immediately interested in the other's refinement.

Neil Beck's brand of handsomeness would be easy for many people to appreciate, but for me, drawn to men with wide jaws and brutish mouths, his looks are out of my usual realm. His dark hair is longer than is the style; his nose is aquiline. He is thin, yet well-muscled; when I look at his lean arms I see the ropy musculature that is his by nature. (I don't have to worry about how many sets of how many reps he does of anything.) What so gets to me about Neil is that despite all his fierceness when we're together, despite his emphatic clasp and the menacing air of his hand posed near my throat, despite all the sexual greed he rushes at me when he crosses my threshold, his gray eyes have never shown anything but warmth. I imagine if I knew him better I would see in these soulful eyes predominantly kindness and melancholy—that I would never glimpse the cunning, the indifference, or the arrogance I've grown accustomed to in the eyes of countless men I've been with.

Finally, sitting up in bed before I've caught my breath, I say, "Conversion therapy. *There's* a challenging profession."

I expect Neil to laugh, but he doesn't. Blunder, I tell myself. He's not ready.

"I got your gift," I say. "I was pretty surprised, as you can imagine. Especially after having not heard from you."

"I'm sorry," he says.

"And that you went to the trouble to find me in Cleveland made it all the more . . ."

"I saw it in a window, and I thought of you."

I ponder this simple equation. "I haven't used it yet."

"You will," he says, as if he were a seer. Then he sits up and looks around for his clothes.

"You're going?" I venture.

"It's late. I have work in the morning."

"I thought you were still a student."

"I'm interning with Yu Ping Chen," he says. "I was very lucky to get a placement with him."

Apparently this name holds some prestige in the world of Chinese medicine. I nod politely. "Can we see each other this weekend?" I ask.

He looks away.

"Is it unreasonable for me to think you tracked me down in Cleveland because you wanted more than a one-night stand?" I can't believe that I hear a faint tremble in my voice. I hope my hearing is better than Neil's.

"No," he says, still not looking at me. "God, no. It's just that I'm disentangling myself from something. I mean someone. She was my assignment from the reparative therapist. It's pretty humiliating to talk about."

I get a sense Neil might cry, so I start to slowly massage his shoulders.

"Alicia. We were engaged. Only for a month, and I broke it off. But it's not . . . taking."

"What do you mean? Is she stalking you or something?"

"In a way. She keeps insisting we go to Dr. Zorides together. I quit seeing him a while ago. *Believe* me, I don't want to ever see him again. If I see Zorides again, I'm afraid I'll undo all the benefit of years of Buddhist meditation."

"How does Alicia know about Zorides? Did you tell her about him?"

"He sort of fixed me up with her." Neil quickly turns red. He grabs onto my hand that is massaging his shoulder. "Can we not talk about this?"

"Okay, but . . ."

"I would love to see you this weekend, Brian, but I think I need one last time with Alicia. I can't leave her in the state she's in now."

"All right."

He turns around and touches my face before he goes. When he's gone I realize I forgot to tell him that while I was in Cleveland my father died.

It's 4:00 AM when I awaken. Neil comes to mind immediately, along with a lurch of fear that I'll never see him again. Trying to fall right back asleep will be impossible, so I remove the bookmark from *Helen Croft: Dawn of a New Season*. Before long, I discover that the Shipley twins are making Helen's life miserable. She doesn't know exactly what to do. Even in Hyde Park, where they would never think of playing with the other children, the twins wander about in their matching plaid knickers and jumpers, their little tams set identically askew. They hold hands and skip in unison until they hear someone comment on their sweet devotion. The other children, sensing the twins' falseness and their ambition, despise them.

One morning in the park, the twins are sitting on a blanket reciting nursery rhymes in alternating couplets.

"I suppose a flogging wouldn't do," says someone on the bench beside Helen. "What a pity."

When Helen turns around, she sees beside her a man in his young middle age. R.W. Dodson has dressed the man in a Donegal tweed waistcoat and given him raven black hair and Nile green eyes.

Helen is rendered speechless. The man's resemblance to the Master of Baybridge Manor is startling. She catches herself up, though, and realizes that this is a different man. He has a fairer complexion than the Master's, and his forehead does not rise quite so nobly from his brow. Yet despite his stern words, the man's eyes are gentle whereas the Master's were bright but often stern.

I stop reading. Of course R. W. Dodson has signaled how the plot will unfold for the remainder of the volume. Although it is for their unfailing predictability that I love my spinster novels, this one gives me an eerie feeling. It's because of Victor and Vanessa. After Avery had his first stroke, he became preoccupied with reconstructing Beryl and me as

163

just such adorable twins. Never mind that even as small children we hated being dressed alike and avoided each other as much as possible. Never mind that from the age of five Beryl dismissed me as ineffectual, while I was embarrassed by her drive and her blunt style in all human interaction. Never mind, too, that Avery had played his part in ensuring our distrust of each other. Our distinct personalities and his role in shaping them fell away as soon as Avery found himself old—as soon as the cheaply-built shopping centers he'd erected in the early sixties began to fall into disrepair and four-story malls appeared just blocks away. It was then that Avery decided he'd been the father of the closest and most devoted twins, twins made of the same cloth as Victor and Vanessa.

Beryl is disciplined and she is an optimist; she will never again think of Avery's sentimental period. But I will not forget it. I will always be jarred by the memory of my father in polyester reminiscing about matching pogo sticks. I will always be sad for having seen this other Avery. And I will always wonder what unimagined reversals we all harbor—what other selves might emerge if, for just a moment, too little oxygen were to reach our brains.

❧ 17 ❧

The last Tuesday in March is cold and rainy. It's too early for me to be awake, let alone outdoors; my whole body tells me so. My joints are stiff, my scalp itches. When I reach St. Mary's Hospital and catch my reflection in the glass of the automated doors, I see that my face is still swollen from sleep. Luis waits for me in the lobby. He is standing, his arms loosely crossed, tapping his fingers against his elbows. "Don't ever get yourself stuck in a Catholic hospital," he says, rushing up to me.

Luis is Catholic. He wears a cross around his neck. I notice he is not wearing it today. "What happened?"

"They ignored the DNR. It was right there, hanging on the foot of his bed, in bold letters, Do Not Resuscitate, and they ignored it. The resident claims the cleaning staff put it somewhere it wasn't supposed to be. Fucking bitch."

"Hey. No need to turn into Gerald over this."

"Sorry. But what is the matter with these people? I think we should get a lawyer. Do you think we should get a lawyer?"

"No. And anyway, it's too late to do any good. The harm has been done. I *told* Jordan that if anything went wrong, he should make sure to get the ambulance to take Frank to Episcopal Downtown. My neighbor Hector works there, and he could've kept an eye on Frank. And anyway, Episcopalianism doesn't pull this kind of shit."

"Jordan is beside himself. It's the worst thing that could've happened, he says. Ignoring Frank's wishes."

"It's horrific," I agree. "Let's go up."

We are alone in the elevator. "And it's not the only thing they did," Luis continues. "He had this terrible infection, we never really found out what it was, but they treated him for PCP; they have no imaginations, they figure we all get PCP. The heart failure, it was probably from the spread of the infection. He was on the wrong antibiotic for a week and a half."

"I thought he was with Doug Janus. I've heard nothing but good about Janus."

"Janus was on vacation," says Luis. "He's back now. He tries to restrain himself in front of Jordan, but you can tell he wants to kill everybody on the floor. Why would a decent doctor want to be attending here?"

"I can't believe you didn't call me," I say.

Luis understands that I am hurt. He squeezes my shoulder. "You had enough on your plate," he says, calming down.

Frank has his own room, and the door is shut. Outside is a stainless steel cart full of cleaning supplies; on the top tray is a box of Latex gloves and a package of paper masks. "We're supposed to put this stuff on every time," says Luis. "So we don't give Frank our germs. Aren't they considerate?" Many times over the years I've put on these gloves, the ones with the light dusting of powder on the inside, but Luis has to help me with the mask. The elastic strap digs into the skin behind my ears, and I feel a moment of claustrophobia when my breath heats up inside the stiff paper shield. Without thinking, I hold the mask away from my face and inhale deeply. Replacing it, I nod to Luis, who has slipped on his gloves, and together we open the door. The reason for its being shut becomes immediately clear. Why should innocent visitors turn their heads and see the confusion of cords and tubes, digital displays, plastic bags of nutrients and saline, and—most unearthly—the bulky respirator required to keep a set of limp lungs expanding and contracting? Lying here because of someone else's will, the will of St. Mary's administration acting as God's representative, Frank Cantore is an absurd and terrifying sight. His face is white, and his lips—stretched around the mouthpiece of the respirator—are parched and colorless. Each time his chest rises and falls, it quivers with the pressure and then the artificial release of the air being forced into his lungs. Behind him, the respirator sounds a mechanical rattle. Sticking out from the sheets, Frank's feet are swollen from edema. His skin looks tough, more like hide—I don't know why this is so. But what makes Frank's appearance absurd is its seemliness, the concession to civility imposed from without. Someone has been shaving him and someone—I shudder to think it must be Jordan—has gelled his hair. It rises from his moist and albescent forehead in countless shiny peaks.

Finally, Luis says, "Jordan must have taken a break. He's probably in the solarium. Or maybe the cafeteria." His voice buzzes a little inside the mask.

I nod. Luis has taken one of Frank's hands, and I take the other. It's bloated, and probably tender to the touch. My hold is light. "Can he feel me touching him?" I ask.

Luis looks up. This is the first question of such a kind, relying upon his superior knowledge, that I have ever asked him. It is usually he who asks me. I see a mix of confusion and pride move across his face. "We think he can," he says, an answer I take to be more superstitious than informed. He bends over Frank and whispers something into his ear. I never thought about the connection between Frank and Luis, if any existed at all, but Luis's eyes are tightly closed, and as he murmurs there is a sense of urgency in the working of his jaw. I don't speak. Rather, I touch Frank's shaven cheek, careful not to upset the tube of the respirator.

When Luis straightens up, I'm surprised he doesn't look at Frank. I find it difficult to *stop* looking at him.

"Let's go find Jordan," Luis says.

"Frank," I say, stupidly raising my voice. "We're going to find Jordan, and then we'll all come back together."

Outside the room, I whip off the mask, and stare at it for a moment. "Jesus fucking Christ," I say.

"Thank you, Pope Paul," responds Luis. Then, "That goes in here." He takes my mask and throws it, along with his own, into a trash receptacle attached to the cart. Next he sets off, and I follow him. "The solarium is at the end of the hall."

166

When we get there, the solarium is empty. "This is it?" I ask. There's only a row of upholstered side chairs lined up under an expanse of dirty window. On the wall at one end is a painting of the adult Jesus among a flock of sheep. On the other is one of Mary holding her baby. Religious kitsch, I think.

"We'll try the cafeteria," says Luis.

"We've gotta get Frank out of here. I'm going to make Jordan come home with me and talk to Hector. Hector will tell us how to do it. How long has Frank been in here, anyway?"

"A while," Luis says. "I think he got here pretty close to when you left for Cleveland."

We share the elevator with several visitors and orderlies, and when we get to the lobby, Luis leads me through a long corridor and two sets of double doors to the cafeteria. As we turn the corner to enter, both of us spot Jordan. He's not alone. He's saying good-bye to a man, a stocky man with an overcoat thrown over his arm, a man perhaps just a few years younger than Jordan. Before they turn in different directions, Jordan kisses the man on the lips. It's clear that each of them is trying to make this kiss, which has by oversight occurred in public, into a fleeting and innocent contact, yet when they pull away from each other I can virtually see the force field they are resisting. The man squeezes Jordan's hand, holds onto it. They press their foreheads together, the man says a few words, and then they reluctantly part. It's merely a stroke of fortune that it's the man and not Jordan who turns to stride past us. Luis and I stand there watching until Jordan disappears into the men's room down the hall.

"Oh, my God," breathes Luis.

"Come on," I say. "We have to get out of here."

We start walking fast. Luis seems to have lost his bearings. He asks someone the way to the front entrance. Once there, we burst out the door, me right on Luis's heels. It has stopped raining, but water drips from the overhang above the entrance. It's windy. I zip my leather jacket, and we walk past the hospital. Inside the doorway of an apartment building, I manage to light a cigarette after three tries.

"Maybe we should just go around the block a few times," Luis suggests.

"What if he comes out? He could see us."

"He won't come out. He stays here twenty-four hours a day. You didn't see the made-up cot in Frank's room?"

"I guess I didn't pay attention."

We walk, and every half block or so Luis says, "Oh, my God," or "I don't believe it."

"It's interesting," I say, exhaling smoke into the moist air.

"Interesting? What kind of crazy thing is that to say? Is this what happens when you teach college, everything becomes interesting? There is nothing interesting about this, Brian."

I don't want to leave Luis while he's so upset, but neither do I want to discuss what we just saw. It's too complicated.

"These things take a long time to understand," I say. "And what if we don't understand it? So what."

"Jordan irons Frank's jeans!" bursts out Luis. "He serves him three-minute eggs in porcelain cups, and once when I was over there he sat on the floor and stroked Frank's foot the whole time. Why are you telling me we don't have to understand this? If we don't understand this, what *should* we try to understand?"

"Calm down. Let's just keep walking. Do you want to go south or north?"

"How long do you think it's been going on?"

"Hardly any time at all," I say, and I know I'm right. "Tell me when you're ready to go back."

"You go," says Luis. "I'll come later. When I can trust myself to keep my mouth shut. Like maybe in a year."

Back at St. Mary's, Jordan has returned to Frank's room. When I enter, he's sitting in a chair by his bed, a mask dangling from his neck, reading to Frank from a paperback book called *Wisdom from the Far East*. When Jordan hears me, he looks up, expecting to see a nurse or an orderly. His demeanor is cool, but when he sees me he abruptly stands, sending the book to the floor, and throws open his arms like the mother of a prodigal son. We embrace for a long time. Jordan's wet cheek presses against my temple, until he lets me go, saying, "Please just stand here with me and look at him. Please just do that for as long as you can. Tell me he looks peaceful."

* * *

Hector Diaz is holding a balled-up paper bag from Tower Records when he answers my knock at his door. He tosses it in the air. "Molly's latest CD," he tells me. "Rosa Ponselle. A double."

"Keep 'em coming," I say. "You're not only her guardian angel, you're mine."

"Yes, well, don't count your chickens."

I roll my eyes. Hector's experiments with American idioms can get irritating.

"No, I mean it. Molly's getting to be a pain in my ass."

"Really?"

"An occasional 'thank you' would not kill her."

I'm not surprised. Molly Winfield was probably polite at first, but I don't doubt she regards Hector as the Mexican in her building who does her favors.

"My group thinks I'm just nice to her because I still feel guilty about Mama." Hector goes to the refrigerator, takes out a seltzer bottle, holds it up in my direction.

"Sure, thanks," I say. "Last time we spoke, you were making fun of that group."

"That was then," says Hector, pouring two glasses of lemon-lime seltzer. "Before Sal."

"Ah-ha," I say, but I'm not much in the mood to find out about Hector's new boyfriend. "Listen, I need to ask you something. You know Jordan down at The Barracks? His partner is in a coma at St. Mary's. He went into cardiac arrest and they revived him, totally ignoring his DNR. But he was pretty sick before, and now he's in a coma. Can we get him transferred to Episcopal Downtown?"

"In a coma? They won't accept him unless there's something we can do for him that St. Mary's can't. And anyway, only his doctor can arrange it."

"But you have a hospice, don't you? Didn't you tell me they opened a hospice?"

"Yes, but . . ."

"It would be more for Jordan. He can't stand what St. Mary's did to Frank. It's a matter of principle; I don't think he wants him to die there. If it were me, I'd feel the same way."

Hector thinks a moment. "When I get in for my shift," he says, "I'll go upstairs and talk to Julie. She's the head of nursing at the hospice."

Maybe it's too transparent a reward, but I ask Hector about his new boyfriend. Sal, he tells me, is an elementary-school teacher whose closest relative, an aunt who lived with him, has died of Parkinson's.

Sal, says Hector, was just as down on the idea of a bereavement group as he, but now they're both glad they joined.

Downstairs in my apartment, I call Beryl's cell phone.

"Hey," she says. "I'm just running out to meet my architect for lunch."

"How are you doing?"

"Okay, considering. It was really hard on Sunday when it was our usual time to talk."

"I bet. Maybe you should go out around then. Go do something with Melissa and Seth. Just be in a different place than usual."

Beryl pauses, then says, "That's a really good idea."

"Look, I need to ask something. Have you talked to Dad's lawyer yet?"

"Several times. Probate's going to take for ever. We have to get through Debbie Shuster's case. It's going to be a nightmare."

"So she's persisting?"

"Oh, you bet."

"Can she be reasoned with?"

"She'll have to be. I'm not yielding."

Probably even Beryl recognizes the offensiveness of her *I'm*.

"How much does she want?"

"A lot," says Beryl, as though I am incapable of grasping the significance of an actual figure.

What I can't bring myself to ask my sister, what is far too humiliating, is if Debbie Shuster's lawsuit will affect both of us, or just her. Instead I say, "Can you give me Dad's lawyer's number?"

I hear a car door slam.

"Beryl, don't drive while you're talking on that thing. I just want the lawyer's number and then you can hang up. Do you have it?"

"Of course," says Beryl. "I just assumed you had it."

"I never asked Dad. He never offered."

Beryl says, "Is it about Debbie Shuster? We need to talk about this, Brian."

I hear the car start up. "It's not about Debbie Shuster. I don't know anything about Dad's will."

"What do you mean?"

"I mean I know nothing about it. I've never seen it. We never talked."

"I can't believe this."

"What did you think?"

"I don't know. I don't know what I thought. I'll send it to you Fed Ex. Will you be home in the morning?"

"Yes."

"I'll send it for 10:00 AM delivery, then. Gee, I had no idea," she adds, as if talking to herself. I hear a car horn. Naturally she's on the road. We say good-bye.

Just before it's time to leave for the Barracks, I call St. Mary's and ask for Frank's room. When Jordan answers, I invite him out to dinner for the next night.

"Brian! Brian, you're a sweetheart to call, but I can't go out to dinner tomorrow. Tomorrow night I'll be dining with my beloved."

It's the affair, I think. The affair is insupportable to someone of Jordan's constancy. Sitting alone in Frank's room, Jordan must have become spooked by the affair. A guilty conscience has distorted his sense of what is real; this is something I believe a guilty conscience can do.

"You need a break," I say. "We'll go down to Greenwich Street. If it's nice, we'll walk around a little and then I'll take you to that Italian place you like."

"He thinks I'm crazy," says Jordan. His voice is faint; he's holding the receiver away.

"Do you want me to ask Luis, too?" I say louder.

There is a rustling, and then a hoarse voice says, "Hello? Hello? Wait a minute."

In a second, Jordan gets back on. "He's still too weak, but you heard him, didn't you? He's officially out of the coma. It happened an hour after you left. The respirator's out, and the poor shubble has a raw throat I can only imagine, and he's disoriented. But they're watching him closely; we got doctors and nurses running in here every five minutes. They identified the infection; they kept trying, even though he was in the coma, and they got it! Talk about restoring your faith. Doesn't this restore your faith in everything, Brian?"

All this resurrecting, I think. The combination therapies, powerful new antibiotics; they've set off second comings throughout my city every single day. Those of us standing off to the side are thought to be cynical or bleak if we expect comas to end in death. Yet all the dramatic

171

recoveries have not restored my faith. Rather, I expect that every event, good or bad, is due to reverse itself at any moment.

"Amazing," I say. "Congratulations."

"Will you tell Luis? And Norman? Tell Norman that if all goes well I'll be back in the kitchen in a couple of days. I'll call him tomorrow."

"Of course," I say. "Luis will be thrilled."

When I call Luis at his sister's, though, he says only, "I guess the mistress will have to wait in the wings a little longer."

When Hector hears what happened to Frank, though, he says, "Bless his soul."

* * *

Next morning the door buzzer wakes me, and I hurry into my pants and run down the stairs. The Fed Ex woman is about to leave and looks annoyed that I showed up after all. Two minutes later, I'm turning the pages of the will. I read my name, *Brian Daryl Moss*—remote in its formality.

Avery has left me half of his estate. *Give, devise, and bequeath* is the term used on the third page of the document. An inventory is attached, but I leave it on the table. I call Beryl's cell phone immediately.

"Beryl? It's me!" My voice betrays me, as it did when I was seven and eight, nine and ten. Still when I was eleven, twelve, and thirteen. I hear the same gooney tone, berserk with enthusiasm, veritably screeching with love of possibility. If I were Missy's schnauzer Fitzhugh, my tail would be a blur of frantic wagging.

"Did you get it?"

"Yes!"

"Brian, honey, you couldn't have been surprised."

She has never before called me honey.

"Oh, come on. You must have wondered, too."

"Not for a second. Dad had a keen sense of fair play."

To this I say nothing. I'm not anxious to sound giddy and ardent again. Also, I know that my father's sense of fair play was exercised only in the realm of money. (It is a realm—I must admit to myself—that is far more picturesque than it was yesterday.)

"At any rate," continues Beryl, "we've got a long battle with Debbie Shuster ahead of us. The money may not be freed up for two or three years. Maybe four. And there will be legal bills."

"I think we should cut our losses with Debbie. I said that to Dad just before he died."

"Can we discuss this tonight? I'm on my way to the cleaners."

"Sure," I say, but I know that Beryl's resilience will wear me down. She will convince me that Debbie Shuster did nothing to enrich Avery's final years and everything to undermine them. She'll turn the pursuit of reprisal into a matter of honor, and in the end I'll concede to go forward with fighting Debbie's lawsuit all the way to court. Why play out the scene? I simply won't call her back.

* * *

It's been nearly three weeks since I've seen or heard from Neil. I've been busy with the usual routine of Tri-Community and The Barracks, and with trips to the library to research a new project (one so shadowy I can barely name it myself). Yet despite my work and my preoccupation, I think of Neil every day. He comes to mind unbidden, from without, a new element in my personal atmosphere. He has settled into my most mundane and private routines, a reassuring witness to my solitude.

Yet, when I go to call Neil, I discover that he has changed his number and that the new one is unlisted. Certainly he has created more enigma around himself than is necessary. I know—can simply tell—that there is nothing of the outlaw in his nature. Why is his number unlisted? Is the ex-fiancée, Alicia, pursuing him so relentlessly? Is Dr. Zorides?

Finally, I get the number for Dr. Yu Ping Chen and call to make an appointment. I ask to see the intern, Neil Beck. In order to get myself to do this, I borrow a technique from Neil's domain, Zen Buddhism. I act as if, as if I were someone with the audacity to do such a thing, as if all action were welcome and none judged, as if I had nothing to lose.

The office is not where I'd expect it to be, in SoHo or on the Upper East Side, but in a shabby building in the theater district. The sign on the door of Suite 304 says Dr. Yu Ping Chen, L.Ac: *Supreme Balance*. Inside the waiting room are three people reading, a tropical fish tank, and some framed charts illustrating a stupefying number of acupuncture points, including one so close to the scrotum that I conclude it must be there for the viewing pleasure of ill-used women.

A receptionist gives me a form consisting of three pages of questions, everything from a checklist of childhood diseases to asking me to describe the kind of weather in which I feel my worst. I fill it out, using the same pseudonym I used when I called to make the appointment.

After a while, I'm ushered into a small room with a treatment table that has a flat pillow on one end and a bolster in the middle. The room has been recently painted white, and there are two black-and-white landscape photos on the wall near the window. There's nowhere to sit, so I lean against the table and wait.

I expect to see Neil in a lab coat, but when he enters he's wearing a denim shirt and chinos. The moment he sees me, he flushes deeply. The flirtatious smile he attempts is ambushed by his extreme self-consciousness. He ends up looking only forlorn, a sight I find so wrenching that I want to put my arms around him. "I'm sorry, but your number's unlisted."

"I keep meaning to have that changed," he says.

"I haven't heard from you. But anyway, I wanted to check out your wares."

He tries to respond in kind, with a knowing look, but he's not up to it. "Can you tell me your complaints?" he manages.

"Anxiety. General malaise. And I'm a terrible sleeper."

He nods solemnly. "Acupuncture can be very effective for anxiety."

"So could some reassurances from you."

"I'm working on it, Brian. Don't think I'm taking you for granted, please. I want to do this as purely as I can."

"Are you having doubts?"

"No. My silence would make it seem so. I apologize."

If the situation were reversed, I think, if I were trying to extricate myself from a relationship in order to enter into one with him, I would not have his discipline nor his virtue; I know I would complicate matters by staying in touch. I'd be afraid not to.

He takes hold of my wrist and the warmth of his hand surprises me. I want more, but I realize he's taking my pulse. He's doing so without a watch. After a moment, he removes his hand.

"So?"

"You can lie down." He lifts the bolster, and when I'm settled on the table he slides it under my knees.

"What can you tell?"

"You smoke."

We laugh. "If I didn't know you, I'd still be able to tell through your pulses. We need to get your qi moving."

He goes to the foot of the table and pushes up the legs of my pants. This is what he does, I think. He pushes up the legs of strangers' pants. Next I hear him tearing a paper wrapper. He inserts a needle in the tender spot to the left of my right ankle. It stings, and I'm embarrassed that I twitch.

"This point is often sensitive," he says.

Once again, I am overwhelmed that this man who is essentially shy, who has established within himself an abiding tact and solicitude, can achieve such command over me.

I wonder how close to the groin he'll put his needles. I'm imagining myself a Buddhist monk, able to resist the projected image of his hands hovering over my fly.

"Obsession or overthinking," he tells me, "injures the pi-spleen."

"Forget it," I say. "Then my pi-spleen must be nothing but a rock of necrosis. Probably should've been removed years ago."

Neil does not respond, and it occurs to me that I'm no better than the students in my seminar who find every excuse to disparage that which is elegant. I see now that their dismissiveness most certainly arises from their sense of intimidation.

"How can you tell where to put the needles?"

"I'm using Spleen 4, Gong Sun; Spleen 3, Tai Bai; and Spleen 6, San Yin Jiao. These are several points to treat anxiety." As he speaks, he inserts a needle in the big toe of my right foot, another on the side of my foot, near the arch but closer again to the big toe, and a third above my left ankle on the right side.

Each needle he's inserting into my skin, sometimes with a little rotation, is being entered into a precise point in an invisible design. I know so little about acupuncture, just the mysterious words most people know, words that include Yin and Yang and meridian. I know, for instance, or can deduce, that all these needles in my foot are along my spleen meridian. What is so compelling is that this intricate network of points is entirely unmanifest. My organs—my liver and kidney and spleen—are merely hidden from *me*, but the blocked or flowing energy upon which Eastern medicine is based is truly invisible.

Neil is quiet, and I think that he is doing what he can to achieve the compositional balance he detects beneath the chaos of my body's disharmony. In this labor, he is like a painter.

At last he says, "All right, Brian." He brings over a lamp on rollers, which he identifies as a magnetic heat lamp, and positions it over my stomach. "I have no right to ask for your patience," he says. This time I hear a fluttering in *his* words. "There is only this feeling we both have, and we've hardly begun to know each other. Of course you'll do what you need to, but I am nonetheless humbly asking for your patience."

"I believe you have the advantage at this particular moment," I say.

He laughs a little. "Let's stop. We're interfering with the treatment. I'm going out now. You'll be here for twenty minutes." He dims the lights and closes the door.

Lying immobile with over a dozen needles in me, I get the sense someone is still in the room. I listen closely for the sound of another person's breathing, but decide there is only me in this remarkably silent room in the middle of Times Square. When Neil comes back, I plan, I'll tell him that there's something S&M about his chosen profession, that if you look at it a certain way, he spends his days constraining people to tables.

The lamp is slowly warming my stomach, its heat passing through the cloth of my shirt. No, I won't make the S&M crack; I'm sick to death of my own little quips. "There is only this feeling we both have," he'd said. I try to think what this remark means and what might be its consequences, but I'm starting to drift. When was the last time I lay on my back, unable to distract myself with the radio or one of my spinster novels? Even living alone, I never take the opportunity to simply exist. And when was the last time someone dimmed the light in my room and softly closed the door? The last time was when my mother settled me down for a nap, then wandered off. "Go to sleep," she'd whisper, "I'll be back." And she always was. This recollection comes to me like a plea from my own memory. Virtually pinned to the table by the needles meant to improve my health, I cannot prevent the memory from rising full bloom. Because I refused to go to my room, Lenore would take me to the day bed in the sun room, cover me with an afghan, and later return, as she'd promised, to lead me again into the woken world.

The warmth from the lamp is growing stronger, and it is a great comfort. Neil has applied his heat to the very center of my body. I know I should plan something to say to him when he returns, but I feel no urgency; my thoughts are devolving into fragments. This peculiar thing that Neil does, this poking people with needles so he can eventually heal them, is taking form, is becoming part of him in my mind.

Eventually the door opens behind me, letting in a shaft of light from the hallway. Then the room itself brightens. I can barely speak, but I must force myself. I have to secure some time alone with Neil; we have to talk.

"How do you feel?" asks a stranger, a woman. I open my eyes as she begins to circle my body, removing needles. She is looking down at me, waiting for my answer.

"Fine," I say. "Everything is good."

* * *

Dark has not quite fallen on my block; it's lighter than it was a week ago at this time. I don't want to enter my building, but where would I go? In this state of mind, I would inflict myself on no one. I took a risk going to see Neil like that, a risk such as I am not used to, and it failed—delivered just the collapse of hope that one dreads when taking a risk. Yes, he asked me to wait, but then he disappeared. Tomorrow will bring what it may, but I honestly don't know where to go from here. The dreariness of my life is presenting itself in my body, in the sudden burden of its weight, even in the lingering soreness of two needle points on my right leg.

On the hallway radiator cover, I see a small package addressed to me. There's a return Diabetes Foundation of America sticker printed with Mosley Wright's name. My longing for Neil has drawn a scrim over this label, and everything else. Nothing quite registers as it should. Nonetheless, I take the package upstairs and open it. Something is wrapped in a letter written on lined paper. Inside the folded paper I find Duchess Regina. She's in perfect condition, not a rhinestone missing from her collar.

The meaning behind the poodle's displacement to my apartment is immediately obvious. Lighting the last cigarette from my pack, I smooth out the letter. It's one page, handwritten in pencil. Charlene Wright died of heart failure in her sleep only six days after she visited the house on Periwinkle Drive. Mosley wants me to pass on Duchess Regina to my sister—he doesn't have her address. He's got some news for me, too. Charlene had a bit of money saved from Floyd's death benefits and from here and there. She has divided this money equally among him, Rudy, LeRoy, and me. 'Mama always said you might be left with nothing,' wrote Mosley. If there's innuendo in this message, I cannot rout it out. The amount is neither trifling nor considerable.

As on the day of my visit, I'm astounded that Charlene would keep anything that would remind her of working for the Moss family. Yet she was clearly not bitter about those years. I never knew if she loved me as I did her, how deeply she understood her role as the closest woman in my life, to what extent the role frightened her as a responsibility on which she had not counted. Yet it was her decision to stay. When her duties far surpassed what her job required, she stayed. She dragged along a sullen six-year-old who had reverted to sucking his thumb for hours on end, endured months of my clinging, my wish to be nothing in life but her shadow. Years later she wearily promised to keep my pot smoking a secret from my father, listened to my snotty opinions and harsh judgments (all probably an affront to her sweet temper), and took me into her home when I'd shown up crying at her door. She stayed until Beryl and I went off to college. And now Charlene Wright, who struggled throughout her life, has given me—a child of privilege—a gift of money. It would be indecent for me to accept this gift, and yet Charlene's having given it confirms that she had loved me from my early childhood until her death.

I want to tell Avery. I want to call and tell him that Charlene Wright has died. My father's treatment of Charlene throughout her years with us had been erratic. A few times he'd aimed his rage at her. When this happened, he performed some good turn the next day—gave her boys a set of tickets to the Cleveland Browns, paid for a new muffler for her ancient Chevy Valiant. He never understood his love for her, and he was never explicit about it or about his feelings of admiration. Yet if I could call him now and tell him Charlene was dead, I would almost certainly hear a half gasp, followed by a choked sound—a failed attempt to find his voice, a near-yelp that would frighten me for its lack of power. It would be close to the sound he'd made when he learned that my mother was dead.

spring

❧ 18 ❧

It took me three drafts to compose the letter to Mosley Wright in which I refused his mother's money. In the end, I told him the truth, that it turned out Charlene's fears for me were unfounded, my father had preferred to reserve his generosity for after he was dead. I wrote to Mosley that this withholding was Avery's way, and had it been otherwise he would have expressed his love and respect for Charlene. I asked Mosley to send me the papers to formalize my forfeiture of his mother's bequest. I told him I'd never forfeit the memories of Charlene's acts of kindness when I was a child, nor would I ever be able to count them.

The same day I mailed this letter, I asked Beryl for the money that has gotten Melissa and me here, to a small hotel just over the Pont Vieux in Albi, France, for spring vacation. I told Beryl the trip was my treat to Melissa, but she'd have to advance me against my inheritance. Beryl agreed. She said maybe the trip would satisfy Missy's wandering bug. She was counting on me, though, to remember my niece's age and rein her in; there should be absolutely no going out on her own.

We will be here for a couple of days, then we're flying from Toulouse to Paris. So far, Melissa and I have yet to determine which of us is meant to care for the other. I rely only upon my status as her uncle and the capacity to point out and describe a few things she might not otherwise notice. Melissa offers up her considerable social ease and her ministerial nature.

We are eating couscous in a tiny Moroccan restaurant on the banks of the river Tarn. Melissa has done a satisfactory job of ordering for us in French. Now she's feeling in charge. "If Toulouse-Lautrec is so famous, Uncle Brian, how come all his work is in this town no one's ever heard of?"

"First of all, you know he was born here," I say. "And when he died, none of the directors of the Paris museums wanted the work he'd left behind in his studio. So his family donated his paintings to this city, and then later when the family died off, more paintings came into the collection. So now they all hang in the Berbie Palace, where we're going tomorrow. It's a palace built by prelates in the thirteenth century. Lucky for Albi the museum is here; tourists would probably not come to this city just for the Berbie Palace."

"It's not fair to act like I'm supposed to know who prelates are."

"Clergymen—high priests. The joke is that all these paintings of prostitutes and lesbians and drunkards hang on the walls of the former archbishop's palace."

Melissa does not react. Could it be that she finds my sense of irony juvenile? "Why *did* he paint all those people?" she asks.

"Why not?" I counter.

"I don't know. Maybe it's just that I think art should be of beautiful things."

I think of the hideous painting of the Acoma Indian chief hanging in Beryl and Seth's living room. Before I can answer, Melissa asks me if she can order wine.

"No. Maybe a taste in Paris."

"But in France even the children drink wine every day."

"Most don't," I correct. "And anyway, they have a different biological make-up. It affects them less."

"When I say stuff like that my dad asks me which study I'm citing."

I particularly dislike this because it sounds like something I would say. "Good thing he's not here, then."

"Come on, Uncle Brian—we're in France! How about I have one glass here and one in Paris, and that's all?"

This is the sort of inclination Beryl wants me to suppress in Melissa—this headlong reach for all that is adult.

"What makes you think this is open for negotiation?" I ask.

"I don't know . . ."

"You Kid, me Adult," I say. I don't know where this comes from until I remember Jordan and Frank's, 'you Tarzan, me Jane.'

I call the waiter over. Having read up on the wines of France before the trip, I know that the reds from nearby Gaillac are excellent. I order a glass for myself and just a taste for Melissa.

Melissa sits up straighter when the waiter comes back. He has mistakenly brought her a full glass, or perhaps my French was inadequate. Missy flushes in anticipation, and before she brings the glass to her lips her eyelids drop shut for a second, a completely sincere gesture; she takes seriously the mileposts of her own experience. She sips, then sucks her lower lip, savoring the taste that remains there. "It's good," she says. "I like it."

"Oh, great!" I say sarcastically.

Melissa drinks more. "It's weird. It's not heated, but it's warm when it goes down. Can I have the rest?" she asks.

"Maybe. See how you do. Drink slowly."

She does, and meanwhile we split a flan. From my place at the table, I can see the river Tarn. It's perfectly still, and the swallows have stopped flying overhead. No boats or barges pass. It's a cold spring evening, and the sky has darkened as we've sat. Brilliant lights appear along the bank and the Pont Vieux.

Crossing the bridge to return to our hotel, Melissa strains up for a moment to steady herself by grasping my shoulder. Her head pointed skyward as she sniffs the night air, she is all sybaritic emotion. I have known, at various times, the sense of bounty that now astonishes her.

* * *

Nothing happens when I pull the door handle designed in the shape of Toulouse-Lautrec's famous monogram. We are early. As we wait, Melissa tells me about one of her friends in Scottsdale, a girl she calls Beppy who would not be able to eat in a French restaurant because she's on a diet of juice, rice, tofu, and multi-vitamins. I'm reminded of the immeasurable distance between America's turn of the twentieth century and France's turn of the nineteenth, and I fear for us all.

In a few minutes, a guard opens the door. On the first floor inside the museum, a clerk is already posted at the cash register in the small gift shop. Melissa lingers there, but I'm eager to enter the galleries. This is something I should have considered—that I'd want to be alone.

"You can stay here if you want to," I tell her. "We can be on our own here, don't you think?"

Melissa agrees so enthusiastically that I realize her parents would never allow this separation in a strange public place. We arrange a time to meet, and I rush through the first gallery, wanting to shake the other tourists who were waiting outside with us.

First I look at Henri's early work, his juvenilia more mature than the works he executed shortly before his death, caricatures of himself urinating or sitting naked on a chamber pot. These paintings are of his father Count Adolphe on horseback or with his falcons, all done in thick brush strokes that shout *oil painting*. By the time he'd painted his mother, Countess Adèle, when he was nineteen, Toulouse-Lautrec had abandoned those stiff strokes. Maman appeared in Henri's painting sitting erect before a single teacup, her solidity conveyed entirely by loose and scratchy brush strokes.

It doesn't take long for me to find Toulouse-Lautrec's Impressionist-influenced paintings of the 1890s: a gentleman reading his paper in the garden, a woman at the piano, another scrutinizing herself in a dressing-table mirror, perfume vials adorning her tabletop. In 1894, Henri painted *In the Sitting Room at Moulins Street*, and to look at this one I sit down. The "Sitting Room" is the social room in the brothel where Henri often stayed, the room where women relaxed or awaited their next assignation. The prostitutes seem resigned, yet ready to strike up a diverting conversation. They sit on velvet sofas with lush circular cushions. One woman stands to the side, lifting her dress, preparing to be examined for syphilis.

Some of Toulouse-Lautrec's best brushwork can be seen in his many paintings of prostitutes. The works of this period are what made me originally want to write about Henri Toulouse-Lautrec. Once again, they are the evidence that this childish and self-debasing little man was also a man of great refinement.

From across the room, I spot La Goulue. It is like recognizing an old friend passing on the street. There she is in an unfinished lithograph with her dancing partner, Valentin the Boneless. The condition of the litho is poor; water stains mark its bottom corner. Yet the edges of La Goulue's body are clear and typically assured. Executing a quadrille kick, La Goulue is rendered in sharp focus, and her bright yellow hair, fashioned in its famous golden helmet, is the only flash of color in the work. This litho sketch is a study for the Moulin Rouge poster that made the club owner Zidler rich and Toulouse-Lautrec famous at the age of twenty-six. More than one version of the poster is here. The fact is, I don't like any of them. In a word, commercial. An absurd criticism for a work that was commissioned as an advertisement, but for me the poster is a blunt and ugly work, despite its strong composition. It is famous because it happens to have captured a prevailing social mood.

In another room I walk over to the sketches in a glass case. To my delight, I spot the drawing *La Goulue Devant Le Tribunal*. I love the story that led up to this courtroom scene of La Goulue in a lion trainer costume taming a poodle. I am leaning over to get a closer view of the light pencil strokes when Melissa appears, announcing herself by pressing her weight into my hip.

"Hi, Uncle Brian. Can I stand here?"

"Sure, honey." Now I'm happy for her company.

"Why's she wearing that costume?"

"The drawing is a satire. You know what that is, right?"

"Sort of."

"Okay, I'll tell you the story. You'll appreciate that some of it is X-rated, or at least PG-13."

"Cool."

"In 1893, the night club the Moulin Rouge held a big ball. Toulouse-Lautrec was pretty famous that year, his work was everywhere, and he was at the ball—in top form, I'm sure. Everyone was wearing clever costumes. But the highlight came when a group of art students carried in their models, one by one. They were all naked, or just about."

"That's sexist, right?"

"You bet. But I'm not finished. A woman named Sarah Brown was the most famous model then, and the art students carried her out on a litter as Cleopatra under a gold net. That's when the ball turned into a drunken riot, and gangs of art students went after the models. No one knows for sure, but the models were probably raped. Next the students went on a rampage. They tore through the streets and demanded free drinks at every bar they passed. Finally, someone called the police and several people were arrested."

"Oh my God, stuff like that happened *then*?"

"Stuff like that has happened from the beginning of time, Missy. Anyway, the artists of Montmartre loved the whole event. They talked about it for days. But there was this one senator who had a lot of power then, Senator Beranger. He was also head of what was called the Moral League, this group trying to repress morally offensive conduct, and he filed a formal complaint."

"He sounds like that senator from North Carolina my dad hates, the one always going ballistic about artists' grants and gays and stuff."

"Hey—excellent. A lot like him, but you have to consider there was real rape in this incident at the ball, so this time the senator's outrage had some justification behind it. Anyway, a trial was held, and Toulouse-Lautrec and his friends got themselves prime places in the visitors' gallery. They figured if they all banded together, no one would get convicted."

"So who won?"

"This is the part where La Goulue comes in." I point to *La Goulue Devant Le Tribunal*. "She was the only witness for the prosecution."

"Wait, I always forget who's the prosecution and whose the defense."

"The prosecution is the side doing the accusing. They called La Goulue to the stand. Supposedly she was dressed like any respectable matron of the day, and she talked about how morally offended she'd been by the nudity at the ball."

"Why'd she do that? I saw those pictures of her in the galleries back there. She was probably nude herself!"

"I bet she wasn't. As far as I know, she never fully took her clothes off at the Moulin Rouge. But probably the answer to your question is that she didn't want the place that paid her salary to be shut down by the Moral League. Whatever her motives, *no one* thought her testimony would be taken seriously. After all, she'd just appeared in newspapers kicking off the Prince of Wales's top hat during her dance. She was a joke."

"So the students got off."

"Nope. The defendants were found guilty and fined. No one could believe it. That's when Toulouse-Lautrec did this drawing of La Goulue appearing in court wearing this costume."

"What did La Goulue do when she saw the drawing?" she asks.

I shrug. "Don't forget, I wasn't there. I'm not *that* old."

Melissa rolls her eyes. "I bet she freaked. I bet she told him to get a life."

"Or the equivalent for the period," I say. "The really awful thing was that Toulouse-Lautrec's canvases showing La Goulue in her glory days went to the Louvre the very same year she died begging on the streets."

"God," says Melissa, and we walk on until we come upon the cane, the hollow wooden cane with the shot glass inside. It's thrilling to see it up close. The cane unscrews in two places, at the very top and about eight inches down. Henri had stored his shot glass in the top section, and he kept his strange concoctions of liquor in the bottom of the cane. At first guess, someone might assume that he used this cane to hide his drinking, but it is more likely that Henri made a show of dismantling the cane to pour himself a drink.

"That is *so* cool," says Melissa. "What a smart idea."

"Alcoholism with a flair," I say.

"It's as if he said to himself, 'Hey, I'm already a dwarf, so I may as well be weird about everything,'" Melissa observes.

This impresses me. "I think there *was* some of that, now that you mention it. The thing is that so often eccentric types are marginal talents. Toulouse-Lautrec was major. Not that I'm in the business of tagging talents," I hasten to add.

A few minutes later, in the gift shop, Melissa lingers over each item for sale. I buy her an English-language museum guide as a souvenir of her visit. She buys a video for Seth and a refrigerator magnet for Beryl. I say nothing about the disparity between the size of the gifts. When we get to Paris, I'll make sure she picks up something nice for Beryl.

We leave to have lunch in the district north of the river, where our hotel is, and all along the walk Melissa creates scenarios in which La Goulue triumphs over Toulouse-Lautrec, rising to ever greater heights of fame as Henri languishes in the sanitarium in Neuilly. By the time we reach the restaurant, Melissa has La Goulue wrapped in sable and accompanied by her string of beautiful children. In turn, she holds them up to peer through a peephole in the door of a padded cell. Inside, a drooling and unkempt little man is drawing on the cement floor. "See Jacques, see Simone, see Maurice, there's the man who did that nasty drawing of Mommy we all hate so much."

The biggest queens at The Barracks would be proud to spin out this little scenario. I tell her she's got a terrific imagination. Beaming, she puts her arm around my waist, and we enter a pretty little café set back from the boulevard.

❧ 19 ❧

I haven't been to Paris in almost twenty years, not since my lonely and undistinguished junior-year semester at the Sorbonne. Melissa has never been here. We're staying at a late-seventeenth-century hotel in the

Marais, and it's expensive enough that we've had to opt for rooms with a shared hallway bath. Melissa loves this aspect of our stay. Over croissants and orange marmalade in the hotel's cramped breakfast room, she speculates about the other guests using the bathroom, one of whom is a teenage boy she spotted in his boxer shorts. She confides that the boy had hair on his legs and she drops her eyelids, not from embarrassment, I realize, but from a charge of recognition that the leg hair of boys has implications for her future.

"Most of the museums are open today," I tell her. "We might be able to fit in two, with a walk and lunch in between. How about the D'Orsay and a smaller one? The Cluny—we could see the unicorn tapestries. Or L'Orangerie. They have some Monets I bet you've seen pictures of."

Melissa doesn't commit, but asks, "What about the Eiffel Tower? Or the cemetery where the famous dead people are buried? I promised my dad I'd have you take a picture of me at Jim Morrison's grave. He has all the Doors' albums."

I'm chastened, although I don't know how I'll bear the Eiffel Tower. I consider suggesting we split up, then remember I don't have the liberty. "How about we go to Père-Lachaise this morning? That's the cemetery. And then we can squeeze in a museum late this afternoon? Maybe we can visit the Eiffel Tower on our last day."

Picking up her tea cup, Melissa sips carefully. Her left hand, slender like Beryl's, rests on the handle of the porcelain pot. In another era, she might have been the subject of one of Henri's more genteel pictures, or of Mary Cassatt's *Lady at the Tea-Table*. I am looking at Missy's hand when someone touches my shoulder.

"*Pardon.* I didn't want you to think I'd forgotten you."

When I first look up I see only the man's denim shirt. It's enough. A sense of dislocation flings me out of time as well as place. Heat envelops my head. I try to speak, allow words to emerge from my mouth, but I am numb from the shock, the magnitude of the compliment, the suddenly incandescent frame around my future. Still, my voice serves me. It doesn't break or stray into one of those sinkholes of nervous ardor that pitted my boyhood. "I *cannot* believe this. When did you get here?"

"This morning. Not entirely a coincidence though. I called The Barracks and your informant Jordan told me you were here, at this hotel. I was on spring break too, the hotel had a cancellation, so . . . the stars were aligned."

"Melissa, this is my friend . . . Neil Beck. Neil, this is my niece, Melissa Edwards."

The breakfast parlor is cramped, so Neil stands, waiting. I've yet to emerge from the nirvana of my displacement. Thoughts are scrambled in the vertigo of the moment. Neil's sudden appearance here must mean he's made a permanent break with Alicia. Delirious as I am, I wonder if he expects us to accept him as our traveling partner. And what about the room arrangements? Is he telling the truth about the cancellation at the Hôtel Amarante, or does he expect to stay with me? He's too tactful, I decide, for that presumption. After all, how could he be sure Melissa knows I'm gay?

There is little question that his coming here will change everything. Finally disgusted with myself for allowing Neil to make me feel provisional in my own life, I had decided on this trip to help myself get over him. Now here he stands—rooted, filled-in, a manifestation of my surrendered daydream.

The sunlight coming through the French windows' sheer curtains in this corner breakfast room is so pleasing it could be christened "Domestic Light." Never have I wanted more to linger over a cup of coffee and a few crumbs on a plate. The bit of orange marmalade left on Melissa's saucer reflects all that is cultivated about French society. There are, however, the practical demands of the moment. Neil still stands before me. "Let's go out to the lobby," I say.

There, Melissa and I sit down on a love seat across from Neil. So far, Melissa has said nothing.

"Missy's really enjoying this hotel," I say helplessly. "Sharing a bathroom with strangers is the height of exotica in her book." I lean into her shoulder to show my affection, to get her to react.

"Look," says Neil. "I certainly don't want to horn in here. Of course, I hope we can spend a little museum time together, but this is my first trip to Paris. There's some just plain old touristy stuff I want to see, and I'm perfectly capable of charting my own way."

"Me too!" says Melissa. "I want to see the touristy stuff, too. Like Jim Morrison's grave for my dad."

"On my list. That and the Eiffel Tower and Notre Dame. And just walking."

Neil leaves to retrieve his bag from Hôtel Amarante's back office and put it in his room.

"Are you okay with this?" I ask Melissa when he's gone. The question is equally to myself. Now that I've absorbed the fact of Neil's presence here in Paris, I'm not sure the grief he caused me should go unpunished.

"I think. He seems nice."

"Let's see how it goes," I tell her. "Don't think you have no say here."

When Neil returns, no one can decide where to go first—it's as if there is no directing adult among us—and so we just walk. First we cross Pont Marie to Île St. Louis. It's after 10:00 AM, and the full sunlight of early morning has given way to gray clouds and a cool drizzle, then glints of faint sunlight again. We appreciate the generous display, the opportunity to see Île St. Louis under this mercurial sky. All our plans can wait, we decide. Today is for walking, for previewing.

Appearing alternately ahead of and between us, Melissa has been claimed by an uncharacteristic step. Neither a walk nor a run, it is some kind of kinetic clamor, an arrhythmic recording of her passing impressions. She regularly stops to train her point-and-shoot camera on a building façade, an easel artist working the tourists, a cruise boat on the Seine—anything that presents itself as other. I'm getting irritated, but Neil has his own point-and-shoot. I find myself thinking that if something comes of Neil and me, I'll have to look elsewhere for a partner in crankiness. My department head Nathan, I decide, would be a good choice for this purpose.

At Quay St-Michel on the Left Bank, we cross the street to the boulevard. Standing on an island along Boulevard St-Michel is a public toilet that Melissa says she wants to use. In the short line, she shifts her weight from one foot to the other. I don't know if she really has to go or just wants the experience. She is not so many years beyond the age where children are fascinated with bathrooms and what goes on in them. Probably the idea of pulling down her pants within a metal stall in the middle of a bustling boulevard in Europe presents a thrill beyond her reckoning. When she's inside the *toilette*, Neil and I are alone for the first time. My surprise at his arrival returns in full force. If I look directly at his face, I'm afraid I'll fall into a place rife with danger. Finally I look anyway, but he's taking in the sights around him.

The opening of the stall door has automated the toilet's noisy flushing and cleaning process. Melissa stands just outside, listening in delight. "Wow, thanks, Uncle Brian."

"Don't mention it. I'm glad to have provided the highlight of your trip."

"The Toulouse-Lautrec Museum was the highlight of my trip."

"Oo-o-o," I say. "You're good. A future in public relations for you."

"No, I *mean* it," Melissa practically whines.

I take out my map. "Let's walk to St. Germaine de Prés," I say. I intend to lead them to the Delacroix Museum, which was his atelier, and if one of them suggests we go inside I will not object.

Rue de Fürstemberg is a lovely square with old-fashioned lampposts and, at this time of year, trees just blooming. The entrance to the atelier is discreet, but when I find it, it's locked. The guidebook confirms that the museum is closed on Tuesdays.

We head back to the boulevard. Drizzle has turned to rain, and we duck inside St-Germain de Prés Church. All the way from Île St. Louis, Melissa has been comparing the fashions of teenage girls in Scottsdale to those of Parisian girls, particularly delineating accessories of French and American origin. As we enter the cathedral's nave, crowned by Gothic vaulting and lined above the arches with frescos portraying the life of Christ, she falls immediately and profoundly silent.

There are very few people in the nave; the three of us hear one another's steps on the stone floor and the least throat clearing with resounding clarity. We walk slowly, staring up at the frescos. Further down, in deep square recesses in the transept and chancel, are ornate tombs. They belong to Benedictines and noblemen entirely unfamiliar to us and, I imagine, to the majority of tourists who enter the church. I am awed, yet at the same time not fully present. With me is this new man in my life, one no longer a stranger in a dark green flight jacket, but Neil Beck who has flown nearly 4,000 miles to be with me, to do whatever the moment calls for, to examine ancient religious icons in a historic French church.

Neil is the first to sit in a pew, from where he looks up at the magnificent ceiling. When I finish examining the wrought-iron grillework in the chancel, I join him, and then Melissa approaches down the center aisle, her expression distant, anonymous, glazed. Heavily, she sits down next to me. The heat of her body fills the slender space between us. She is extremely still. Neil continues to scan the ceiling, and I'm looking again at the frescos when I become aware that Melissa, beside but not quite touching me, is trembling. Infinitesimal shudders have overcome her, and I find myself reluctant to turn in her direction. Instead, I put my arm around her shoulders, and she breaks into convulsive weeping. When she hears her amplified sobs reverberate in the vast transept, she buries her face in my jacket to stifle herself. I draw her closer. She is crying, I believe, because Scottsdale gives her the Desert Pavilion Mall, built when she was five years old, and Paris gives her this eleventh-century Romanesque church housing the remains of ancient strangers. She is lost, quite probably for the first time in her life, to dread.

"You're tired," I finally whisper. "Let's go get some lunch."

"Burger King," says Neil. "I'd love a Paris Whopper."

He is dipping into a reserve of wisdom that, without conceding it to myself, I've hoped to one day discover in a lover.

The rain has stopped, so after lunch we resume our walk. Melissa has brightened some, though she still anchors herself with glimpses of the familiar. Along the way to the Sorbonne she pauses to look in the windows of clothing stores. Heading back, she is pleased when we drop into Shakespeare & Company, the English-language bookstore Seth made her promise to visit. There she picks up a paperback copy of *The Giver*, the same edition she was reading during the time of Avery's death in Cleveland. Spotting it here among other titles she recognizes prods her back to herself. She wants to buy this copy simply because it's sold here, but changes her mind when she determines the conversion from francs equals $21.00.

It's past four when we cross Pont au Double and approach Notre Dame. Neil gives me a look; do we dare? Melissa is watching some tourists watch a mime whose character keeps falling asleep while he's supposed to be digging a ditch. I point out to her the flying buttresses and remind her of Victor Hugo's story, but she doesn't bite.

Throughout the day I've been astonished by the rapid changing of Melissa's moods; within the course of five minutes she has been impetuous and brimming with enthusiasm, then downcast and querulous. I remember Beryl's advice not to overstimulate her—as though we could avoid the flow of society or the evocation of history delivered by French cities. Yet now I regret that she has been overstimulated, and I want to get her back to the hotel. We leave Neil in the line to climb Notre Dame's tower. Closer to the Marais, Melissa asks if we can go into a secondhand clothes store, but I tell her it's nap time. She needs a nap, I think, as much as a toddler might.

At the Hôtel Amarante, I tell the clerk that I will be staying in Neil Beck's room. We arrange that I will pay for my own room for tonight. Beyond that, the clerk waves off my concern. This is April, he tells me. He'll flip the sign on the door to *Chambre Disponible*, and it won't be half an hour before the hotel is filled again.

Neil's room turns out to be identical to mine, on the floor above. It faces a courtyard and is blessedly quiet at this hour before dinner. The room is clean, the bed made, and I don't see Neil's bag until I open the wardrobe. I have yet to fully believe he has joined me, that for the first time we will sleep together for consecutive nights. But what am I going to do about *Helen Croft: Dawn of a New Season*? I'll read it now, I decide, while he's inching along in the long line of people waiting to climb up the south tower of Notre Dame.

Naturally the man in the Donegal tweed waistcoat, the one who sits beside Helen on a bench in Hyde Park, turns out to be the rector of a Sussex parish. On the modest salary he allows himself from the parish tithes, Rector Ian Morton has come to London. He is staying with old friends across the park and plans to spend several days visiting orphanages to see how the one in his parish might be improved. Sitting next to Helen on the bench in Hyde Park, not far from the Shipleys' home, he shakes his head over her twins. He has just come from an orphanage in which a yard full of shabbily dressed children gets barely a whit of kind attention all day. Rector Ian Morton studies the beautifully groomed Shipley twins, now chanting to a hand-clapping game, and says, "Reprehensible inequities. And these two seem only too aware of their advantages."

Helen looks at him in astonishment. She can't believe this harsh judgment is coming from the lips of a rector. Then she looks again at her charges and says, "I can't abide them."

"Oh, dear," says Rector Morton. "Have we just confessed the unspeakable to each other?"

But there seems to be no going back. From their place on the ornate iron bench, Helen Croft and Rector Morton discuss the quality of effete self-consciousness they find abhorrent in the Shipley twins. The class system, they claim, is responsible, as it is for so many ills in modern England. Amid this discussion, R. W. Dodson reminds his readers of Rector Morton's raven black hair and Nile green eyes. I learn too that

Helen is grateful she washed her hair that morning and knows that it now frames her cheeks in soft waves.

Just as I'm turning the page to find out how Rector Ian Morton can possibly secure another meeting before returning to Sussex, there is a clicking at the door, and Neil walks in.

"Well," he says, "here he is. Lying here waiting for me, just like I'd wished for when I finally got up to the top of the tower."

As he comes over to the bed, only a few steps from the door, I barely have time to slip *Helen Croft: Dawn of a New Season* under the bedspread. As I do so, I glimpse the unfortunate tag line, "the last in the popular romantic trilogy."

Neil lies down. "Jet lag finally got me."

"I'm surprised you held up this long."

He closes his eyes.

"You're here," I say.

"Yes, I'm here."

"Are you happy you're here?"

"The question is, are *you* happy I'm here?"

"I'm too busy being stunned."

"I know, I'm a little stunned, too. But how else could I get you to forgive me for what I've put you through? I had to do something big."

"This is fairly big."

"Mmmm. By design."

"So are you deprogrammed? Have you unconverted?"

Neil rolls over, reaches for me, then interrupts himself. "Ouch." He lifts up and removes *Helen Croft: Dawn of a New Season* from under the cover. "What's this?"

"My other side," I say, holding out my hand to reclaim the book.

Neil keeps it long enough to read aloud the title and "the last in the popular romantic trilogy."

Why did I take the chance of this happening? The devil of self-sabotage travels to Paris.

Neil gives me back the book. He looks genuinely pleased. "It's okay. I practice Zen meditation, so I'm well beyond judging. 'Mindfulness is to be aware without judgment.'"

"You shit," I say, and the reality of ourselves together in this room so far from home seems to strike us both at once.

At eight o'clock, we meet Melissa in the hotel lobby, a small room whose walls are crammed with framed watercolors, appreciative letters from past guests, and bookshelves filled with outdated travel guides. Melissa has changed into a black cotton knit dress and sandals with outsized soles, but her face is puffy and a sleep fold runs down her right cheek. The back of her blonde hair is tangled. At the nearby bistro where we go for dinner, she speaks little, and when she does her voice is muffled, far away. She tells us she had the deepest sleep she's ever had, a thousand dreams, including one in which the tombs from the church we visited kept sprouting up beside the desert cactus of her backyard in Scottsdale.

I've gotten her to try bouillabaisse, but she dislikes it, complains it tastes of something like licorice. It's anise, I tell her, and ask if she wants a steak sandwich. She shakes her head no and slumps a little in her seat.

When Neil gets up to go to the bathroom, I ask, "Is this because of Neil? Your mood?"

Her eyes well up. "No." Her voice is that of a younger child. "I like him."

I believe her. "Are you homesick, sweetie?"

Again, she shakes her head.

"Is it still from this afternoon?"

Almost imperceptibly, she nods. "There are . . ." The tears spill over. I wait.

"There are so many . . ." She pauses, then blurts out in a phlegmy voice, "*people* in the world!"

How can I convey to my niece, her whole life spent in Scottsdale—unwittingly consigned to a group of one or two percent of the world's wealthiest—that yes, there are millions and millions of people, that people, so easy to achieve, are one of the earth's few boundless resources, but their multiplicity doesn't detract from the singular importance of her own life? How can I convey this when I felt the same way the first time I saw New York, felt sure that the sheer bulk of all those lives declared my own immaterial?

"I'm surprised you didn't feel hit by this when you went to Nogales. It's pretty populated there."

"I did, but it was different."

She doesn't elaborate, but leaves her seat and stands before me. I push back in my chair so she can sit on my lap. Then Neil returns.

"Missy," Neil says, claiming her nickname. "Want to go down to the Seine and watch the tour boats?"

"I think she's still tired," I say. "How about we go back to the hotel and Melissa just listens to the CDs she brought? How 'bout we all have a quiet night?"

It's after eleven when Neil and I decide to go out. Sex had been different than what it was in the beginning; some degree of hesitancy had turned it sweet and languid. To be expected, I reason, everything is evolving. Going out seems the thing to do. I'm worried about Melissa, but I hear the TV in her room; she's testing her French, as she did in the Albi hotel. We rap on the door and let her know we're going out for an hour or so.

We find ourselves on Rue des Rosiers, the old Jewish quarter, a place whose history is so dark that I cannot imagine it in daylight, can barely think of it as an integral part of this city that—it must be said—has not counted people of the Semitic race a cherished part of its population. At this hour, there are very few Orthodox men on the street, and no women. The several men wear payess, and two or three rush along with their eyes on their feet. They carry packages from Goldenberger's or other kosher delis that have closed and reopened their doors more than once in history. Neil asks me what I know about the activities of the Jewish Quarter in Toulouse-Lautrec's time, and I admit I know nothing. This ignorance, I reflect, is one reason I had so little chance of becoming an art historian. I lack the sense of omniscience that is required to project scope. I never considered what was going on in the Jewish quarter in the late nineteenth century while Lautrec was draining the contents of his hollow cane and painting the quadrille dancers at the Moulin Rouge just a few miles away.

Before we know it, the Jewish Quarter has yielded to a street full of gay restaurants and bars and stores with rainbow decals stuck to their windows. I know the Marais includes Paris's gay neighborhood—I chose to stay here for this reason—but I didn't remember that it so closely abuts the Orthodox community.

"Boy, is this ever strange," says Neil.

"I wonder if there's been trouble," I say.

"I bet they just totally ignore each other. Probably we don't exist for the Orthodox, and vice versa."

We're looking in windows as we talk. Surely somewhere in Paris are the equivalent of the black-windowed bars and bookstores along West Street in New York, but this block does not house them. Smiling, well-dressed couples sit eating expensive food at small tables. The restaurant in front of us, *L'Endroit De Réunion*, has a large mahogany bar. Men watch their own and one another's reflections in the immense antique mirror behind this bar. We decide to go in.

The stools are taken, so we stand in the loose row of men gathered behind them. Most patrons speak a pure and musical French. We also hear some French-accented English and some American-accented French. Neil orders a draft and I order a Bordeaux. The two of us are conspicuous for our casual dress. Cashmere pullovers and Armani jackets are the uniform here. If we were in New York, these men would be doctors or corporate attorneys or real estate developers on Beryl's scale, but here the connection to wealth is probably older; there are lineages here.

I try to envision Jordan flipping his hamburgers and Luis showing off his abs in this establishment. I tell Neil about the two of them. His hand is on my shoulder as he listens. When I tell him about the Pamper Yourself vibrating heat mattress covered by green flocking, he rears back his head and laughs. I own this laugh for having evoked it, and I'm overjoyed. I go on to describe Frank's coma and his extraordinary recovery. I tell Neil how angry we all were at St. Mary's for ignoring Frank's DNR, then how we had to reverse ourselves and be grateful to them. Neil nods. I'm sure he has his share of such stories; maybe so many he decided to go straight, to enter conversion therapy.

Two men in front of us have cleared the bar, and for the first time I notice the bartender. He could have been imported from the Shackle for the purpose of occupying those few men in this bar who harbor another nature behind their staid appearances. He's probably Israeli, maybe Arab. He has a great deal of curly black hair and on his right bicep is a tattoo of a serpent coiled around a knife. I hear someone greet him as Avi. He turns to us with a pouty gaze, a smile in the rarefied vernacular that is his world. His gaze lingers on Neil, then he looks away, occupies himself with some regulars, but I see him sneak a second look at Neil. In another time and place, without Neil beside me, *I* might easily have attracted Avi's eye. He would have played me as he's now playing Neil. Suddenly I feel shorter than my five feet, ten and a half inches— maybe the shortest man in the room. There's no question that Neil has registered the bartender's attention. He has kept looking at me, but I can see, with utter familiarity from my own experience, that he's been affected by Avi's fleeting appraisal. Neil is probably not even aware that he now stands straighter, brushes the hair off his forehead in a seductive manner. I remind myself that he has recently come home, back to the fold; he must be both relieved and charged up.

There will be others to contend with on both our sides, but why think of them now?

Neil puts his half empty glass on the bar and suggests we leave.

We go on to Place de Voges, the oldest square in Paris, once the royal square of King Henri IV, a plaza of buildings with arcades and steeply pitched roofs. A couple of cafés are still open. It's a cool night, and we settle at a table under an infrared light. From our seats, we look out at the park in the center of the square. The evening's intermittent rains have brought out the scent of grass. We each order a Kir.

Neil tells me the story of his conversion therapy. He speaks low, but without a trace of apology in his voice. He repeats what he'd told me about wanting to conform, about his loneliness when he was studying in China, then tells me how he felt toward the beginning of the therapy, when he'd had hopes for its success. For the first time in his life, he said, he'd walked around in the anticipation of having no shame. He stopped worrying about the eventuality of coming out to friends or to interested women. He let his interactions go where they may. With the help of Dr. Zorides, he began to date women. Dr. Zorides understood Neil's shame. He did not actively condemn Neil's homoerotic feelings, but was firm that their work together was to be focused on the objective of teaching Neil to resist those feelings. After a while, Neil began to enjoy sex with the few women he dated, to imagine himself married. He went home to northern Virginia and told his parents he was going straight. Over the years his parents had grown accustomed to their son liking men, and if they'd never warmed to the concept, neither were they sanguine about the announcement that he was now straight. His brother, an oral surgeon in Milwaukee, greeted the news with little interest. No one expressed skepticism, but no one was impressed.

Neil continued to enjoy a new freedom to mix in ever-larger groups. If those groups sometimes included gay men, he did as the other straight men in the group—he showed no acknowledgment of their difference, embraced their inclusion entirely. He felt little temptation, and in fact assumed a slight air of bemusement in their company.

"Do you want another Kir?" I ask, and order us both a second. I can no longer smell the park grass, but it's a joy to occasionally look over at the spring flowers and the sand paths, the fountains and statues, all presided over by medieval buildings obscured in the dark.

Then Neil tells me about Alicia, whom he met in Dr. Zorides' Tuesday night group. Eight months into therapy, Dr. Zorides began to talk about this group, and he mentioned it every week during his and Neil's individual session. It was a coed group that he facilitated, he said, and he explained the uses of group therapy over that of individual treatment. Neil is certain that Dr. Zorides had a particular interest in introducing him to Alicia, a lively and intent young member of the group who, despite being in a conducive setting, gave no hint of her true fragility. When Neil began to date her, he was pleased with himself and always happy to be seen in her presence. Unfailingly, she knew what to wear, what to say, how to show her pleasure in Neil's attentions. He took her to plays and to concerts, and he relished most the intermissions, when they leaned together along a balustrade or spoke in hushed tones near the bar. Then Neil could see men glancing at Alicia, women admiring them as a pair.

Just as I'm wondering where this will lead, Neil tells me that one day he realized he was playing a game as superficial as any he'd played as a gay man, and that he was being fundamentally dishonest with himself in order to play it. The shame he'd felt before, says Neil, was nothing compared to the vicious sense of remorse that overcame him now. When he expressed his doubts to Dr. Zorides, he found that Dr. Zorides' sympathy had its limits. Once again, Neil experienced inner chaos, a turmoil so far removed from Chinese medicine's principles of wholeness that he doubted even his career path. And right as he was beginning to face that his treatment was failing, that it had in fact been destructive, Alicia asked him to marry her. Halfway through his second Kir, Neil says that the details of the rest of the story are not very illuminating. It was during that time, he says, that he began to go to the West Street bars, and also that he met me.

The likelihood of his now being converted to heterosexuality, he assures me, is considerably below zero. We're quiet for a bit. I stretch my legs over the stone pavement. I'm happy Neil told this story, but I don't have any questions.

Then Neil wants to know more about me. He wants to know my plans. He leans forward and looks at me in such a way that for the first time I see his objective view of me. He finds me interesting and is curious to find out why I'm working below my potential. This may or may not be my projection—Neil's the one with experience in psychotherapy, but I realize it would not be a good idea to tell Neil I'm not by nature a planner.

"For now," I say, "I'm going to stay at Tri-Community. There are some problems there, but I've decided to stick it out for a while. And I've started a new project. I can work on it between my class and The Barracks."

Neil does not respond to the mention of The Barracks. "You only have one class at Tri-Community, right?"

I tense at the implied judgment. "Their Humanities Department is bare bones. The number of classes I teach varies. This year I only have one, but next year I'll have two, maybe three."

Neil nods. He reaches across the table for my hand. I'm not a fan of public displays of affection, but I don't pull back. "What's your new project?" he asks. There is only kindness in his voice, and a respect I haven't earned.

"A gleam in the eye, really, something having to do with maternal influence on the painters of the era I've written about before, the Belle Époque. Sounds pretty hokey, I realize, but what I envision is definitely not sentimental."

Neil starts to respond, but I put two hundred francs on the table and tell him I'm getting nervous about Melissa.

On the Hôtel Amarante's second floor, I press my ear to the door and hear nothing. Melissa is a child with a habit of illicit roaming, and I have left her alone in a foreign city. Intuition tells me, though, that her new fear—her awakening existential fear—has for now eclipsed her bold streak. Just as we've arranged, she'll meet us in the hotel breakfast room at 8:30 tomorrow morning, and once again she'll be pleased when the waitress sets down the basket of fresh croissants and bread and a porcelain teapot just for her.

Beryl has written to thank me for taking Melissa to France. Her note says that Melissa has measurably benefited from the trip, that there is a new emotional maturity about her, even a new self-discipline. The writing is calligraphic script. Beryl doesn't know calligraphy. She's hired someone.

I answer Beryl on a postcard of an apple-cheeked young woman, a tedious Renoir. A shop clerk at the D'Orsay had accidentally slipped it in with my own card purchases.

Dear Beryl,

It was my pleasure to take Melissa with me to France. She's a lovely girl, and I enjoyed her. She's curious and warm and gives me faith, especially after a long semester at Tri-Community, that there are still some open-hearted kids out there, kids whose enthusiasm doesn't embarrass them.

I want to add *as mine for years embarrassed you,* but I end it there and sign off *Love, Brian.*

Beryl's letter was signed *Always,* so my closing ups the ante. I decide to mail the card before I can change my mind or look too hard at why I didn't so much as mention Neil when Melissa has surely told Beryl all about him.

When the three of us arrived back at Newark International Airport two weeks ago, Melissa had hugged us both for a long time before she boarded her connecting flight to Phoenix. She promised she would send pictures of Neil and me together at the entrance to the Picasso Museum, and told us she would keep a duplicate on the most prominent spot of her bulletin board at home. "Prime real estate," Melissa had told us Beryl called this spot, and she'd rolled her eyes. I haven't spoken to Missy since our return. She's back at school, busy with gymnastics and water ballet. I can't help feeling bereft—an idler left in the wake of a thirteen-year-old's busy life.

My own routine will soon change. On my first night back at The Barracks, Jordan was not there. Norman Brinsky was fiercely flapping patties onto Jordan's grill.

After Frank was released from St. Mary's, Jordan took him on a trip. Not to the Nile, not to the Himalayas, but on a gay cruise featuring nightly cabaret. Just a week-long cruise to Barbados, but before Jordan left, he quit the Barracks. For the last year, Frank has been trying to get him to become, like himself, a salesman for Hudson Rug and Carpet. It will be a practical move for Jordan. He is past fifty and uninsured; Hudson Rug and Carpet can protect him.

Luis has been moping around all week, and he is threatening to quit. I've cut limes, changed CDs, mixed drinks, and poured beer on tap, as usual. As much as civility demands, I've spoken to Gerald from Sony and his awful crowd. I've heard some urgent secrets. But I know that my routine is provisional. Without Jordan wandering out of the kitchen, spatula in hand, brow perspiring, ready to unloose his robust laugh, I too will leave the Barracks.

Walking to the mailbox with my card to Beryl, I see the roller bladers have returned. Men with iron asses glide by on the street. I light a cigarette. Someone touches my arm. "Those'll be the death of you, dollface. Rubbers every time, meanwhile puffin' away like there's no tomorrow. I love it."

I know from past springs, this is Seraphina's favorite season. She's wearing a halter top with a daisy pattern. I blow smoke not too far from her face. "Nice to see you, Seraphina."

"Has no one ever told you, darling, that your body is a temple?"

"Not until this very moment. And how are you?"

"Splendid. Seraphina blooms in spring. Unfortunately, so do all the crazies. Poor Molly. Can you imagine? Of all the people for it to happen to! Why couldn't it have happened to me? Did you hear if he was well endowed? Oh, never mind, sweetie, I guess you couldn't have just burst forth and asked. That would've been a tad insensitive."

"Is this an exercise in mind reading, Seraphina?"

"Oh come *on*, sweetie. You *have* to know. She lives right below you. The whole block knows."

I shake my head no.

Seraphina can barely contain her excitement over the responsibility with which she's been charged. She's dancing in place. "Then of course only the long version will do," she says. "Let's find a stoop."

We sit down on the second step of a stoop two doors down. I think it's unseemly for adults to sit on strangers' stoops, but Seraphina is perfectly relaxed. She stretches her legs and crosses her ankles. She's wearing seventies-style espadrilles, probably from some thrift store. They're too small. "Light up another, honey," she instructs, and I do.

"It started 'round about 1:30 this morning. Where were you? Oh, please, I don't want to know. Those bars are so dirty, I don't know how you stand them."

"Sera, I do have one or two things I'd like to do today."

"All right, all right. Around 1:30, Molly woke up hearing a voice. She thought maybe she'd left the radio on. But when she checked, it was off."

"Who told you this?"

"Hector. Every word. Molly called him while it was happening, but he was on his late shift. She told him the whole thing this morning."

"Go on."

"You can just imagine how frightened poor Molly was. It's not the radio, it's not the TV, and the voice sounds as close as the next room. A man's voice, talking and laughing. Not to anyone, mind you, just talking and laughing like he's at a cocktail party for one. Molly said he sounded quite contented. But of course that didn't ease her fears. She stayed there in bed, and from what Hector said, it was some form of deep-breathing she does that got her ready to cope. She got up and went to the back window, and there he was. Stark naked on her garden chair, talking to no one about Ted Koppel's hair."

"Oh, come on!"

"Darling, Seraphina would lie to you in a heartbeat, but Hector Diaz would not. You can confirm every word with him. The man is talking up a blue streak, he gets on to how WNBC News should fire Sue Simmons for looking hateful and being too fat for her cheesy suit jackets and how Janice Huff is signaling the FBI with the angles she uses to point out cold fronts. By now about five people are sticking their heads out the window. Someone yells down at the man that the police are on their way, but he doesn't even look up. Where *were* you, anyway? Oh, don't answer, we must respect each other's post-midnight civil liberties."

"I'm a heavy sleeper," I say.

"Certainly, dear. Well, next the police come. But they must go through Molly's apartment to get to the garden. Can you imagine, three burly officers at the door: 'Police, ma'am. We're sorry to disturb you, but we need entry. Your neighbors have reported an intruder.'" Seraphina gives a little shiver of pleasure.

At one time, this would have been fantasy material. I just nod for Seraphina to continue.

"She put on a robe and let them in. What could she do? Official police business, she didn't want to get slapped with an obstruction of justice charge. Besides, there was a naked man in her backyard."

"So they went through her apartment?"

"It was the only way. They were very polite, Hector said. Molly let them out the garden door, closed and locked it, then watched at the back window. The officers shined their flashlight on the man like they didn't believe their eyes that he was really naked. Then they turned it off when they saw his penis all purply there in the night. No one deserves a spotlight on his dick, dollface, not even a hardened criminal." Seraphina's expression is solemn, even reverent. "By now everybody is hanging out their windows, Hector included. Everybody but you, who would rather indulge in wholly transitory moments of ecstasy at places of ill repute."

"Forgive me my frailties, Mother Superior," I say.

"Absolved, my child. So the first officer, Hector says he was a real cutie, he naturally enough asked the man where his clothes were. To the extent that the poor man could register that people do tend to wear clothes at all times when they are out of doors, he could not say. All the officers persisted, of course. Where are your clothes, where were you last, how did you get in this garden? The man could not remember. He just kept talking about how heathens and anarchists had taken control of News Channel 4."

"Oh my God, this is unbelievable. I can't believe I slept through this whole thing. I hate myself."

"Whatever you say, darling. Shall I continue?"

"That's right, Seraphina, make me beg for it."

"A little periodic begging is good for the soul. Fosters humility, a quality in short supply in our culture."

"Do please go on, Seraphina."

"The man simply had no memory of anything, least of all ever having had any clothes. But Hector says Molly told him the officers treated the whole episode like business as usual. Naturally, they had to arrest him. I mean, I suppose there are laws against sitting naked in other people's gardens."

"More than one," I tell Seraphina.

"Who can possibly guess what happened to his clothes or how he got in Molly's garden? But the problem is, there he was naked, with no way out to the squad car except through Molly's apartment."

"Oh, God."

"Yes indeed, honeypot. You'd think one of the officers would have offered him his shirt to cover his privates. Perhaps there is a regulation against lending official NYPD clothing to suspected criminals."

"No doubt," I say, but I am remembering the quite unofficial use I have made of NYPD-registered handcuffs. "So what happened?"

"The cute one knocked on Molly's door and explained the predicament. He apologized, but said there was no other alternative than to bring the naked man through her apartment. He asked if she happened to have any men's trousers on hand, and, as I hear it, Molly was none too gracious in her response. In the end, she cut up a three-ply, thirty gallon Hefty trash bag and gave it to the officer. By the time the man had established it around his waist, Molly had put on opera to calm herself and the man, who had finally shut up, made his exit to Cecilia Bartoli singing Rossini."

"Horrendous," I say.

"Tales of the City Manhattan-style. One must have a flourishing imagination just to accept reality in our little hometown. But of course we wouldn't have it any other way, would we?"

I snuff out my cigarette on the step, then get up to toss the butt curbside. Seraphina rises, too.

"You've left me speechless, Seraphina," I say.

"I'm so sorry, Brian. But then I love the strong, silent type." She cocks her head fetchingly and heads off toward her building at the end of the block.

I go the opposite way, to the corner mailbox, where I was headed in the first place.

❧ 21 ❦

The weekend before I return to Tri-Community, before the Wednesday my class's term papers are due—including Damon Craig's on "why it's okay for women to paint family scenes"—I meet Beryl in Cleveland. We have sold Avery's house for close to eleven times what he paid for it in the sixties, and the closing is Monday. Beryl seems to regard our profit as some kind of an accomplishment, rather than the simple result of real estate appreciation that it is.

It's a clear Saturday afternoon and the house and yard are full of furniture and household items affixed with red price tags. We've hired Millman Brothers' Liquidators. Most of the buyers are from Cleveland's west side, not far from where Charlene had lived. They come in large family cars, and leave with strange combinations of purchases: the Shaker sideboard and my third cousin Geoffrey's rugby trophies.

The woman from Millman's who is running the sale is Doreen Hubbard. She sits with a cash box, calculator, and portable credit card machine at a card table in the foyer. She is too old for this job. Every time she extends her hand to accept money, I see her tremor.

I'm not sure of my role at this sale, or even if I should be here. I go to smoke a cigarette by the kitchen door. Beryl comes in, high on the action, on the marketability of our father's possessions. "Aren't you interested? Don't you want to see who gets what?"

"Remember our sidewalk sale?" I ask. "The one where you sold Duchess Regina to Charlene?"

"Mmm. What about it?"

"I remember we tried to sell Mom's college diploma."

"Oh, God."

"Yeah, I know, but some family just walked out with all of Geoffrey Weiss's rugby trophies. So go figure."

"Still."

"I wonder if Mom's diploma is around here somewhere. I wouldn't mind having it."

"They put all the unsaleables down in the basement."

Beryl wanders off, and as I follow her on my way to the basement, she approaches a woman in a turban examining *The Confessions of St. Augustine* from Avery's Harvard classics. "We're selling those together, as a set," I hear her tell the woman, who promptly returns St. Augustine to the fifty-volume library.

There's a wet bar in the basement, and on its counter are two big cardboard boxes full of worthless or broken items. Rummaging around, I find the cardboard tube with velveteen lining that I remember from our sidewalk sale so many years ago. I'm careful when I remove and unroll the parchment diploma from the University of Chicago. *Lenore Stella Rubin, Bachelor of Arts, 1945.* This was my mother's, I confirm for myself, just as I've always done whenever I've run across something that belonged to her.

I go up to find Beryl, show her our mother's diploma that I can't believe she overlooked. In the foyer, Doreen Hubbard is going through the receipts. "What do you have there?" she asks me when she spies the piece of parchment.

"Nothing for the sale," I say. "Just a diploma."

"May I see it?"

How did this pushy old woman end up running our sale, I wonder. Still, I go over to show her the diploma. Maybe it's pride.

Doreen Hubbard is breathing through her mouth. Must be a respiratory problem of some sort, but her dropped jaw makes her look a little moronic. When she unrolls the diploma, her eyes tear up. I put out my hand for her to give it back.

"I'm sorry," she says. "You know, I was a friend of your mother's."

This can't be. My mother was a glamorous woman. Her hair shone and she wore a black cocktail dress and a Persian lamb jacket with a mink collar. She had those clip-on emerald earrings. I press the diploma to my chest.

"Maybe I shouldn't have said anything. It was another lifetime ago."

"That's okay," I tell her, but walk away.

When I go upstairs to call Neil from my old bedroom, a woman is there, examining the bottom side of my mattress. It's necessary to find Beryl and borrow her cell phone. Much as I hate cell phones, I find myself walking down to the end of Periwinkle Drive, talking to Neil on Beryl's.

"I'm so glad you're there."

"When are you coming home?"

"Tomorrow night."

"I can't believe how much I miss you," he says. "It's scary."

"I know. I wish you were here."

"Is it hard?"

"Just strange. The woman from the liquidators says she was a friend of my mother's."

"You are *kidding*. You have to find out more."

"No I don't."

"Brian, then why did you tell me?"

"Just . . . I don't know. I feel displaced. I mean, time-wise, too."

Neil sighs. "There's something about you," he says, "that makes me want to anchor you forever."

"Straps or rope? I'm game."

"You know I'm not talking about sex."

Is it the distance that's so emboldening Neil? What do I say? The temperature is climbing into the seventies, yet I'm suddenly cold.

"Sorry. I'm being an asshole. I'm really sorry; I don't want to blow this. Can we. . . ?"

That's it, not even a crackle, and Neil is no longer there. The battery is dead.

For the rest of the afternoon, I wander around, stay out of Doreen Hubbard's way. The woman I'd seen in my room before did not buy the mattress, so I go in to take a look, see what might have made her reject it. (Maybe one of my twenty-year-old porn magazines is still there, stuck between the mattress and box spring.)

A young man with a buzz cut—maybe nineteen or twenty—is tapping the side of my bookshelf to see if the oak is solid.

"There's some good stuff at this sale," the young man says.

"You think?" I've lifted my mattress and I'm poking at the underside.

"Well, compared to that one on Brentwood. At least this family had a modicum of taste. Did you go to the one on Brentwood?"

"No."

"Don't bother. Unless you're in the market for a fifteen-year-old eight piece dining set from Michaelson's "Orient Collection." The buffet has touch-to-open doors with inlaid fake mother-of-pearl dragon heads. The whole set is claret red lacquer."

This of course clears up any doubt I might have had.

"Brian Moss," I say, and extend my hand. "Actually, this is the house I grew up in. This is my old room."

"Philip Dobbs," he says. "Jeez, I'm sorry. You should've stopped me."

"What are you looking for?"

"A few things. I just signed a lease on an apartment down by University Circle."

"The museum area. I used to take Saturday classes at the Institute. I live in New York now."

At the mention of New York, Philip turns to me full view. I smile. His eyes in particular show his youth. They look to be precisely the same size and shape, a symmetry I rarely see in people out of their twenties. He wears a goatee and a rivet earring, a uniform of sorts; it testifies to some experience. He's neither good nor bad looking. At a glance, I can tell he's incomparably more confident and stable than I was at his age. This makes me feel cheated and turned on at the same time.

"Are you going to get that? It's well built, I can testify."

"It seems so," says Philip. He crouches down to remove my boyhood books from the bottom shelf, the John Tunis and Matt Christopher sports novels, Time-Life's *The Post-Impressionist Years*, a set of Hardy Boys mysteries, three volumes from the Junior Classics library: *Treasure Island, The Last of the Mohicans, Robinson Crusoe.* These last three my father called priming for his Harvard Classics. I'd started each one, but each had left me heavy-hearted that the glorious tenets of manhood had been established with no consideration for me. It was clear the tales would be full of bleak and pleasureless victories, so I'd put them back on the shelves unread, just as I'd known Avery had done with The Harvard Classics.

Philip taps the inside of the shelf back. "Good," he says. He rises, faces me, slides his right hand into the front pocket of his jeans. He's wearing a good white shirt. The fingers of his left hand flutter against his stomach. He looks me over and smiles, his intention unmistakable.

I'm aroused by Philip's temerity. He knows this is the house I grew up in. It's easy to surmise there's been a recent illness or death in my family, and yet he's hitting on me in my boyhood room. He's younger even than Damon Craig. It would take a second for me to close and lock the door. The opportunity itself is seductive.

It's Philip, though, who takes command by going toward the door. Yet watching him from behind, the stirrings I've felt somehow drain away. I realize I'm not with him, there is no mutual tempo here, I cannot stay the course of whatever time we'd spend together in my locked room.

"I'm sorry if I gave off mixed messages, Philip, but it would just be too bizarre for me. It's not you." I walk past him. "Sorry," I repeat. "Good luck with your new apartment."

Just past six, Beryl is in the kitchen, drinking soda from a can. "Someone bought the glasses," she says. "The green tumblers and the water glasses, too. Did you find the diploma?"

"Yes. I'm taking it home."

"That's fine with me. University of Chicago, wasn't it?"

"Yes."

"Dad would never have married a stupid woman."

This doesn't warrant a response. Opening the kitchen door to the backyard, I light a cigarette and position myself at the threshold.

"I need to thank you again. About Missy. Whatever you did, however you were, it stuck."

"She's easy to be with."

"Novel description. But I'll admit, she is easier now."

"Maybe you and Seth shouldn't give her so many things," I say. "It oppresses her. It makes her want to escape."

"Thank you for your wise counsel. So much for expressing my gratitude."

"I'm sorry if you don't want to hear it." I've startled myself by picking this fight.

"Excuse me, Brian, but when was the last time you were a parent?"

"Every Wednesday for the past seven years."

"For an incredible, back-breaking ninety minutes at a stretch."

"You don't have to be a parent to know something about parenting."

"And how did you gain your insight, Dr. Moss?"

"Can we stop? You *know* it's just because we're here. It's my fault, I apologize. Let's be good to ourselves and give it a rest."

"Plus you could've *told* me that your boyfriend was coming along. Maybe I'm not the redneck arch conservative Mormon-John Bircher-Orthodox-Jehovah's Witness you think I am."

I grind out my cigarette on the first of the flagstone steps leading to Avery's half-acre backyard.

The swing door from the dining room opens with a squeak. "That's just about it," Doreen Hubbard announces. "Very successful first day. The weather helped, but honestly I've run sales in the most perfect weather where a single thing has sold. It's quality that sells."

"My father had good taste," Beryl says. "Would you like a ginger ale? Or some wine?"

Doreen Hubbard accepts, and Beryl unearths a stack of Dixie cups from a bottom cupboard. She fills two with Merlot. "Brian?" she asks.

"Okay," I say, but I remain standing while Beryl and Doreen Hubbard sit.

"Are you keeping your mother's diploma, Brian?"

"I'll take it back. Not that I know exactly what to do with it."

Doreen Hubbard stares into the middle distance. There is the problem of her gaping mouth. "I know I shouldn't have said anything," she comments.

"Excuse me?" says Beryl.

"Don't worry about it," I tell Doreen, failing to sound nonchalant.

"Something I should know?" Beryl asks.

"It's nothing." There's no doubt she'll persist, though, so I say, "Mrs. Hubbard knew Mom once."

"You're kidding! What a complete coincidence." Beryl's whole countenance changes. Her tone invites intimacy. "How well did you know her?"

"We were good friends, actually. Three of us from the University of Chicago. Your mother, Marcia Sorenson—she was her roommate who moved to Pittsburgh—and me. I got married to a fellow from Euclid, and Lenore came here to apply to graduate school. Then she met your father."

"My God," says Beryl. "Brian, did you know all this?"

"No." I'm trying to reconcile the idea of Doreen Hubbard, this old woman who wears too much cheap jewelry and apparently supports herself working for Millman Brothers' Liquidators, going to the University of Chicago. In my mother's era, that school was a hotbed of intellectualism: Saul Bellow, Philip Roth, Susan Sontag—they all went there.

"We drifted apart for some time, but we were getting close again when the accident happened." Doreen struggles to keep her voice steady, takes more than a sip of wine. "My husband and I were at the funeral."

"This is kind of amazing," says Beryl.

"Our father didn't let us go to the funeral," I say.

"I know, I remember. I always respected your father. Your mother married much better than I did. You probably figured that out." Doreen's cup is empty now, and Beryl refills it three-quarters to the top. "It would've been interesting to see what would have happened to her."

"What do you mean?" asks Beryl.

"After she came back from Pittsburgh."

Beryl glances at me. She doesn't know what to make of Doreen Hubbard.

"I think I'll go clean up out there," I say. Yet I can't quite get myself going.

"Your mother was something of a wild card. She could've really succeeded, or . . . she could've ended up more in my situation. I wonder if we would have remained friends."

No, you never would have remained friends with my mother, I think. Lenore Moss had about her a mystery and self-possession that was commanding. She was destined to attract another kind of person into her orbit.

"No use in speculating," I say.

"What do you mean?" asks Beryl. "Succeeded at what?"

Doreen looks guiltily at her plastic cup. "Oh, my."

"Mrs. Hubbard, you get me and my brother all worked up by telling us what we don't necessarily need to know, and now you're being coy."

This is harsh, but I don't intervene.

"I'm so sorry," says Doreen. "I'm not trying to be coy. I was never very good in these situations." Her tremor has intensified; she might well have Parkinson's. I think she might cry, and there's a new raspy quality to her breathing. The wine could not have been good for her.

I lean over to hand her a paper napkin. "Let's just all calm down. We have another full day tomorrow."

"*Brian.*"

"You poor kids," says Doreen Hubbard. "And your father did such a good job with you. That's obvious."

Right, I think, *Ms. Uncivil* and *Mr. Overgrown Boy.*

"I'm sorry to upset you," Beryl says to Mrs. Hubbard, "but I'd still like to know what you meant about my mother being successful or not."

"*I* might know," I volunteer.

"Oh yes?"

"Before you came here last time, when Dad was fairly loosened up on his meds, he told me some things. He told me that when Lenore went to Pittsburgh it was to decide if she would divorce him."

Beryl's eyes widen. I shared my childhood with her, and it's easy to know what she's feeling. Foremost, she is disturbed that Avery took me into his confidence.

"I'm sure he didn't want to upset you. Or me, for that matter," I say. "But since we're doing this now, he also told me that after the accident her old roommate—I guess it was this Marcia Sorenson—told Dad that she *had* decided to divorce him. Maybe telling him was her warped idea of consolation, I don't know. Anyway, it's not hard to imagine Lenore's state of mind at the time she got into the accident."

"Is this all true?" Beryl asks Doreen Hubbard, until this morning a complete stranger.

"Yes. She was planning to go back to school," says Doreen.

"What?" I ask.

"Your dad didn't tell you that?"

"No. I'm not sure he knew."

"He knew. Marcia told him. Lenore had been accepted to Berkeley's graduate art history program."

Beryl nods in a slow, deliberate way, as if she'd suspected as much all along. She's still nodding when she looks at me. *Well, that would explain you.*

Mrs. Hubbard appears quite lost in herself. She gets up to leave, but once she moves out from behind the table, she steps forward, then inadvertently back. I go to help her.

"I wasn't sure you were the same Mosses until I got here," she explains. "I'm sorry."

"She was willing to take us *that* far away," muses Beryl. "To California. Daddy would've raised hell."

Helping Doreen Hubbard steadily cross the floor, I say only, "She would've had her hands full with two five-year-olds."

The brace of my hand on Mrs. Hubbard's arm is too steady to allow her to tumble, but when she tries to answer she pitches forward a bit. She doesn't try to speak again.

Naturally my mother was going to take us with her, I say to myself. Hadn't she always returned to wake me from my nap, to let me trail her around as she did her housework?

Yet I think of how oppressive the sight of me must have been every time Avery took Lenore out for the night—how my mother must have heard me wailing and looked back from the driveway to see the shape of my forehead, cleaved like an outsized leech to the little bubbled glass square at the bottom of our front door.

❧ 22 ❧

When I return from Cleveland, Hector Diaz is sitting on our stoop. He jumps up as soon as I emerge from the cab, then takes my heavy backpack from me. "What are we going to do without Molly?" he immediately asks. "The garden'll go to hell. We'll have to buy our own diva CDs. And who knows *what* could move in down there."

"Not another death. Please."

"No, no she's fine. Just moving. Abandoning us for Sussex."

"Sussex!"

I'd finished the trilogy on the plane. I can resume my life knowing that Helen Croft is, and always will be, pregnant with her and the raven-haired rector's first child. She has turned the rectory cottage into an inviting home, and when she and the rector go out for their morning constitutional, they pass by vines of morning glories climbing up the cottage wall, a throng of purple and violet blooms inclining east.

"West Sussex, to be precise."

"She was *that* shaken by the naked man? Imagine."

Hector returns my backpack, walks me up the stoop. "She's seventy-six, Brian. Put yourself in her place. She has a first cousin in Sussex who just lost her husband. They're going to buy a cottage together."

"When is all this happening?"

"At the end of the month. We'll do something. Seraphina is already planning. She's been to an English tea place. She's taken notes."

"Oh, God. Yin and Yang have tea."

"Seraphina is planning a variation. A choice between tea and mint juleps."

"Good idea," I say. "Necessary idea."

"Molly's been here the longest," Hector says. "Doesn't it feel like our house mother is leaving? Although, between you and me and the lamppost, the errands were getting to be a bit much."

"Good one," I say, referring to Hector's idiom.

"Thank you. But don't misunderstand me. I will seriously miss Molly Winfield."

"I'm sad to see her go," I say, thinking mostly of Mrs. Winfield's garden and her music. "But you were always her favorite." I pat Hector's cheek and turn to walk up the stairs to my apartment.

At The Aegean the next morning, I tell Neil about Philip Dobbs. One point of recalling the incident is to confirm that we are everywhere, even tucked away in one's childhood home in Cleveland. It seems a good point to make, given Neil's recent emergence from conversion therapy. I say nothing, of course, about my flickers of attraction to Philip. Neil probably knows the interest was not entirely unilateral. But the real reason I want to tell him about the little episode is to impress him with my fidelity. Neither of ours will last, so we may as well bask in the moment.

Athos comes over with the menus. Always the host of my solitude, he's never seen me with a single person. Tonight I'm revealed. When we came in, I'd introduced the two of them, they'd shaken hands, Athos had told me I was the best, and the ceremony had ended there. Now I can't seem to look at this man who over the years has handed me countless $8.95 dinner specials.

"Molly Winfield's moving," I tell Neil.

"The opera nut?"

"The very one. I wish she'd donate her sound system to the building."

"Oh, *that's* nice."

"I do feel bad, but if I were her, I'd leave too."

Then I tell Neil the story that Seraphina told me right before I left for Cleveland, the tale of the naked man in Molly's garden.

Athos returns for our order. We're both having French toast. Athos gives Neil what seems to me a pointedly bored look. Possessiveness is everywhere, in myriad forms.

"Have you thought about taking her apartment?" asks Neil.

"God no, I can't do that."

"Why not?"

"For one thing, I can't afford it. Her rent will go up substantially, even under rent stabilization laws, and it's a two bedroom."

"You told me you're inheriting from your father."

"The money's tied up."

I wonder if Neil is beginning to worry that I'm negative, which I am.

"I think it's a real opportunity. I'd try to get it, if I could." Neil blushes as soon as he says this. "If I were you, I mean."

Neil shares an apartment in Kipp's Bay with two roommates. One is also studying acupuncture; the other is a woman in the chorus of a Broadway musical.

"My apartment could use some work," I say defensively.

"Brian, it's not that; I wasn't criticizing your apartment. None of this is really my business anyway."

"It affects you," I say. I hadn't thought of this until now; where I live affects the experience of someone else. In all the years I've been in New York, this has never been quite true.

"Think about it. It's worth looking into. You love that garden, and it could be yours!" Neil gives me his singular smile, a smile that transports me to the deep interior of a place I'm still trying to identify.

When Athos sets down our French toast, the Aegean's excellent challah French toast, he may or may not observe a transformative energy passing between the two of us, a vitality like qi, and just as difficult to describe. It is my new responsibility not to care what Athos notices.

"Two bedrooms with garden," I say. "In Chelsea, that has an exalted ring to it."

* * *

A new flat weave carpet has been laid down in my classroom. Its acrid smell rises off the floor, but I'm too impressed to be bothered by it. Someone actually cared enough to authorize the removal of the carpet with the scratched-up swastika. I wonder if it was Nat, if he leveraged his several grains of influence to make this new carpet his triumph of the year.

"This is a pleasant surprise," I say, when I walk in at a few minutes past two. Three students are there, under a fifth of the class. It's our last meeting, and most of them have handed in their final papers. I've graded the papers, and they're in the folder I'm carrying. The students who are absent, who don't mind insulting me with their absence, have apparently resolved to settle for the final grade I'll post next week. Whatever comments I've made on their papers will go unread. The students who are here, Felina Diamond—who enjoys challenging me but is unskilled at it—Damon Craig, and Maggie Cho probably all feel sorry for me. Their sense of decency has prevailed on them to show up while their classmates are finishing other papers or smoking and teaching themselves Three Card Monty on the sunny side of the building's roof. It's an unfortunate turn of events not only because it so starkly illustrates my failure, but because now I'll have to discuss their papers with them.

"Do the other classrooms have new carpets?" I ask, stalling.

Felina shrugs. Maggie says this is the only one.

"Good," I say. "They got it. I'm glad to see they finally got it."

"It was pretty gross," says Maggie.

"It's easy to be cavalier with symbols. But this was serious business, and I'm glad to see the school recognized it."

Felina yawns. "Sorry," she says.

"Should we wait a few minutes?" I ask.

214

They look at me. Damon says, "I know this seems bad, Mr. Moss, but a lot of people have an Accounting Practices final next period. It's four credits."

"Then let's talk about your papers, why don't we?" I remove the pile from my folder and search out Maggie, Felina, and Damon's. The handling of this situation calls for some improvising. None of these papers is in the least distinguished, and one is unacceptable. I can either discuss them openly with extreme tact—with lies, even—or discuss each individually while the others wait in the hall or leave early. The choice, I decide, should be theirs.

"Individual," says Felina, whose paper on Toulouse-Lautrec was unacceptable. She agrees to go first. Maggie will return in fifteen minutes, Damon fifteen minutes after that.

I place *Henri Toulouse-Lautrec (1864-1901)* before us. "What font did you use for this, Felina?"

"I think its name is Impact."

"Well, it made one." The font's roman is actually boldface, and the stylized letters crash together, making it as difficult to read Felina's paper as it has been all semester to respond to her sweeping and uninformed attacks on world societies. "I won't dwell on its unreadability, since I didn't talk to the class about presentation. That was my fault."

Felina begins to twist her hair, braiding it, then letting it go. She knows what's coming.

"And it's obvious that it's three pages shorter than the minimum requirement."

"That's because I thought I'd hit all the major points of his life."

"But what we really have to talk about is the point of view. Or lack thereof. I actually expected a strong point of view from you, Felina. You usually have one in class."

"I know, but I thought this was supposed to be *academic*."

"Academic papers have points of view. On the list of individual artists, I asked you to take and support a critical perspective on the artist's work."

"Well, like, I didn't *know*. You didn't *say* that."

She's using my reason to accept her font, Impact, as precedent for my accepting her paper.

"Even if you didn't read the assignment, there are some things you're expected to know. The assumption of a critical perspective was woven into every conversation the class had about these papers. Didn't you write any critical papers in high school?"

"A couple. Mr. Moss, I'm not just saying this to be defensive, but I don't think this is fair, because you told the class that you're like practically in love with Toulouse-Lautrec, and so it's not really fair to expect me to know as much as you."

Clearly Felina has decided her motive in choosing Lautrec has backfired.

"I'm not arguing with how much you know. Your paper's unacceptable because it's three pages shorter than the assigned minimum length and it's completely lacking a thesis. I'm sorry."

"Can I do it over? This is going to make me fail your class."

"The semester's over."

"I should've taken an Incomplete! This is so unfair!"

There's no point in arguing with her that taking an Incomplete would have been simply postponing the inevitable if this is anywhere near the paper she was going to turn in. "I'm sorry, Felina, but this is not much more than a book report, a thorough summary. You can do better than this."

"I know! I can! Please, Mr. Moss, just give me three days."

"To do the semester's main paper?"

"There's this whole other part of me you haven't seen!"

"And why didn't you choose to show it?" Why, I want to add, do you hold your motivation in reserve until a crisis occurs? Nearly all my students discover the most consummate version of themselves only when they're facing the consequences of not having discovered it earlier.

"I could've. I just had all this pressure from my other classes and I didn't realize yours was supposed to be pressured, too."

There's nowhere to go with this one. I hand Felina her paper.

"I can't believe you're doing this." Her voice has risen an octave. She heads for the doorway, then turns around. With a keen and lavish deliberation, she says, "You know, you really, *really* suck."

In a few minutes, Damon comes in.

"I thought Maggie was next."

"She says to say she's truly sorry. She thinks she left her home test for Business Communication in Starbucks, and she has class at four. I'm supposed to get her paper from you."

"All righty." This expression, which I've never used in my life, is my armor. Without it, I'd cry or throw chairs around the room. "Should we get started, then?"

"Sure. I know it's not the best paper you've ever read in your life, but I have a question."

"Good. Questions are good." This comes out to the same beat as *all righty.* "Want to start, then?"

"I read that essay, 'Why Have There Been No Great Women Artists?'"

"I'm glad. It's considered the first art history article from a feminist perspective. If that's 100% indisputable, I'm not sure, but it made a pretty big impression."

"I'll admit I didn't completely get it, but it made me mad."

"I thought it might."

"But then I read it again after I turned my paper in."

"Really?" This is more than any teacher can reasonably ask.

"And Sue did, too. What made her mad was that art schools in the nineteenth century were so much better than they are now. She says she feels cheated because they were more serious and they taught much more anatomy."

"Yes, Damon, but part of Nochlin's point is that women were barred from drawing the nude model—male *or* female."

Damon performs his signature gesture with his hair, squeezing a handful at the top of his head. "I know. I guess Sue wants art school to be a combination of then and now."

"That would probably be ideal."

"Anyway, I wanted to ask you if I could redo my paper. After I read the essay again, I decided it didn't make sense. My paper, I mean."

Damon's paper, which he'd titled "Mistresses of the Domestic Scene," had been true to his promise and within the realm of my expectations. In defense of his thesis, that women are inherent nurturers and therefore the most reliable chroniclers of domesticity, Damon had called upon the work of the nineteenth- and early twentieth-century artists Mary Cassatt, Berthe Morisot, Marie Bracquemond, and Eva Gonzales. His paper did not include any reference to Suzanne Valadon, the outlaw who dared to paint naked female models—sometime plain ones—without emphasizing their sexuality. And probably only to please me, Damon had discussed Rosa Bonheur, best known for her horse paintings, on whom Linda Nochlin focused at the end of her article. Without addressing a single aspect of Bonheur's complex relationship to her

217

femininity, without commenting on the total command she had of her subject matter, and without any supportive evidence whatsoever, Damon had determined that Rosa Bonheur never grew out of her adolescent obsession with horses. He'd concluded that Bonheur's case of arrested development had put her in a category of her own, outside serious consideration among the others. This was just one of several wholly defective arguments, yet in general there was too much vigor in Damon's paper for me to outright fail him.

"What do you mean? You decided you didn't explain yourself well, or something more?"

"More. I might have been wrong."

"I didn't know that I'd stressed wrong and right in connection with these papers."

"Well, I changed my mind. And my paper was no good anyway, right?"

"It has some promise, Damon. You clearly did some homework. But I've read better argued ideas. Tell me about changing your mind."

"It was all that stuff the article said about institutional discrimination against women. What was acceptable to paint and what wasn't, and, like you said, how they didn't have a chance at the same training men had. I really hadn't thought enough about that, I admit. But remember what got me hot on this topic in the first place—that Sue is being discriminated against for the opposite, exactly *for* painting domestic scenes."

"Makes for a pretty interesting contrast, doesn't it?"

"And so that's why I want to do my paper over. Because, like you say, it's an interesting contrast."

"How *is* Sue?" (Apart from motivating your every move, I think.)

"Pretty good. She says that going against the tide will end up making her a better artist."

I nod. "And things at your parents'? How's that working out?"

"Okay. I'm planning to transfer next year. I wanna go to NYU. I'm worried I won't get in, but I'm going to try."

Damon is not about to confide in me again. After all, last time he'd done so it had ended with me looking down at his crotch. Just something that happened, beyond judgment, I believe, in Damon's eyes, but why should he take a chance again? Nor do I want to take the same chance.

"All right, Damon. If you really think you have something unique to say, and you can articulate your point of view more convincingly than you did in this paper, you can have another chance. But the paper needs to be in my box a week from today."

He may not get into NYU, I think, but I won't be the obstacle.

"I really appreciate it, Mr. Moss," says Damon. "And . . . other stuff you've done. Not just this."

"But do me a favor, Damon. Don't let this get around—my letting you do the paper over. I wouldn't tell, for instance, Felina Diamond."

"You think I talk to Felina? Give me *some* credit."

* * *

"A little dissolute, don't you think?" asks Nathan Weinstein.

I'm smoking near the building's entrance as Nat walks toward me, papers sticking out of his open briefcase, their edges flopping against his wrist.

I smile and exhale a gorgeous stream of smoke, a B-52 jet stream, masculine and suave. "The dissolute don't teach at Tri-Community. They throw wine bottles into the Seine at three in the morning and eat the richest patisserie for breakfast. They urinate on the cornerstones of venerated academies and bring male prostitutes to their mothers' garden parties."

"Sounds divine," says Nat. "But listen, I have some news." He winks and gestures for me to follow him to his office.

"I was just going to run back in to get something and then leave."

He holds the door open for me. "Come."

Inside Nat's office are piles of student papers, administrative forms, publishers' review copies, AV equipment, theater props. He pushes away a crowded in-box and leans against the corner of his desk. "It's good. Casey's out."

"You're kidding."

"And it wasn't pretty. Embezzlement."

We slap palms. "*Knew* he was a slime-bucket!"

"Until he's replaced, I'm in a nice little position. And so, with the power vested in me, I hereby vanquish 'Art and the Digital Revolution'."

"You're a wizard, Nathan Weinstein. What else?"

"It remains to be seen. But the Board is doing some reshaping. We're always going to stop at associate degree, but if they want to get kids into decent four-year colleges, be able to offer more transferable credits, they'll have to do better with the liberal arts."

"Shit."

"What?"

"I was thinking of quitting. Next week, actually, after the last staff meeting."

"Ho-hum. Must be that time. Every three months I can expect at least one of you to threaten to quit."

"Can you blame us? Aren't our complaints legitimate?"

"Very. But only one of you has a Ph.D, and he's done zero in his field since he got it twelve years ago."

This is the closest I've ever seen Nat come to playing hardball.

"Actually, I have more power vested in me. I have the power to make you department chair," Nat tells me. "*And* give you better classes. I'm stepping down. I'll keep my courses here, but I'm going to pick up a couple of new ones at Rutgers. Instructor level, but serious drama courses."

"That's wonderful, Nat."

"So what about it, Brian? You've quit the Barracks. What are you planning?"

Here it is again: planning. Nat has given me an offer that would require committing to a plan. Loss would come of accepting his offer— loss of the freedom to contemplate other possibilities. To be expected somewhere is not to be free to be expected elsewhere. Our purview is determined, in part, by where we place our bodies.

"Brian, are you with me here? Ask me some questions. I need a decision from you by early next week. Don't make me have to pass this offer on to Rupert."

I groan. Rupert Connelly is a compulsive talker who drives us both crazy. Nat has twice told him in my presence, "Land the plane already!"

"I'm going to consider it," I say.

Nat looks as nonplused as I feel. "Well, good. Put a list of questions together. Call me over the weekend. Better yet, can we meet for dinner? I can't bear sitting in my underwear eating a single more Lean Cuisine while Sam's out on the Potomac wearing a tuxedo and eating rack of lamb."

We make an arrangement, and I leave, chain smoking all the way to the Path train.

At home, I take out my graduate school Xerox of "Why Have There Been No Great Women Artists?" It is brittle and dusty and bears the imprint of the photography book that's been pressed against it for fifteen years. The first highlighted phrase I come to is "always a model, never an artist." True, of course. A hundred years ago La Goulue, Jane Avril, and the others had their own ambitions. In history, they have only stories that ended badly.

The story of Toulouse-Lautrec's life ended badly, too; he died a miserable death in much the same setting into which he was born. But his art was another matter. The making of his art depended only on his comparative sobriety and a few extra francs from his mother. Given these, his future was limitless.

Édouard Vuillard lived with his mother his whole life; she was his greatest supporter.

Claude Monet's mother died when he was seventeen; his aunt had so much faith in him that she bought his way out of the army on the condition he enroll at the *Belle Artistes* to pursue painting.

When I was a boy, I visited the Cleveland Museum of Art where I examined the work of these men. I'd had my own ambitions, but my father told me that good competitors know when to concede, and I suspect now that he was right; he saved me a good deal of wretched unhappiness.

My mother was born fifty-four years after La Goulue, fifty-six after Jane Avril. She had more opportunities than they, fewer than she'd have today. But right before she died, Lenore Rubin Moss was poised to determine her own future. She might have been arranging to leave me and Beryl behind to do so. This is a pivotal detail that we will never know. I did learn something from Lenore's old friend Doreen Hubbard, though. I learned that my mother was not the sort of person who would have indulged the affliction of my longing for her; she would have prepared me for an independent existence—however I balked, however the process of nudging me away might have pained her.

* * *

The day before summer begins is bright, not quite hot, and Molly Winfield's garden is in its glory. Her seven-variety iris garden is the showiest, the centerpiece, but there are foxgloves and periwinkles, and short rows of lupine. There are different kinds of grasses, too, and by her apartment's back door, out of view from my apartment window, a wide garden of herbs: sage, basil, thyme, mustard, mint. Neil and I stand in the stone path, and Molly and Hector sit on her pair of iron garden chairs. Seraphina has just arrived, and she is putting something in the kitchen.

Last week I arranged to take over Molly Winfield's lease. A living room, a big bedroom, a small bedroom, the garden. I'll move at the end of this month. Except for the books, nothing is coming with me. My Murphy bed stays behind in the studio. Over the next few weeks, Neil will help me shop for furniture. He's staying with his roommates; the question did not even come up. Still, we'll decide on furniture together.

"It was where Hector is sitting, actually," Molly is saying. "I have not sat there since. Brian, would you like me to leave these chairs here? They're good English garden chairs, but they seem a bit tarnished, now."

Hector shifts in his seat, then looks over his shoulder as if the naked man's aura still hovers there. "I don't know," he reflects. "If it were me, I'd be a little leery . . ."

"Magical thinking," I say. "What do you think, Hector? The chair is going to start drawing every schizophrenic in the city?"

"No . . ." says Hector, "just the naked ones."

We laugh, but Molly Winfield's smile is only vague and polite. Our joke has been her trauma, and I think we come to realize it at once.

"Mint juleps, anyone?" asks Seraphina, appearing at the garden door with a bottle of bourbon in her hand. "Fresh mint from the garden, thanks to Mrs. Winfield. Mint juleps and watercress sandwiches, what could be more sublime?"

We all moan. In a few minutes Seraphina serves us, and Hector rises to give her his seat. She makes herself comfortable next to Molly's chair, and the rest of us—Hector and Neil and me—sit cross-legged in a half circle around them on the stone path. For nearly sixteen years this garden has given me the greatest pleasure, yet this is the first time I've sat in it. My new perspective, level with the flower blossoms, is jarring.

"You make a nice mint julep," I tell Seraphina.

"My. Compliment from a bartender. I'm honored."

"Former," I say. "I've quit."

"I'm absolutely green," says Seraphina. "The life of a housewife is the only life worth living."

Molly Winfield, I notice, shifts just barely away from Seraphina.

"Quite possibly true," I say, "but I've decided to take an offer to head the Humanities department at Tri-Community. I'm not going to tell you it's the thought of those rapt and impressionable young people that convinced me. But I'm going to try it out, and I have some work of my own in mind. Something still gelling, but I'm going ahead with it."

"Wonderful, Brian," says Molly. "Lovely news."

"It's funny," I continue, "you can be stuck in the same place for years, like I was stuck at the Barracks, and then suddenly some force from without says 'walk away,' and you do. It's kind of wonderful how that can happen."

"My force from without was quite off the trolley track," says Molly, "but I suppose I should be grateful to him."

"It's a good decision," Hector puts in, "and you can have an even bigger garden in Sussex."

"But you boys," says Molly, "you must start thinking about where you will settle, too. Let me be an example to you. They will invade your garden and run naked through your living room to make your redundancy absolutely clear."

"We gentlemen and ladies," corrects Seraphina, "are deeply urban creatures." Mint julep in hand, she gestures to us all. "Maybe we'll just take up permanent residence here in this building, and in your beautiful garden. We'll divide up the planting and weeding according to whose arthritis is in recession."

Not an altogether unpleasant prospect. I watch Neil lean back, cross his ankles, and incline his face toward the sun. Mrs. Winfield smiles. She gets up to go inside, and when she returns she is accompanied by the first notes of Callas singing the aria from *Samson and Delilah*. She walks with great care, as if afraid any motion might disrupt the sweet notes that have entered her garden like an ache in bones. The rest of us don't move, except for when I lie down next to Neil on the stone path, close my eyes, and drop my hand to the moist humus Molly has spread beneath her white bearded irises—perennials I'll inherit along with all the others.